"THE TERRANS HAVE CAUSED NO END OF TROUBLE FOR OUR PEOPLE. . . ."

Viela looked back over his shoulder at Bantu as they rode away from the fisherfolk with their burden of death. "The Terrans prey upon those who are greedy and insecure. Do you not see that they must be forced to leave Ardel?"

Bantu did not answer his fellow Healer.

The Terrans will not harm any more of my people, vowed Viela as he rode toward Port Freewind. *There shall be no more unnecessary deaths, no more magical Terran houses that fly above our keeps, no more towers of metal in the wasteland, no more Terran potions. I will find a way to drive all of the Terrans from Ardel. Then rain and wind and time will erase them from our land and our memories. . . .*

HEALER

KRIS JENSEN

DAW BOOKS, INC.

DONALD A. WOLLHEIM, FOUNDER

375 Hudson Street, New York, NY 10014

ELIZABETH R. WOLLHEIM
SHEILA E. GILBERT
PUBLISHERS

First Printing, October 1993

1 2 3 4 5 6 7 8 9

DAW TRADEMARK REGISTERED
U.S. PAT. OFF. AND FOREIGN COUNTRIES
—MARCA REGISTRADA
HECHO EN U.S.A.

PRINTED IN THE U.S.A.

For Larry, who groks.

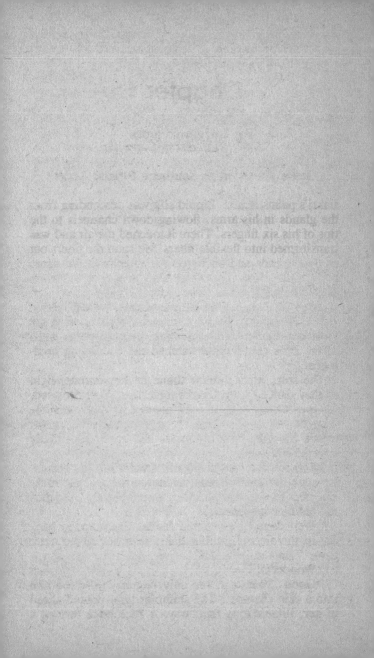

Chapter 1

Jessic Caves, High Southern Desert, Ardel

Ilakri's palms itched. Liquid silk was descending from the glands in his arms, flowing down channels to the tips of his six fingers. There it touched the air and was transformed into flexible fibers. He spun the fibers out in fine threads and anchored the threads to the damp wall of the cave. Then he began to weave a cocoon about the body of his mate, Yaro.

Their other mate, the Mother Jaella, waited behind Ilakri. A ball of glowing shimmer-light floated in the air above her head, illuminating the gold-green walls of the little alcove. She watched the cocooning in silence.

The soft, white threads shone in the shimmer-light as they danced from Ilakri's fingertips. Yaro drowsed, his eyes closed and his back pressed against the stone wall of the cave, while the cocoon's gentle prison bound his legs, then his hands and arms, and finally covered his face.

Ilakri felt the last of the silk drain from his glands. He spun the final threads, anchored them to the rock. The cocoon was completed. It would protect Yaro during his metamorphosis.

"Well done," whispered Jaella. She stepped back out of the alcove, pulling Ilakri with her to the outer cave. "How do you feel?"

"Wonderful!"

"Good. Your task has only begun." She led him into a side chamber. The shimmer-light floated ahead of her, illuminating their way. A rock edge formed a natural couch against the back wall of this small cave. The ledge was strewn with the shaggy pelts of wool-deer and goats and a prized silver tol fur. Jars and pouches waited in shadowed niches in the stone above the couch. Jaella took a flask and two cups from one of them. She filled the cups with dark amber liquid from the flask and offered one to Ilakri. "Sit, and drink."

"Thank you, Mother." Ilakri sipped from his cup. The warm liquid smelled of flowers, and was sweet and silky on his tongue. He swallowed, felt its warmth spread through his chest.

"You must call me Jaella now. You are no longer a youngling, Ilakri. You are a Master, with the rights and the obligations that come with leading a trine." Jaella offered him more of the drink. He covered his cup with the palm of his left hand. "Yaro and I are depending on you to secure our trine's status within the clan."

Ilakri watched her warily. Liquid fire seemed to dance down his arms. His empty silk glands burned. "I am a herder, as was Yaro, as you were before him. How can I bring status to the trine?"

"You must earn it, just as Yaro and I did when we completed our first metamorphoses. You entered the cocoon as a youngling and emerged as a Master, to mate with us and take your place at the head of our trine. You have fulfilled the first obligation, that of cocooning Yaro. While he undergoes his metamorphosis to Motherhood, and the younglings grow within me, you must fulfill the second obligation. Only then will you have earned your new position."

"What must I do?" Ilakri set aside his cup. He pressed his palms against his burning forearms, left to right and right to left, and willed the pain to cease.

Jaella drained her cup, then filled it and Ilakri's again. "Drink the *gris am*. It will close the glands and give you strength."

He did as she bade him. The liquid slid easily down his throat. "What is the second obligation?"

"You must go to the sacred ruins in the cliffs to the west, and there you must seek out a relic. You must carry it westward to the sea, and then follow the shore northward, until you find a village of the fisherfolk. There you will trade the relic for things of value."

Ilakri's arms no longer burned. Instead his mind was aflame. The ruins were forbidden territory. When he was a youngling, he had heard tales around the evening fires, frightening stories of the dangers that awaited those who trespassed in the ruins. Now Jaella expected him to go there alone! "How can I safely enter the ruins? What sort of relic should I take? What will the fishers have that I might trade for?"

"I cannot answer any of your questions. You must face the test of the ruins alone, and decide for yourself what will have value to our trine and to the clan. What you bring back to us will determine the status of the trine while you are its leader.

"There is one thing more. You must return before our younglings are born."

Ilakri stared at Jaella. A halo of light surrounded her body, a soft topaz glow that moved as she moved. He reached for her, and she clasped his hands.

"You must go now, Ilakri. You have no time to waste. I will rest and watch over Yaro while you are gone. Return to us quickly, Master." She pushed him away. He turned and stumbled from her warm and homey cave into the main cavern.

Distant voices echoed through the chamber. Ilakri heard the sounds but not the words. He moved like a sleepwalker through the dank cave, following the smooth path that countless feet had worn in its stone floor. The darkness was oppressive; he conjured a tiny ball of shimmer-light to float above his head. It cast a weak sphere of illumination that moved with him through the cavern.

Bright arcs of light emanated from some alcoves and side caves, but Ilakri stopped at none of them. No one called to him. He passed the younglings' cave without hailing his old friends there. They would not welcome him. As an adult he no longer held a place in their games and amusements. That part of his life was over. He would find new companions now.

The golden haze that he had first seen around Jaella's body moved with him and colored everything with a soft topaz glow. It disturbed him, made him look twice at the stones, the mosses, and the people that he passed. He lifted his right hand and stared at the aura that enveloped it. He could not erase the glow from his perceptions, even when he closed his eyes.

Full water skins hung from pegs near the main cavern's entrance. Ilakri took one without thinking about it. No one ever left the caves without water.

The entrance, which sloped upward and faced northwest, was in shadow. He scrambled up the incline, then crouched in the broad, low opening, surveying the steep slope down to the bottom of the arroyo. The narrow, rude steps cut in the stone were littered with pebbles, as if no one had passed that way in a long time. The trail leading up the scarp to the heights where the herders kept their goats and wooldeer was clear of debris.

Ilakri crawled from the safety of the cave into the open air, but stayed in shadow. He stood up and felt the pressure of rough, dry stone against his newly-metamorphosed feet. His Master's cloak was more confining than youngling's garb, but seemed appropriate to his changed body. He tugged at the sash with one six-fingered hand and waited for his eyes to become accustomed to the light.

The midday sun was bright. Its golden globe hung high in the southern sky, but not high enough to light the southeastern wall of the arroyo. Even in the shadows, the auras that surrounded everything disrupted Ilakri's depth perception. He leaned forward to look at the steps, trying to judge their height. Then he carefully lowered his left foot to the first step. A pebble slipped between two of his foot's broad pads and rubbed against the tender new tissue. He drew his foot back and sat down at the mouth of the cavern. Jaella had given him a pair of soft boots along with other new clothes. Ilakri had never worn boots. He took them from his pocket, stroked the heavy goathide soles and the soft uppers of scraped and tanned wool-deer skin. Jaella had made them herself, and he sensed some of her aura when he touched them.

Ilakri picked the pebble from his foot, tossed it into the arroyo. Then he pulled on the boots and struggled with the lacings that bound them to his legs. He had to rewrap the right one twice before he was satisfied that the boots would stay on.

He slowly climbed down the steps, searching for the most stable footing on the loose rock. Soon the slope became a vertical drop. He pressed his right shoulder to the wall and hoped he would not fall. Halfway down he stopped to rest and count the remaining steps on his fingers. *Five hands plus three,* he thought, although there might be more. The shadows at the bottom were deep.

The steps ended too soon. Ilakri stared at the sheer drop that seemed as deep as he was tall. He had no rope, no ladder. He sat down, dangled his legs over the edge, and was surprised to see that his feet almost touched the arroyo floor. His legs had grown during the metamorphosis; he was taller, tall enough to slip off the step and land on his feet with only a minor stumble.

The ground was littered with fallen rock and other debris swept from the heights by the winter rains. Ilakri trod carefully, stepping over small obstacles and climbing around large ones. The dry canyon widened as he moved northward. He tried to stay close to the sunny west wall. Once he disturbed a basking lizard.

It disappeared under a rock. He walked well away from it; the blue lizards were sometimes poisonous.

He moved slowly, as if through a dream, not quite connected with the movements of his new body and the unfamiliar features of the landscape. The hazy auras that surrounded everything no longer surprised him. His thoughts were focused on the task ahead—conquering the ruins, and then the trek far to the west and north, to the sea and the fisher village.

Chapter 2

The iron bar would not move. It was an ordinary hexagonal cylinder, no larger than Sinykin Inda's littlest finger, and it stood on end on his desk. He stared at the iron's dull gray surface and willed the cylinder to tip over. He imagined one of his fingers reaching out, touching the cool metal, pushing against it just hard enough to tumble it to its side. Its position did not change. Inda, physician and former assistant administrator of the spaceport, drew a deep breath and closed his eyes.

The air in the mountains was cold, even within the stone walls of the Iron Keep. Especially within the Iron Keep. Inda shivered, from excitement and fear as much as from the chill. The passageway was dark and dusty. He stood at its end, facing a smooth wooden door, and considered returning to the dubious safety of his room. Instead he reached out with his mind, let his thoughts touch the hidden iron bar that controlled the door's latch, turned the bar, listened for the click. Then he pushed open the door and began climbing the staircase. . . .

That climb two months ago had nearly cost his life. Fear still tightened his chest when he thought of the tower and the psychic powers of the Ardellans who worked there. Nor could he forget that instant of magic when he had moved the iron bar and opened the latch with a thought. The dingy white walls of his office, the ranked vials of vaccine on the table, were less real to him than that memory of power.

Yet he could not re-create that momentary magic. He had tried again and again, at home and in the safety of his spaceport office, but he was unable to move any object with his thoughts alone. Inda feared he had forever lost that wondrous power. With his eyes still closed, he envisioned the iron cylinder tipping, falling, clattering to its side on the desk. Nothing happened. He muttered an oath, slammed his palm against the corner of his desk, heard the soft thud of the metal bar falling. Dull pain cramped the base of his thumb. The comm console behind him beeped as an incoming message was added to the queue.

Rubbing his hand, Inda turned his back on Ardellan magic and faced Terran technology. He tapped the keypad to access his mail. The first message, from the technical office of the Interstellar Trade Commission, did not warrant an immediate response. Another tap routed it to short-term memory. Inda rarely generated hard copy; it was too expensive on a world that produced no paper of its own.

A bulletin from medical was short and to the point. "STOP BY THE INFIRMARY FOR YOUR MANDATORY VACCINATION AGAINST THE ARDELLAN FLU." The Ardellan flu was one of a handful of nonterrestrial diseases that crossed species lines to affect humans. It had produced a mild illness in Terrans at the spaceport last season, and had killed many Ardellans in their cities and keeps. Inda had developed a simple vaccine, then had traveled to the keeps to collect tissue and blood samples from Ardellans. His tests had proved the vaccine safe for the natives, yet now they had no access to it. The spaceport's administrator, frightened by the Ardellans' previously undocumented psychic powers, had closed the compound after Inda's trip outside. Ardellans were forbidden to enter it, and Terrans were forbidden to leave.

Plague season was coming soon; Inda feared that many Ardellans would die before its end. His vaccine, carefully prepared and stockpiled in hundred-dose vials in the lab, was being wasted on people who had no need for it. He erased the bulletin with a stab of his finger and a curse.

Inda's eyes widened when he saw the dateline on the third message. The Trade Commission Secretary's name and seal appeared above encrypted text. Inda's fingers flew over the numeric pad, automatically entering his security code. Characters danced and flickered on his viewer. He smiled. This might be it at last—official notification of his appointment as the Terran Union's envoy to the Ardellan people. He would once again have authority to travel beyond the spaceport gate. He could carry the vaccine to the Ardellans himself.

Inda's smile faded as the characters finished sorting themselves into readable text.

2262:9/14, TERRAN CALENDAR
SECURITY/SCRAMBLED
TO: SINYKIN INDA, MD
FROM: HOWARD SANDSMARK, SECRETARY,
      INTERSTELLAR TRADE COMMISSION
PLEASED WITH YOUR SUCCESS IN DEVELOPING VACCINE. DISSEMINATE TO NATIVE HEALERS BY WHATEVER MEANS AVAILABLE. IMPERATIVE THIS OFFICE REMAIN UNINVOLVED.

POLITICAL CLIMATE MAKES IT UNWISE TO APPOINT AN ENVOY AT THIS TIME.

NAGASHIMI-BOEM CORP YESTERDAY RECEIVED JUDGMENT AGAINST THOR'S MOON MINING COLONY FOR NONDELIVERY OF CONTRACTED ORES. TRADE COMMISSION ORDERED TO ABANDON FACILITY IN FAVOR OF NAGASHIMI-BOEM. STATUS OF ARDELLAN BASE THREATENED UNLESS TITANIUM MINING COMMENCES IMMEDIATELY.

MINERS SHOULD ARRIVE WITH FINAL SHIPMENT OF EQUIPMENT 9/18. MAINTAIN

POSITIVE CONTACTS WITH NATIVE LEADERS
TO ENSURE SMOOTH COMMENCEMENT OF
MINING OPERATIONS.

UNDERSTAND YOUR PROBLEMS WITH AD-
MINISTRATION. WIDER POLITICAL CONSID-
ERATIONS MAKE IT DIFFICULT FOR ME TO
INTERVENE. HANDLE AS YOU SEE FIT.
ENDMESSAGE
AUTOWIPE

Inda blinked as his viewer returned to blank screen.
His right hand stroked the frown lines on his brow. He
closed his eyes and tried to will away his headache. *By
all the ancient gods,* he thought, *what is Sandsmark
doing to me? He entices me to this post with his promise
to appoint me envoy, then abandons me to the mercies
of an incompetent administrator. He orders me
to vaccinate the Ardellans, then warns me that he cannot defend me if I break the travel ban. Bureaucrats!*

The news about Nagashimi-BOEM and the mining
colony was even more alarming. The interstellar corporation was well known for its exploitation of native
populations and their mineral resources. Nagashimi-
BOEM operatives had been involved in the deaths of
several Ardellans before the Terran Union signed an
exclusive trade agreement that forced the corporation
to abandon its claim to the planet's resources.

Inda's fingers tapped the keys once more, entering
the code for his wife's office in Maintenance and Engineering. He wanted to apprise her of this latest development before he made any decisions.

"Chief Durant's office." Jer Robinson, Elissa's
clerk, looked up from his desk. He was a tall man;
even with the vid-phone's camera set to maximum
field, the edge of the screen clipped his forehead below the hairline. "Hello, Dr. Inda. What can we do
for you?"

"Is Elissa in?"

Robinson shook his head. "She's testing equipment in the mine room. Shall I patch you through?"

"No. I'll walk over and talk with her. I can use the exercise."

Robinson laughed. "I could use more of that myself. My partner says that if I gain any more weight, I'll have to pay extra for my ticket off this planet."

"You'll just have to convince Elissa to build you that anti-grav belt," said Inda before he cut the connection. Robinson's weight problem and the mythical anti-grav belt was a long-standing joke, actively encouraged by Robinson. Two centuries ago he might have parlayed his strength into a fortune on Terra's gaming fields; in this age his great size often was a liability. Robinson had turned this trick of fate into a social advantage.

The wind outside the medical building was cold and heavy with moisture. Inda skirted a spring puddle as he strode across the pavement. Piles of snow on either side of the walkway had been diminished by sunlight and the play of children. Here the rubble of a snow fort withered, there the packed snow of a slide melted to slush. Spring rains would soon wash away the last evidence of winter.

Inda looked across the landing field at the two great windmills that provided most of the installation's power. In the last winter storm the right tower had tumbled and nearly killed Elissa. Now it was erect again, blades turning in the wind driving its squeaky shaft. The windmills stood as twin idols guarding the road that led to Ardel's titanium mines. Their steel towers reminded Inda that all gods, even technological gods, sometimes exacted sacrifices.

A makeshift fence stretched across the front of the compound, from the stable's corral to the agricultural center's enclosure. A simple gate barred the trail to the FreeMasters' guildhall and Alu Keep. For the first four years of Terran occupancy Inda had never seen the gate closed; FreeMasters were welcomed at the compound and Terrans, adhering to the trade agreement, only left it with permission from the Ardellans. Yet when Inda had returned from his trip into the mountains ten weeks ago, he had found the gate—and the compound—sealed. Terrans were to stay inside, Ardellans outside, by decree of Administrator Anna Griswold.

Neither calm discussion nor angry rhetoric had persuaded Griswold to lift the restriction against mixing with the Ardellans. Inda had been depending on the appointment as envoy to set him outside her jurisdiction. Then he could carry his vaccine to the Ardellan keeps and villages and train their Healers to administer it. Griswold's ramshackle fence was not strong enough to keep a determined person from entering or leaving the compound. Inda saw it as a symbolic barrier, a reminder that crossing it would allow Griswold to charge him with insubordination and to request that he be recalled from Ardel.

Howard Sandsmark wanted the vaccine distributed to the Ardellans, but he would commit neither himself nor his power as Secretary of the Trade Commission to force Griswold's hand. His message had said, "Handle as you see fit." "It's your ass, not mine," was Inda's loose translation. He wondered if Elissa would agree.

Elissa's office was located in the tech building, a huge hangar opening onto the near side of the landing field. It housed Maintenance and Engineering, and was the sturdiest, best-equipped building on the base. The Trade Commission cut expenses wherever it could, except in the maintenance of its ships.

The landing field was empty, the hangar doors closed. Inda entered the building through a human-sized door and climbed the stairs to the gallery of offices that ringed the open work space. Trucks and heavy equipment, drums of solvent and huge loops of cable lined the walls below. Engineers in bright orange jackets worked among them. The hangar was cold.

Inda waved to Jer Robinson as he passed the clerk's office. He stopped at the drink dispenser, punched up a cup of black coffee for Elissa and herbal tea for himself. Offering in hand, he walked to the mine room.

The door opened into a glass-walled cubicle that gave him a view of the projection room. Elissa sat in one of a half-dozen contoured chairs arranged in a ring in the room's center. Her right hand gripped the end of an oversized joystick that extended downward from the ceiling. A black net glove covered her left arm from fingers to elbow, and opaque goggles hid her eyes. The toes and heels of her boots were locked into stirrups attached to a sensor pad on the floor. A rainbow festoon of slender cables connected her glove and goggles to the central processor.

Inda watched Elissa's movements for a moment, wondering which of the pieces of heavy mining equipment she was testing. Her left hand manipulated unseen buttons and levers, while her right swung the joystick in wide arcs and her feet shifted on the sensor pad. She moved in her chair as she would if she rode in the control cabin of one of the giant mining excavators.

The coffee was getting cold. Inda set it on the desk and entered a greeting on the keypad. His message was projected onto the inside of Elissa's goggles, along the upper edge where it didn't interfere with the scene she was viewing. Elissa flashed the "task terminated" response, and began shutting down the vehicle's systems. Disconnecting from the sensory network took less than three minutes.

"Coffee," said Elissa as she entered the booth. Inda handed her the cup. She raked the fingers of her left hand through her hair, fluffing chestnut curls matted by the goggles' straps. She sipped, and shrugged. "I like it cold."

"You're used to it cold. I can get you another."

"This is fine." She smiled. "What brings you here? Do you want to ride the spook?"

Inda laughed. "Riding the spook" was engineers' slang for hooking into the mine room's computer network. Sensors at the mine site delivered data to the central processor, and it projected a holographic image of the mine and its equipment inside the miners' goggles. The miners used the processor's controls to manipulate that virtual image. Their actions were translated exactly to the mine site, moving the trucks and 'dozers and the huge crane as they specified. To anyone not hooked into the network, they appeared to be handling invisible controls in unseen cockpits.

"I like to watch you work. How are the tests going?"

"The depth perception translator needs adjustment," said Elissa as she tapped some codes in at the keyboard. "I'll have to get a tech in to help me check it."

"I thought you weren't supposed to run the equipment without a tech present." Inda was concerned. Elissa usually followed protocols to the letter. He looked more carefully at her face, noticed the tiny lines stress had etched around her eyes and mouth. She was working too hard.

"Everyone is busy today. Half of my team is completing testing at the mill. The miners will be here before the end of the week, and all the equipment must be up and running when they arrive. We have to ship our first load of titanium in ten days."

"Then you've heard from the Trade Commission," said Inda. "I received a message from Sandsmark today."

"Your appointment? Has it come through?" Elissa finished her coffee and added the cup to the untidy pile of empties waiting to be returned to the dispenser.

"No." Inda shook his head. He was feeling frustrated by Sandsmark's political games. It was beginning to look as if the promised appointment as envoy

would never materialize. "Sandsmark warned me that
Nagashimi-BOEM and some of the other big corporations are trying to discredit him and the Trade Commission. They've taken control of the base on Thor's
moon. They might try to take Ardel if we can't deliver
the titanium on time. Sandsmark is fighting to keep
this planet out of Nagashimi-BOEM's hands. He won't
appoint an envoy until he's sure Ardel is secure.

"He did ask me to distribute the plague vaccine to
the Ardellans, but he warned me not to expect any
help from him if I run into trouble with Griswold."

Elissa crinkled her nose as if she smelled something
distasteful. "Now that's useful." She had a gift for
sarcasm. "How are you supposed to get the vaccine
to the Ardellans without violating Griswold's restrictions? Did Sandsmark have any ideas?"

" 'By whatever means available.' I'm on my own
for now."

"Then you must do what you can without his help.
Go talk with Griswold. Plague season is coming.
Surely she'll let the Healers come to your lab. You can
give them equipment and teach them how to administer the vaccine. Convince her."

"Easy to say, Lissie, but difficult to do." Inda took
her hand. "I've been thinking of leaving the compound without permission."

Elissa pulled her fingers from his and stepped away.
"Griswold will have you recalled if you set foot outside the fence. You know she's been waiting for that.
Only Sandsmark's support saved you from recall last
time you left the compound."

"The plague killed hundreds of Ardellans last year.
I'll do whatever I must to prevent more deaths."

"Even if it creates havoc in my life and Jaime's?
He's your son, Sinykin. How can you risk splitting
up our family? Jaime ran away last time you left the
compound. He wanted to follow you into the mountains. What will he do if you're forced to leave Ar-

del? I couldn't abandon my contract here to go with you.''

"I wouldn't expect you to do that." Inda stepped closer and laid a reassuring hand on her shoulder. "I'll talk with Griswold. Perhaps I can convince her to open the compound again."

"Try." Elissa hugged him. "Now go. I have work to do."

Inda walked out of the dim tech building into bright sunlight. He squinted against the snow glare, saw something moving out beyond the gate. An alep and rider were approaching from the nearby FreeMasters' guildhall, probably bearing a message. Inda hurried toward the gate.

Two members of the spaceport's meager security force were talking in the gate house. Inda stopped at the window to greet them.

"Hello, Juan, Moshe. Do you have a recorder ready?" Although Inda and several others at the spaceport spoke Ardellan and a number of the FreeMasters spoke Terran standard, neither group was yet able to read the other's writing. The Ardellans inscribed their scrolls with complex runes, each representing a word or phrase. Until the planned cross-cultural dictionary was ready, all messages from the natives were recorded in Ardellan and in Standard, if the messenger was fluent in the Terran language.

"Here it is, Dr. Inda," said Moshe Steinmetz, offering up the tiny disk recorder. "Will you take the message yourself?"

"Yes, thank you," said Inda. He clipped the recorder to his belt and stepped up to the gate.

The alep was plodding down the rutted road on all six of its flat-footed legs. Inda had ridden aleps and knew the speeds of which they were capable. They often ran on smooth ground, their central pair of legs folded against their bellies. He preferred riding at the slower, more stable six-legged gait.

This animal's shaggy winter coat was matted and gray with dirt. It would shed its fur in clumps when the weather warmed, and reveal the distinctive pattern of its undercoat. Now the alep's color gave no clue to its, or its rider's, identity.

The rider was bundled in a voluminous brown cloak, the heavy hood pulled forward to hide his face. He was not a FreeMaster; they wore gray or silver cloaks. Full sleeves covered his hands, and only the soles of his soft leather boots showed below the cloak's hem. Inda watched and waited, wondering who this might be.

The alep stopped ten meters from the gate, and its rider lifted his right arm in greeting. The sleeve of his cloak fell back, revealing a hand held palm-outward, the six fingers spread around the circular palm to form a sunburst.

"May the great sun shine on you today, Healer Inda!" called the rider in the bell-like tones of the local Ardellan dialect.

"And on you, Master," replied Inda, returning the gesture as best he could with four fingers and a thumb.

"Do you not know me?" The rider swept back his hood, revealing sparkling gray eyes and a youthful face capped by fine straw-colored hair.

"Septi!" Master Septi, a member of Clan Alu, was a musician of high reputation and a close companion of Inda's Ardellan friend, Ertis. "It is good to see you. How has your House fared this winter?"

"Torma and the younglings are well." Septi dismounted, then led his alep to the gate.

"And Ertis? Is he also well?"

"He is eagerly awaiting the emergence of his new mate from the cocoon. By midsummer Ertis will be a Mother, with a gaggle of younglings to care for."

Inda tried to envision the slender, frail historian as a female—round of body, with tentacles supplementing her arms and a half-dozen helpless younglings clinging to her. The image did not seem realistic.

"I have brought you a message." Septi reached inside his cloak and produced a scroll of writing cloth. He read the runes first in Ardellan.

"From Jeryl, Mentor of Clan Alu, to Healer Inda of the Terran compound. May the great sun shine on you this day.

"My friend Hanra-bae, Master Healer of Port Freewind, sends word that the warm winds have come to the shore, and plague season is beginning. He fears for the lives of his people. Sixteen hands of Mothers died in the fisher village during the last plague season, and twice as many younglings were deformed by the illness.

"Is your plague-stopper ready? Will you ride to Port Freewind and teach the Master Healer how to use it? Alu will provide the necessary mounts and pack animals, and a guide and escort.

"I would welcome your presence at Alu Keep before you begin this journey."

Septi repeated the message in carefully-accented Standard, then paused for Inda's reply.

"The vaccine is ready," Inda said in Ardellan. "I do not know if I will be allowed to bring it out of the compound myself. Perhaps the Master Healer could come here, and I could teach him how to use it."

"I will take that message back to Jeryl. By the time Hanra-bae is contacted, and travels here and then returns to Port Freewind, many of the fishers may have fallen ill. It would be better if you could go to him."

"I know." Inda offered up both hands in the Ardellan gesture that begged forgiveness. "I must talk with my superior. Return here tomorrow with a spare alep, and I will give you my answer then."

"I will return," said Septi. He swung up into the saddle and turned his alep away from the gate. "I wish you good luck," he said in Standard before he rode away.

"Ride in sunshine," called Inda. He unclipped the recorder, removed the disk and slipped it into his pocket, and returned the machine to Steinmetz on his way to the administration building.

Griswold's office was on the second floor of the building, just down the hall from the office formerly occupied by Inda. Until recently Inda had been Assistant Administrator and head of the spaceport's Science Division. Now his friend Jeff Grund occupied both the office and the administrative post. Inda stopped outside Grund's door, considered knocking, realized he was attempting to postpone his confrontation with Griswold. He walked on.

Griswold's door was closed. The white plaque centered just above eye level read, "Anna Griswold, Administrator." Below it hung a holograph of two freighters on the landing field, with the huge hangar in the background. The interplay of light and shadow on the ships' pocked hulls made it one of Griswold's best.

Inda knocked.

"Come," said Griswold in her low, soft, not quite feminine voice.

Inda turned the knob, fleetingly wondering how Griswold would react if he could open this door with a thought. Would she banish him from the compound for practicing Ardellan magic? "Good afternoon, Anna. Do you have a moment for me?"

"Certainly." She entered a code at her keyboard, then pushed the pad aside and faced him across a bare patch of desk. More holos, and a dozen old-fashioned photographs, covered the wall behind her. There were no landscapes, no portraits, no candid shots of people. All the images were studies of made things—buildings, spacecraft, tools. They were all very good.

"Sit down, Sinykin. Would you like some tea?"

"No, thank you." Inda dropped into the chair that some of Griswold's subordinates jokingly called "the seat of inquisition." He noticed the dark circles under the Administrator's eyes, the new strands of white in her steel-gray hair. "You look tired, Anna. Have you been getting enough sleep?"

"Do you ask that as a physician, or as my former assistant?"

"As a physician and a coworker. The health of everyone at the compound concerns me, as does the health of the Ardellans." Inda unzipped his jacket, and removed the disk recording from his pocket. "I received a message from Jeryl today."

"Yes?"

"Plague season has come to the coast. Jeryl fears that there will be many more deaths this year than last." Inda saw the muscles of Griswold's jaw tense. Her eyes narrowed and she pressed her lips tightly together. She would not be easily convinced, but he had promised Elissa that he would try. "Jeryl would like me to vaccinate the Ardellans, beginning in the coastal city of Port Freewind."

"You are needed here, Dr. Inda." Griswold emphasized his title. "I cannot spare you. If the plague is indeed worse this year, we will need you to care for our people."

Inda shook his head. "You know that this virus only causes mild symptoms in humans. I'm surprised that it affects us at all. One day some doctoral student will come here to research its cross-species effects and write a dissertation.

"Everyone in the compound is being vaccinated, and the rest of the medical staff is competent to handle any problems that might arise. You won't need me. The Ardellans will."

Griswold rose and refilled her cup at the beverage dispenser. "There are other things to consider here. Three Terrans have died under strange circumstances while interacting with the Ardellans."

"Those deaths occurred years ago, and have been explained to the Trade Commission's satisfaction."

"But not to my satisfaction. These Ardellans have powers which we don't understand. You experienced

Ardellan treachery in the Iron Keep, yet you continue to defend these people." She walked to the window and looked out across the landing field. "I cannot allow you to leave the compound. It's too dangerous. We don't know enough about what goes on out there. The Ardellans won't even allow you to carry a weapon. I won't be responsible for your death."

"Then let the Healers come here."

Griswold turned back to face him. "Why should we let those superstitious herbalists bring their 'magic' into the compound?"

"Careful, Administrator. Your prejudice is showing. Herbal medicine and psychic healing are often effective for the Ardellans." Inda caught the fleeting look of disapproval on Griswold's face. "The Healers are open to trying our methods where theirs have been unsuccessful. They want to learn how to make and administer our vaccine. I can provide them with administration equipment and a supply of the vaccine for now, and they can come back later to learn how it is made. They are really quite sophisticated. Some of them rightly view us as barbarians. After all, it was a Terran who violated the trade agreement and brought powered weapons to Ardel."

"I cannot allow them to enter the compound."

"Why not? What harm could it do?"

"We have ten days to prepare our first shipment of titanium. If we aren't ready on time, we could lose this base to Nagashimi-BOEM. A single Ardellan saboteur . . ."

Inda stopped trying to hide his anger. "Why would the Ardellans want Nagashimi-BOEM to have this base? They refused to negotiate with the corporation's representatives five years ago. Several Ardellans died because of Nagashimi-BOEM!"

"I don't trust them," said Griswold. She walked back to her desk and sat down. "I won't have them on the base."

"Anna, we could keep the Healers under guard,

even allow only one at a time into the compound. What harm could they do with Security watching them?''

"Do you know the limits of their powers?" she demanded. "I don't. I will risk neither this base nor its personnel. The Ardellans stay outside the gate.''

Inda rose. "Then I am once more applying for permission to leave the compound on a humanitarian medical mission. I will take full responsibility for my actions, and for any harm that may come to my person. You are required by regulations to consider this request. Good day, Administrator.'' He turned and strode from the room, certain that even Elissa would believe he had tried his best to change Griswold's mind. Yet he knew there were other solutions he might have tried, compromises that might have been acceptable to the Administrator. His desire to return to that world beyond the gate had kept him from voicing them.

Chapter 3

Terran Spaceport, Ardel

The shoreline of the northern continent was lengthy and jagged. Inda stared at the map on his terminal's viewer, picking out the tiny characters that designated population centers. It was impossible to tell which was Port Freewind. He touched his light wand to the option that would magnify the display and transfer it to the large wall screen. Nothing happened.

The miners get all the new equipment, he thought, *while Research and Medicine struggle with these outdated units. When will they send me that voice comprehension module?* He checked his command list, tapped the alternate key sequence. The map appeared on the wall.

Port Freewind seemed to be the largest of the fisher communities. It sprawled on the shore of the estuary where the White River flowed into the Storm Sea. The river's wide mouth provided a natural harbor, a safe haven from the wild open waters.

Jeryl had not said how long the trip would take. Inda queried the computer; the distance to Port Freewind was almost three hundred kilometers straight across country. If they rode swiftly, they could cover that distance in three days. It would be so much easier if they could take a shuttle, but Jeryl would no longer allow even small ships to land outside the spaceport. Terran ships too often foreshadowed Ardellan deaths.

Deaths were what Inda hoped to prevent. His vaccine might save lives, prevent deformities, help keep the plague from decimating the dwindling native population. He had witnessed too many deaths, Ardellan and Terran, in his five years on Ardel. He touched the holo-cube that rested on the corner of his desk, and the images inside came to life. He and Elissa and Jaime moved and laughed and hugged one another, yet Sinykin felt more sorrow than joy as he watched the scene. Elissa smiled with her mouth, but her eyes belied any happiness. Their depths were sorrowful, as their daughter Miranda's eyes had been near the end of her long illness. Miranda's absence from the scene was a reminder that even Inda's healing skills could not save everyone.

Enough! There were other deaths that he could prevent. He would do whatever he must to see that the Ardellans were vaccinated against this plague. He released the holo-cube, was already requesting a hard copy of the map as the figures stopped moving. The printer whirred.

"Sinykin?" Jeff Grund, the spaceport's meteorologist, stood in the doorway. His broad shoulders nearly filled the opening. "May I come in?"

Inda nodded. "Did Griswold deputize you to talk me out of my 'madness'?"

"No. I haven't seen her today. Elissa called me." Grund strode across the room and dropped into the chair beside Inda's desk. It creaked a single protest as he leaned back. "She's worried about you. She said you were talking about leaving the compound. What's going on?"

"Plague season has started. Jeryl wants his people to be vaccinated, and Griswold won't allow the Healers inside the compound so that I can teach them how to administer the vaccine."

The printer spat the multicolored map onto the counter behind the desk. Grund leaned forward to look at it, eliciting another complaint from the chair. "So you'll take the vaccine to them, with or without Griswold's permission."

"I've applied for official leave to undertake a humanitarian medical mission," said Inda.

"Griswold will probably deny your request. And if you set foot outside the gate without her permission, she will have you recalled."

"She can try. The Union has a long history of supporting humanitarian missions." Grund was Inda's friend; he had known for weeks that vaccinating the Ardellans was Inda's primary aim. Why was he issuing this warning now? "I believe that Griswold would lose an arbitration hearing." Inda tried to sound more certain than he felt. Sandsmark could not protect him, yet right now no one but he and Elissa knew that.

"Strictly speaking, Griswold can make a case that 'humanitarian missions' apply only to humans," Grund replied. "The Ardellans are dealing with a plague that has been with them for generations. They have their own Healers, their own medicines. She could accuse you of interfering with the natural course of development in a lower-class civilization.

"Even if the Union did decide in your favor, the damage would already have been done. If Griswold petitions for your recall, you'll have to leave Ardel until the matter is settled. Elissa is bound by her contract; she and Jaime will have to stay here.

"And the Union may not be able to save you. The bureaucrats are scrambling to keep this base out of the hands of Nagashimi-BOEM. We received word this morning that Sandsmark is on his way here with Austin Duerst and a team of corporate engineers to inspect the mine."

Inda ground his teeth at the sound of Duerst's name. The legendary VP headed Nagashimi-BOEM's Resource Development division. Under Duerst's guidance the corporation had acquired more materials sources than its three competitors combined, often under less than ethical circumstances. Duerst's office had been implicated in the deaths of several Ardellans, but the Union had been unable to prove a connection. His impending visit to the compound explained at least part of Griswold's paranoia. She was right to fear sabotage, but she should expect it of Duerst's people, not of the Ardellans.

"Sandsmark wants the Ardellans to have this vaccine. Do you know of any other way I can get it to them?"

Grund had no answer. He picked up the holo-cube, and the little family came to life once again. "Haven't Elissa and Jaime lost enough? Will you risk your post and their security on a vaccine that hasn't been proven to work?"

Inda watched the image of Elissa hugging Jaime, and knew what he would be risking by making this trip. "I've seen deformed younglings who will never be metamorphosed into Masters. I've spoken with FreeMasters who have lost their mates to plague, who have lost their Houses and their younglings and had the courses of their lives forever altered. The vaccine is the Ardellans' only chance. They have asked for my help. I cannot withhold it and still call myself a physician."

Grund nodded. "I know that, and I'm sure Elissa knows it. That does not solve the problem. I ask this as a friend, Sinykin. How will you protect your family if you leave the spaceport without Griswold's permission?"

"Elissa's never needed my protection. She'll be fine, and she can take care of Jaime without my help." The words seemed cold and insensitive, even to Inda.

"Well, that's something for you and Elissa to work out." Grund set the holo-cube back on the desk and rose. "Let me know Griswold's decision." He walked from the room without looking back.

Inda picked up the map and folded it into precise rectangles as he contemplated Grund's words. Elissa had always been self-sufficient. The question was not whether she could care for herself and Jaime; it was whether it was reasonable to expect her to do so. Their contract called for shared responsibilities and joint decisions on family matters. He was denying her the right to take part in this decision. He told himself it was to protect her and Jaime, so that her position at the spaceport could not be challenged. Yet deep down he knew that he would let nothing, not even the needs of his family, keep him from returning to that mysterious and magical world beyond the compound.

The map fit neatly into a clear plastic slipcase. He tucked it into the outer pocket of his pack and began to gather the administration equipment he would need. The vials of vaccine were packed in a foam-lined aluminum box with a hinged lid and a locking latch. Each vial, inserted into an air-pressure vaccination gun, would innoculate one hundred Ardellans. Oral vaccine could be administered more easily, but he did not yet know enough Ardellan biochemistry to insure that the vaccine would not be broken down by their digestive systems. Old-fashioned injection seemed the easiest route. He had tested the vaccine on blood and tissue samples from a number of individuals and was reasonably certain there would be no allergic reactions.

A dozen of the vaccination guns, with extra cylinders of compressed air, went into the pack along with some emergency supplies. Most medications would be of no use to the Ardellans. Inda had watched their Healers work; they could effect more cures with their mind-powers than he could with a bag full of drugs. Bandages, synthetic skin, and sutures might be useful. He dropped steri-paks of each into the pack.

Iron was the trade metal among Ardellans, so he tossed a half-dozen small iron bars into the pouch. He packed nothing that required a source of electrical power. The Ardellans had always banned powered weapons; a few unscrupulous Terrans had ignored the restriction. Now all electrical power sources were forbidden. A bioluminescent lantern with extra packets of chemicals to renew its light took up the last space in the pack. Inda slipped his journal and a few pens into the pocket with the map. He was ready.

The summons to Griswold's office came at 16:30.

Inda stopped at the desk of the administrative secretary, Lindy Zapata, and waited while she buzzed Griswold's office.

"Send him in," said the Administrator.

Griswold met Inda at the door. "Good afternoon, Sinykin. Thank you for being so prompt." She led him to the pair of comfortable chairs near the window. A teapot and two mugs were waiting on the table. Griswold sat, poured tea for both of them, and handed him a mug before she spoke.

"I envy you your trip to Alu Keep. I've never been there, you know. I haven't been outside this compound since the day I arrived on Ardel."

"Few Terrans have traveled beyond the fence," said Inda. "The Ardellans are understandably cautious about inviting us into their settlements."

"They still hold us responsible for the killings five years ago, don't they?"

Inda shrugged. "Three Ardellans were murdered by Terran weapons. Does that give them reason to trust us?"

"No, of course not." Griswold sipped her tea. "Tell me about Alu Keep."

"I described it in my report." This uncharacteristic probing made Inda wary. "What else do you want to know?"

"What does the keep look like? How was it built? How old is it?"

"It's a village of stone buildings enclosed by a high stone wall. I can't guess at how they built it. Many of the stone blocks are huge. I spent some time in one of the Houses and didn't see any seams or mortared joints. It was as if the House had been carved from a solid piece of stone. The outer walls of the buildings seem weathered by centuries of wind and rain. The keep has been there for a long time.''

Griswold nodded. She was facing Inda, but her eyes were focused beyond him, on a world of memory or imagination. "I'd like to photograph the keep. I made holographic records of archeological sites before I signed on with the Trade Commission. It was interesting work. No two cultures have quite the same kinds of homes, or build things in the same ways.''

Inda felt a surge of hope. Griswold was thinking of leaving the compound herself; surely she would allow him to take his vaccine to the Ardellans. "I'm certain that Jeryl could arrange for you to visit Alu Keep. The current ban on power sources would prohibit holographic equipment, but if you have a manually-operated camera you could take photographs.''

"Perhaps some day when travel is safer I shall discuss it with him. I am not inclined to take unnecessary risks, and it would not be appropriate for me to leave the compound now. Secretary Sandsmark is on his way to inspect the mine, and Austin Duerst of Nagashimi-BOEM is coming with him. We shall all be very busy readying the base for their visit and preparing our first shipment of titanium ore.'' She refilled her mug and offered more tea to Inda. He declined; he had hardly tasted the tea. His stomach was a knot of tension as he waited for Griswold to announce her decision.

"I understand how important this medical mission is to you.''

"It is important to the Ardellans, Anna. This vaccine will save lives. Hundreds of Mothers and younglings died last year. Many others suffered terrible deformities. Our vaccine can keep that from happening again.''

"Your vaccine has not yet been tested," said Griswold. "You don't know that it will prevent illness in the Ardellans. I wish I could grant you permission to go out and test it. The situation here is too unstable to allow that right now. Perhaps after Sandsmark's visit . . .''

"By then it may be too late." Inda's tension turned to anger as he realized that Griswold was not going to let him leave the base. "You are condemning these people to another year of pain and suffering!"

"I am only postponing the experimental trial of this vaccine for a few weeks."

"The insects that carry the plague are already hatching in the coastal waters."

"Then they should kill the insects. Perhaps a pesticide . . ."

Inda was exasperated. "Anna, you can't be serious!"

"No, not really." She shrugged apologetically. "Don't the insects have a natural predator that could be released in the area? There must be another way to control the spread of this plague."

"The insects have their own role in the biosphere. Perhaps their population could be controlled, but we would have to study the situation extensively before deciding what measures to take." Inda decided to make one last plea. "The vaccine won't disrupt the ecosphere. It's the simplest solution, Anna. Please let me go."

She shook her head. "After Sandsmark's visit. Not until then."

Inda swallowed his anger and put on an acquiescent face. "All right. I'll hold you to your word. I expect to walk through the gate as soon as Sandsmark's ship lifts off."

"Done."

"Elissa is very busy getting ready for this inspection," said Inda. His pulse was racing. He was not accustomed to prevaricating. "My work is caught up right now. I'd like to take a few days off to spend with Jaime."

"That's no problem. Make sure your department knows about the inspection."

"I'll route a memo to all personnel." He rose and started toward the door, then turned back as if he had forgotten something. "Septi is coming for my answer tomorrow morning. I'll be meeting him at the gate at dawn."

"Fine," said Griswold. She had returned to her desk and was already hard at work.

Elissa cycled the equipment to standby and locked the projection room before walking back to her office. Jer Robinson was already gone. He had left her a note about the coming inspection. She scanned it, decided that the problem could wait until morning, and set it aside. Her jacket was hanging on a peg beside the door. She put it on, turned out the light, and closed the door as she left.

Only the safety lights were on in the hangar. They shed minimal illumination along the walkways and on the stairs. Bulky equipment loomed even larger in the dimness, casting huge black shadows across the hangar floor and up the far wall. Elissa felt at home here, even in the shadows. She knew every cubic meter of the building as if she had built it herself.

The steel stairs rang as she trod on them. The noise echoed in the hangar, and then Elissa heard another sound, faint and unfamiliar, on the floor below. She stopped to listen, heard only the soft whir of the ineffectual heating plant. "You've been working too hard," she muttered to herself, and continued on her way.

She stopped at the outer door, turned back to look into the now-quiet hangar, and thought about calling Security. They had searched the building before and never turned up more than a nest of mice or a stray coney seeking shelter from the cold. Either would explain the sound she had heard. She decided not to bother Security. They would expect her to wait while they conducted the search. She opened the door and stepped out into the cold night air.

The sun had set hours ago, and the smaller of Ardel's two moons had already risen. Elissa walked the narrow pathway across the compound to the family housing units.

Light shone from the big front window of their apartment. Elissa looked in, saw Jaime running toward the kitchen. She smiled. It was good to be home. She would step across the threshold and forget about Sandsmark and the inspection until morning.

"Jaime! Sinykin! What's for dinner?" she called as she pulled off her orange jacket and put it away. She smelled fresh garlic and rosemary. The viewer in the entertainment center displayed a page of text from Tony Hillerman's *Talking God*. Sinykin must have been reading it. Classic mystery novels were Elissa's passion; she was rarely able to interest Sinykin in them. She had not had much time to read lately. Perhaps after Sandsmark's visit they could read one together.

"Mom!" Jaime stuck his head around the corner and smiled at her. "I thought you'd never get home. Dad said I couldn't eat until you got here!"

"I made brown rice and lentils with onions, and fresh broccoli," said Sinykin. "It'll be ready in a few minutes. Would you prefer tea or coffee?"

Elissa strode into the kitchen. The room was less messy than usual; Jaime was stuffing onion peels and broccoli stems into the composter, and Sinykin had confined his culinary efforts to two pots, which was one less than he customarily used. The table was set, and a fragrant tea was steeping in the pot.

"Tea, I think," she said. "I've had too much coffee today."

"Too much cold coffee," said Sinykin, laughing. "Jaime, please get me the cheese."

"Did you work hard today, Mom? You should sit down and rest." Jaime's words sounded muffled. His head, both arms, and most of his torso were in the cooler, where he was searching for the missing cheese. "Are you sure we have some?"

"Look behind the bowl of ground-plums."

"Found it!" Jaime surfaced, the package of ersatz cheddar clutched triumphantly in one hand. The other was stuffing a sweet ground-plum into his mouth. He kicked the cooler door shut. "Can I have some hot chocolate?"

"Before bedtime," said Elissa. She sat at the table and watched Inda grate cheese over the rice mixture. "Are you studying with Tommy tonight?"

Jaime nodded. "We have to do a special project on Beluki artifacts. Ms. Griswold brought her holograph collection to school today and showed us what they look like. She's seen more than thirty of them! They're weird."

"What did you learn about the Beluki?" asked Inda as he brought the food to the table.

"They were all over the galaxy five thousand years ago, and then they just disappeared. We've found the ruins of their cities on lots of planets, but nobody knows what happened to them." Jaime scooped two spoonfuls of the sticky rice mixture onto his plate, then passed the bowl to Elissa. "Some people spend their whole lives studying the Beluki. I think it would be fun to do that."

Elissa nodded. "Xeno-archaeologists go to school for many years before they are allowed to work at Beluki ruins or handle the artifacts. Which sort of artifacts did Ms. Griswold show you?"

"One that was shiny green, like one of the glazes we used on our pottery in craft class. It was long and thin, and had a funny bump on the end." He speared a dark green broccoli floret, looked at it as if considering the advisability of cutting it in half, then stuffed the whole piece into his mouth. He had to chew for quite a while before he could swallow and speak again. "They were lots of different colors—blue and pink and sort of sunset colors. They were funny shapes, too. Some looked like clubs, and some were big rings, and some were kind of squiggly. They were all shiny, though.''

Inda smiled. "Did Ms. Griswold tell you that the artifacts are divided into classes by shape and color?''

Jaime nodded. "And no one knows what they were used for. That's what our project is. We have to learn the different classes, and try to guess what they were for.''

"That'll be fun," said Elissa. "I did the same kind of project when I was in school.''

"Students your age have wonderful imaginations,'' added Sinykin. "These class projects give the scholars lots of unique ideas about the Beluki and their artifacts.''

"Teacher said that the best reports would be sent on to the Beluki Institute on Titan.'' Jaime stuffed one last piece of broccoli into his mouth and pushed his empty plate away. "Can I go now?'' he mumbled around the broccoli.

"Of course. When will you be home?''

"I might spend the night. Is that all right?''

"If Tommy's mother says it is.'' Elissa knew that her friend Marta Grund would send Jaime home if his visit became inconvenient. "Call us if you decide to stay.''

"I will.'' He grabbed his jacket from the closet and stuffed a handful of textbook disks into his pocket as he headed for the door.

"I wish I had half his energy,'' said Inda. He sighed. "Did you resolve the problem with the depth perception translator?''

Elissa shook her head. "I'm not sure what's wrong. It's just a little out of spec. We haven't been able to track down the anomaly yet. Rys and I are going to work on it tomorrow.''

"What about the mill? Is the work on schedule?''

"It is. The crew had a good day today. They should finish up in the morning, and be able to start testing the equipment before the miners arrive.''

"That's great. I wish Nagashimi-BOEM wasn't breathing down our necks. Someone connected with that corporation really wants this base."

Elissa nodded. A long time ago Sinykin had read her some passages from the journal of Sarah Anders, the first Terran envoy on Ardel. Anders had been a capable negotiator, yet her mission to establish a trade agreement with the Ardellans had been sabotaged and nearly thwarted by operatives she suspected of working for Nagashimi-BOEM. Elissa had been chilled by the corporation's ruthless pursuit of exploitable resources and greater profits. Now it was evident that Nagashimi-BOEM still coveted Ardel's plentiful titanium reserves.

"My team is committed to meeting the terms of that contract," said Elissa. "We'll do everything we can to keep Nagashimi-BOEM off Ardel."

Inda nodded. "Those corporate bureaucrats are ruthless. They'd crush the natives in their rush to exploit Ardel's resources." He stood and began to clear the table.

Elissa watched Sinykin, wondering how long he would avoid the topic of his visit to the Administrator's office. She decided not to wait for him to broach the subject. "Speaking of the native population, how did Griswold take your suggestion that she allow the Healers to visit your lab?"

"She was more concerned about the Ardellans than I had expected." He turned away to dump food scraps into the composter.

"What does that mean?" He was being evasive. Elissa gulped the rest of her tea, then carried the cup to the cleaner.

Inda shrugged. "You know how suspicious she is."

Elissa took the plate from his hand and dropped it into the cleaner along with the cup. "Don't avoid giving me an answer. What did she say?"

"She's afraid the Healers might try to sabotage the

mine. Isn't that ludicrous? The Ardellans don't want
Nagashimi-BOEM to take control of the spaceport!''

"You don't know that for certain. Jeryl and Clan
Alu may be happy dealing with the Terran Union, but
you've told me that the guilds aren't content. Perhaps
they would send someone . . .'' Sabotage? The idea
was incredible. Still, that noise she'd heard in the hangar . . . perhaps she should call Security after all. But
first she wanted to know what Sinykin planned to do.
"Are you going to leave the compound?''

His mysterious black eyes had always intrigued her.
Sometimes she looked into them and glimpsed his
soul; other times she saw only a reflection of herself.
Tonight his pupils were dark mirrors.

"I'm leaving at dawn tomorrow.'' He touched her
hand. "I have to go, Lissie. People will die if I don't
bring them the vaccine.''

"Do you have Griswold's permission?''

He shook his head. "She said she'd consider it after
Sandsmark and Duerst complete their inspection. I
can't wait that long. The Ardellans can't wait that
long.''

Elissa was angry. "You'll leave me here to cope
with Jaime and the mine and the inspection . . . and
Griswold! She will surely have you recalled.''

"I'm sorry, Lissie. I'm not doing this to hurt you or
Jaime.'' He reached for her, and she pushed him away.
"It wasn't an easy decision for me to make.''

"How can you abandon your family like this?''
Elissa heard the words and immediately regretted say-
ing them. Sinykin was not abandoning her or Jaime.
His work was important to him and to the Ardellans.
She turned away, walked to the window and pretended
to stare out at the landing field. Her voice was very
quiet when she spoke again. "Take a transceiver with
you. I don't want us to be out of touch with each
other.''

"You know I can't do that, Elissa.''

He was standing behind her, so close that she could

smell the faint scent of his depilatory. Reflex and long familiarity urged her to lean back, to press her shoulder blades against his chest and pull his arms around her, but she was too angry to surrender to it. She watched his shadowy reflection on the windowpane and wished that he would stay with her, yet she would not use threats to keep him from leaving.

Inda touched her hair, let his fingers trail through the soft curls. "A transceiver might be mistaken for a weapon. I don't dare carry one. I'll send you a message every day, have one of the FreeMasters deliver it to the gate, and you can give him messages to bring back to me. Will that do?"

She wanted to say no, to tell him that her only wish was to have him in her bed every night. Instead she nodded. Then she drew a deep breath and stepped away from him.

"I'm going to call Security," she said. "I heard a noise in the hangar tonight. Harwood will probably want to search the building. I'll have to go back and wait until they're finished."

"All right," said Inda. "I'll wait up for you."

"The building is clean, Chief Durant," said Security Chief Alec Harwood. "Joswyn spotted a coney behind one of the trucks. We'll set out some live traps in the morning. There was nothing else out of the ordinary."

Elissa smiled and offered her hand. Harwood took it between both of his. "Thanks for coming out so late, Alec. I'm sorry to have bothered you for nothing." She liked this big, gruff man. He reminded her of the clichéd police officer of another century's fiction rather than of the conniving security operative of popular holofilms.

"It's never a bother, and it's never nothing, Elissa. Call me any time."

"I will," she said as she walked with him to the

door. He waited as she locked the building behind them.

"I'll see you at the staff meeting tomorrow." He took the walkway to the right, toward the quarters for unpartnered staff.

"Thanks again," Elissa called after him. She started down the path toward home, then turned back and walked onto the landing field instead.

The smaller moon, dubbed "Junior" by Jaime's classmates and Museos by the astronomers, was high in the sky. His sister satellite, much larger Hecate, was just rising. She was nearly full and looked huge and yellow as she climbed above the horizon. Elissa could pick out the two most distinctive landmarks on Hecate's dappled surface, the broad reflective plane of Cerridwen's Cauldron, and the narrow shadow of Lingam Mountain.

Nagashimi-BOEM had built a space station to purify Ardel's titanium and ship it to the stars. The station orbited above Hecate's airless peaks and craters, waiting for the first shipment of ore. Soon the silence of Ardel's skies would be broken by the daily arrival and departure of intra-system freight hoppers. The big interstellar jump-ships would come more often, bringing visitors and luxuries to the spaceport and taking away Ardellan trade goods. This little backwater base would become a center of commerce.

Elissa did not look forward to the change. The prospect brought back memories of her childhood on Titan Station, memories of pain and longing and aloneness. The big ships had come and gone at Titan Station every day. Elissa had watched them day in and day out, as she waited for her father's ship to dock. It had often seemed that she spent all her time waiting. Then he would arrive, laughing and hugging her and kissing her mother, and for a few days they would be a family. All too soon the ship would call him back to pilot it to some distant star. Elissa and her mother would be alone again, watching and waiting.

She had come to love the big ships as her father had, but she had always been determined that they would not separate her from her family. She had chosen a career in engineering, as had her mother, and then she had married Sinykin. His career usually took him no farther away than the base hospital. Their home was stable, their family secure.

Until last fall, when Sinykin traveled to Alu Keep. He was gone for weeks that time, and now he would go again. A hard knot of sadness settled at the center of Elissa's chest as she considered it. Despite her careful plans, her life was falling into the pattern she had been trying to avoid.

Yet she would not try to stop Sinykin from taking his vaccine to the Ardellans. It was too important to him and to those who might otherwise die of this terrible plague.

She knew there were other things drawing Sinykin to the Ardellans, things that he could not or would not share with her. He had learned something from these aliens when he journeyed among them. She had seen its shadow in his eyes, and felt its presence between them when they made love. Now it was pulling him inexorably back to that world beyond the gate.

Chapter 4

Salt Flats, Southern Desert, Ardel

Ilakri sat on the salt crust of the ancient seabed and stared at the cliffs to the south. First-moon, bright and nearly full, traversed the sky above his head. Her light streamed down on the packed salt crystals and on his hunched body. The crystals' tiny, uniform facets scattered the moonbeams across the plain, making the night almost as bright as day. Ilakri could see better than he had in sunlight, when heat rising from the salt's surface had made the air shimmer and distant images waver.

The ruins began where the salt flat touched the base of the cliff. Skeletal remnants of metal towers lay like broken offerings at the feet of strange gods. Buildings of more durable material climbed diagonally up the face of the cliff. The largest nestled in a broad, shallow cavern that pocked the bottom of the cliff's facade. Shadows darkened the cave; Ilakri would not enter it until daylight. He watched and waited and wondered what purpose the towers had filled and who had lived in the strange, shiny houses.

Moonlight illuminated the broad stairway cut into the stone above the cave. Shadows danced on the steps like ghosts. Ilakri shivered and hugged his knees. He closed his eyes, and his head fell forward as consciousness slipped away from him.

They were laughing at him, the strange beings with bright clothing and too many legs. He didn't know how he knew they were laughing; he just knew. He heard no sound. They never spoke, not in any way he could understand. They just looked at one another and then at him, and he knew things.

They wanted him to find it. The long, dark, twisted thing. It was the color of scarletberries, only darker. And it was shiny, not metal-shiny like the towers, but soft-shiny like the walls of their houses.

It would be in the third building. They told him that, and then they showed him how to find it. They took him past the first house, where other bright beings laughed and talked and did strange things at the walls and tables. He saw them speak, and he heard no sound. They took him through the second house, where more people did other strange things. These beings were smaller and more fragile, but they also wore bright clothing and had too many legs. Then they led him into the third house. It was empty, as if it had been abandoned long ago.

They showed him where the long, dark, twisted thing lay covered with dust and fine powdered salt. It had been waiting for a long, long time, waiting for him or someone like him to find it and carry it away. It was special, unique, a thing of value. He looked at it and tried to understand what it was and what it could do. It remained a mystery. He could only know what they told him, and they would not tell him anything more about it.

They laughed again, the people with the bright clothes and too many arms, and then they told him what to do with the twisted thing and where to take it, and then they left him to find his way back to the salt flat alone.

Ilakri awakened before dawn. He stayed on the plain, relishing the last moments of coolness as he watched the sun rise. The shadows, and the ghosts, had left the ruins. Now he saw only disintegrating buildings and piles of fallen masonry. The pathways up the cliff's face were strewn with rubble, as if no one had climbed them in a hundred lifetimes. Perhaps no one had.

A kite circled lazily overhead, beginning its search for a morning meal. Ilakri was the only visible prey on the salt flat, and the kite was not large enough to threaten him. Ilakri sat perfectly still and watched the bird glide in tightening circles above him. The sunlight glinted on its shiny blue tail feathers. It dropped lower and lower, hoping that Ilakri was a victim of heat and thirst, a fresh corpse and an easy meal. Finally Ilakri tired of the game and reached for his water skin. He stretched and drank as the kite circled once more. Then it turned back to the heights above the ruins, to search for other prey.

Ilakri rose and stretched again, and looked about at the barren landscape. His stomach was empty, and for the first time since emerging from the cocoon in Yaro's cave his thoughts turned to food. All the youngling's fat that had accumulated on his body was gone, used up in the lengthening of his legs and the transformation of a pair of tentacles into arms. He was thin, as were most of the Masters he knew, and he was hungry. He began to regret leaving the cave without a pack and some bread and jerky. He gulped more water, knowing that it would only temporarily quiet his stomach.

The ruins beckoned him. He thought of the strange relic, the long, dark, twisted thing that the spirits had shown him in his dream, and he knew where to seek for it. The ruins beckoned, and his hunger receded. His only purpose was to find the relic.

Ilakri walked toward the crumbling buildings. He avoided the broken metal that lay disintegrating at the foot of the cliff and the red streaks of rust that discolored the salt around it. The towers looked as if they had been tumbled from the heights above the ruins, as if someone had plucked them up, crushed them, and scattered them like gaming tiles across the salt. The metal in them was weakened and decaying, but it was still powerful enough to make Ilakri uncomfortable. He longed to be away from it soon.

The first building stood before the high mouth of the shallow cavern. It was little more than a pile of rubble. Its roof had caved in long ago, and two of the walls had followed. The back and one side wall were still standing, covered with dust and white with salt. Ilakri walked past the ruin and moved into the shell of the second building. It also had lost most of its roof and parts of three walls. He carefully picked his way through the remaining debris. His feet sent up little plumes of dust and powdery salt that settled on the hem of his cloak and across his new boots.

There was an opening in the far wall. Ilakri stopped before it. He was suddenly fearful of these ruins and of the spirits that inhabited them. Jaella had not warned him about the ghosts. What if something was wrong, with him or the dream or the spirits? What if he could not find the relic that they had chosen for him? If he found it, could the spirits use it to take possession of his mind or body? This was too strange, too frightening. Ilakri wanted to run away from this place, to return to the safety of Yaro's cave and Jaella's warm arms. He turned from the opening in the wall, intent on retracing his steps across the room. His feet would not move.

Ilakri closed his eyes. He could see the spirits in his mind as he had seen them in his dream, laughing and showing him what to do. He knew that they would not allow him to leave the ruins unless that long, twisted relic was in his hands. Heart pounding, fingers cold, knees stiff with fright, he turned back to face the opening in the wall.

The third building was nearly intact. Light streamed in through a hole in the front wall. Ilakri bent low and stepped through the passage. His boots touched dust that had not been disturbed in many seasons and sent a cloud of it swirling through the sunbeams. He moved forward, slowly, searching the floor for the long, dark, twisted thing that the ghosts had shown him. He did not find it.

The dream had been accurate, perfectly accurate, until now. Panic bloomed in Ilakri's chest, filling his throat and pushing downward to sour his stomach. He could not leave the ruins unless he took the relic with him. It must be here! He began his search again at the far corner of the room, on his knees this time, his cloak dragging behind him. The dust made him cough, and the powdery salt burned his eyes. He patted and prodded and shifted the pieces of debris one at a time, until his fingers were coated with dust and salt and sweat. He covered half the room that way and still did not find the relic.

Ilakri sat on his haunches and stared through the hole in the wall. Someone could have taken the relic away long ago. Perhaps the spirits were playing with him. He should rise right now and walk out of this building, out of the ruins, out to the salt flat and home to the safety of the caves. He wanted to stand, but the spirits would not let him move. He sat frozen, watching the sunbeam that streamed in through the hole. His gaze followed it down to the jagged patch of brightness it spilled across the floor. There, there! He scrambled through the dust on hands and knees, reached for the strange long dusty lump. His hand closed on something hard and cold. He pulled it closer, brushed the dirt from it, saw its dark red color and twisted shape. He clutched it to his chest, then rose and ran from the building.

He tripped and fell twice before he escaped from the ruins. Then he was out on the salt flat, in the bright sunshine and the heat, with the relic held tightly in both hands. His heart was still beating fast. Dirt streaked his cloak and the creases of his face. He had far to travel, to the west and then to the north, as the spirits had shown him in his dream. They had said he would find a fisher village, and in the village he would meet the Master to whom he was to give the relic. He would know the Master by his strange speech and his five-fingered hands.

Chapter 5

Terran Spaceport, Ardel

Sinykin carefully disentangled himself from Elissa's arms before he slipped from their bed. He pulled the coverlet up over her bare shoulder, bent and kissed her gently on the cheek. She did not move. He tiptoed from the room and ten minutes later had washed, dressed, and eaten.

His two packs were waiting beside the door. He inspected his gear one last time, checked the vials of vaccine, the tiny cylinders of compressed air and the vaccination guns. Warm clothing, extra boots, and dietary supplements filled the second pack. He had tried to prepare for any eventuality, although he knew from experience it was a futile effort.

Jaime had spent the night with his friend Tommy. Inda regretted the lost chance for a hug, but dared not stay until Jaime returned home. He put on his parka, shouldered the heavier pack and grabbed the other by the carry strap, and let himself out through the front door.

The lights that illuminated the walkways were still shining, but their glow was washed out by the sky's brightness. It was that eerie time between full night and dawn, when darkness flees the coming sun and moon and stars fade from sight. The air was calm, and the world was peaceful. Inda walked the path toward the gate, awaiting the arrival of dawn and Septi.

Two bored and sleepy security officers were watching Inda from the gate house. He slowly approached them, intent on appearing casual. Anticipation made his heart pound and his knees wobble. The magic of Ardel lay just beyond that ramshackle fence and its locked gate.

One of the guards opened the upper half of the split door and leaned out. "Isn't it a little early to be hiking, Dr. Inda?" she called.

"I'm expecting a messenger from the FreeMasters Guild to meet me at the gate at dawn," he replied. The guard's name was Coni Mattrisch; he had removed a polyp from her vocal cords last year. Her voice was still an octave low and a little hoarse. Sexy, Elissa said. "Administration cleared the visit. I discussed it with Griswold yesterday."

"There's a note here," said the other officer. Inda could not see his face and did not recognize his voice. "Just says you're to give the Ardellan a message. What's in the packs?"

"Emergency medical supplies." Inda looked down the road toward Alu Keep, willing Septi to appear. He wanted to leave the compound quickly, before Mattrisch and her companion became suspicious and called for additional Security personnel.

"Nothin' about supplies in the note."

"Drop it, Heditsian," said Mattrisch. Her voice had a hard edge. "Dr. Inda says it's medical supplies. You want to search the packs out here?"

Heditsian said nothing.

Mattrisch smiled. "Nice sunrise behind you, Doc."

Inda turned to look at the distant mountains. The sky behind the peaks was rose-colored, shading upward to violet and deepening hues of blue. The sun would be up soon. Where was Septi? There would be trouble if Heditsian decided to press the issue of the packs.

"It certainly is beautiful. Does every dawn look like this?" asked Inda.

"Only when the weather is clear. Rider coming!" Mattrisch opened the gate house door and stepped out-

side. She walked over and reached for the pack in Inda's right hand. "Can I carry that for you?"

"No, thanks," said Inda. His heart was racing. "I
can manage. This will only take a moment. No need
for you to come out in the cold."

"It's my job, Dr. Inda. It looks like your friend
has brought a spare mount." She snagged the pack's
strap and tugged it from his hand. He tried to take it
back, realized the move looked suspicious, let his
hand drop.

"I wasn't sure how heavy the gear would be. I
warned him to bring an extra animal to carry the
packs." Inda disliked lying to Mattrisch. He followed her to the gate, wondering how quickly she
would see through his deceit and try to bar his way.
He hoped that she had not yet learned to understand
Ardellan.

Septi's mount plodded slowly toward the compound, its six legs moving in a complicated rhythm.
The other alep seemed larger and sturdier. It trod
along on only four feet, its central pair of legs folded
up against its belly. Septi held its single rein; a small
saddle was already on its back.

Inda pressed his hands against the fence rail to keep
them from shaking. He was not sure what he had
expected—to walk through the gate and ride away
from the compound unchallenged? What a naive
thought! He let the heavy pack slip from his back and
called to Septi in Ardellan.

"Bring that pack animal up to the gate, Free-
Master. The medical equipment I have for you is
heavy." He turned to Mattrisch, addressed her in
Terran Standard. "We'll have to open the gate. This
pack is heavy, and the equipment in it might be damaged if I drop it. I don't want to risk passing it over
the fence."

Mattrisch nodded and turned back to the gate house.
"We're going to open the gate," she called to Heditsian.

"Not supposed to!" he yelled.

"Just have to get the gear onto the pack animal," explained Inda. His hands were shaking as he watched Mattrisch punch in the security code. A light flashed on the lock panel. She slid the gate to one side, and Inda stepped through the opening and greeted Septi.

"I am coming with you," he said in Ardellan as he fastened the heavy pack to the straps at the back of the spare mount's saddle. Mattrisch was standing beside Inda, holding the other pack. Her smiled faded as she watched him work. Inda knew she was becoming suspicious. He continued talking quietly to Septi. "Say nothing. We must ride away quickly, before this one can stop me. I do not have permission to leave the compound."

Septi lifted one hand to signify that he understood, then turned his mount away from the gate. He dropped the second mount's rein, and Inda snatched it up.

"Here, let me have that pack," he said to Mattrisch as he tugged it from her hand. "It has to go on the other side of the saddle." He slipped it onto his shoulder, then ducked under the alep's neck and stepped to its far side. Mattrisch tried to follow him, but he turned the animal to block her path. He mounted in a swift scramble, turned and kicked at Mattrisch's shoulder. She stumbled into the fence. "Sorry, Coni," said Inda as he tugged at the rein, swinging his mount's head away from the compound.

Septi was already moving down the trail toward Alu Keep. Inda followed, urging his mount to a dangerous four-legged run. Heditsian yelled something incomprehensible from the gate house. An alarm sounded. Inda looked back, saw Mattrisch pursuing him on foot and Heditsian stepping from the gate house, weapon in hand. Other Security personnel were running toward the gate.

Inda turned his back on the compound. He fastened his eyes on the trail, bent low against his mount's neck, and whispered a prayer that Elissa would forgive him.

Ahead lay Alu Keep and the plague victims, and magic.

Inda had seen Alu Keep once before. His thoughts returned to that trip—the day-long ride, the force of the midwinter blizzard that had struck them in the late afternoon, and his surprise when the keep's great wall had loomed out of the swirling snow to dwarf him and his alep. This ride was different. The sun warmed his shoulders, and the wind carried the green scents of spring. The day was longer, the trail was clear, and the aleps moved more swiftly than they could those few weeks ago.

The evening was bright with the sun's last rays when Septi led Inda to a hilltop overlooking the keep. A patchwork quilt of orchards and fields, some with furrows still harboring pockets of snow, spread before him. Water ran swiftly in ditches, blocked here and there by ice and debris so that it formed little ponds and spillways. Several younglings were driving a herd of borras toward Alu's broad gates.

The keep's wall was no less impressive for being seen from a distance, in daylight. It wrapped like a membrane around the buildings and residents of Alu Keep, here bulging out to allow room for growth, there rising to echo the shape of the land around it, always protecting its contents from the dangerous threats of the elements and predators. The huge wooden gates stood open. They looked to Inda like warm arms welcoming home beloved friends. He urged his mount down the hill and followed the borras through the archway and into the stableyard. Septi rode in just behind him.

Inda dismounted stiffly. He straightened slowly, working the kinks out of his back by stretching his arms and rolling his shoulders. A youngling trundled from the stable on stubby legs, tentacles flailing, and took the rein from Inda's hand. It started to lead the alep away.

"Hey!" Inda called, and, "I need my pack," before the youngling's startled look made him realize that he was speaking Terran Standard instead of Ardellan. He tried again. "Please do not take the alep. I must remove my pack from the saddle."

The youngling's eyestalks dipped; it had understood him. It unfastened the pack and brought it to him.

"Thank you," he said.

"Of course, Master," replied the youngling before it led the alep into the stable. Another youngling followed it with Septi's mount.

Evening's long shadows were darkening the narrow roads of the keep. Inda followed Septi down a graveled path, past stone Houses that were all curves and rounded corners and oddly-shaped patches of lighted windows. They passed House Actaan, where he had stayed with Historian Ertis just ten weeks ago. Beyond Actaan they walked up a hill toward an open circle of ground and the imposing two-story clanhall behind it.

"Jeryl will be waiting for us," said Septi as they climbed the stone steps to the clanhall. The heavy wooden door opened before them, showing Inda a dark and cavernous hall. Septi lifted his right hand and blinked, and a ball of shimmer-light appeared to float above his palm. Inda's breath caught in his throat.

"Surely you have seen Ertis conjure shimmer-light?" asked Septi.

"Many times." Inda was thrilled to see the magic, but he tried to pass his excitement off as surprise. "I wasn't expecting it now."

"What were you not expecting, Healer Inda?" Jeryl emerged from a side room and raised his hand in greeting. Flames flared in the wall sconces, casting long shadows across the floor. "We are pleased that you chose to visit Alu Keep. Welcome to our clanhall."

"I was pleased to receive your invitation," replied

Inda. The magic was all around him now, in Septi's shimmer-light and the cool flames in the wall sconces; in the ancient stone of the building's walls; in the easily perceptible auras, so different from the vague auras of humans, that surrounded Jeryl and Septi. This time he had a special magic of his own to share with them. "I have brought you the plague-stopper, the vaccine that should keep your people from succumbing to the plague."

"No!" Another Master, his hands extended in a warding gesture, stepped into the hall behind Jeryl. He was the oldest Ardellan Inda had ever seen, stick-thin of body, his face etched and furrowed by innumerable cares, his fine white hair standing out like a translucent halo about his head. His bearing was imperious, his pale eyes were bright with intelligence and anger. Age had not weakened him. It had made him more powerful.

Jeryl turned and answered the warding gesture with one of his own. "Viela, not even you may treat a guest in such a manner."

Viela did not accept the rebuke. "Terrans bring with them pain and suffering. I will not acknowledge this one as a guest."

"It is not your place to deny him." Jeryl's voice had lost its warmth. "The council of elders approved Healer Inda's visit. You have no authority to interfere with their wishes."

"I am Alu's Healer. The health of this clan is my responsibility!"

"So it is," replied Jeryl. "Perhaps you should return to the Healer's compound and see to your patients."

The old Healer's anger was a red heat in the cold hall. Inda took a deep breath and stepped forward to confront Viela. "I have not come to harm your people or to usurp your power. The plague-stopper has been thoroughly tested on Terrans. It is compatible with the blood and tissue samples I collected from your people.

I will teach you to administer it yourself, and supply you with everything you need."

Viela raised his hands against Inda. His sleeves slipped back to reveal blue tattoos that spiraled up each of his arms. The sapphire lines seemed to glow in the hall's dim light. "You ask me to trust you, Terran. What have you done to earn my trust? You visited the Iron Keep and brought destruction upon it. Now we have no metals of our own, and we must trade with you for iron and copper."

"The power-hungry leaders of the Miners Guild destroyed themselves and ruined part of their keep," said Jeryl. "Inda was not the cause of it."

"So say you. I know what I know. Terrans have spread death and destruction across Ardel!" Viela turned his palms inward, and Inda was suddenly afraid. He had watched Ardellans conjure destruction of their own, had seen them create fireballs between their palms and send them flying across a room to burn and maim an enemy. He would never forget the acrid odor of ozone and the stench of burned flesh. Griswold was correct; there was danger beyond the gates of the Terran compound.

"Enough!" Jeryl stepped in front of Inda and answered Viela's threat with one of his own. "You will not interfere with the wishes of the council. Tomorrow Healer Inda will administer the plague-stopper to all who desire it. Then he and Septi will travel to Port Freewind. You have nothing more to do with the matter."

Viela stared at Jeryl. Neither of them moved for a long time. Then Viela dropped his hands. "My apprentices and I will not accept the plague-stopper. Do what you will; we will not help you." He stalked past Jeryl and Inda. The clanhall door slammed behind him.

Jeryl turned and addressed Inda as if their conversation had not been interrupted. "Have you eaten? Septi, take Healer Inda's packs to his room, and then join us in the kitchen.'' He led Inda to a warm and cheery room at the back of the clanhall.

Inda unzipped his parka and hung it on a peg near the door. Then he joined Jeryl before the broad hearth and let the gentle heat of the banked fire warm his body and spirit. Jeryl offered him a mug of fragrant tea, which Inda gratefully accepted. Inda was greatly disturbed by the argument with Viela and by the old Healer's accusations. He wanted to help the Ardellans, not to harm them, yet his presence at Alu Keep was already causing dissension within the clan.

Three younglings bustled around a long table in the center of the room, setting out platters and bowls of food. One opened the stone door of a warming oven beside the fireplace and pulled out a whole roast fowl. Inda turned away from the carcass, trying to hide his distaste. He never ate flesh. There was fresh bread and a pile of roasted tubers on the table, plenty of food that he could eat. A youngling put out plates and the oddly-shaped metal utensils that served the Ardellans as spoons and forks. Inda realized he had forgotten to pack his flatware; he would have to struggle with utensils designed for a circular palm and six opposable fingers until he returned to the spaceport.

"Does the roast fowl trouble you, Healer Inda?" asked Jeryl. "I can have it removed from the table."

Inda was disconcerted. He had hoped that Jeryl would not notice his aversion. "I do not eat flesh, but I do not object to others doing so."

Jeryl looked puzzled. "Sarah Anders followed no such prohibition. Roast fowl was one of her favorite dishes."

Inda shrugged. "Many Terrans eat meat. Others eat only fish and plant products. Some will eat no animal products at all. It is a matter of personal choice."

"That should not surprise me. Many of our Healers

do not eat flesh. Perhaps the prohibition is one of the mysteries all Healers share.''

"Perhaps,'' said Inda, "although I doubt that your esteemed Healer would acknowledge such a kinship between us.''

The younglings seemed to be finished at the table. Jeryl pulled up a bench and sat down. "Come and eat. Septi will join us when he is finished upstairs.''

Inda filled a plate with warm nutbread, bright red preserves, and a steaming tuber. Jeryl tore a leg from the roast fowl and helped himself to a huge spoonful of boiled grain. He moved the bowl to the far side of the table, away from Inda.

"You should not eat this grain,'' he said. "It made Sarah Anders ill.''

"Ertis warned me about it when we were visiting the Iron Keep.'' Inda launched an awkward attack on the tuber with his knobby-handled utensil. "Has the Iron Keep truly been destroyed?''

"Parts of it.''

Jeryl seemed reluctant to say more. Inda wanted to know the fate of the miners who had imprisoned him in their keep, but he did not press the Mentor for more information. There were others he could ask. Surely Ertis or Septi would know the details and be willing to reveal them. Instead he questioned Jeryl about the coming trip. "I am looking forward to visiting Port Freewind. Will we be traveling along the river to the coast and then up to the port, or will we ride cross-country through the forests?''

"You will take the caravan trail north to the great river road, follow that halfway to the sea, and then cut north again through the woodlands to the White River. The river will take you straight to Port Freewind. This will be the fastest and safest route.''

Inda was losing his battle with the tuber. His utensil was made of a soft metal, probably silver, and had no sharp edges. Its spoonlike bowl ended in three narrow tines, and there was a single heavy prong along the underside of the bowl. The handle was a sculpted knob that was difficult for him to grip. He stopped trying to be tidy and grasped the tuber in his left hand, pierced its thick skin with the heavy prong, and pushed. The skin split, revealing the starchy yellow meat inside. "I had expected that you would be traveling with me."

"I have business to attend to here at the keep. Septi is our finest translator. He knows the route, and will guide you well. You can depend on him."

"Thank you, Mentor," said Septi from the doorway. He was watching Inda struggle with the tuber. "Would you like a knife and fork, Healer?"

"Yes," said Inda, "but I forgot to pack them."

"I have a set that you may use." Septi rummaged in a cabinet at the far end of the room, then returned to the table with a small cloth-wrapped package. He handed it to Inda. "These belonged to Sarah Anders."

The package contained a worn set of standard issue stainless steel flatware. The metal alone would have great value to the Ardellans; it could make several fine knife blades. Inda was surprised that it had not been traded to the Metalsmiths Guild. "Thank you, Septi. May I take them with me on our journey?"

"Certainly," said Septi as he sat down beside Inda and began to fill his plate. "I would like to have them back when you are through with them."

"I will return them to you. I know that steel has great value on Ardel."

Septi shrugged. "I treasure them because they belonged to Sarah Anders. I served her when I was a youngling. She taught me your language, and that skill made me a valuable member of my clan. It insured that I would be chosen to become a Master and have a House of my own."

"You do speak Standard very well." Inda stabbed the tuber and began slicing it into bite-sized pieces. "I wish my Ardellan was as good. But it serves me well enough for most things. Will I truly need a translator on this trip?''

Jeryl reached for the bowl of boiled grain. ''The fisherfolk speak a dialect that may be difficult for you to understand, and they have no one who speaks your language. You would be in great difficulty if you made the journey alone.''

''Then I am grateful that Septi has agreed to accompany me,'' said Inda.

They ate in companionable silence for a while. Finally Inda pushed his plate aside and poured another mug of tea. He liked the fruity smell and faint cinnamon taste of the rich red brew. He sipped the tea, and watched Jeryl ladle preserves onto a chunk of bread. The Mentor was wearing a blue wool tunic over a loose shirt of soft gray fabric that matched the color of his eyes. His silver hair was less unruly than Viela's. A circular enameled pendant hung from a thong about his neck.

''The colors of your medallion are quite beautiful,'' said Inda. ''The pattern reminds me of some I have seen on the front walls of Houses in the keep. Does it have a particular meaning?''

''It is the mountain and sun design,'' responded Jeryl. ''It represents a pledge I made at winter solstice. I promised to return to the mountains at high summer and make a sacrifice of thanksgiving, as my ancestors once did.''

Inda nodded. ''My ancestors also made seasonal sacrifices, most often at the great rivers of their land.''

''Some Terrans continue the honored custom of sacrifice,'' whispered Septi.

''Not all sacrifices are intentional.'' Jeryl drained his mug in one gulp. ''Perhaps you should take Healer Inda to see the mourning wall. I will meet you both at sunrise.'' He rose and strode from the room.

Inda turned to Septi. ''The mourning wall? What is that?''

"It is the oldest portion of Alu Keep's wall, behind the clanhall. We take the burial urns of our dead Mothers there, and place them in niches in the wall. If a Master dies before his time, or a Healer or a Mentor dies, his body is cremated just as a Mother's would be, and his urn joins the others in the wall. Sarah Anders' urn is there, near the urn of Jeryl's murdered mate."

Unanticipated sweat chilled the palms of Inda's hands. He wanted to see Anders' urn, to touch it. He wanted to acknowledge the power of the woman he had come to know through reading her journal and hearing the story of her mysterious death among these aliens. He followed Septi to the door, stopped there to pull on his parka before stepping into the cold night air.

The clanhall's back stoop was shadowed. Inda glimpsed sparkling stars in the strip of black sky visible between building and wall; then Septi conjured a ball of shimmer-light and the stars were no longer the most wondrous thing to be seen.

The stone wall was three meters high, and disappeared into darkness to the left and right. Its lower half was carved with row after row of niches, and each one held a stone urn. Septi led Inda across the narrow cart track toward the wall. Gravel crunched beneath their feet. A cold wind ruffled Inda's hair. The shimmer-light floated above them, illuminating a broad circle on the wall.

Inda was captivated by the urns. They were all about the same size, but their shapes varied from squat to broad-bellied to slender, from round to square to asymmetrical, from smooth and flowing to harsh and angular. Each one was beautiful.

Inda sighed. "I would like to see them in daylight, so that I could appreciate their colors."

"They are quite impressive in full light." Septi brought the shimmer-light closer, and the urns that were touched by the light answered it with a glow of their own. They shone with subtle colors—soft blues and greens, lavenders, deep browns, reds and grays and golds. Here and there the crystal face of a pale pink urn glittered. The colors were as varied as the shapes. Some of them seemed to change as Inda watched them.

"Come." Septi walked along the wall to the right.

Inda followed. He reached out and touched the ancient stone, let his fingers trail along it. They brushed over a figure incised in the rock beneath one of the niches. He stopped and traced it with his index finger. "What is this?"

"A rune. It tells us something of the person's life or death. That one is the figure 'happy home.' "

"And you carve them beneath each urn?"

Septi shrugged. "It is a memorial. You can read the history of Clan Alu in the runes upon this wall."

"Which is Sarah Anders' urn?"

"Here." Septi pointed to a beautiful round moss-green urn. He stroked it, and a sapphire cloud swirled across its surface. The urn began to glow with a soft light, becoming almost translucent.

"May I touch it?" asked Inda.

Septi stepped aside. "She is one of your people. I think she would welcome your touch."

The stone of the urn felt warm and smooth and soft against his fingertips, like a woman's skin. Inda caressed it, and the sapphire cloud moved for him. It slipped beneath his hand, beckoning his palm to touch it. He pressed his hand to the stone urn and felt Anders' presence even more strongly than he had when he was reading her journal. Her words, her thoughts, her actions came alive for him in that moment. She was no longer the legendary trade attaché who had died under mysterious circumstances. She was a living person, a friend, a guide, a human revered by these aliens.

"What does the rune say?" whispered Inda as he traced it.

"Honor."

Inda felt Sarah Anders' presence all around him. She had lived and died for Alu and its people. He wondered if he would be worthy of her legacy. Could he truly become a part of Ardel, as she had before him?

Chapter 6

Elissa Durrant turned her head, her eyes tracking movement above the rock-strewn plain. A kite was flying in broad circles, its wings cutting the air with slow, powerful strokes. Those wings suddenly snapped back along its body and the kite dove straight toward the ground. It disappeared behind a boulder, rose an instant later with a struggling coney in its talons, circled once and turned toward a distant rock pile. The coney had not yet shed its white winter fur, camouflage gone awry with the early onset of spring. The wasteland was unforgiving; those who lived here did so on its terms.

The truck's engines purred. Elissa adjusted the air/fuel ratio, considered speeding after the kite's swift shadow. Ardel allowed her few opportunities to test her racing skills.

"Ready to recalibrate the ground-level sensors?" asked the tech, his words clear and precise through her earjack.

"Yes, Rys. Let's go." Elissa touched a control, felt the big truck turn. Her view shifted to the vast oval of the mine site, laid out where the titanium sands were richest. She moved a finger and the mining graphics came on line, overlaying the virtual image with a rainbow of transparent color. Red marked the richest deposits of titanium, violet and blue the areas of lower concentration, and green the surrounding titanium-free rock.

The truck's enclosed cab was six meters off the ground, too high to give Elissa a view of potholes and small boulders. She shifted her hand and the display inside her goggles changed. Sensors near the wheels of the big truck produced an image of the surrounding land, giving her a three-dimensional view of obstacles. Another truck and an immense 'dozer crouched a half-kilometer away, in the shadow of the huge mining shovel. Elissa drove her truck toward its twin, slowly traversing the rough terrain.

"Excellent," said Rys. "Now park it."

She turned the truck again, began backing it carefully next to the 'dozer. The 'dozer's cab was even farther from the ground than the truck's, and its broad blade was fashioned to shift huge quantities of rubble around the site. The 'dozer was dwarfed by the mining shovel, with its articulated arm and scoop that could lift twenty tons of ore in one bite and dump it into a truck's long, deep bed. Elissa's palms itched to control one of those great machines. "Will there be time to work on the 'dozer?"

"Tomorrow. Straighten out the third set of wheels or you'll jackknife the back section," warned Rhys.

Elissa's hands caressed the controls, making minute adjustments as she jockeyed the truck into position. This was her equipment; she had supervised its assembly, wired most of the sensors herself. It would be in perfect order before she allowed the miners to touch it. "Done," she said, cutting the engine's power. "What's the readout?"

"Alignment is ideal, all the sensors are working, and the depth perception translator is calibrated to spec."

Elissa tapped a stud on the joystick in her right hand, and "task terminated" paraded across the inner rim of her goggles. She pulled her left arm free of the black net glove, straightened her elbow and spread her cramped fingers. Her legs were stiff, and her back ached. Ten hours was too long to spend in one chair, no matter how anatomically correct its design. No wonder the miners worked in six-hour shifts. "Thanks,

Rys. That's all for today. We'll start again in the morning."

Rys switched the controls to standby. "Board says there're three messages for you, Chief. See you tomorrow."

Elissa waved at him as he left the booth. She slipped the toes of her boots from their stirrups and rose, stretching. Then she strode past the board, chose instead to walk down the hall to her office and access the communications net. Jer Robinson had already left his desk. Elissa checked her watch, realized she was probably the only person in the building. She had worked through supper again. It was always daytime in the projection room.

She punched up Marta Grund's home number on the vid-phone, smiled when Marta's husband answered. "Hello, Jeff. Is Jaime there? I've been working . . ."

"And you lost track of the time." Jeff laughed. "Yes, he's here. He and Tommy talked me into roasting a chicken tonight. Marta worked late, too, so it was just the three of us for dinner. The boys are studying now. Do you want to speak with Jaime?"

"No, I'll stop by and get him in a few minutes. Thank you for feeding him."

"You've done the same for Tommy often enough."

Elissa nodded and grinned. "I'm glad to have such helpful neighbors."

"Friends," corrected Jeff.

"Good friends," said Elissa as she broke the connection.

Her terminal's mail indicator flashed. She keyed in an access code, brought up the messages. Two were voice mail; the other was a formal memo under the Administrator's seal.

The first message was from Security Chief Harwood. "My crew live-trapped two coneys in the hangar this morning. That should take care of your mysterious noises. Call me if you hear anything more."

Elissa smiled as she overrode the save/reply function and skipped to the next recording.

"Chief, this is Herve. We finished installing equipment at the mill this morning and began testing this afternoon. We should complete the tests tomorrow. I'll transmit the results as soon as we have them. Let me know when you have a date for the inspection." The work at the titanium mill was right on schedule. Administrator Griswold would be pleased.

The memo from Griswold came up next. It was dated that morning but had no priority flag. Elissa scanned it, then slowly read it again.

2262:9/16, 1010 HRS LOCAL TIME
TO: ELISSA DURANT, CHIEF ENGINEER
FROM: ANNA GRISWOLD, ADMINISTRATOR,
     TERRAN UNION SPACEPORT, ARDEL
COMMUNICATION FROM INTERSTELLAR TRANSPORT *NAIROBI* CONFIRMS ARRIVAL OF MINERS ON 9/18 AT APPROXIMATELY 1430 HRS. FINAL TESTING AT MINE SITE AND MILL MUST BE COMPLETED BY THAT TIME. BRIEFING WILL BE HELD IMMEDIATELY AFTER MINERS DISEMBARK, WITH MINING TO COMMENCE AT 1800 HRS.

TRADE COMMISSION SECRETARY SANDSMARK AND AUSTIN DUERST OF NAGASHIMI-BOEM SCHEDULED TO ARRIVE BETWEEN 9/22 1700 HRS AND 9/24 600 HRS. WILL NOTIFY YOU OF APPROXIMATE LANDING TIME WHEN CONFIRMATION RECEIVED FROM NAGASHIMI'S *WHITE CRANE*. INSPECTION OF MINE SITE AND MILL FACILITIES WILL COMMENCE AT SANDSMARK'S CONVENIENCE.

DR. SINYKIN INDA ABANDONED HIS POST THIS MORNING AND LEFT COMPOUND IN DEFIANCE OF ADMINISTRATOR'S INSTRUCTIONS. DR. JAMAL ADDAMI REPLACES HIM AS CHIEF MEDICAL OFFICER. DR. INDA'S IMME-

DIATE RECALL FROM ARDEL HAS BEEN RE-
QUESTED.
ENDMESSAGE

Elissa leaned one elbow on the desk and pressed her
forehead into the palm of her upturned hand. She was
too tired to deal with Griswold tonight. She would
send Sinykin word of the recall request in the morning, and then file a grievance in his name. If he could
return to the compound before Secretary Sandsmark
arrived, they might be able to convince Sandsmark to
overrule Griswold and let Sinykin stay on Ardel. Elissa
refused to consider the alternatives right now. Keeping
the family together was more important than maintaining her contract with the Union, but she was nearing
completion of the biggest project of her career, and
she would not abandon it. That meant staying on Ardel
even if Sinykin was forced to leave. Jaime would lose
one or the other of his parents, at least for a while,
unless they could change Griswold's mind.

She turned out the lights and left the office. The
hangar's safety lights guided her past Robinson's desk
and onto the second floor walkway. A rectangle of
brightness in the shop area below caught her attention.
She leaned over the rail, saw light and someone moving around in the machine shop. She was about to
shout a greeting when the light was switched off. An
unfamiliar figure walked away from the shop.

Elissa ran to the stairs, clambered down them. Her
boots made the metal treads ring. The intruder looked
back and then moved quickly toward the door.

"Stop!" cried Elissa. She jumped over the last three
steps, made a jarring landing on the plasticrete floor
despite bent knees and cushioned insoles. Her prey
stopped before the door, reached up and tapped the
switch for the hangar's main lights. Elissa blinked in
the sudden brightness.

"Who goes there!" called the intruder.

"Coni?" Elissa's heart pounded as she ran to the door.

"Chief Durant! You startled me. I thought everyone had left the building." Coni Mattrisch brushed a stray hair from her face. "For a moment I thought I'd discovered the source of your mysterious late-night noises. Do you often work this late?"

"Too often. Did you come to check the traps?"

Mattrisch nodded. She flicked off the lights, then opened the door and held it for Elissa. She stifled a yawn. "It's been a long day. I'm going to get some food and then turn in."

"I think I'll do the same," said Elissa. The adrenaline rush had left her shaking. She needed food and sleep before she would be able to think clearly. In the morning she would deal with Anna Griswold and Sinykin's recall order.

Chapter 7

Alu Keep, Ardel

A wooden bed strewn with furs and woven blankets, a single intricately carved chair, and a small wooden table furnished Sinykin Inda's room on the second floor of Alu's clanhall. A tiny charcoal brazier, its fumes venting through a slit beneath the window, provided minimal warmth. A pair of candles in fanciful wooden holders cast flickering light upon the table. Inda sat there, bent over a sheet of paper. His right hand moved in precise strokes as he signed a letter and addressed it to Anna Griswold.

Inda leaned back in his chair and read through the letter. "I could not delay this medical mission any longer," he had written. "I take full responsibility for my actions in leaving the spaceport. No other personnel were involved in my decision. There was no collusion, no conspiracy to disobey your orders.

"Mass vaccinations will take place at Alu Keep this morning. I will be leaving Alu today or tomorrow and traveling to Port Freewind on the coast of the Storm Sea. I will vaccinate as many Ardellans as I can during the trip, and I will supply vaccine and administration equipment to any Healers who are willing to learn how to use it. I should be able to complete the vaccination program at Port Freewind and return to the spaceport within ten days.

"Please tender my apologies to Security Officer Mattrisch. I took advantage of our relationship as physician and patient when I approached her post at the gate. She was not aware of my intention to leave the compound and attempted to keep me from doing so. Officer Mattrisch behaved in a professional manner at all times. The actions I took on the morning of 2262:9/16 were entirely my own, and I accept the consequences of those actions.

> "Sinykin Inda,
> Chief Medical Officer
> Xenobiologist
> Terran Spaceport, Ardel"

The sky was beginning to brighten as Inda folded and sealed the letter. He picked up a second letter addressed to "Elissa Durant—Personal and Confidential," and slipped both into his pocket.

Morning smells of baking bread and brewing tea drifted up the stairwell and enticed him to the kitchen. Jeryl and Septi were already eating, and a gaggle of younglings and the rotund kitchenmaster were bustling about their morning's business. They had set a place for Inda, complete with Sarah Anders' flatware.

"May the great sun shine on you today, Master Inda. You must eat quickly," said Jeryl between bites. "Younglings are already waiting for you to give them the plague-stopper. They are on their way to work in the fields and at the stables."

"The vaccinations will not take long," said Inda. He used the technical Terran word; he hoped to convince the Ardellans to adopt it instead of using the imprecise term "plague-stopper." He poured a mug of tea, then pulled out his letters and placed them on the table. "Can someone take these to the spaceport today? They contain important messages for Administrator Griswold and for my mate."

Septi scooped them up and tucked them into his cloak. "Enric is riding to the FreeMasters' guildhall after midday. I will see that he takes them with him. The FreeMasters will deliver them to the spaceport."

"Thank you. Give Enric my greetings and wish him a speedy journey for me." Inda filled his plate with fresh bread and fruit. He followed Jeryl's lead and ate without ceremony.

After breakfast, Inda found several hundred younglings waiting in the open circle in front of the clanhall. Most of them wore only brightly colored sashes or belts hung with strange implements. They seemed inured to the cold. Their pale, ovoid bodies were perched on pairs of stumpy legs that ended in sturdy round feet. Four tentacles ringed each torso at shoulder level, and two eyes were mounted on short stalks at the top of each youngling's body. The eyestalks moved independently, turning and twisting, sometimes crossing each other. Inda looked down from the clanhall's porch on a disquieting sea of roving eyeballs and flailing tentacles.

"These are our brightest, most promising younglings," said Jeryl. "Many of them will be Masters one day, if they escape the deformities caused by the plague."

"The vaccine should enable most of them to do so." Inda was dismayed by the crowd's size. It would take him all morning to vaccinate these younglings, even using the pressure guns. "I had hoped your Healer would want to do this himself. I brought plenty of equipment for him and his staff."

Jeryl lifted a hand in dismissal. "Viela will have nothing to do with Terrans and their tools. He is a stubborn old borra who puts his own prejudices before the good of the clan." He pointed to a pair of Masters who were wading through the throng of younglings toward the clanhall's steps. One wore the gray cloak of a FreeMaster, and the other was dressed in the same blue wool fabric as Jeryl wore. "These two will help you. The Freemaster is my new apprentice, Aakar. The other is Serla, newly made Master of House Bellar. Neither has any pressing duties, so you may have them for the entire day."

Inda introduced himself to his new assistants in Ardellan. Serla lifted his hand in the traditional greeting, but Aakar offered his palm in a weird imitation of a handshake. "Welcome to Alu Keep," he said in heavily accented Terran Standard.

"Thank you," replied Inda. His hand touched Aakar's and a tingling electricity spread across his palm. He pulled his hand back too quickly. "Come, let me show you what we will do."

Inda helped Serla and Aakar clean their hands with germicidal towelettes. Then he tore open three of the steri-paks, inserted a vial of vaccine and a cylinder of compressed air into each of the shiny steel vaccination guns, and handed one to Serla and another to Aakar. The grips were shaped for human hands and did not fit well in Ardellan palms.

"Everyone should be vaccinated. Which of you will be first?" asked Inda.

Jeryl stepped forward.

"Pull up your sleeve, please." Inda pulled a germicidal swab from a dispenser and wiped it across Jeryl's upper arm. Then he addressed his assistants. "Choose a fleshy spot, either on an arm or a leg, and cleanse it well. Then press the mouth of the gun against the skin and touch the blue stud. A single dose of vaccine will be forced through the skin by a puff of compressed air."

Inda's gun hissed, and Jeryl jumped away. "It stings," he said, rubbing his upper arm.

"Yes, it does. If your arm puffs up or turns a strange color, or if you feel ill, come and see me at once. Otherwise, we are finished with you." Inda smiled. "You may pull down your sleeve now."

Jeryl watched Inda vaccinate Aakar and Serla before retreating into the clanhall.

Inda supervised Aakar and Serla as they vaccinated their first younglings. He showed them the reload indicator on the top of the gun. "When this turns red, we must put in a new vial and cylinder. Your gun will not work until we do that. Bring it to me as soon as you see the red marker. Now, let's start on the young-lings.''

They worked quickly and without incident. The younglings were disorganized but cooperative. By mid-morning the last one limped away from the clanhall's circle, rubbing a tiny golden bruise on its upper leg. It made no complaint; none of them had. A moment of pain meant nothing when it might prevent a lifetime of deformity.

''Have we time for a cup of tea before we vaccinate the Masters and Mothers?'' asked Serla. ''My mouth is parched.''

''And I need more vaccine.'' Akar showed Inda the nearly empty vial. Inda could not pry it loose from the dispenser. His fingers were chilled and would not grip the smooth vial. He had been too busy to notice the cold. The idea of warming himself by the kitchen hearth and wrapping his hands about a warm mug of tea was inviting.

''Help me with the packs, and I'll reload your guns in the kitchen. Then you can tell me where we will find the Masters,'' said Inda.

''Two of them are here. Can we offer any assis-tance?''

Inda heard the familiar voice and looked up. He smiled when he saw the Master standing with Septi in the clanhall's doorway. ''Ertis! Historian, it is good to see you.'' Inda pushed his equipment into Aakar's hands and ran to greet his friend. ''I feared we would never meet again after the guards took you from the Iron Keep. Are you well? When did you return to Alu? Has anyone told you what happened to me after you left the keep?''

Ertis touched Inda's hands. ''You are cold! Come into the kitchen, Sinykin, and I will answer your ques-tions and you may answer mine. Jeryl brought me word of your escape from the Iron Keep. I would have come to see you at the spaceport, but I have been busy with events in my own House.''

They walked through the clanhall and past the meeting hall where Jeryl was conferring with a group of Masters. Septi followed with Aakar and Serla, helping them carry Inda's gear.

Inda did not take his eyes from his friend. Ertis' copper-colored tunic and leggings and his soft gold shirt were as familiar to the Terran as his own coveralls. The Historian looked older and thinner than when Inda had last seen him, but his color was much improved, and his eyes sparkled.

"You have recovered your health," said Inda. "I had thought you would not survive the trip down the mountainside. Yet here you are, looking as well as you did when we began our journey. I hope that the time you spent with me brought no harm upon your House."

Ertis shrugged. "My life follows the expected path. naOflea is cocooned in the Mother's chamber of my House. Mother Poola will soon be fertile, and Oflea will burst from the cocoon to become Master of House Actaan. Then I will remove my Historian's garb for the last time and begin the next phase of my life.

"I leave my guild a fine legacy—two unique tales that will be passed to Historians for all time to come. The first is the story of your sojourn with me among the weather-workers of the Iron Keep. Already that tale has spread through all the clans, as the Historians describe the destruction of the keep's great tower. Some clansfolk who do not know Terrans said that the tower's disintegration was your doing. We tell them the truth, that the weather-workers destroyed themselves."

Inda sat at the kitchen's long table, his cold fingers clutching a mug of tea, and listened to Ertis' tales. The Historian's voice took him back to his first night at Alu Keep, when he had first encountered Ardellan magic. He closed his eyes and remembered touching the living stone of House Actaan and hearing the music of Septi's shell-pipe and Ertis' harp. The House had come alive around him then, each part of it glowing with an aura of its own.

He suddenly was aware that magic was with him in the clanhall. Life filled the kitchen's walls and the wooden table and the stone tiles of the floor. Auras built up through years of use surrounded everything. The auras glowed with residual energy left by the hands and tentacles that had carved the wood, worked the stone, washed the platters, filled the cups. Inda felt the presence of Septi across the room and knew that Aakar and Serla stood behind him. Ertis' aura glowed like topaz fog all around the Historian's body; Septi's was a translucent white cloud. The angry kitchenmaster's aura blushed ruby red as he reprimanded a youngling at the hearth.

"And the other story?" asked Inda in a hushed voice.

"That tale is not yet complete. It begins on a cold midwinter's day, when Jeryl, Mentor of Clan Alu, made a rash vow. His people were dying. Many Houses in Alu Keep stood empty, their family lines extinguished. Jeryl asked a boon of the great amber sun and offered a pledge in exchange. If he could rediscover the long-forgotten secret to repopulating Alu's Houses, he would return to the mountains at midsummer and make a sacrifice." Ertis paused to sip his tea. "Jeryl found such a secret, hidden in the text of an ancient scroll. On the day that I cocooned naOflea, he cocooned naMieck. Now they both rest in the Mother's chamber of House Actaan. If Mieck emerges from the cocoon as a whole and healthy adult, he will become the new Master of House Ratrou and the founder of a new family line."

Inda nodded. "Then that is the pledge represented by Jeryl's medallion."

"That is so," said Septi. He put the vaccination guns on the table before Inda. "Midday approaches, and there are many Masters and Mothers to vaccinate."

"Yes, of course." Inda sighed as he set aside his mug. He touched the cold Terran steel, and his perceptions of the magic around him changed. The table was only wood, the floor tiles only worn stone. The loss was a sharp pain in the center of his chest. He tugged the empty vial from the gun, inserted a full one, and changed the compressed air cylinder. Then he handed the gun to Aakar and prepared the second one for Serla.

"Healer Inda, you should stay here and visit with Master Ertis," said Aakar as he pulled on his gray wool cloak. "Serla and I will go out and vaccinate the Masters and Mothers. We can send a youngling for you if we need your help."

"Some of the Masters are planning to come here for their vaccinations. It would be best if you stay here," added Septi. "And you must vaccinate the kitchen staff, and Ertis, and me."

Inda laughed. "Then pull up your sleeve, Master Septi, and show me your arm. I will be glad to do the honors for you." He brandished the vaccination gun with his right hand and reached for a swab with his left.

"Beware of the sting!" Jeryl cautioned as he led two other Masters into the kitchen. "I bring you more customers for your vaccine, Healer Inda. These are GuildMaster Reass and his apprentice, Beral, of the Metalsmiths Guild. They are anxious to sample Terran magic."

"I will be with you in a moment, Mentor." Inda pressed the gun to Septi's arm and touched the firing stud. The Ardellan flinched as the puff of air pushed a tiny dose of vaccine through his skin. He looked down at the single drop of golden blood, watched Inda wipe it away with another swab.

"Less pain than the bite of a night-flier," said Septi.

"But if it should itch or swell, you must come and see me." Inda pulled another swab from the dispenser. "Who will be next?"

"I will," said the GuildMaster.

Inda stared at the Ardellan's weathered face, at his distinctive tunic and leggings of Metalsmiths' red, at the leather thong that bound his long gray hair. He should have recognized the name: Reass . . . leader of Ardel's most powerful guild. "We met not too long ago, GuildMaster, at the FreeMasters' guildhall. You may not remember me, as you were occupied with other matters at the time. I believe we were not introduced. I am Sinykin Inda."

"I do remember you," said Reass. "I remember that you were concerned about my argument with the FreeMasters and that you tried to aid me when my hands were burned."

"Have they healed well?"

Reass offered them, palms upward, to Inda. The physician looked in vain for scars. The skin of the smith's hands was smooth and unblemished, showing no signs of his years at the forge or the burns that had blistered his palms just after midwinter. "Your capacity for regeneration is remarkable. I cannot tell that you suffered any injury."

"Will your magic truly cure the plague?" asked Beral.

Inda swabbed Ertis' arm with germicide. "The vaccine is not a cure. It will make you immune to the plague, so that even if you are infected, you will not become ill."

"I dispute that statement!" Alu's Healer stood in the kitchen doorway, arms bared to show spiraled blue tattoos. A copper medallion shone on his thin chest. His exclamation caught everyone's attention. Younglings stopped working; even the kitchenmaster turned away from his pots to stare at Viela. "The Terran's magic is evil. It will make you all ill!"

Jeryl crossed the room in three swift strides and confronted Viela. "I grow tired of your prejudice and your baseless accusations, Healer. The Terran is here to aid us. My apprentice and I were vaccinated this morning, and we have come to no harm from it.''

"Others have been harmed." Viela reached behind him, pulled a youngling forward by one tentacle. He pointed to a small golden bruise at the top of its leg. "This youngling carries the Terran's mark, and it is ill. It came to me at midmorning, complaining of fever and pain.''

Inda set down his vaccination gun and motioned the youngling forward. It seemed reluctant to leave Viela's side. Inda sat, bringing his eyes level with the youngling's. "Come, little one. I will not harm you. How do you feel?''

It limped forward on unsteady legs, extended a tentacle to brace itself on the table's edge. "Sick, Master. Hot. Sore.''

"Plague," said Viela.

"Or one of a hand of other illnesses that trouble younglings," countered Jeryl. "It has no rash. Its tentacles and eyestalks are not shriveled.''

Viela was not deterred. "The rash is the final stage of the illness. Before it appears, the youngling's fever will increase, and that will cause its tentacles and eyestalks to become deformed. By tomorrow it will be having convulsions. This is the fault of that Terran. His 'magic' spreads the plague!''

"Sometimes the vaccine causes a mild illness and, rarely, a serious reaction," said Inda. He stroked and soothed the youngling with his left hand as he palpated its bruised leg with his right. The vaccination site was no warmer than the rest of the youngling's body. He pressed the bruise, and the youngling did not flinch. "The reaction is always most intense at the site where the vaccine enters the tissues. The area will swell and feel hot and be painful to the touch. This youngling exhibits none of those symptoms.''

"Lies!" shouted Viela. His anger showed in the ruby glow of his aura. "The youngling has been infected with the plague!''

Reass stepped to Viela's side, pressed a hand to his shoulder. "Calm yourself, littermate. You were always the most excitable of my siblings. I had hoped the years would have improved your temper, but I see that you are still as irritable as a ribbon-snake and as stubborn as a recalcitrant borra."

Viela shoved Reass' hand away. "And you are still enamored of all things Terran. Open your eyes, littermate! They come not to help us but to conquer and destroy us."

"You are a fool, Viela." Reass turned away from his sibling. The GuildMaster's face was twisted into an expression that Inda could not read. "I will no longer claim to be kin of yours."

"That is no loss to me," said Viela. He turned his attention to Jeryl. "I forbid any further vaccinations."

"You do not have the power, Healer." Jeryl bent down and addressed the youngling. "What is your name?"

"naFiira."

"Are you certain that you feel ill?"

"Yes, Mentor." naFiira's left eyestalk trembled.

"When did you begin to feel sick?"

"After the Terran worked his evil magic!" shouted Viela.

Jeryl turned on him. "Hold your tongue, Healer, or I will have you escorted from this room!" He stared at Viela for a long time before he turned back to the youngling.

"Now, naFiira, when did your illness begin?"

naFiira's other eyestalk began to tremble. "This morning, Mentor."

"Before or after you ate your morning meal?"

"Before, Mentor."

"And did you receive the plague-stopper before or after you ate?"

naFiira looked at Viela. He would not answer.

"Tell me," demanded Jeryl.

The youngling's eyestalks crossed as he tried to watch both Viela and Jeryl. "After, Mentor."

"So you felt ill before you were given the plague-stopper?"

naFiira's words were hardly audible. "Yes, Mentor."

Jeryl straightened up. "You are dismissed, naFiira. You have done well. Return to the infirmary and ask the Healer's apprentice to give you something for your fever."

The youngling almost ran from the room, staying well out of Viela's reach as he passed the Healer. Viela's ruby aura had darkened, and rage shone in his bright eyes and twisted mouth. He raised his hands in a gesture of power. The sapphire spirals on his arms glowed as he spoke.

"Heed my words, Mentor. I am sworn to protect the health of Clan Alu. I will no longer permit a Terran Healer to practice his arts in Alu Keep! Send him and his fake 'plague-stopper' back to the wasteland. Let him poison his own people with his alien remedies!"

Jeryl lifted his hands in answer. Sparks flew from his fingertips. Inda's heart lurched as he remembered another argument and the conjured flames that had blistered Reass' palms.

"Lower your hands, Viela." Jeryl pronounced each word carefully, as if its edges were honed and a slip of the tongue might lacerate him. "You have knowingly made false accusations against the Terran. You have forfeited all rights as Healer of Clan Alu. I will convene the council of elders, and they will decide what further action is required."

"None!" cried Viela. Power flashed from his fingertips. The sapphire tattoos snaked up and down his arms. "I resign my position as Healer of Clan Alu, and revoke the conditions of my pledge. Tomorrow I will return to my guildhall in Berrut."

"Then you are required to have a new Healer assigned to Alu. We will expect him to arrive within four days, in keeping with the laws.''

''It is apparent that Alu has no need of Ardellan Healers! That is what I will tell my GuildMaster when he asks me why I have returned to the hall. I doubt that any Healer will choose to serve a clan that employs a Terran.'' Viela lowered his hands and turned away from Jeryl.

''You have not been dismissed, Healer!'' A streak of fire leapt from Jeryl's palms and sped past Viela's ear. Inda gasped. Viela did not move. ''You will send another Healer to Clan Alu!''

Viela looked back over his shoulder. ''If the GuildMaster can find a Healer who is willing to serve Alu, you shall have him.'' He strode from the room.

Jeryl dropped his hands.

Inda sighed, let his taut muscles relax. He slumped on the bench.

''Viela is a fool,'' said Reass. ''He walks away from the most powerful clan on Ardel.''

''Viela has never cared for that kind of power.'' Jeryl walked to the hearth, poured a mug of tea. ''He wants only the power of the old ways, the strengths of tradition and history. That does not make him a fool.''

''But it has made him view me as an enemy,'' said Inda, ''and he is correct. Terrans have brought much harm to your people. The Iron Keep would still be whole if not for us.''

''That was not your doing,'' said Jeryl. ''The weather-workers brought destruction on themselves.''

''They were trying to protect their livelihood,'' protested Inda.

''By destroying your spaceport and driving all Terrans from Ardel.'' Reass poured more tea. ''It was not a reasonable solution. We must adapt to your presence and use what you offer to the best advantage of our people. That is why I invite you to come to Berrut with your vaccine.''

''I am committed to making the trip to Port Freewind. That will use up most of the vaccine I brought with me." Reass' aura darkened; Inda feared his answer was precipitating another angry scene. "If you will send your Healers to the spaceport after I return, I will supply them with vaccine and equipment and teach them how to use it. They can vaccinate the people of Berrut themselves."

"Our Healers would be pleased to do that," said Reass. "Unlike Viela, they will accept changes that make their people's lives easier."

Inda turned away from the others. Despite their reassurances, he felt the weight of Ardellan losses: Jeryl's mate cut down by a Terran weapon, Alu's previous Mentor and his apprentice killed before Sarah Anders' eyes, the many dead and injured in the Iron Keep. He tried to balance that against an increased standard of living and improved health care for the survivors. There were too many immeasurables: lost traditions, changed political and economic relationships, disrupted lives. And there were lives changed or lost on the Terran side.

Above all, there was the magic. His fingers slipped into his pocket, wrapped around the little iron bar hidden there. Tonight, alone in his room, he would attempt the magic again.

Now there were vaccinations to be completed. He picked up the gun, reached for a swab. "Who is next?" he asked.

Chapter 8

Salt River, Southern Desert, Ardel

Ilakri pulled the stopper from his water skin, lifted the spout to his lips, tipped his head back, and drank. A single swallow of warm, sour water dribbled into his mouth. He held it there a moment before letting it run down his parched throat.

He was tired. The midday sun and the warm westerly breeze had made his new clothes too warm. He slipped off his cloak and wrapped it around the twisted red relic that he clutched in his left hand. The cloak's hem and his new boots were stiff and white with salt. He tried to brush the powder away, but it had permeated the cloth and leather.

His belly demanded food. He no longer had water to quiet it. There was water nearby, lapping at the banks of the stream beside the trail and filling the salt sea a short walk to the west. All of it was contaminated. Nothing lived here.

He turned northward, toward the land of the fishers. The terrain sloped up and away from the river, dry dirt and rock climbing to meet the blue-green sky. Ilakri had no idea what was beyond this hill. The huge pile of earth and stone might hide a lush valley or more desert. He would not know until he reached the top.

Ilakri scrambled up the slope, cradling his bundled cloak and the relic against his side. Halfway up the hill, his left foot came down on a loose stone. He fell forward, his knees and right hand hitting the dirt hard. Skin tore on his palm; wet heat spread across it. The legging on his left knee was torn and sticky when he struggled to his feet. Salt made the scrape burn.

He continued the climb more slowly, testing his footing with each step. Golden blood dripped from his palm and oozed from his tender knee. He tore a strip of cloth from the bottom of his new tunic and wrapped his hand with it. He could do nothing for his leg.

The hill was higher or he was more exhausted than he had thought. The climb seemed endless. At last he reached the hill's crest and could look down at the next valley . . . more bare dirt strewn with rock and rubble. Beyond it was another hill, higher than the one on which he stood. He sighed. It was going to be a long afternoon.

Halfway up the third hill Ilakri slipped and fell again. He had no energy to rise this time. He lay in the dirt, his head cradled on his bandaged hand, the relic pressed against his belly. Ilakri closed his eyes. The visions began even before he was asleep.

They were still laughing at him. He heard no sound, but he knew they found his plight amusing. The bright colors of their clothing flashed in the sunlight as they passed him on their way up the hill. He tried to count their arms and legs, knew only that they had more than he. Too many.

They laughed and beckoned to him to follow. A part of him rose and floated after them to the top of the hill. The bright beings did not stop there, did not look down into the narrow, rocky valley or up at the next desolate hillside. They turned to the northeast, danced along an almost invisible path between the boulders. Ilakri followed, skimming over the ground, never quite touching anything. He shivered despite the afternoon's warmth. His body called to him, warning him to return soon or it would die. The bright beings beckoned. He pursued them.

What had seemed a hill became a narrow ridge. They moved in single file along it, laughing and talking in a language Ilakri could neither hear nor understand. Their speech filled his mind, but he could not decipher the words. He followed, peering this way and that, trying to see where the snaking column of colorful beings was leading. Too many arms waved and too many legs danced; he saw nothing but their movement. He heard nothing at all, not even the wind that moved the grasses. . . .

Grass! He saw the deep red blades of spring growth here and there among the rocks. Then he saw a low shrub, its yellow-green leaves unfurling in sunlight. He should hear the branches brushing against each other in the breeze, smell the growing plants and the water that gave them life. He bent to feel grass, felt nothing, smelled nothing, heard nothing. He shivered.

The bright beings had disappeared. He was alone on the ridge, looking northward at the rich, multihued tapestry of a distant forest. Bushes dotted the rolling hills between him and the trees. Plants extended new stems into the light, spreading leaves of pale green or darkest red. A plentiful supply of water and food awaited him in those hills and in the forest beyond. If he could reach it, he would survive.

Ilakri's body called to him once more. Its voice was weak and distant. Ilakri turned about, looking for the path back to his body. Nothing looked familiar. Had he come this way, or that? There were no footprints to guide him, no bright people with too many arms to beckon him home. He was cold and afraid.

His body called again. Ilakri tried to answer, but his mind could make no sound. He concentrated, tried again. Again he made no noise and heard no response from his body. Ilakri floated above the narrow ridge, trying to remember from which direction he had come, trying to guess where his body lay. He cast first one way then the other with no success.

Fear grew in Ilakri's mind, became panic and confusion. His body might be dying, might already be

*dead. He might be doomed to roam these hills forever,
seeking a body that no longer existed. Had the bright
spirits stolen his soul?*

*No! Ilakri summoned all his energy and called to his
body once more. No sound disturbed the stillness in
his mind. He listened quietly, reached out, searched
for a sign. He circled the ridge, circled again, wider,
searching. Another circle, and another, and he heard
the faint call. Ilakri followed it back along the ridge,
memorizing landmarks as he passed them. He still
could not stop shivering.*

Ilakri was cold. He felt warm sunlight on his back,
yet he could not stop shivering. His body was stiff and
slow to respond. He rolled over, used one shaking
hand to unwrap his cloak from the relic and cover himself with it. His other hand ached. He smelled old
blood.

His ears buzzed. He shook his head. The buzzing
did not stop. Ilakri opened first one eye, then the other.
A cloud of tiny red insects was swarming above his
body. A few broke away from the group, flew down
to land on the stiff legging near his sore knee. He
brushed them off, waved the rest away with both
hands. He struggled to sit up. His thirst was almost
overpowering.

He knew where to find water and food. He clambered to his feet, wincing as scabs cracked and tore
on his skinned knee. He settled the cloak about his
shoulders, grabbed the relic and pressed it against his
complaining belly. Then he began to climb. The hill
seemed twice as high as it had before he slept.

Chapter 9

Terran Spaceport, Ardel

The huge shovel moved forward on giant treads. Elissa scanned the graphics display on her goggles, looking for the deep red overlay that identified the highest concentrations of titanium. She chose a patch of ore, dropped the dipper to the ground, maneuvered the articulated arm. The huge bucket began to fill with dark, mineral-rich sand ten meters below her seat in the cab.

The shovel's weight and load balance graphics automatically replaced the ore display. The yellow line of the weight gauge moved up—five tons, ten, fifteen. Elissa's fingers touched controls; the boom began to hoist the bucket. Sand trickled out between the dipper's tines. The orange holographic display showed her how the load balance was shifting as the bucket moved. She tipped the dipper backward and to the right, and the ore settled into the dipper's hollow. The display leveled and changed from orange to green; the load was stable and the shovel's center of gravity was within safe limits.

Elissa slowly backed the shovel away from the sandy oval of the mine. She switched to wheel-level sensors, watched until they told her the treads had reached firm ground. She backed a few meters more, then swung the boom in the wide arc that would deliver the load to the waiting truck. Elissa winced when she saw the ground ahead, where two previous loads of black sand were spread across the dirt. She cleared her goggles, then brought up the sensors' graphic display and had it overlay the virtual image of the truck and the surrounding landscape.

The shovel faced the truck's box straight on. Elissa manipulated controls with her hands and feet, and the shovel's articulated boom hoisted the bucket eight meters into the air, high enough to clear the side of the truck's box. She held her breath and watched the display for any sign of instability; she had lost the first load here, when the bucket had opened prematurely and poured ore onto the sand.

This time the controls held, and Elissa inched the vehicle forward. The shovel's slow-moving treads ground over the spilled ore, pressing it into the wasteland's dry soil. Elissa's fingers tensed as the bucket passed over the second spill. "Third time's a charm," she whispered. Up, over the mound of black sand, boom holding steady, load stable, nothing to worry about. Sensors showed clear ground ahead, the truck bed just where she expected it to be. She extended the bucket toward the truck.

The graphics changed, colors shifting from green to red as the sensors warned her of an unstable load. Elissa's hands moved quickly, not quickly enough. The boom dropped, the bucket opened, the ore spilled just short of the truck's box. Elissa swore as the shovel continued to move. She hit the power interrupt, swore again when it had no effect. Rys' voice reached her through the ear jack; she spared no attention for his words. Her fingers and feet moved on the controls as she fought to turn the huge shovel away from the truck. The empty bucket fell, hitting the ground with enough power to shake the shovel's cab. The dipper's tines jammed straight into the rock-hard soil. The shovel stopped moving with a screech of tearing metal that made Elissa shudder.

"Are you all right?"

Elissa stripped off the goggles and glove, disconnected herself from the projection equipment. "I'm fine. The damned shovel went berserk. Call Herve at the mill, see if he can spare a couple of men. Have them drive down to the mine right away. I'll run the repair-bot from here. Have the computer perform diagnostics on all the shovel's systems immediately.''

"Already started, Chief." Rys handed Elissa a mug of coffee. His long, pale fingers and manicured nails beat a nervous tattoo on the edge of the keypad.

"What time is it?" asked Elissa. The coffee was cold, as always.

Rhys shrugged. He was small and perpetually agitated, and now he seemed more anxious than usual. "20:12. Too late to reach Herve at the mill. They finished testing today and headed back to the base."

"Then contact him at home. Tell him I want a crew at the mine at dawn." Elissa gulped one swallow of coffee, set the rest aside. She looked pointedly at Rys' drumming fingers; the motion stopped. "Have them take the big truck and whatever spare sensors we have in stock. They'll also need the spare boom and a welder."

"How bad is the damage?" Rys turned a stylus over and over in his hand.

"Bad." *Too bad*, thought Elissa, *to be just a glitch in the system. Something is very wrong in that control program.* "We'll have to do a lot of physical repairs tomorrow, and I want the software checked from beginning to end. Nevarre supervised the installation; get her in here first thing in the morning. And let Harwood know what's going on."

Rys nodded. Elissa strode past him and down the hall to her office. Robinson had left the light on for her. She checked her terminal for mail, was relieved to see nothing in the queue. A message from Griswold would have been the perfect end to a truly bad day.

Elissa glanced at her notes for the grievance she was

filing on behalf of Sinykin, decided she was too tired
to wrestle with the half-finished complaint. Jaime was
waiting for her. It was time to go home.

The night was dark and cold. Jaime ran to the door
ahead of Elissa, keyed in his entry code. After a short,
fierce battle the handle bent to his will and the door
opened.

"Dad?" Jaime dropped his pack inside the door,
left his parka in the middle of the room. "Dad, are
you here?"

"Your father isn't on the base, Jaime. You know
he had to go away for a while." Elissa shrugged off
her jacket, hung it and Jaime's parka in the closet.
She saw Sinykin's spare coat, ran her fingers over
the sleeve, wished she could be touching his arm
instead. What part of her mind had changed his status
in her life from partner to "your father"? A few
days ago they were handling crises together; now she
was alone, explaining Sinykin's absence to their son.
This was not the life she had envisioned for any of
them.

Jaime ran into the kitchen. Elissa heard a door slam,
something crash to the floor and shatter. Then Jaime
cried out, that incoherent mix of fear and pain that
always made her heart race. She ran.

She found him on the floor, sitting amid shards of
broken crockery. Blood welled from a cut on his finger. He looked at it, then squinted up at her. He was
frowning.

"I want Dad to fix it."

"Don't pout," she said. She bent, helped him to
his feet. She brushed the pottery slivers from his
clothes, then walked him to a chair. A drop of blood
splattered on the floor.

" 'Don't touch it," said Jaime as she reached for
his finger. "I want my father to take care of me. He's
the doctor."

Elissa could see that the wound was little more than

a scratch, a minor event in an active childhood. She took Sinykin's first aid kit from the cupboard, found a sterile swab, a tube of ointment, and a bandage. She set them on the table before Jaime.

"Your father isn't here. I can bandage your finger, or you can clean it and bandage it yourself," she said. She wanted to reach for Jaime, knew he would push her away. Sinykin had always taken care of him when he was hurt. Had Jaime's nine-year-old brain reasoned that an injury would bring his father running to his aid? No, she was sure he hadn't meant to hurt himself. It was an accident.

"Your dad loves you, Jaime, and he wants to take care of you. He knows that you're safe here, with me and all the other people at the spaceport looking after you." She watched him swab his finger with antiseptic. He winced.

"It stings, Mom."

"It stings when your father does it, too." The cut had almost stopped bleeding. "Your dad left the compound so that he could help some other people who don't have anyone to take care of them right now. He'll be back when you really need him."

Jaime wrapped the bandage around his finger. It looked sloppy, but it would serve its purpose. He looked up at Elissa and smiled, proudly showing off his finger.

"Maybe I can be a doctor, too. Can I have some hot chocolate now?"

"Of course. Go get ready for bed, and I'll make it for you." She cleaned up the broken pottery and the first aid supplies, then heated chocolate for both of them. Her letter to Sinykin was still on the table, decorated with a single drop of Jaime's blood. *I'll have to explain that before I seal the letter*, she thought. *What will hurt Sinykin most: knowing that he wasn't here when Jaime needed him, or learning that Griswold has replaced him with Addami? Will he care that she is having him recalled? A few days ago I thought*

*I knew him and what he wanted from life. Now he
seems as unknowable to me as the Ardellans with whom
he chooses to travel. Is this the time when he won't
return to us?* She sighed as she set the pair of blue
mugs on the table.

Chapter 10

Alu Keep, Ardel

A single candle illuminated one corner of the guest room in Alu Keep's clanhall. Coals glowed dull red in the brazier beneath the window, radiating heat but no light to brighten the shadows. Inda sat at the small wooden table, his shoulders pressed against the carved back of the room's single chair. His fingers brushed the embroidered cloth that covered the table, exploring its soft, nubby texture. The colors of the intricate stitches were muted in the dim light.

He took the cloth from the table and carefully folded it. Then he reached into his pocket and touched the slender iron bar that he had carried with him from the spaceport. He held it in his palm for a moment, then brought it out and stood it on end on the table's smooth top.

The bar was no larger than his smallest finger, the same size and shape as the bars that opened the clanhall's door latches. Inda had watched Ardellans trip such latches with a thought a dozen times since he had entered the keep. He had seen doors swing open without being touched and wall sconces light at a Master's blink. He had witnessed what he could only describe as magic.

It was not the events themselves that were magic. Doors often opened without a touch in Terran buildings; artificial illumination could be adjusted with a word or a wave. He could explain those events with sensors and electronics, technology that could be metered and measured.

How did one quantify a thought, a desire, a command? Could one define Ardellan magic by measuring brain waves or electrical fields? Inda couldn't guess at the source of the Ardellans' power; he only knew that it existed, and that once, in the Iron Keep, he had been able to perform the same magic. He wanted to do it again.

He pushed his chair back so that no part of his body touched the table. His feet were flat on the floor and his hands lay open, palms upward in his lap. He closed his eyes and thought about the iron bar. He thought about reaching out, touching the bar with the tip of a finger, watching it tumble over onto the table. He thought about the cold, hard, smooth surface of the metal touching his skin, thought about the way it would press back against his finger until he exerted enough pressure to push over the bar. He imagined the bar falling, hitting the table with a thud. He thought about it again and again, visualizing the touching, the pushing, the tipping, the falling. He concentrated all his energy on moving the bar.

A knock on the door disrupted his visualization.

Inda opened his eyes. The bar still stood upright on the table. It had not moved. He looked around the shadowed room, wishing he had more candles. Inda took a deep breath, tried to flush the frustration from his mind so that his Ardellan visitor would not sense it.

"Come in," he called.

The door opened, casting a long rectangle of light and shadow across the floor. The Ardellan was a dark cutout inside the bright outline of the doorway. Inda could not make out his features.

"You need more light," said the visitor in Terran Standard. A flame flared in one of the wall sconces, and half of the room's shadows vanished. The Ardellan stepped into the light. The door closed behind him though he did not touch it.

The heavily-accented Standard spoken by Jeryl's ap-

prentice was unmistakable. "It is good to see you
again, Aakar," said Inda in the same language. "Your
Standard is very good. Did you learn it from Sarah
Anders?"

Aakar shrugged. "I never met Master Anders. I
know her urn well; Septi and I visit the mourning wall
often. Septi and Jeryl have been teaching me your language."

"You are an apt pupil. Thank you again for helping
with the vaccinations today."

"It was an interesting experience," said Aakar,
"but I did not come to speak of that. I bring you a
message from Jeryl."

"I am pleased to receive a message from Alu's Mentor." Inda smiled. Jeryl had told him of Aakar's second vocation as Alu's librarian. Tonight dust streaked
Aakar's sleeves and leggings and smudged his face.
His long gray FreeMaster's cloak was askew, and the
ends of a half-dozen scrolls poked from one tunic
pocket. He must have been working among the ancient
texts when Jeryl called him.

Aakar wiped one hand on his tunic and lifted it in a
gesture of greeting. "From Jeryl, Mentor of Clan Alu, to
Healer Inda. May the great sun shine on you. I have decided to accompany you to Port Freewind. We will leave
tomorrow morning, as you had planned. I will meet you
in the clanhall's kitchen at dawn."

"This is an unexpected and pleasant change of
plans. I look forward to traveling with Jeryl. Please
express my gratitude to the Mentor."

"I shall do so." Aakar dropped his hand, pointed
to the iron bar. "That is a fine piece of metal. Are
you planning to have it made into a knife?"

"No." Inda studied the dusty librarian for a moment. How much did he really know about Terrans?
"I have been trying to move it with only my
thoughts."

Aakar gazed at the floor. He seemed uncomfortable.
"I have been told that Terrans are like younglings,

who cannot move a thing without touching it. Is it true that you cannot open our doors?''

"It is true. I must use the younglings' handle. Once, in the Iron Keep, my mind opened a door that had no handle. I have tried many times but I have not been able to repeat that feat.''

"And you cannot make shimmer-light?''

"I have never tried.''

Aakar stared at him. ''That is strange. Moving an object is both a simple and a difficult thing. You must have knowledge, and will, and energy—all three in adequate amounts—before you can accomplish it. Watch your piece of metal.'' The FreeMaster closed his eyes and tilted his head to one side. The iron bar rose three centimeters above the tabletop, turned on its side, and slowly floated down to rest on the table again. ''Making shimmer-light is easier than moving an object or opening a door. Even some younglings can learn to do it. That is how we know that they are mature enough to be cocooned and become Masters. If you opened a door, you surely could learn to make shimmer-light.''

"No one has explained to me how it is done.'' Dare he ask for a demonstration? Sarah Anders had made shimmer-light once, under Jeryl's tutelage. She had described the event in her journal; Inda remembered reading the entry three times as he tried to decide whether it was truth or fiction. Then Ertis had made shimmer-light for him, and he knew that Sarah had not lied.

It had not occurred to Inda to ask an Ardellan for lessons. He rose and offered his hands to Aakar, palms upward. ''Will you teach me how to make shimmer-light?''

Aakar shrugged. ''Sit,'' he commanded. ''Be comfortable. Relax your body. Think of nothing.

"Let your hands fall open on your legs. Keep the palms upward.''

The librarian was quiet for a moment. Inda listened

to the wind outside the shutters, a coal crackling in the brazier, the hiss and pop of a candle flame, the pounding of his own heart. All else was silence.

"Your body is warm. That warmth comes from deep inside you, from a place of light and energy and power. A place of fire, a flame that warms but does not burn, a flame that is controlled. Seek inside yourself for that flame. Find it and observe it."

Again Aakar was silent. This time Inda spared no thought for the noises of the night and the room. He focused all his attention inward. It was easy to visualize the flame. Inda saw it brightly burning in the center of his chest, just as Sarah had described it in her journal. The flame's base was pale yellow, its flickering tip a soft orange-gold. It was tiny, yet it shed enough light to make his entire body glow.

"Once you have found the flame, you must touch it. Slowly, carefully, with the gentlest of intentions, you must reach out to the flame. See yourself cradling it in the palm of your hand, allowing it to rest there. Do not try to hold it, do not try to possess it. Just allow it to exist."

This was more difficult. Inda reached for the flame, but it eluded him. Time after time he imagined his palm cupped beneath the bright tongue of fire. Each time the flame evaded his hand.

The flame never moved from its place in his chest. It seemed to be the spark of life that was the center of his being, yet it would not bend to his will. It appeared to flee from his imaginary hand, but it was his hand that moved rather than the flame.

"Relax," Aakar advised him. "This is not a youngling's contest, to see who can do a thing quickest. This is a matter that takes a Master's skill and patience."

Inda tried again. He considered Sarah's description of her experience, how she had coaxed the flame into her palm. This time he offered his imaginary hand to the flame. He made his palm an inviting nest, a place of warmth and safety, a refuge instead of a prison. He visualized the hand resting against his chest, enticing the flame outward to meet it.

"Slowly open your eyes," whispered Aakar. "Look down at your right hand. Do not move."

A tiny tongue of shimmer-light flickered in the palm of Inda's hand. He stared at it, afraid even to breathe. His hand twitched. The flame did not disappear.

"Raise your hand."

Inda brought his hand up, held it before his face. He had to breathe now. The moving air did not disturb the flame. He turned his hand from side to side, examined the tiny bit of fire that seemed at home in his palm. It felt warm, not hot, where it touched his skin. It moved like a true flame, its color and shape constantly changing.

Inda felt Sarah Anders' presence as strongly as he had when he had touched her urn. She seemed to be with him now, watching the shimmer-light in his palm, showing him how to feed it energy.

"It is so small," he said to Aakar. "Can I make it grow? Could it be as large as the balls of shimmer-light I've seen Masters conjure?"

"With practice you can learn to make a larger flame. Remember that making shimmer-light requires energy. You must learn to control and channel the energy of your body and mind into the flame. Only then will you be able to conjure shimmer-light whenever you wish, in whatever amount you need."

Inda nodded. He was already feeling tired. He closed his eyes, visualized the flame rejoining the spark of life within his chest. Sarah's spirit slipped away with the flame, leaving him with the knowledge that he could always call upon her by touching her urn or conjuring shimmer-light or reading her journal.

"I see that you know better than to unnecessarily rob your body of its strength. If you continue to use good judgment when you practice, you will soon develop the strength and skill to move objects and open doors.'' Aakar touched Inda's shoulder. ''Jeryl will be pleased to hear of your progress.''

''Must you tell him?'' Inda was reluctant to inform the Mentor of his new ability. He wanted to practice in secret for a while. Perhaps when he had more skill, he would conjure shimmer-light for Jeryl. Now he looked at his empty palm and doubted that the tiny flame had ever been there. He knew that the spirit of Sarah Anders was not real. It had been created by his desire to have known her, and fed by his readings of her journal and his visit to the mourning wall. Now they had both created shimmer-light. ''I would rather not tell Jeryl until I have had more practice.''

Aakar shrugged. ''It is wise not to boast of untried skills. I will say nothing.'' The door opened behind him. ''You are tired. I will leave you now.''

''Thank you for teaching me,'' said Inda. Aakar had given him a gift so great that Inda could not put a value on it. ''Perhaps someday I can find a way to repay you.''

''You already have.'' Aakar stopped in the doorway and looked back over his shoulder at Inda. ''Today you vaccinated me against the plague that killed my mate.''

The sleeping platform was hard, but the furs were warm and Inda was exhausted. He was asleep and dreaming five minutes after Aakar left the room.

Inda stood on the crest of a hill. Sunbeams warmed his back, but his body cast no shadow. Sarah Anders walked toward him through a field of younglings' eyeballs that twisted and turned on their stalks, waving like flowers in a breeze. She led Inda's daughter Miranda. Sarah's left hand clutched Miranda's right. Miranda laughed and skipped and held out her left hand to her father. A single tongue of shimmer-light danced in her palm.

The eyeballs parted, drew away from Sarah and Miranda, disappeared beyond the horizon. Stone walls grew up around the pair, walls like those of the Iron

Keep's tower. A staircase appeared. Inda looked down the stairs. The faces of Sarah and Miranda stared up at him. He felt the cold stone of the wall against his back, heard the ominous chanting of the weather-workers in the tower room above. There was danger here.

Miranda and Sarah extended their arms, offering him the shimmer-light that nestled in their palms. He reached for them, an impossibly long stretch of his arm. His fingers passed through Sarah's hand. He tried to touch Miranda, found her to be as insubstantial as her companion.

The tower dissolved around them, leaving Sarah and Miranda standing on a beach. The bright sun warmed them, and waves lapped the sand at their feet. Inda watched them from the top of a dune. Miranda drew patterns in the sand with her tiny bare toes. She was dressed for swimming. Sarah still held Miranda's hand. They offered Inda another gift, something more precious than shimmer-light. It was wrapped in a cloak of shadows and hidden from his sight. He reached for it, and it disappeared. Sarah and Miranda turned away from him and ran, laughing, into the sea.

The morning light had the bright, clear quality of spring sunshine, though the air retained the cold crispness of winter. Inda was glad he had worn his insulated parka and gloves. Septi and Jeryl walked beside him on the keep's main road, their cloaks thrown open and their hair disheveled by the wind. A group of younglings wearing only brown sashes worked to clear the remnants of last year's crops from a garden patch. Alu was preparing for a season of warmth and growth.

Septi spoke quietly to Jeryl. "Mieck will be emerging from his cocoon in only a few days. He will have no mate to guide him, no family line to join. You should be here in case he needs you."

"Mieck will have many friends to help him," replied Jeryl. "Healer Inda cannot make this journey without protection. There are those who would try to keep him from vaccinating our people. My status as Mentor of Alu and my FreeMaster's skills will keep them at bay."

Could last night's dream have been a warning? wondered Inda. He turned to Jeryl. "Of whom should I be afraid? Reass? He was not pleased when I refused his invitation to come to Berrut and vaccinate his guild members. Would he harm me?"

"No. He will send his Healers to learn from you, as you suggested. It would give him greater status if he could bring you to Berrut, and he is one who always seeks status. It would also provide him with an opportunity to discuss the trade agreement with you. I am certain he has a proposal that would benefit the Metalsmiths Guild and undermine Clan Alu's power."

"And such a proposal could not be discussed in the presence of Alu's Mentor," said Inda.

Jeryl shrugged. "Not without inviting immediate dispute. Reass has learned to be wary of me."

"With good reason. You need fear no one when you ride with Jeryl." Septi tried one more plea. "I should travel with you and Healer Inda. You do not have the gift of the fisherfolk's speech. Who will translate for you?"

"GuildMaster Arien will meet us at Bentwater. This is the time of his spring trip to arrange the warm season's caravan schedule. He will be our guide and translator."

Arien! Inda was pleased. The GuildMaster had brought him safely out of imprisonment in the Iron Keep and delivered him to the spaceport. He owed Arien a great debt; perhaps he could repay it on this trip.

Jeryl touched Septi's arm. "You must stay here and wait for messages from the other Terrans. You know our route. If Healer Inda's people need to reach him you will know where to find us. You will be our messenger."

Septi did not seem pleased, but he kept silent.

The younglings had taken most of Inda's and Jeryl's gear and supplies to the stable. Inda carried only his medkit, with its irreplaceable vials of vaccine. Mounts and pack animals were loaded and waiting for him and Jeryl when they reached the gate. At the corral several younglings were harnessing a pair of borras to a small cart.

"Are we taking the cart with us?" asked Inda.

"No," said Jeryl. "That is Viela's cart. He is preparing to return to his guildhall in Berrut."

As if on cue, the Healer strode from behind a wall. A gaggle of younglings burdened with misshapen bundles and covered baskets followed him.

"May sunset find you in Berrut, Healer," called Jeryl. "For your sake I hope that your journey is swift."

Viela turned, made a warding gesture. "I have been told that you ride with the Terran. Be warned, Mentor. I carry word of your treachery to the Healers Guild. The GuildMaster will not countenance alien interference in our ways. Ride swiftly, and watch your back." He turned and stalked to his cart.

Inda stopped a few meters from the corral. "Did he mean that? Will the other Healers be upset enough to come hunting for us?"

"Viela always means what he says. When faced with confrontations, cooler heads usually prevail. He will try to convince his guildmates in Berrut that your vaccine is harmful. Some among them may agree, but most will want to see for themselves. They may follow us to investigate the truth of Viela's claim." Jeryl shrugged. "Do you fear their questions?"

"No, not at all," said Inda. He feared other things, such as the flames these Ardellans could conjure from their fingertips and cast across a room. He was glad that Jeryl would ride beside him and Arien would meet them at Bentwater. They possessed powers that he could only think of as magic, and they would protect him. He pulled off his right glove, looked at the skin of his palm. He could still feel the warmth of the shimmer-light that he had coaxed into his hand. A tiny bit of Ardel's magic was now a part of him.

Inda mounted and guided his alep out through the keep's wide gate. Alu's orchards and fields were spread before him. Beyond them sprawled the wasteland and the spaceport, with its acres of pavement, its fences and buildings, its cables and towers and antennae. His family was there, safe among the Terran technology. Magic was real in Alu Keep. Inda had yet to make it real at the spaceport. He felt the warmth in his palm, wondered if he could take the shimmer-light back with him, or if he would be forced to choose between remaining here with the magic and returning to his old life.

Chapter 11

Terran Spaceport, Ardel

The vid-phone in the Durant-Inda kitchen beeped just after dawn. Elissa was sitting at the table, enjoying the only warm cup of coffee she was likely to get that day. She opened the line for audio only. "Chief Durant."

"This is Coni Mattrisch at the gate. A messenger just arrived with two letters from Dr. Inda. Yours is marked 'personal and confidential,' and the Free-Master won't let me accept it. Do you want to come out and get it?"

"I'll be right there," said Elissa. She cleared the line, looked up to see Jaime standing in the doorway.

"Can I come along?" he asked, rubbing the sleep from his eyes with balled fists.

"Of course. Get dressed." Elissa gulped half the coffee, then reluctantly left the mug on the table and went to find her boots and parka.

Jaime met her at the front door. She made him put on boots and gloves before they strode out into the chilly morning air.

The FreeMaster was waiting for them at the gate. Jaime ran ahead to meet him, offered his hand in a five-fingered imitation of the Ardellan salute. The FreeMaster raised his hand in answer. Coni Mattrisch left the gate house and joined Elissa.

"You look familiar," said Jaime. "Are you the FreeMaster who came to take my dad on his first trip?"

"I am Ramis. I remember you. You are Jaime."

"Yes!" Jamie turned to Elissa. "Mom, he remembers me!"

"That's nice, Jaime." Elissa offered her hand to Ramis. "Have you brought me a letter from Dr. Inda?"

Ramis gave her the plain blue envelope. "This came from Alu yesterday."

"Have you seen my dad?" asked Jaime. He had climbed onto the bottom rung of the gate and was leaning over, trying to pet Ramis' alep.

"No. He did not come to our guildhall."

Elissa pulled off her right glove. Her name was written on the envelope in Sinykin's precise script. She ran the tip of her finger over the letters. A single drop of moisture smeared the "D" in Durant. She sighed, folded the envelope, and exchanged it for the one in her pocket. "Can you see that this is delivered to Dr. Inda as soon as possible?"

"I'll have to report that," said Mattrisch. Her voice was huskier than usual.

"It doesn't matter," replied Elissa. "I'll give Griswold a copy if she wants it." She turned back to Ramis. "Can you deliver it?"

Ramis shrugged and took the envelope. "Someone will take it to Alu."

"Thank you. It is very important."

"May the great sun smile on you and on Healer Inda today." Ramis mounted and turned his alep away from the spaceport.

"Good-bye!" shouted Jaime from his perch on the gate.

"Come," said Elissa. "Let's go make breakfast."

"And read Dad's letter?" Jaime jumped down and ran ahead.

"And read Dad's letter."

They left Coni Mattrisch standing at the gate.

"You'll have to be off the system while I run parallel diagnostics," said Joli Nevarre. She smiled, showing the tiny golden sapphire set in her right front tooth. Its color was a perfect match for her eyes. She always wore yellow or gold coveralls; they looked rich against her warm brown skin. "You can use the repair-bot, but all the other vehicles will have to be switched to manual control."

Elissa nodded, resisting the urge to brush the lint from her faded gray coveralls and pat her disheveled curls into place. "Santiago and his team are out at the mine. They can check the manual systems and make certain they're operating at spec. I'll monitor from here."

"Good. I'll call Rys when I have some results." Nevarre walked out of the mine room, leaving behind the faint scent of orange blossoms.

"Rys, shut down everything but the repair-bot," said Elissa. "Has Herve reached the site?"

"He just checked in, Chief. You can pick him up on channel two."

The controls for the repair and maintenance robot were more elaborate than those for the vehicles. Elissa settled into the operator's chair, slipped on the gloves and goggles, and jacked the com-unit into her ear. She had a clear view of the mine and its equipment through the robot's sensors. Herve Santiago and a member of his crew were scrambling over the shovel's boom, inspecting the damaged joint. Another engineer was climbing the caged ladder to the control cabin nine meters above the ground. The truck she had almost hit was gone; someone had moved it over next to the 'dozer.

"I think we'd better replace the boom," said Santiago's companion. "We can repair the damage, but it'll be easier to do it at the base."

"Let me contact Chief Durant and get her opinion before you start disassembly," said Santiago.

"I'm already here, Herve." Elissa rolled the robot forward on its three sturdy, wheeled legs. The huge treaded tires left deep impressions in the sand. The robot was only three meters tall, but one of its six arms could be extended six meters beyond its body.

Sensors at the end of the arm allowed Elissa to peer over the engineer's shoulder at the broken joint.

A steel bolt thicker than a human femur had snapped, letting one corner of the bucket separate from the boom. Another bolt had bent, but the boom and the bucket seemed to be intact. Elissa touched a control, switched from virtual reality to a graphic image of the stressed and damaged joint. The robot's particle diffraction sensors came on line, showed her a three-dimensional view of the interior structure of the boom.

Santiago ran a hand over the sheared surface of the bolt. "This metal shouldn't have been torn apart by that accident. The shovel is designed to dig this earth."

"The dipper was built to handle the loose titanium sands," said Elissa. "You know how expensive it is to ship these things. The manufacturer would have been instructed to make it as lightweight as possible. It's not meant for digging hard-packed soil and rock."

"I suppose not . . . but I'd like to have the metallurgist run this bolt and the bent one through a battery of tests. And she should check the other bolts for hidden damage."

"That's a reasonable precaution. Have her check the boom and the bucket, too." Elissa withdrew the inspection sensors, extended two of the robot's maintenance arms. "Now if you'll get off this boom, I'll start detaching the bucket. All the vehicles have been switched to manual control, so you can begin testing them. I want you to check every system on the trucks and the 'dozer."

Santiago was already on the ground, directing his engineers. "Genesee, you and Li take truck one. Ejma and Hart, truck two. I'll take the 'dozer. Run them through the standard check first, from sensors through controls and engine operations. Then we'll take them out on the desert and run them around a bit."

Elissa began cutting through the bent bolt. She envied the other engineers this chance to drive the trucks without "the spook" as an intermediary. "Herve," she said with mock sternness.

"Yes, Chief?"

"No racing, Herve."

"No, Chief."

She heard him laughing as he walked toward the 'dozer.

Olduvai touched down at 1447 hours. Elissa and Jer Robinson watched the shuttle's landing from the wide hangar doorway. The pilot was skilled; she brought the shuttle in from the west and dropped her lightly to the field with minimal retro firing. *Olduvai* was an older model, her skin pocked and rippled by the debris encountered in atmosphere and around space stations. Elissa had repaired many like her at Titan Station, had scoured their hulls in her maintenance bug or suited up and crawled into their engines. She missed working on the shuttles and the bigger ships.

The door opened, the ramp dropped to the ground, and two dozen miners with duffels on their shoulders strode out onto the field.

Robinson whistled. "That is the tallest woman I have ever seen!"

"I'd say by the insignia on her sleeve, she's their crew chief." Elissa laughed. "You'd better watch yourself. You could be in trouble if Tanyeesha hears about that whistle."

"Tanyeesha is not a jealous woman," protested Robinson, "and what she doesn't know won't annoy her. So we won't tell her, all right?"

Elissa decided not to protest this fine example of illogic. "Drive the cart, Jer. Let's not make them carry those duffels all the way to their quarters." She walked out to greet the miners.

"I'm Jan Mboya, chief of this crew," said the tall woman, offering her hand to Elissa. "This is my assistant, Mammo Selati."

Elissa shook hands with each of them. Mboya was

nearly two meters tall and so slender that it seemed a breeze might break her in two. Her hands were narrow, her fingers were long and tapered, and her brown eyes turned up at the outer corners. Selati was shorter, rounder, with meaty hands, kinky black hair, and full lips. He grinned as Elissa greeted them.

"Welcome to Ardel. I'm Chief Maintenance Engineer Durant. Please call me Elissa. If you'll place your luggage in the cart, my clerk will take it to your quarters. The rest of your crew can have a few hours to settle in there. Administrator Griswold has scheduled an immediate briefing, and she would like both of you to attend."

Mboya tossed her duffel into the cart. "We want to begin work as soon as possible. We have heard rumors that there are problems with your facility, and that you may be forced to cede this base to Nagashimi-BOEM. We have no desire to work for that corporation; nor do we wish to be marooned on a base under its control. *Nairobi* will stay in orbit until we are certain the mine and its equipment are operational and that you will be able to meet the conditions of our contract."

Elissa guessed that a dismantled shovel and malfunctioning control program would not satisfy Mboya. "What happens if we don't live up to your expectations?"

"Then we will return to *Nairobi* and seek another assignment. Kenyan mining teams are in great demand; our training center cannot fill all the positions that are available."

"But I'm sure everything is ready for us," said Selati. He smiled. "We have heard these rumors before, and they are almost always baseless."

Elissa's mouth was suddenly dry. Sandsmark and the Nagashimi-BOEM representative were coming to inspect the mine in a few days. They expected to find the miners hard at work, the mill taking in truckloads of sand and spewing out high-quality ore. If that first shipment was not ready in seven days, the Union would probably lose the mine and the spaceport to Nagashimi-BOEM. Then Sinykin's recall would be meaningless. The entire staff would be replaced by Nagashimi-BOEM employees. Elissa could not bear to think of the chaos that would cause in her life and the lives of her friends. She had nothing to say as she led the miners across the field to the administration building.

Lindy Zapata was waiting at the reception desk on the second floor. "Everyone is in the conference room, Chief Durant. The Administrator said you were to go right in."

The conference room was at the end of a long hall lined with framed photographs. Most of them were Griswold's work, taken with one or another of her antique cameras and developed, printed, and framed by her. Elissa had passed them so often that she no longer noticed them. Neither Mboya nor Selati made any comment.

Griswold was seated at the far end of the conference room's long table. She rose as Elissa and the miners entered the room.

"Welcome to Ardel," she said. She pointed to the two chairs on her right. "Please be seated. I'm Anna Griswold, Administrator of this facility. This is my senior staff. Jeff Grund, Science Division; Alex Harwood, Security; Joli Nevarre, Information Services; and you've met Durant."

Mboya nodded as she sat. "I am Jan Mboya, and this is my assistant, Mammo Selati." She reached for a mug and the server at the table's center. "Is this coffee?"

"As near to it as you'll get on this base," said Grund.

Mboya filled her mug and passed the server to Selati. He poured, sipped, and grinned. "It'll do. At least it's hot."

"How soon can we inspect the facilities and begin work?" asked Mboya.

Griswold looked at Elissa. "You can tour the facilities today. Chief Durant, have the repairs on the shovel been completed?"

"The damaged boom is being replaced right now," replied Elissa. She turned to Mboya. "We had an accident with the shovel yesterday. I was testing it from the mine room and having some problems with the sensors on the bucket. On my third run I lost control of the shovel, and a bolt sheared between the boom and the dipper."

"Was it your error or a problem with the equipment?" asked Mboya.

"It felt like an equipment problem. I immediately shut down the spook and called in a repair crew and Dr. Nevarre. We inspected the damage this morning and removed the boom and bucket. Santiago's crew tested the manual controls on the trucks and the 'dozer. Everything checked out above spec. I'm going to test the shovel after this meeting. At this point we think the problem is in the spook."

Nevarre nodded. "That isn't confirmed yet. My diagnostic programs are still running. So far they show some inconsistencies that I can't account for. The virtual reality firmware is very complex. It could take several days to track down and correct the problem."

"We don't have several days to spare," said Griswold. "Nagashimi's *White Crane* is due to arrive on the twenty-second. Howard Sandsmark and Austin Duerst will be aboard. They want to inspect a working mine and witness the delivery of our first shipment of ore to the Nagashimi-BOEM reduction facility orbiting Hecate."

Harwood entered some notes at the keyboard of his memo pad. "Let's be realistic about this. Chances are we won't have that shipment ready in time to fulfill our contract with Nagashimi-BOEM. Can the Union's legal department get us an extension?"

"The courts, and Nagashimi-BOEM, have been quite unforgiving of late," commented Selati. "A

Kenyan mining team working on Thor's moon found their employer had changed quite suddenly from the Terran Union to Nagashimi-BOEM.''

"I've seen a report of that incident," said Elissa. "It sets a nasty precedent. We could lose this base if we're not ready to ship on schedule."

Griswold poured another mug of coffee. "Has anyone considered that these problems might be the result of sabotage? Five years ago Nagashimi-BOEM made an attempt to gain control of Ardel's titanium resources.''

"Would they really try that again?" asked Nevarre.

"I think they would. Now they'd get a spaceport, a mill, and the mine. They'd have to compensate the Union for the facilities, but they would earn that back very quickly," said Griswold. "I think its very likely that we're dealing with one or more saboteurs."

Grund shrugged. "I suppose it's possible. I don't like to think that one of my neighbors is an industrial spy."

"I don't think we should discuss this outside this room." Harwood folded his memo pad and tucked it into his pocket. "I'll start a discreet investigation today. I don't want to panic the staff or cause our saboteur, if he exists, to go into hiding."

"He may already have left the grounds," said Griswold. She was watching Elissa. "There are Ardellans who don't want the Union on their planet. They may have found an ally on our staff, someone who was willing to sabotage the mining equipment in order to help them. Perhaps you should begin by investigating everyone who has close ties with the Ardellans."

That's Sinykin, thought Elissa, *and no one else. Can she really believe he would do this?*

"Those Ardellans want to be rid of all Terrans. They wouldn't be willing to trade the Union for Nagashimi-BOEM," said Grund. "I think it's more likely we're dealing with an agent of the corporation."

"Perhaps." Griswold sounded skeptical. "I'll send

a message to Sandsmark informing him of these developments. Meanwhile, let's get that equipment repaired as quickly as possible. Chief Durant, please conduct a tour of the virtual reality facility for miners Mboya and Selati and their crew. Dr. Nevarre, let me know as soon as you complete your diagnostics. Dr. Grund and his staff will be at your disposal. Call on them if you need help with the analysis.

"Chief Harwood, I want you to double the guard on the gate. Absolutely no Ardellans are to be allowed into the compound. And if Dr. Inda returns, he is to be taken into custody."

Butterflies filled Elissa's stomach. This was worse than censure, worse even than recall. Griswold was planning to arrest Sinykin and charge him with sabotage.

Chapter 12

Healers' Guildhall, Berrut, Ardel

Viela guided his borras to one side of the narrow, rutted track to make room for a merchant's cart. It was one more inconvenience in a day of trials. Animals were not allowed on Berrut's streets; instead they used the walled tracks that extended like spokes from the city's center, running behind the shops and guildhalls. Traffic had impeded Viela's progress toward the Healers' Guildhall all morning. Now his cart shuddered and slowed again. Viela cursed as he heard the right wheel scrape against the track's stone wall.

"You are in a foul mood, Healer," called the merchant as he passed Viela.

"Too many insolent tradesmen have troubled me today! Take your goods elsewhere and let me get on with my business." The Healer tugged at the reins, urging his borras back into the center of the track. Cart wheels bounced across ruts, jostling the load of jars and baskets inside the cart. Something clattered and fell. Viela cursed again.

The next gate was painted with the Healers' insignia. Viela stopped the cart, then leaned over and tugged the bell pull that hung against the wall. He listened to the thud of the clapper against the wooden gong and remembered the first time he had heard that sound. The gate had opened then to reveal a courtyard filled with neat herb gardens and floral borders, with blooming fruit trees and lush conifers. Younglings had been tending the plants and working in the stable. A mere youngling himself, naViela had gasped when he

first saw the guildhall's yellow stone walls and three
stories of lighted windows.

Now the creaking gate swung wide, reminding Viela
that he and it had aged. He turned his borras into the
courtyard of the Healers' compound. A youngling
pushed the gate closed behind him.

"Shall I stable the borras?" asked the youngling.

"Yes, and get some help to unload the cart. I do not
want to find any of my jars broken or my baskets missing when I inspect my baggage this evening." Viela
stretched his right leg, then his left. His joints ached
from spending more than a day in the jouncing cart.
He climbed down from the wooden bench and stepped
carefully between the courtyard's puddles and piles of
dung. The hem of his cloak was caked with mud and
his boots were already ruined, but he was determined
to suffer no more indignities. The muddy road from
Alu Keep had mired the cart twice, and Viela had had
to push it out himself. All in all, he had to agree with
the merchant. His mood was foul.

The condition of the courtyard and guildhall did
nothing to improve his disposition. The herb gardens
were overgrown, and the once stately scarlet conifers
that lined the fence were shedding their needles in
clumps. Broken windows, boarded from the inside,
dotted the guildhall's three-story stone facade. A hand
of shutters hung askew. Piled garbage and manure
steamed near the stable door.

Viela disdained the guildhall's wooden knocker and
hit the weathered door with his palm. The warped
wood rattled in its frame. A small panel slid aside,
and a disembodied eye peered at him. Viela showed
his Healer's token and the door opened, squawking as
wood rubbed against stone. The youngling inside had
only one eye; the other stalk was shriveled. *A victim
of the plague,* thought Viela. *This youngling should
not be wearing an apprentice's sash. It belongs in the
fields, toiling with the other malformed younglings.*

Viela stepped across the warped threshhold. The youngling closed and barred the door behind him.

The building looked no better inside than it had outside. The yellow stone walls were streaked with soot. Bunches of drying herbs hung from the rafters, and crumpled bits of leaves were mixed with the dust in the room's corners. A small fire smoldered on the hearth. The room was drafty and cold.

"May I take your cloak, Healer?" asked the deformed youngling.

"No. Tell GuildMaster Kelta that Healer Viela requests a moment of his time." Viela crossed to the hearth and found a pot of tea on the warmer. He pulled a mug from the rack, wiped it with the cleanest corner of his tunic, and filled it. The tea was weak and lukewarm, but it was a welcome change from the cold food he had eaten on the trail.

The Healers Guild had once been prosperous. Bright tapestries had decorated these walls when Viela was an apprentice. The hall had been crowded with younglings and apprentice Healers vying for the attention of their teachers. Merchants and GuildMasters had arrived daily with gifts of food and goods to exchange for healing powders and potions. The Healers, with the powerful Messengers and the wealthy Metalworkers, had exerted great influence in Ardel's ruling Assembly. Then the Terrans came, and the face of the world changed.

Power now rested with Clan Alu and the Free-Masters Guild, both allied with the Terrans. The Healers lived in poverty, guarding their ancient secrets and waiting for the wheel to turn again. Viela looked around the decrepit guildhall and remembered its former glory. He would do whatever was necessary to turn the wheel and rid Ardel of the Terrans.

Footsteps sounded on the stairs. They were too lively to be Kelta's. Viela turned and saw Bantu, the GuildMaster's assistant, coming toward him. "May the great sun shine on you this day, Healer Bantu. I bring news of Clan Alu. Is the GuildMaster able to see me?''

Bantu straightened his disheveled tunic before raising a hand in greeting. Even the tattoos on his arms seemed disordered. ''It is good to see you, Viela. The GuildMaster welcomes news from outside Berrut. He has had a difficult winter and now rarely leaves his rooms. He spends much time resting, but he is awake now. I will take you to him.''

Viela followed Bantu up the steps, lifting the muddy hem of his cloak so that it would not attract more dirt. The second floor was filthier than the first. One of the windows opening onto the corridor had been boarded over, and cobwebs festooned several doorways. ''How many Healers live here now?'' asked Viela.

Bantu shrugged. ''Most of the hall is empty. We have five Healers who practice in the infirmary and three apprentices who study with them. Two other Healers spent the winter searching through the ancient scrolls in our library. They soon will return to their clans. We manage to feed two hands of younglings, and old Hesra the herbalist is still alive. Myself, and the GuildMaster. That is all.'' He stopped outside an open door.

''It is sad indeed that we have been reduced to this,'' commented Viela.

''It is a disgrace!'' The GuildMaster's voice was full and harsh, not at all the voice of an aged and failing Master. ''Come in, Viela, and give us your news. What has happened at Alu Keep?''

Kelta sat beside a glowing brazier on the far side of the cluttered room. His legs were wrapped in one dusty fur and another covered his shoulders. What little hair he still possessed stood straight up from the center of his head like a tuft of white grass. A tattered scroll was spread across his lap. He used a strip of red cloth to mark his place, then carefully rerolled the ancient manuscript. His hand shook as he set the scroll on a nearby table, but when he looked up his gaze was steady.

Viela felt like an apprentice as he bowed to his old teacher. "I have resigned my post with Clan Alu, GuildMaster, and revoked my pledge as Alu's Healer. My resignation was accepted by Jeryl, Mentor of Alu. I ask to be allowed to return to the guildhall."

"You have been with Alu for many seasons," said Kelta. He pressed his palms together. "Its people have become your people. What has made you angry enough to turn your back on them?"

"Clan Alu has betrayed the Healers and all Ardellans, GuildMaster. Alu has accepted the ministrations of a Terran who calls himself a Healer!"

Bantu stepped forward. "What?" he cried, and a pale ruby flush spread through his aura.

Kelta spared his assistant a withering glance before turning back and waiting in silence for Viela to continue.

"The Terran brought Alu a 'plague-stopper,' a potion he called a vaccine. He claims it will keep those who accept it from falling ill with the plague."

"You did not believe him?" asked Kelta.

"It is contrary to everything you taught me, GuildMaster. I warned Alu's elders that the Terran's potion would make their people ill, and I forbade them to accept it. The elders would not listen to me. Jeryl would not listen. He defied me, and then the rest of the clan defied me. Reass was there, and even he allowed the Terran to press the potion into his arm with alien magic. I could no longer stay at Alu Keep."

"You were right to leave," said Kelta. "The Healers Guild cannot permit such insubordination among the clans. We have always protected and cared for our people. We know what is best for them."

Viela shrugged. "Jeryl of Alu no longer believes that."

"Alu has caused us much grief these past few seasons."

"Since the Terrans came," muttered Viela.

"Yes, since the Terrans came." Kelta smoothed the fur on his lap. "Now Alu has no Healer. Its elders may find that is too great a price to pay for friendship with the Terrans and for their vaccine."

"Jeryl invoked the ancient law," said Viela. "He demanded that the guild send Alu a new Healer within four days."

"No." Kelta threw off his furs and leaned forward in his chair. "Alu has broken faith with us. We are under no obligation to provide them with a Healer. Let them find a Healer among the Terrans."

"I have more to tell you," said Viela. Bantu paced the floor behind him. "Hanra-bae has asked the Terran to bring his potion to Port Freewind. Jeryl and the Terran are already on their way there."

"I forbid it!" growled Kelta. "The Terrans have attempted to spread their influence too far. I will not allow them to contaminate the fishers." He pressed his palms together again, intertwining the fingers of his two hands. "I must ride to Port Freewind. I will forbid Hanra-bae to accept the Terran potion."

Bantu stepped to Kelta's side. "You cannot undertake such a journey, GuildMaster. Your health . . . let me go. I can reach Port Freewind in time to meet with Master Healer Hanra-bae and convince him that the Terran potion is dangerous."

Kelta patted Bantu's hand. "Do not be concerned for my health. I am not feeble. This challenge will make me young again. You may ride with me if you like, but you will not keep me in Berrut while a Terran usurps the responsibilities of the Healers Guild. I will leave for Port Freewind in the morning."

By evening all of Viela's gear had been carried up to a cold, dusty room on the second floor of the guild-hall. He was given a small bucket of coal for the brazier and oil for the single lamp. The tiny room, with its hard sleeping platform and musty furs, was a poor exchange for the fine chambers that had been his at Alu Keep. Foraging night-mice rustled through the debris in the dark corridor outside the door. Viela's pharmacopoeia was still sealed in jars and baskets; he decided to leave it there until he could clean out the room and set traps for the tiny marauders.

He had expected the guildhall to be a refuge from the disappointment he had experienced at Alu Keep. Instead it proved to be a further disillusionment. Now he had no other home, unless the guild assigned him to a new post. He thought about staying in Berrut and trying to put the hall in order. By tradition that duty fell to the GuildMaster's assistant, and Bantu would certainly resent Viela's interference.

Bantu had changed in the years since he and Viela had been students together. He had become unkempt in appearance, his housekeeping slovenly. Viela wondered if his teaching and healing skills had also deteriorated. Bantu seemed to him a poor choice to succeed Kelta as leader of the Healers Guild. Kelta's judgment should be questioned if he truly believed Bantu to be the best of the Healers.

Darkness was falling and Viela was lighting his lamp when a youngling announced dinner. The Healer set aside his half-empty pack and walked downstairs to a simple meal of boiled tubers and cold bread. He sat at the long table near the hearth and listened to the banter of the other Healers and their students. The tea was weak, the preserves were too sweet, and the dried ground-plums left a bitter aftertaste. Perhaps the quality of the food explained why Kelta and Bantu failed to appear. Eventually two younglings carried a tray up to Kelta's room.

The hearth seemed to be the only warm place in the guildhall. Viela sat on the yellow hearthstone with his back to the fire, sipping tea. He had a clear view of the kitchen, the main hall, and the staircase to the second floor. A youngling went up, empty-tentacled, then came down with a tray of dirty bowls and plates.

Bantu followed. He stopped beside the door and put on a heavy cloak before stepping outside.

Viela finished his tea and fastened his cloak before he followed Bantu into the night. The air was cold and still, and clouds obscured the stars and diffused the moons' light. Viela picked his way across the courtyard to the compound's main gate, slipped through it into yellow street. A turn to the right would take him to Berrut's center and the great assembly hall where Ardel's ruling council met. Bantu had turned to the left, was walking in the shadows close to the wall. Viela pulled his hood up to hide his face and followed.

Bantu turned into gray street, where the bare limbs of fruit trees made a latticework arch above the road. The high wall ended, and Viela walked beside a decorative garden where stone paths and low benches separated banks of plants that would soon fill the spring air with delightful scents. Bantu ignored the garden and crossed the street to the Inn of the Blue Door.

The inn had no first floor windows facing the street. Viela remembered that the common room opened onto an enclosed court, but there was no path from the street to the courtyard. He would have to follow Bantu into the inn.

The blue door opened before him, and light and warmth spilled out to welcome him into the inn. The common room was filled with small tables at which Masters ate and drank and talked. Younglings tended the fire in the big hearth and carried trays of food and pots of spiced cider and tea to the laden sideboard. The appetizing odors made Viela regret his disappointing dinner.

Bantu was sitting with two other Masters at a table near the far wall. One of his companions wore the red tunic and leggings of the Metalsmiths. His long gray hair was bound back with a leather thong. Viela knew him without seeing his face—Reass, who had betrayed their kinship and Ardel's interests in his pursuit of Terran wealth. The other Master wore merchant's gold.

The three had neither the relaxed attitudes nor the calm auras of friends sharing an evening's conversation. They leaned close together and spoke earnestly about something; Viela was too far away to hear their words. He helped himself to a mug of cider and took a seat in a secluded corner where he could observe Bantu and his companions without being seen.

They talked for a long time with much waving of hands and quiet remonstrations. Once Reass pressed his palm against Bantu's chest, and Bantu violently shook his head. The merchant calmed them, and soon they seemed to reach an agreement. They shared a last pot of tea, and then Bantu left the inn.

Viela stayed a while longer, though he could enjoy neither the spiced cider nor the inn's warmth. Bitter thoughts spoiled his pleasure. The Terrans had once again touched his life, wrenching it from its expected path. Bantu plotted with Reass and the merchant. What mischief were the Terran sympathizers planning?

Viela could not allow Kelta to ride to Port Freewind with only Bantu for an escort. He swallowed the last of the cider and left a small iron ring on the table as payment for the innkeeper. Then he fastened his cloak and left the inn. He would need a good night's sleep if he was to be ready to ride in the morning.

Chapter 13

Nagashimi's *White Crane*

The stateroom's com-unit announced an incoming message. Howard Sandsmark, Secretary of the Terran Union's Interstellar Trade Commission, rolled from his bed into the three-wheeled chair that served as his legs aboard ship. He hid his truncated thighs beneath the chair's plastiform shield, then jacked the control cable into the socket in his left hip. He twitched a muscle. The chair silently glided across the dark room to the comm console.

The unit emitted a second discreet tone. Sandsmark stopped his chair before the console's glowing red indicator, pressed his thumb to the ident reader, then watched the message's luminous characters scroll slowly up the wall. He grunted when he saw the salutation, grunted again as he read the text.

2262:9/18, TERRAN CALENDAR
SECURITY/SCRAMBLED
TO: HOWARD SANDSMARK, SECRETARY
    INTERSTELLAR TRADE COMMISSION
    NAGASHIMI'S *WHITE CRANE*
FROM: ANNA GRISWOLD, ADMINISTRATOR
      TERRAN UNION SPACEPORT, ARDEL
  MINERS ARRIVED 1500 HRS LOCAL TIME TODAY. UNABLE TO BEGIN WORK. MINING SHOVEL DAMAGED ON 9/17; SABOTAGE SUSPECTED. INVESTIGATION IN PROGRESS. SINYKIN INDA LEFT TERRAN COMPOUND UNDER SUSPICIOUS CIRCUMSTANCES.

DELAY ARRIVAL OF *WHITE CRANE* AND IN-
SPECTION OF MINE IF POSSIBLE. CONTACT-
ING LEGAL DEPT TO REQUEST EXTENSION OF
DELIVERY DATE FOR FIRST SHIPMENT OF TI-
TANIUM ORE. APPRECIATE YOUR ASSIS-
TANCE.
ENDMESSAGE
AUTOWIPE

The text disappeared, leaving behind a smooth white
wall and a glowing green indicator on the keypad.

"Lights, thirty percent brightness," said Sandsmark.

The room complied.

A series of minor muscle twitches moved his chair
back, turned it, made it glide to the bed. He considered the narrow but comfortable gel-filled mattress and
the cooling sheets for a moment, turned the chair again
and directed it to the desk.

His personal computer lay, closed and locked, on
the narrow plastiform shelf. He touched his thumb to
the lock and the cover rolled off the recessed keypad.
"Operating," said the machine's androgynous voice.

"List current power status," commanded Sandsmark.

"Eight point two three hours at maximum efficiency
on currently installed battery pack."

Sandsmark reached over, checked the indicator on
the spare pack, was reassured that it still held a full
charge. This ship was owned by the corporation that
wanted to acquire Ardel's titanium mines. Despite
Austin Duerst's assurances that this was simply an inspection tour, Sandsmark trusted neither Duerst nor
Duerst's employer, Nagashimi-BOEM. He would not
jack into the ship's power system and jeopardize the
integrity of his programming or data bases.

"Access Ardellan data file, subject headings only,
in chronological order. Visual display."

The viewer slid up and began to glow. Sandsmark

scanned the lines of text that slowly scrolled up its surface.

The Ardellan situation had been a particularly large thorn in Sandsmark's side since Sarah Anders' unexplained death on the planet five years earlier. The Union's governing board had not been satisfied by Sandsmark's official report of that event. The board had suspected that the Ardellans were responsible for Anders' death and the deaths of several mercenaries; those suspicions were correct, and Sandsmark could not reveal the mitigating circumstances. He'd fought hard to keep the board from withdrawing the Union presence from Ardel; only his political power had kept the mining contract from falling to Nagashimi-BOEM. Sandsmark knew there was more at stake on Ardel than a titanium mine.

Sandsmark stopped the computer's scrolling, called up an excerpt from Anders' journal, and read half of it. Her reports on the natives' psychic abilities and of her own attempts to learn their skills still made his palms sweat, although he had read them countless times since her death and finally, with Sinykin Inda's verifying testimony, had come to believe them.

He restarted the display, skimming more history of the Ardellan project as it scrolled past. Construction of the spaceport had begun less than a year after Anders' death. Months later, Sandsmark had carefully chosen the spaceport's executive staff. He had hoped that the diverse group would evolve into a balanced working team. Anna Griswold, an old friend and a cautious and capable Administrator, would protect her people above all else. He chose Sinykin Inda to assist her because of Inda's idealism and concern for the Ardellans. Sandsmark had hoped that Inda might be able to temper some of Griswold's decisions. He also had expected that Inda would one day succeed Anders as envoy.

It had soon become clear that this strategy was not working. Griswold and Inda were in conflict over most issues that concerned the natives. They argued constantly and bombarded Sandsmark's office with memos, Griswold's demanding that Inda be recalled, Inda's requesting confirmation of his appointment as envoy and open support for his work with the natives.

Meanwhile, Austin Duerst had continued to search out natural resources for Nagashimi-BOEM. Thor's moon mining colony was the corporation's latest acquisition, and Sandsmark feared that the Ardellan mine would be its next. Griswold's "sabotage" almost certainly was connected to Duerst. Sandsmark knew of no way to delay the *White Crane*'s arrival at Ardel or Duerst's inspection of the mining facility. His best hope of protecting the Ardellan mine would be to find proof of Duerst's complicity, proof that would convince a court that Nagashimi-BOEM had violated its contract with the Union. He hoped to find the evidence he needed in his meticulous records of the Ardellan project.

"Access personnel files in chronological order by date of assignment. Visual display."

A holo of Sarah Anders' face appeared on the screen.

Austin Duerst's glance swept down the length of Captain Lori Suwa's dark hair, past the curve of her breasts and the gentle swell of her hips, and on to the toes that peeked from her straw zori. Under other circumstances he would have liked to see more of the slender body she hid beneath her leisure time yukata. He had long ago learned to keep such diversions in their place. All that really mattered to him was power, power over his subordinates and power within the complex executive structure of Nagashimi-BOEM. That especially included power over the Japanese employees who had come into the conglomerate as part of Nagashimi Interstellar Drives. The politics of power within Braddock-Owen Extraterrestrial Mining had consumed much of Duerst's adult life. He would have been CEO of the corporation by now if not for the merger with Nagashimi. He made certain that every Nagashimi employee he met recognized the nature and extent of his power. Now he clasped his hands behind him and let his gaze slowly travel back to Suwa's face as he waited for her to speak.

Suwa stepped out of her quarters and let the door slip closed behind her. "Ah, Mr. Duerst! I am sorry that you have been forced to seek me out. Was my first officer unable to help you?"

"I do not deal with subordinates in matters of security, Captain." Duerst let his hands drop to his sides and took a small step forward, forcing the shorter Suwa to choose between craning her neck to look at him and stepping aside. She moved, and found her back pressed against the closed door. A tiny smile curled the corners of Duerst's mouth. "I just received a message from Hecate Station in the Ardellan system. It is imperative that I reach Ardel within the next thirty-six hours."

Imperative, indeed, that he reach what would be the site of his triumph as soon as possible. The Union's mining equipment had been sabotaged on schedule; when the Union could not deliver its first shipment of titanium ore on time, he would take possession of the mine and the spaceport in the name of Nagashimi-BOEM. In that instant he would wipe out the defeat he had suffered five years ago, when Sarah Anders had managed to wrest Ardel and its valuable titanium reserves from his hands. "This ship is capable of considerably greater speed than that at which we are currently traveling. In the interests of Nagashimi-BOEM and our joint mission, I suggest that you increase velocity immediately."

"I share your concern for our mission, Mr. Duerst. However this is a passenger vessel. My primary assignment as Captain of this ship is to safely deliver my passengers to their destination. I understand your desire for haste and would like to please you. I cannot, however, do anything to risk either my ship or my passengers.'' Suwa raised her right hand and held her thumb a millimeter from the door's access control. ''I must unfortunately ask you to pardon me, as I am off duty at this time. If you have any further questions please direct them to the bridge. Someone there will be able to help you.'' She pressed the control and stepped backward as the door slid open. It closed again with a smooth motion, leaving Duerst standing in the empty corridor.

White Crane's dining room was combined with a small, elegant lounge. A viewport covered one wall and a third of the ceiling; with the jump shield rolled back and the lights turned low the stars seemed close enough to touch. Sandsmark sat before the port, sipping brandy and gazing at the magnificent view.

''Can I bring you anything else, sir?'' asked the white-liveried waiter.

Sandsmark shook his head. ''I'll wait for the others.'' *White Crane* was a private yacht, adapted for chauffeuring Nagashimi-BOEM executives to and from the interstellar corporation's many holdings. The ship was too luxurious for Sandsmark's taste; he had spent years in the field on many undeveloped planets, often living in rude shelters without plumbing and heat. Even after he had lost his legs, he'd felt no need for servants.

''Enjoy the view now,'' said someone behind him. Sandsmark turned, saw Captain Suwa in the doorway. She stepped into the lounge. ''We will be closing the shield after dinner. Our last jump is tonight.''

''What's our ETA at Ardel?''

''9/23, with shuttle touchdown between 900 and 1100 hours local time. Will that meet your needs?'' Lori Suwa spoke in the precise, polite standard used by most of Nagashimi's Japanese employees. Her impassive features were not classically oriental—her eyes were slightly rounded, her cheekbones unexpectedly prominent. She hid most of her dark hair beneath her Captain's cap.

"That arrival time should suffice," said Sandsmark. He turned his chair away from the viewport and faced Suwa. "Will you have a drink with me?"

"If fruit juice is acceptable. I am on duty after dinner." Suwa signaled the waiter; he returned a moment later with a tall glass of something clear and red. "Has Mr. Duerst been called?" she asked him.

"Yes, Captain. He is on his way up."

"Then we shall be seated." She followed the waiter to the table, let him seat her at its head. The ship's chair had already been removed from the place to her left. Sandsmark was maneuvering into that spot when Duerst strode into the lounge.

"Good evening, Sandsmark; Captain." Austin Duerst nodded to each of them, then took the seat on Suwa's right. His tall, slender body moved with an ease that Sandsmark envied. "I apologize for my tardiness; I was attending to an unexpected communication."

"Not a serious problem, I hope," said Sandsmark.

"No, no. Just a minor question that needed clarification." Duerst shot a pointed glance in Suwa's direction, then ordered wine from the waiter standing at his elbow.

"Perhaps we should avoid discussing business this evening, gentlemen?" suggested Suwa.

"Whatever suits you, Captain," said Duerst coldly. He turned to Sandsmark. "There are many other interesting topics for dinner conversation. I recently received a report on the great strides being made in medical research at the new Titan University facility. Have you heard about their revolutionary nerve implantation techniques?"

"No, I have not."

Suwa signaled the waiter to begin serving dinner. "Tell us about these advances."

"The physicians there have developed a special

growth medium for the regeneration of nerve fibers.
They can remove a single nerve cell from a subject,
place it in the medium, and stimulate it to produce the
required length of healthy nerve fiber. Then, using
surgical micromachines inserted through tiny incisions
in the subject's body, they can thread the new nerve
into place. They have restored limb function for several paralyzed patients.''

"Fascinating," commented Sandsmark. "Do you
have a special interest in this type of surgery?''

"I try to keep abreast of technical developments in
all fields. One never knows when a particular piece of
information will offer a solution to a problem," Duerst
replied. "Perhaps you should make the trip to Titan.
You might one day walk again.''

Sandsmark shrugged. He had lost the use of his legs
ten years ago, during his final mission as a field operative for the Trade Commission. Only his physicians
knew that the useless limbs had been amputated soon
after, to keep him from succumbing to a dangerous
bone infection. Successive infections, ulcers, and skin
grafts had made prosthetic legs an impossibility. His
staff and friends believed him to be a vain man who
hid withered legs inside his wheeled chairs and hover
carts rather than walk in awkward braces. He preferred
to let them think that. He did not want to face their
concern or their pity. "I have little time to spare from
my work. I am sure that recovery and rehabilitation
after such a procedure would be a very long process.''

"Would it not be worth it, to have the use of your
legs again?'' asked Captain Suwa.

"Perhaps, although I am quite used to my life as it
is now. Perhaps when I retire. . . .''

Duerst laughed. "I have never known a bureaucrat
to willingly retire.''

The waiter stopped beside Captain Suwa, bent down
to whisper a message in her ear. She nodded.

"Gentlemen, please excuse me.'' Suwa pushed back

her chair and rose, leaving an untouched steak on her plate. "I am required on the bridge."

"Certainly, Captain," said Sandsmark. "I hope it is not a serious problem. Will you be able to rejoin us?"

"I cannot say. Please do not delay your meal. Good evening." She made a minute bow to each of them before she left the table.

Duerst cut a generous bite from his steak. "Now that our chaperone has left us, we can return to topics of mutual interest. What news have you received from Ardel? Have the miners begun work?"

Sandsmark swallowed the last of his brandy, set the glass on the table. His gaze caught and held Duerst's; his expression dared the other to look away. "I doubt that I am as well-informed as you are about events at the titanium mine."

Duerst smiled. "How could that be? The provisions of our contract with the Terran Union forbid us to keep any personnel on Ardel. We would, of course, adhere to that contract. We do not wish to lose such a lucrative source of titanium ore. Several other corporations would be quick to bid for the contract if we were in default. Then we would be left with an expensive reduction facility orbiting the larger moon and no raw material to feed it."

"Nagashimi-BOEM is always careful to remain within the letter of the law." Sandsmark pushed his plate aside; he had lost his appetite. "The appearance of compliance is a useful fiction. It often satisfies the politicians."

"And the courts," said Duerst. "Judges rule in favor of those who appear to have fulfilled their contracts, especially when the other party has observably failed to meet its obligations. If Ardel's mines were unable to ship ore to Hecate Station by the contracted deadline, for example, the court would almost certainly cede the facility to Nagashimi-BOEM."

He knows about the damaged mining equipment,

thought Sandsmark. *Duerst probably ordered the sabotage.* "The mine and spaceport might be more trouble to you than it would be worth. The Ardellans have put many restrictions on our movements and on the equipment we import. You should be glad someone else is doing the hard work and shipping clean ore up to your processing plant."

"I think your operatives don't know how to negotiate with natives." Duerst poured himself another glass of wine. "Had Nagashimi-BOEM written the trade agreement, we would now be manufacturing ship hulls on the moon Hecate. Ardel's surface is sparsely populated. It could support a large human settlement, perhaps a complete colony. And there's iron and copper in the mountains. The Ardellans just don't have the technology to dig it out. This planet could become one of Nagashimi-BOEM's largest industrial centers."

"What if the Ardellans refused to allow that?"

Duerst cut into his steak with slow, deliberate motions. "We would change their minds."

Sandsmark suppressed a momentary urge to gut Duerst with his steak knife. The man had no perceptible conscience. He proposed doing to Ardel the very things that Sarah Anders had died to prevent. He had to be stopped, and to do that Sandsmark would have to find Nagashimi-BOEM's operative at the spaceport and prove his connection to the sabotage before the first ore shipment was due.

Chapter 14

Storm Sea, Ardel

Ilakri stumbled northward along the edge of the forest, trying to keep the trees to his right and open grassland to his left. The soil beneath his boots was soft and sometimes shifted like sand. He fought to stay on his feet, his breath coming in quick gasps and his heart thudding in his chest. The light, cool wind brought sea sounds from the west and dried the sweat on his body, making his skin clammy. Grasses swayed and leaves rustled beside his path. He paid them no attention.

The tender muscles of his torn palm were swollen and aching; his knees burned where the skin had been scraped away. He spared no thought or energy for healing the wounds. Blood pounded in his ears; his head was heavy and the back of it pained him. He felt flushed and feverish one moment, chilled the next. Still he clutched the ancient, twisted red relic with his good hand and kept walking, following the Master with the five-fingered hands. He moved in a daze, certain that he was dreaming or hallucinating.

The strange Master never spoke. Ilakri listened, waiting for the Master's words of wisdom, but he heard nothing. Ilakri hurried his steps, trying to catch the Master's attention. The Master never turned, never looked at Ilakri. He only strode northward, leaving no tracks in the sandy soil.

Why must I do this? Ilakri asked himself. *Why must I pursue this Master who does not acknowledge my existence?*

*I could drop this relic, turn, and make my way south
again, to the Salt River and home. Jaella and Yaro are
waiting for me in the warm caves. Jaella's body is
plump with our younglings by now, and Yaro will soon
be ready to leave the cocoon.*

*I should go back. I have failed in my task; I will
never reach the fisher lands. If I return now, I will
have no goods to bring status to our trine, but I
will be with Jaella and Yaro when our younglings are
born.*

No! There was no sound, just the sense of the command piercing Ilakri's thoughts. The five-fingered
Master did not turn, did not look at him. Ilakri stopped
moving. He closed his eyes, and the bright beings with
too many legs became visible once again. They danced
around him, waving their many arms to urge him forward. He began to walk, following in the path of the
Master.

Afternoon sunlight flooded Ilakri's face, making him
blink and squint. He was too tired to walk. He wanted
to fling out his arms, fall flat on his face in the dirt.
He wanted to sleep.

He could not rest. The bright beings with too many
arms and too many legs still compelled him to move
northward along the edge of the forest, toward the land
of the fishers.

Fever wracked his body. Sweat beaded his brow,
soaked his tunic. He felt the plague working in his
limbs, making them tremble. His lungs ached with the
effort of breathing. Pain filled his body, but it did not
slow his steps.

He knew that the plague would kill him. The bright
beings told him that his life was of no importance.
Only the relic mattered. He lived only to carry the
relic to Port Freewind and to deliver it to the five-
fingered Master.

Chapter 15

Sinykin Inda leaned forward in his saddle and pressed his hand to his alep's strong neck. He felt thick muscles bunching beneath the skin, wondered if they tensed as his own did. He rolled his shoulders to loosen the knot in his upper back. When he straightened up, he heard the gentle popping of shifting vertebrae. He sighed.

Jeryl, mounted on a small gray alep, was disappearing around a curve in the trail ahead. Inda felt a momentary panic as the alep's tail vanished from sight. He was wary of being left alone in the wilderness. He and Jeryl had ridden all day without seeing another sentient being. The fishers now seemed more myth than reality. Riding through alien forests and meadows, occasionally viewing strange river fauna, Inda had become aware that he was an exile in a sometimes hostile land. He did not regret his decision to leave the spaceport, but he had no intention of being left on his own. He kneed his alep forward.

Jeryl was waiting just around the bend. Inda passed him in a rush, almost rode headlong into a group of brightly-dressed people walking toward him on the trail. He tugged hard at his rein, and the alep circled back and stopped beside Jeryl's mount.

"Are these fishers?" asked Inda, looking over the dignified parade. The line of people extended back up a hill, where the trail disappeared among a cluster of buildings that might be their village.

"These are the fishers of Bentwater," said Jeryl in

a hushed and solemn tone. He pointed to a large object
being carried in the procession. "This is a funeral
parade, and that is the body of one of the fishers. They
have all come out of the village to celebrate her death.
We must not go any farther until the ceremony is
over."

The funeral procession moved like a graceful, colorful snake down the muddy trail toward the riverbank. The Mothers, barefoot and dancing in their
robes of yellow and gold and green, led the way. A
half-dozen Masters followed them, carrying the corpse
aloft on a platform of rope twined between two slender
wooden poles. The Mother's emaciated body was
wrapped from feet to neck in a shroud of fine blue
linen, the same shade of blue as the delicate tattooed
lines that swirled across her pale forehead and down
her sunken cheeks. Her eyes were open.

Other Masters and younglings followed, shaking rattles and striking polished sticks together. The instruments produced a soft, chaotic sound that blended with
the noises of wind and water and forest.

The last person in the procession wore the gray
hooded cloak of a FreeMaster. He stopped before Jeryl
and Inda, and beckoned them to follow him.

"Dismount and leave your alep here," whispered
Jeryl. "We will honor the fishers by witnessing their
ceremony."

The aleps stood quietly as they climbed from the
saddles. The FreeMaster did not wait for them; they
had to walk quickly to catch up with the procession.
Inda slipped in a muddy rut, and Jeryl grabbed his
arm to keep him from falling. Inda righted himself,
took a deep breath. The heavy, musty odor of moist
earth mixed with the clean scents of the river and
greening vegetation, filling his nostrils with the smells
of life. The air was warming, and a few scattered
clouds sailed the brilliant sky. Reflected sunlight
danced on the river's surface. The gentle rhythm of the
rattles and clicking sticks merged into a kind of music.

Inda slowed his pace, fell into step beside Jeryl and the hooded FreeMaster.

The Mothers had reached the narrow piers that jutted from the riverbank out over the water. A dozen small boats were docked between the piers, tied bow and stern to pillars as thick as tree trunks. Other elongated craft, just wide enough to seat one person, lay overturned on the bank. A collection of paddles and oars leaned against a rack near the piers.

The Mothers ignored the boats, danced out to the end of one pier, and returned bearing a woven wicker coffin. Strips of golden cloth had been threaded through the wickerwork, their loose ends making a bright fringe at the coffin's head and foot. The Mothers set the beautiful coffin on the riverbank in front of the bearers of the corpse. They removed the coffin's curved lid and stepped aside.

No words had been spoken. The Masters carried the body forward in silence, half of them standing to one side of the coffin and half to the other. They knelt, bringing the platform down until it, and the corpse, rested on top of the open coffin. A Mother stepped up and carefully drew out one of the wooden poles; the rope platform collapsed and the blue-shrouded body slipped into the golden wicker basket. The Masters withdrew, taking with them the other pole and the ropes.

The Mothers came forward again, this time with offerings in their hands. They bent and placed flowers and shells and tiny wrapped packages inside the basket with the body. They touched the dead one's face, traced her tattoos with their fingertips. Their hands lingered on her shrouded limbs, stroking them one last time.

Then they settled the lid on the basket, tying it securely with the golden fringe at head and foot.

The music stopped.

In the sudden silence Inda saw a large bird flying above the river, its pale blue breast making it almost invisible against the sky. The bird circled twice, then dove into the water and emerged with a gleaming fish in its beak. It flipped the fish into the air, caught it neatly by the head, and swallowed it whole. The bird shrieked once before settling in a tree on the far riverbank.

The Masters stepped up to the coffin again. They had removed their boots and rolled up their leggings. Now they bent and picked up the basket. They carried it into the water. It floated like a little wicker boat, riding low, the water almost reaching the lid. The Masters released the coffin, and one of them pushed it into deeper water. The current caught it, turning it slowly end for end before tugging it downriver.

The world was no longer silent. Water lapped at the riverbank and around the small boats, pushing them against the stout pillars of the piers. The sounds were not like those of the ocean, but they reminded Inda of the dream that had troubled his last night in Alu Keep. He closed his eyes and summoned the vision of Sarah Anders and Miranda standing on the shore, waves breaking over their bare feet. He remembered reaching for them, remembered how they turned away from him and ran into the sea. The water had claimed them, just as it was claiming the body of this Mother.

He watched with the others until the coffin was out of sight.

Their aleps were waiting under the trees, grazing on new leaves and red shoots of spring grass. The animals stood patiently while Inda captured their dangling reins, then let him lead them back to the trail. Jeryl was there, talking with the hooded FreeMaster.

"When did you arrive in Bentwater?"

"Yesterday, just before Mother Lipran died." The FreeMaster reached up and stroked the long nose of Inda's mount. "I was telling Mother Tikran and the village council of the Terran's visit when Lipran's death cry interrupted us. That put an end to our talks. The fishers know that Inda is coming, but they do not know what to expect of him.''

''Nor do I know what to expect of them,'' said Inda. He leaned forward and peered into the FreeMaster's shadowed face. ''Arien? GuildMaster, I am pleased to see you again. Jeryl told me that you would join us on this trip.''

Arien swept back his hood, revealing disheveled straw-colored hair and piercing gray eyes. ''I always travel to Port Freewind in the spring to arrange the summer's caravan schedule. It is fortuitous that our paths are the same.''

''Experience tells me that few things involving you happen by chance.'' Inda offered his palms to Arien. ''I owe you a great debt, GuildMaster. Without your help I would never have escaped from the Iron Keep.''

''You owe me nothing, Healer Inda. The debt is Jeryl's and Clan Alu's.''

''True,'' said Jeryl. ''I hope to repay that debt on this trip.''

Most of the fishers had gone up to the village, but one stopped beside Arien. She looked at Jeryl, then at Inda, but spoke only to Arien in words that Inda could not understand. Her look had not been threatening, and Inda felt no fear. The Mother spoke again. Arien replied in the same guttural dialect that she had used. He pressed his palm to Inda's chest and spoke again, more indecipherable words bracketing ''Terran'' and ''Sinykin Inda.'' Then he repeated the procedure with Jeryl, who managed a couple of words in response. The Mother replied in kind.

Arien translated for Inda and Jeryl. ''This is Tikran, eldest of Bentwater's Mothers. She and the Mothers' council would like to meet with Healer Inda at this time. We are to follow her to the council house.''

Tikran led them up the gentle slope toward the village. The low hill lifted the small timbered homes and workshops out of the White River's flood plain. The river wrapped around the hill to the north and west, giving the village its name—Bentwater. To the south was the great forest through which Inda and Jeryl had ridden, and to the east lay Bentwater's fields and grazing meadows.

The village square at the hill's crest was paved with an irregular patchwork of red and gray stones. Most had been worn smooth by years, perhaps centuries, of traffic. Some were cracked, others chipped. Here and there tufts of grass or tiny white bell-shaped flowers poked between the jagged slabs. A single youngling was hard at work tugging out the trespassing plants.

Four Mothers awaited them before the long, low council house. Their robes of gold cloth fluttered in the breeze. Tikran stopped beside the first Mother and motioned Inda forward. She pointed to his chest, spoke more words he did not understand. Then she touched the Mother's shoulder.

"Elehran," she said.

Inda raised his hand and greeted her. "May the great sun smile on you, Elehran." She had blue eyes, the first Inda had seen among the Ardellans.

They continued down the line of Mothers. Inda was introduced to tall, slender Kimran; to Diiran, whose hair was the same shade of gold as her robe; and to Minaran, who lifted her fingers to Inda's face but could not bring herself to touch him. Inda greeted each Mother in turn, offering polite wishes that he feared they did not understand. None of them said a word.

For the first time Inda felt like an alien among Ardellans. Sarah Anders had never met the fishers; her journal had not prepared him for a culture so different from that of the keeps. He did not know how to relate to these tattooed Mothers. The language barrier was daunting. For the first time he doubted that he could make himself understood.

Tikran introduced Jeryl to the Mothers in the same manner she had used with Inda. Jeryl greeted them, and they answered him in kind.

When the introductions were finished, Elehran

turned and ducked through the low doorway into the council house. The others followed, until Tikran was left standing alone with Inda and the FreeMasters. She spoke to Arien, who translated for his companions.

"We are to enter the council house and be seated to the left of the door."

"What about the aleps?" asked Inda.

"Leave them here. The youngling will watch them."

Inda crossed the threshhold and stepped down into the dim council house. There was no furniture in the single room. Fur-covered seating platforms lined the walls. Ventilation slits under the eaves provided fresh air but little light. There was no ceiling; many un-identifiable objects hung from the broad beams that supported the roof. Faint rustling sounds from above made Inda uneasy.

The Mothers had already taken places on the far side of the room. Inda stepped to the left and sat down. Jeryl and Arien joined him.

"I will translate the inquiries of the Mothers and your answers," said Arien. "All people are equal in-side the council house. You are allowed to question the Mothers; they will answer you as best they can. If there is anything you do not understand, ask me for an explanation. I am here to help you."

A tongue of shimmer-light appeared in the center of the floor as Arien finished speaking. It grew slowly into a sphere that illuminated the far corners of the council house and the faces of the five Mothers. There was more rustling in the rafters. Inda looked up, saw tiny yellow eyes peering at him from behind bunches of drying foliage. He saw a clawed foot no bigger than the tip of his finger, a twitching gray nose surrounded by bristling whiskers. He could not guess how many of the little beasts lived among the beams.

Tikran asked a question.

"Why have you come to Bentwater?"

"I am traveling to Port Freewind at the request of Master Healer Hanra-bae. I am bringing him a vaccine against the plague. We came to Bentwater to meet GuildMaster Arien. He is to be our guide and translator." The cold of the stone bench penetrated the furs and Inda's coveralls and chilled the backs of his thighs. His spirit was chilled by the alienness of these Mothers.

In the keeps the eldest Masters ruled their clans, and Mothers raised younglings. Here the Mothers were a powerful force in the community. Inda observed the strength in their expressions, the directness of their questions, and the way they weighed his answers. Kimran watched him and did not speak; Minaran asked about his travels on Ardel. Elehran and Diiran seemed skeptical about his vaccine. They asked for many details about its manufacture and administration, and they did not seem satisfied with the answers.

Inda tried to quell the frustration he felt at being unable to communicate directly with the fishers. He explained as best he could to Arien, in both Ardellan and Terran Standard, then watched the Mothers' faces as Arien attempted to translate technical information into a language that had no words for Terran technology. Jeryl tried to help; he described the injection he had received, bared his arm to show them smooth, unblemished skin. Their expressions did not change. Inda feared they would not let him vaccinate the villagers.

When the questions stopped, one of the tiny rafter-dwellers emitted a high squeal and jumped from its hiding place, legs spread in all four directions. Folds of skin on each side of its body stretched, caught the air, let it glide down to the bench beside Tikran. She petted it before it scurried out through a chink in the wall. Then she spoke.

"The Mothers wish to consider what you have told them," Arien translated. "We are expected to spend the night in Tikran's home; the youngling outside will guide us there. We should leave now."

"May I thank them for their kind attention?" asked Inda.

"It is best just to go." Arien rose and turned toward the door. "We will talk outside."

Septi was waiting in Tikran's common room when Inda and the others arrived. He jumped up from a bench near the fire and raised a hand in greeting. His wrinkled tunic and mud-spattered boots and leggings testified to a swift ride from Alu Keep. He pulled a crumpled blue envelope from his sash and offered it to Inda. "I bring you a message from the spaceport."

"Thank you," said Inda. He took the envelope, smoothed it between his palms, read his name in Elissa's neat block printing. Jeryl offered him a dagger; Inda used it to slit the envelope, then returned it to the Mentor. He pulled a single sheet of quadrille-lined paper from the envelope and unfolded it.

The brownish drop of blood caught his eye. He scanned the letter looking for an explanation, found a description of Jaime's accident in the postscript. His hand shook as he slowly read the letter again.

Jeryl turned to Septi. "How were things at Alu when you left? Had Mieck emerged from his cocoon?"

"Nothing has changed at the keep. Ertis still waits for Oflea and Mieck to complete their metamorphoses. Viela has abandoned Alu, and the Healers Guild had not yet sent a replacement when this message arrived." Septi returned to his seat at the hearth. "Ramis brought the message from the spaceport. He said Inda's mate and youngling were unhappy."

"He is perceptive." Inda stripped off his parka and hung it on a peg near the door. "My mate is displeased because I left the spaceport without our superior's permission. My child is sad because he injured himself and I wasn't there to care for him. And there was an accident at the mine. No one was hurt, but some of the equipment was damaged."

Jeryl reached for Inda's arm but drew his hand back

without touching the Terran. "This letter has upset you."

Inda nodded. "This day has been disconcerting. I didn't know it would be so difficult to communicate with the fishers. I fear they won't accept the vaccine." Had he made this trip, risked breaking up his family, for nothing? He had lost his post as the spaceport's Chief Medical Officer, and Griswold had already requested his recall from Ardel. Sandsmark would be no help—his last message had made that clear. Inda had known from the start that this trip was a gamble. If the fishers would not accept the vaccine, he might just as well have stayed at the spaceport instead of angering Griswold and abandoning Jaime and Elissa. "Will we have as much trouble making the fishers of Port Freewind understand us?"

Arien shrugged. "Hanra-bae knows clan-speech, and so do the Mothers of Port Freewind's council. Their city is a major trading center."

"And Hanra-bae has told them about your vaccine. He would not have sent for you if he were not ready to have his people vaccinated," said Jeryl. "The Mothers of Bentwater are conservative. They do not speak for all of the fishers. Do not be discouraged if they reject you."

"I must send a reply to Elissa." Inda turned to Septi. "Will you be returning in the morning? Would you take back a message for me?"

"Certainly. I would leave tonight, but my alep needs to rest."

Jeryl looked at Septi and made a gesture Inda had not seen before. "And you need to wash. Did you bring a change of clothes?"

"In my pack."

"Then come, we shall find a youngling to heat some water. I want to wash off the trail dust and change my tunic before dinner."

"I will join you," said Arien, hefting his pack and following the others down a dim passageway.

Inda sat near the hearth and let the fire warm his cold feet. His boots were caked with dried mud from the trek to the riverbank. He closed his eyes, saw again the dead Mother in her wicker casket. Death had become his companion on this trip. He held shimmer-light in his palm thanks to Aakar, a librarian made FreeMaster by the plague-death of his mate. He dreamed of gifts given him by his dead daughter Miranda and by Sarah Anders.

He had set out to save Ardellan lives. The price was more dear than he had expected. Inda stared at the blue paper of Elissa's letter, at the spot of Jaime's blood amid Elissa's careful printing. There was an unfamiliar ache in his chest. He lifted his hand, concentrated, drew the flame from his center. He felt its warmth in his palm before he saw the tongue of shimmer-light dancing there.

Chapter 16

Terran Spaceport, Ardel

Elissa muttered a vile epithet under her breath. "Are you certain?" she asked, looking over the diagnostic printout that Joli Nevarre had given her.

"Absolutely. There is nothing wrong with the spook. We've checked the hardware, the firmware, and the software. I ran the diagnostics a second time just to be sure we hadn't missed something." Nevarre brushed a bit of lint from the sleeve of her yellow coveralls. "I'm sorry, Elissa. The problem must be in the sensors or in the controls of the vehicles and the other equipment."

"We checked the controls yesterday at the mine site." Herve Santiago looked across the conference table at Jan Mboya. "You were out there with me. Was there anything strange in the way those trucks or the shovel handled?"

Mboya shrugged. "Everything seemed fine to me. The boom camera was recording most of the day." She touched a button and the holographic monitor at the end of the table came alive. It projected an image of the shovel's huge bucket dropping to the sandy oval of the mine. The dipper tipped forward, its tines cutting into the earth. Sand flowed back into the bucket. The boom shifted, and the dipper began to lift its load.

"I ran the shovel through all its paces to test the repaired boom and the dipper," said Mboya. She pointed to the image of the moving bucket. "That load weighed over eighteen tons. You can see that the equipment is performing at spec."

The scene shifted as the shovel turned. The 'dozer moved in the background, shoving a jumble of boulders away from the mine's edge. One of the huge trucks pulled into view, then parked with its bed perpendicular to the shovel.

Mboya looked at Elissa. "There was no recurrence of the problems you reported during your test of the virtual control equipment. I was able to deliver the entire load to the truck bed without incident. I moved five loads of ore in all."

"Then the problem has to be in the spook," said Elissa. "You must have missed something, Joli."

"Impossible! There's nothing wrong with the spook." Nevarre reached for the printout. "The sensors might be malfunctioning."

"No." Elissa shook her head. "Sensor data is transmitted simultaneously to the spook and to the gauges in the cabs. The driver sees the same information, whether she controls the equipment manually from the cab or by remote from the mine room. If the sensors were causing problems, we would have seen it in the manual tests yesterday."

"My crew drove the 'dozer and those trucks all over the site," said Santiago. "The vehicles responded perfectly, and the sensor readings matched what the drivers were seeing. The sensors are in perfect order."

Jeff Grund leaned forward and turned off the holographic display. "What if both the sensors and the spook are working correctly? If there's nothing wrong with the vehicle controls, we have only one option. Something is interrupting or altering communications between the spook and the vehicles."

"How could that be?" asked Alec Harwood.

"The data stream is transmitted to and from the spook by radio link." Elissa leaned back in her chair and considered Grund's suggestion. "We have several communications options: microwave transmitters, which require repeater towers; forty kilometers of optical fiber cable; or radio transmitters. The radio link was the least expensive choice.''

''And the easiest to interfere with,'' commented Harwood.

''No, not really,'' said Grund. ''A determined person can find a way to sabotage any method of communication. The simplest way is to cut into a cable and use a computer to alter the data stream. We have cable in our system, running from the antenna on the roof of the engineering building to the spook.'' Grund picked up his stylus and began drawing on his memo pad's screen. ''If a saboteur spliced his own computer into that cable, he could program it to interrupt the data stream and alter it before sending it on to the spook. In fact the device could work in either direction—from the spook to the equipment, or from the equipment to the spook.''

Anna Griswold spoke for the first time. ''Let's not jump to conclusions. What evidence do we have that our problem is caused by such a device?''

''No direct evidence,'' said Elissa, ''but this scenario would explain all the problems we've been having.''

''So would operator error.'' Mboya gave Elissa an apologetic look. ''The problem could have been with you. How much training have you had on the spook?''

Grund laughed. ''Elissa knows that equipment inside and out.''

''You can 'ride the spook' yourself after the meeting,'' offered Elissa. ''I'd be glad if you found the problem was with me. Then we could start mining today.''

''I think we should investigate both of these possibilities. Can you set up some kind of a test?'' asked Griswold.

Elissa looked at Herve Santiago. ''We could station personnel in the cabs of all the vehicles and give them cameras like the one on the shovel's boom.''

Santiago nodded. ''They wouldn't touch the controls; they'd just observe and record. You could control the equipment through the spook.''

"Jeff, can you rig the spook with some kind of holographic recorder? I want to document the images that the operators see in their goggles. Work with Joli; make sure you're getting information directly from the data stream. Then we'll be able to tell whether the problem is in the stream or the operator.''

"Certainly, Elissa. We can handle that.'' Grund cleared his screen and began a new drawing. "I'm also going to trace the cabling from the antenna to the spook to check for unauthorized taps.''

"My team will operate the virtual reality equipment,'' said Mboya.

"Yes, you'll take your assigned places in the mine room.'' Elissa made some notes. "I want to be there, too. I'll control the repair-bot.''

Griswold looked skeptical. "What information can you gather from these recordings?''

"The view from the cab of a vehicle should be identical to the image projected in the mine room,'' said Grund. "If the recordings don't match, something is interfering with the data stream. We'll confirm the method of sabotage, even if we can't identify the saboteur.''

"But we'll lose a day of mining time.'' Mboya's fingers drummed on the table. "We're short as it is. I want to move as much ore as possible during the test.''

Elissa nodded. "If you can get it into the trucks, we'll get it to the mill.''

"What about security?'' asked Griswold.

Harwood nodded. "Until further notice no one is to discuss this test with anyone who is not present at this meeting. If we do have a saboteur on the base, we don't want to tip him off. We're not dealing with some missing medical supplies or purloined chickens; this is a major security breach.''

"Let's announce that we've solved the problem and that we're going to start mining tomorrow,'' suggested

Elissa. "If this really is sabotage, that should guarantee more problems during the test. The saboteur might inadvertently identify himself."

"It's possible. My people will monitor the test on both ends and watch personnel on the base for any unusual or suspicious behavior," said Harwood. He pushed back his chair and rose. "If you're all clear on your assignments, I think we can adjourn."

Griswold shook her head. "Wait a moment, Alec. I want to see you and Chief Durant in my office. The rest of you may go."

Damn Griswold, and damn Sinykin for putting me in this position, thought Elissa. It angered her to be called into the Administrator's office as if she were a recalcitrant child told to stay after school. Her stomach had turned sour and her hands were shaking. She stopped at the beverage dispenser for coffee despite the pain in her gut, then stilled her trembling fingers by wrapping them around the warm mug. She sat on the near side of Griswold's broad desk, beside Alec Harwood.

Griswold filled a delicate china cup with coffee, then carried it on its saucer to her desk. She sat and sipped before she spoke. "Have you received any further communications from Dr. Inda?"

"Only the letter three days ago," said Elissa. *Griswold would know if any messages had come through the gate. Does she think Sinykin and I have a secret rendezvous or some hidden transmitters?* "He promised to send another message with one of the Free-Masters when he reached the fisher community."

"So you do not expect to hear from him for several days?"

Elissa nodded.

"I see." Griswold leaned forward, picked up a sheet of paper. "I received your grievance form yesterday. I have reviewed it, even though it cannot be filed until

Dr. Inda signs it. A copy has been forwarded to Secretary Sandsmark along with my recommendations.''

"And what would those be?'' asked Harwood.

"That Dr. Inda be relieved of his position and removed from Ardel pending the results of an investigation into the sabotage at this base.''

Elissa clenched her teeth. Tension gathered in the muscles of her jaw, spread down her neck and across her shoulders. She put her mug aside and sat straight in her chair, her fingers gripping the arms, her feet firmly planted on the floor. "Are you accusing Sinykin of being a saboteur?''

Griswold shook her head. Her face was a mask—no expression showing except a peculiar light in her eyes. "I have only said that the situation needs to be investigated. It may be a coincidence that Dr. Inda left the spaceport just before the sabotage became evident. However, he is guilty of insubordination and of violating the orders of his superior. Under the circumstances, his actions are suspect.''

"He is conducting a humanitarian medical mission!''

"So he claims,'' said Griswold.

"Security is investigating everyone connected with this base,'' said Harwood. "No one is above suspicion at this time. I suggest we wait until tomorrow's tests are completed before we begin accusing people of sabotage.''

"If the mining equipment fails to function properly tomorrow, we won't have a base to protect. We'll be forced to default on our contract with Nagashimi-BOEM. The corporation will take possession of the spaceport and the mine.'' Griswold turned away to stare out the window at the landing field and the distant wind generators. "Five years of hard work wasted.''

Harwood looked at Elissa. "I'd be more concerned if it turned out to be faulty equipment rather than sabotage. Then we'd have no recourse. Nagashimi-BOEM would gain control of the base and we'd all be out of work. If we can prove that the equipment's been sabotaged and that the corporation instigated it, we have a chance to keep the installation under Union control.''

''The Ardellans might have bribed someone to disrupt our operations,'' said Griswold.

A bitter laugh escaped Elissa's lips. She remembered the excerpts from Sarah Anders' journal, the gruesome Ardellan deaths caused by suspected Nagashimi-BOEM operatives. ''Why would the Ardellans want to exchange Union control for Nagashimi-BOEM's? So that the corporation can take over the base and let its people run free through the countryside, toting weapons and power equipment into the keeps and cities? That makes no sense. The Ardellans who wanted us gone tried to turn our entire base into useless rubble. They wanted all Terrans to leave Ardel.

''This sabotage carries the mark of money and power. I think someone on this base found corporate bribes difficult to resist. I can tell you right now it wasn't Sinykin. He cares for the safety and comfort of the Ardellans above all else. He wouldn't do anything that might cause them harm.''

''But would he do something to help them even if it might harm the Union or the base?'' asked Griswold.

Elissa had no answer.

Chapter 17

Red Spring Way Station, Caravan Trail, Ardel

The Healers Viela, Kelta, and Bantu rode into the way station's tiny yard at dusk. Gravel and last season's seed pods crunched under the feet of their weary aleps. The thirsty animals perked up, snorting and tugging at the reins when they smelled the mineral spring's heavy odor. Their noise disturbed a hand of scrawny wood-hens pecking at spilled grain in the corral. The hens screeched and took flight, setting off a cacophony in the surrounding forest. The sounds died away with the last of the day, and darkness obscured the station yard.

Viela conjured a ball of shimmer-light. The station house was dark. Muddy footprints on the flagstone porch and fresh manure in the corral told him that the way station had had recent visitors. He dismounted near the fence, cursing under his breath because of the pain in his joints, and wrapped his alep's rein around a post. Then he walked back to help Kelta.

"My body also aches," said the GuildMaster as he slipped from the saddle. Viela caught him and gingerly set him on his feet beside his alep. He was shocked by the fragility of Kelta's body.

"You should go inside and rest, GuildMaster. I will care for the mounts." Viela turned to Bantu, who was making an awkward descent from his alep's back. "I saw a pile of wood beside the station house, and there is fresh water at the spring. Lay a fire and make us some tea."

"I must see to the needs of the GuildMaster."

Kelta grunted. "That is what Viela asked you to do. This Guildmaster wants to warm his cold feet beside a fire and drink a hot mug of tea. If you are unable to provide that, Viela will see to it. You can care for the aleps."

"No. I will do it." Bantu handed his mount's rein to Viela, then took Kelta's arm and helped him toward the stone building.

Viela led the aleps into the corral. A small three-sided shelter beside the gate held a few broken pieces of tack and a bin of grain. One of the aleps nudged the bin's lid as Viela removed the animal's saddle. The others stood quietly as he stripped off their gear and hung it on pegs in the shelter. He gave them each fresh water and a measure of grain. The aleps seemed content, so he gathered up the packs and lugged them to the station house.

Kelta was ensconced on a bench near the hearth. Tinder crackled beneath a pair of logs as tiny red tongues of flame devoured it. Then the logs' dry bark caught fire, producing light but little heat as it flared.

"Bantu is fetching water," said Kelta. "If you are half as tired as I am, we should both go to sleep now."

Viela looked at the dusty sleeping platforms and shrugged. "This is not the most hospitable place I have spent a night."

"Nor the least hospitable, I imagine. Have you visited the Iron Keep? Those miners do not know how to treat a guest." Kelta shrugged and tucked his hands into the full sleeves of his woolen shirt. "I am cold."

"The weather will become warmer as we move toward the ocean," said Viela. "I have never visited the miners, but I spent some time in a fisher village when I was an apprentice. The fishers will make us welcome."

Bantu stumbled through the door, a wooden bucket hanging from one hand and a dead conifer bough clutched in the other. "We will soon have more heat," he said, setting the bucket on the floor. He walked to the hearth, broke off a length of the bough, and fed it to the fire. Flames jumped and danced as the dry needles flared, and the room filled with the pleasant scent of burning resin.

Viela was restless. He had never been able to sleep when he was cold. His limbs were chilled, and he could not get warm despite the fire, the heavy furs, and his clothing. *It is the nature of an old body,* he thought, *to always be uncomfortable. That is why the old ones welcome death.*

His sleeping platform was near the door and farthest from the hearth, so he could hear the aleps if anything disturbed them. He lay on his back on the hard wooden platform, one fur wrapped about his body and another spread over it, and he listened to the quiet hiss of the coals in the fireplace and the rustle of leaves outside. Kelta lay still and silent, and Bantu's breathing was barely audible.

Viela widened his perceptions to the area outside the station house. His mind touched the drowsing aleps in the corral, the wood-hens in their hidden nests, a kite sitting high in a conifer watching the ground for nightmice. The spring bubbled inside its stone-walled circle, and tree limbs swayed in the breeze.

His mind reached farther. When he touched a familiar aura, he sat up, spilling furs onto the floor. "Reass," he whispered as he groped for his cloak. He pulled it on, then slipped quietly out the door.

First moon was overhead, casting meager light on the yard and the corral. Viela crossed the yard and waited at the edge of the trail for his sibling. Soon he heard the heavy breathing of overburdened aleps. A moment later two tired mounts carried Reass and his companion out of the forest's deep shadows.

Viela raised his hands in a warding gesture. "Do not turn in here," he said quietly. "The station house is occupied. There is no room for you or your animals."

"I see only four aleps in the corral," responded Reass. "Our mounts require water and food. You cannot bar us from the way station."

"I can, and I do. You and your companion . . ."

"I am Mikal, GuildMaster of the Merchants!"

"You and Mikal must seek shelter elsewhere. Kelta, GuildMaster of the Healers, sleeps in this station house. He is not to be disturbed." Viela struggled to keep his voice and manner calm. He knew now why Bantu had met with Reass and Mikal that night at the Inn of the Blue Door. Bantu was a traitor to the Healers Guild and to all of Ardel. "What is your destination?"

"Port Freewind," said Mikal, though Reass had gestured for him to keep silent. "And we shall arrive there before you do."

"It will not matter." Viela's voice rose. "The fishers will not listen to you. Only Kelta can advise Hanrabae about the Terran vaccine. You are making this trip for naught."

Reass shrugged. "We care not whether the fishers accept the vaccine. I was vaccinated at Alu Keep and have not been harmed by it. My guild and Mikal's wish to welcome the Terran and his vaccine to Berrut. We will escort him there so that he can vaccinate all the smiths and merchants, and any others who wish it. We will not continue to lose our Mothers and younglings to a plague that you Healers can neither prevent nor cure." He dismounted and began walking his alep toward the corral.

"You will not stay here!" Viela snatched the rein from Reass' hand. "Fetch water for your animals, and then return to the trail."

"You cannot bar us from a public way station." Reass turned on Viela, lifting both hands in a gesture of power.

"Your threats do not impress me, Reass." Viela dropped the rein and raised his hands. "I have power of my own!"

The station house door burst open, and Kelta stepped into the moonlight. "Put down your hands! Viela, must I remind you of your Healer's oath?"

"Yes, Viela, put down your hands. You are no match for me!" shouted Reass.

Kelta strode across the yard and confronted Reass. "You court disaster, Smith. If you continue this attack, we Healers will no longer serve your guild. Can you rely on the Terrans to treat all of the Metalsmiths' ills?"

Reass did not change his stance. Mikal, still mounted, leaned down and addressed Kelta. "You Healers eat food from our gardens and grain from our fields. How long will your guild survive if we no longer feed you? Stop serving us and you will starve."

"What of your promises to me!" shouted Bantu from the station house's doorway. Viela and Kelta turned and stared at him. "I have your oath that the Healers Guild will prosper."

"When you become GuildMaster," said Reass. "We will no longer support a guild ruled by this ancient Healer. Once the guild is yours and you aid us in our dealings with the Terrans, we will support you."

Rage reddened Viela's aura and his vision. He turned on Reass, raising his hands with all six fingers extended and the palms facing the smith. Power surged in his chest, fed by unreasoning anger. Unmindful of Reass' power-gathering stance, Viela concentrated on channeling energy down his arms and into his hands. He did not have the skill of a FreeMaster, but he believed he could raise enough power to disable Reass and keep him away from the Terran for a time. Then he saw the sparks leave Reass' fingertips, saw the blue flash of power, and knew that he was too late. He braced himself for the burning impact of Reass' attack.

"No!" Kelta, hands raised in a warding gesture, stepped between Reass and Viela. Reass' energy bolt struck the GuildMaster's chest, sending up a tiny flame as it scorched his cloak. His aura sparkled, then grew dim as the energy discharged into the earth. Kelta collapsed in a heap on the gravel. The only outward sign of the attack was the blackened spot on his chest.

Mikal leaned down, grabbed Reass by the shoulder. "Mount! We must ride now!" Reass stood still for a moment, then turned and scrambled into his saddle. He and Mikal guided their aleps from the yard without a backward glance.

Viela was already on his knees beside Kelta. Bantu ran to join him. The GuildMaster's breathing was shallow and irregular; he lay with his head thrown back, his eyes closed and his mouth open. Pain colored his otherwise white aura, spreading its muddy green cloud outward from the burn on his chest.

"Help me carry him," said Viela. They made a cradle of their arms and lifted Kelta from the ground. There seemed to be no weight to his body. He moaned twice before they reached the station house, but his eyes did not open.

They placed him on the sleeping platform nearest the hearth. Bantu added wood to the fire, building it into a bright, crackling blaze. Viela bent over his Guildmaster, holding his palms just above Kelta's chest. He felt the tingling contact as his hands penetrated Kelta's aura. His Healer's senses came alive; he closed his eyes and let his extended awareness explore the wound.

A patch of scorched skin blistered behind the burned spot on Kelta's tunic. That damage was minor—most of the energy of Reass' attack had passed through Kelta's skin and into the blood-cleansing organ beneath it. The organ, already stressed by Kelta's advanced age and the long day's ride, had ruptured. Golden fluid was leaking into the surrounding tissues, putting pressure on his lungs. If the organ could not be mended, Kelta would surely die before dawn of blood loss or suffocation.

Viela sensed Bantu's hands joining his, felt the other

Healer explore the wound and reach the same conclusion. "We must help Kelta heal the ruptured tissues, beginning with the innermost layer," said Viela.

Bantu disagreed. "The wound is too deep, the damage too great. We cannot heal him."

"Would you stand by and watch him die?"

"I served him in life, and I will ease his way in death." Bantu placed one hand on Kelta's forehead. "First I must wake him, so that he can pass his GuildMaster's badge to the new leader of the Healers Guild. You will be my witness that all is done according to tradition."

Viela pushed Bantu away from the platform. "You claim to be a Healer? Leave my presence, or I will surely kill you. I would rather not do that; it would waste energy that I will need to heal Kelta."

"Kelta is old. His time is over." Bantu reached for the copper medallion that was Kelta's badge of power. "I have trained with him for many seasons. It is time for me to become Guildmaster in his place."

The medallion slipped away from Bantu's fingers. Kelta's chest moved; a harsh cough brought a bubble of fluid to his lips. His eyes opened. He stared at Bantu, but his fingers clutched Viela's hand.

"You served me for a long time, Bantu," whispered Kelta, "but I believe . . . at the end . . . you set your own interests above mine and our guild's. You will not succeed me as GuildMaster." He tugged at Viela's fingers, guiding them to the medallion. "Viela will lead the Healers Guild. . . ."

Another cough shook Kelta's body, further opening the wound. Viela pressed his palms to Kelta's chest, willing the bleeding to stop and beginning the slow job of cell regeneration. He tried to knit the torn places together and searched for a way to ease the pressure on Kelta's lungs. His efforts were too little and too late. Kelta sighed and released the spirit from his body. It swept through Viela and out, carrying its death cry back to the guildhall in Berrut.

For a long time Viela stood over the empty husk that had been Kelta, the GuildMaster's medallion clasped between his tingling palms. He had never sought to lead the Healers Guild. He had only tried to be a good Healer, to uphold the traditions of his craft and his people. Now, thanks to the greed of Reass and Mikal and the influence of the Terrans, he held the guild's, and possibly Ardel's, future in his hands.

Chapter 18

Red Spring Way Station, Caravan Trail, Ardel

It was after dawn when Viela stepped away from Kelta's makeshift bier. "You must take the GuildMaster back to Berrut," he said to Bantu. "The rest of the guild will have felt his death cry. They will be expecting you to return with his body for the cremation."

Bantu's aura seethed with the colors of anger and dashed hopes. "And what will you be doing? It is your place as GuildMaster to escort your predecessor's remains back to the guildhall."

Viela lifted the GuildMaster's medallion, settled its leather thong about his neck. The copper disk felt heavy on his chest. "My responsibilities lie elsewhere today. I must pursue Reass. You were the Guild-Master's assistant. You should tend to his body."

"You shall not command me as you would a youngling." Bantu's face was flushed and his speech rushed. "The badge of power was promised to me. I do not recognize your right to hold it."

"Do you recognize Kelta's right to bestow it as he saw fit? Or do you challenge the oldest tradition of our guild?" Wrath stiffened Viela's jaw, wrapped bands of tension around his chest and forehead. He took a breath, tried to curb his rage. He wanted to store its power, to save it until he could expend it against Reass.

"The right of challenge is also an ancient tradition," said Bantu. "I will follow you until you return to Berrut, and there I will challenge you before the assembled Healers. We shall see if they support your succession, or mine.''

Viela was weary of Bantu's posturings. "And what of the great respect you professed for Kelta? Will you leave his body to rot while you follow me to Port Freewind? Will you deny him the honor of a funeral and a place in the mourning wall with his ancestors?''

"I will honor Kelta by being party to the revenge that is his due. I will pursue Reass with you.'' Bantu brought the blanket from his own bed and spread it over the platform next to Kelta's body. He slipped his arms under Kelta and gently lifted him onto the blanket. Then he wrapped its soft folds around the body, tucking in the loose ends. "We can carry Kelta with us. We surely will find a FreeMaster who can perform the cremation at Bentwater or Port Freewind.''

"You will have to tie him to his alep," said Viela. "It is not dignified.''

Bantu shrugged. "There is little dignity in death.''

The day was warm, with a clear sky and a gentle breeze. Viela rode swiftly. Bantu followed, leading the alep that carried Kelta's body.

They reached Bentwater's piers before midday. Most of the boats were out on the river, their Masters fishing the cold, swift-moving water for spawning silver-backs and red-tails. A single ancient dugout had been left overturned on the bank.

Viela turned away from the river, followed the trail up the hill into the village. The air was filled with the chatter of younglings cultivating garden patches, mending trellises, and repairing roofs. Their banter changed tone when the Healers passed and Kelta's body moved upwind of them.

"Who died?'' called a youngling.

Viela turned and stared. He had forgotten how forward fishers were. Their younglings had no manners. "That is not your concern. My name is Viela, and I am GuildMaster of the Healers. I would like to speak with a member of the Mothers' council and with the village Healer.''

"I am the Healer," said the youngling. It scrambled out of the herb garden, tentacles frantically adjusting its faded blue sash. "I am only an apprentice, but Bentwater has no other Healer. I welcome you to our village, GuildMaster. Is the dead one a friend of yours?''

Bantu dismounted. "He was our GuildMaster. He had an accident last night.''

"He was murdered," corrected Viela. "We pursue his killer. Has Reass of the Metalsmiths passed through Bentwater?''

"Several times," replied the youngling. "Why?''

Viela gritted his teeth. He was about to growl at the youngling when a Mother stepped in front of it.

"I am Tikran," she said, offering her hands in greeting. "I am eldest of Bentwater's Mothers. Why have you brought a dead person into our village?''

Bantu stepped forward to answer her. "We pursue the one who caused our GuildMaster's death. You may know him. He is called Reass, and he is leader of the Metalsmiths. Has he passed through your village since sunset yesterday?''

"He was here with a companion just after dawn today. They stayed only long enough to water their aleps.'' Tikran walked over to Kelta's mount. She reached for but did not quite touch the old Healer's wrapped body. "This one has been dead too long. He already stinks. We must consign him to the river now.''

"It is our custom to cremate our dead," said Viela. "Is there a FreeMaster in the village?''

"No." Tikran shrugged. "Two FreeMasters visited us a few days ago, but they went on to Port Freewind. You will have to give the body to the water.''

Viela waved his hand in a gesture of negation. "We cannot. We must follow the tradition of our clans and our guild. The Healers will expect us to return with Kelta's ashes and place them in the mourning wall.''

''Will you carry the body all the way to Port Freewind?'' Tikran's expression was incredulous. ''That is nearly two days' ride. Your GuildMaster will putrefy before you reach the town.''

Other Mothers had gathered on the upwind side of the square to watch Viela and Bantu. One of them walked out to speak with Tikran.

''I have sent the younglings for a coffin and the funeral instruments.''

''Mount,'' said Viela to Bantu.

''What?''

''Mount now, or I will leave you behind!'' Viela leaned down, pushed Bantu toward his alep. ''You can ride with me, or you can turn back and take Kelta's body to Berrut. If you stay here, they will throw the body into the river and it will be swept out to sea to be eaten by the creatures of the deep!''

The Mothers were already working at the knots that tied Kelta to his saddle. ''Get away from the GuildMaster!'' cried Bantu, shuddering. The alep's rein slipped from his hand as he scrambled onto his mount. He bent low, reaching for it. ''I will care for Kelta. He will not be eaten!''

Viela spun his own animal around, scooped up the other's rein, and tossed it to Bantu. ''You must ride swiftly if you intend to come with me. The Terran will reach Port Freewind soon, and Reass is also a half-day ahead of us. Each of them is dangerous. Who knows what damage they will do together.''

''They will harm no one,'' cried Bantu as he kneed his alep to a speedier four-legged gait.

''The Terrans have caused no end of trouble for our people.'' Viela looked back over his shoulder at the fishers. They made no move to pursue him and Bantu. ''Kelta would still be alive if the Terrans had not corrupted Reass and some of the other GuildMasters. They prey on those who are greedy and insecure. Do you not see that they must be forced to leave Ardel?''

Bantu did not answer him.

Neither Reass nor the Terrans will harm any more of my people, vowed Viela as he rode toward Port Freewind. *There shall be no more unnecessary deaths, no more magical Terran houses that fly above our keeps, no more towers of metal in the wasteland, no more Terran potions. I will find a way to drive all of the Terrans from Ardel. Then rain and wind and time will erase them from our land and from our memories.*

Chapter 19

Nagashimi's *White Crane*

Austin Duerst tried to shift his position on the stateroom's narrow mattress without disturbing the young steward who shared his bed. Her naked body was pressed against his left side, a thin film of sweat forming where their skin touched. Duerst's shoulder pillowed her head and her long, silky hair flowed over his tingling arm. He wiggled his fingers and shrugged, trying without success to dislodge her before his arm became numb. Her name was Susi, and she had been a nimble and enthusiastic partner. She had provided him with a fine evening's entertainment, but now he was restless and he wanted her to leave. He sighed. Susi made a small noise and rolled away from him.

The lights were dimmed to twenty percent brightness, enough illumination to titillate, too little to reveal any but the most obvious flaws. Duerst slipped his arm from beneath Susi's neck and let his gaze stray down the curve of her back and across the weighty roundness of her buttocks. Her thighs were heavier than he liked. One could only guess what was hidden beneath the unisex cut of a Nagashimi uniform.

Duerst sighed again and sat up. The amber light was glowing on the com-unit, informing him that a message had come in while the audio signal was turned off. "Lights fifty percent brightness," he commanded. He shook Susi.

She opened one eye and peered at him. "Again?"

He patted her buttocks. "I have work to do. Go back to your quarters."

"All right."

She stood up, yawned, and stretched. Duerst watched her dress, feeling a twinge of arousal as she bent before him, her breasts hanging down. He turned aside, reached for his dressing gown.

Susi let herself out. Duerst crossed to the closing door and secured it before he approached the comm console. He thumbed the reader.

2262:9/21, TERRAN CALENDAR
SECURITY/SCRAMBLED
TO: AUSTIN DUERST
    NAGASHIMI'S *WHITE CRANE*
FROM: JACKPOLE
      HECATE STATION
WORD FROM SURFACE INDICATES MINING SCHEDULED TO BEGIN 9/22. CONTACT EXPECTS TO DELAY THAT AT LEAST ONE DAY. SABOTAGE SUSPECTED BUT UNION OFFICIALS THUS FAR UNABLE TO LOCATE SOURCE.

STATION CREW LOOKING FORWARD TO YOUR VISIT. TESTING OF REDUCTION FACILITY COMPLETED; HOPPERS READY TO BEGIN TRANSPORTING ORE. PERSONNEL ANXIOUS TO TAKE POSSESSION OF ARDELLAN SPACEPORT AND MINE.

CONGRATULATIONS ON ANOTHER VICTORY FOR BOEM.
ENDMESSAGE
AUTOWIPE

Duerst laughed. The felicitations were a bit premature, but Jackpole was an enthusiastic supporter of the corporation and his supervisor. He would be waiting at the air lock with a bottle of bourbon and a pair of glasses when Duerst's transport docked at Hecate Station. Until then, there were things Jackpole could do that would help ensure Nagashimi-BOEM's acquisition of the Ardellan facility. Duerst sat before the com-unit and began to compose his reply.

Chapter 20

Black mesh gloves sheathed Jan Mboya's arms to the elbows. Ribbon cables, a rainbow of wires encased in transparent plastic, trailed from the gloves to a clip on Mboya's chair and then to the spook's central processor. Black goggles hid her eyes, and her toes and heels were fastened to the floor with metal clamps and more cable.

This room looks like the modern version of a medieval torture chamber, thought Elissa. She gazed at the dangling wires, the ring of joysticks hanging from the ceiling, the cartons of clamps and cable ends that filled the mine room's corners. A collection of fried memory tabs marched across one windowsill like a cadre of army ants. Grund's data stream recorders crouched behind each of the chairs awaiting activation. Fingerprints trailed through the dust on their black metal surfaces. *At least there aren't any empty coffee mugs on the floor. Why do installations always look like this? Just once, can't we hide all the wires, clean up the debris, organize the spare parts. . . .*

Then something would go wrong, and we'd have to tear it apart anyway. Ridiculous! Elissa settled into the empty chair between Mboya and Mammo Selati. Across the room George Asfaw adjusted his goggles, while Tanyetta Jones slipped her boots into the clamps on her chair's sensor pads. The team was ready to begin mining.

Elissa pulled on the gloves that controlled the repairbot's many arms. She slipped the intercom jack into her ear, pushed her toes into the boot clamps, looked once more around the room.

"You there, Joli?"

"Yes, Elissa. Alec Harwood is with me. We'll monitor the test from the control booth."

"All right, then." She settled the goggles over her eyes, blinked at the sudden darkness. "Let's go."

The sunny plain and blue sky of the mine site appeared on the inside surface of her goggles. Elissa blinked again, then turned her head. The scene shifted, tracking an arc along the horizon. She saw one of the trucks, then the big shovel. It was creeping toward the sandy mine, its heavy treads slowly rolling on their crawlers. Elissa shifted her feet, started the repair-bot moving to meet the shovel.

"Not too close," said Jan Mboya. "Keep enough distance so that you can watch all the equipment."

"Right." Elissa turned the robot forty-five degrees, and located the 'dozer and the second truck. "I can see all of you now. Are you ready to start digging?"

"Yes. Mammo, bring that truck around and line it up for loading." Mboya directed the team with quiet competence, just as she controlled the shovel. "Those rocks in the northeast sector need to be moved, Tanyetta. See if the 'dozer can push them up and out. George, line up your truck behind Mammo's. I want you to take his place as soon as he leaves with his load."

Elissa moved in closer to watch the trucks drive into position next to the shovel. She touched a control, added the graphic overlay for ore quality to the display on her goggles. The patch of sand in front of the shovel appeared to change color, becoming the deep red that denoted a high concentration of titanium. Mboya was going to dig some of the site's richest ore.

The shovel stopped moving forward. Its boxy body slowly turned thirty degrees, then the boom extended the enormous dipper. Gears turned, the great winch whined, and cables lowered the dipper to the earth.

The shovel crept forward, pushing the dipper's tines into the sand. The bucket filled with the high-grade ore.

The winch complained again as it wound the heavy cables and lifted the dipper. Elissa held her breath as the shovel rotated once more on its giant gears, turning until its boom was perpendicular to Selati's truck. The bucket hovered above the truck bed for a moment. Then the bottom dropped open and the ore poured into the bed.

Elissa was elated. She watched the bucket close, the shovel turn back to scoop up another load. "Joli, how did that look to you?"

"Perfect!"

"It's only the first load," said Mboya. "Let me move a dozen before you begin to celebrate."

"Yes," said Harwood. "And let's see how the trucks handle with full beds. They've only been tested empty."

The shovel dumped a second load into the bed of Selati's truck. "Just one more," said Selati. "I don't want to overload it on the first trip. My weight gauge shows we're at half capacity now."

"Fine." Mboya dropped one more dipper full of ore into the truck. "Go! George, get your truck up here before I have the next load ready."

Elissa watched as Selati's truck pulled away from the edge of the mine. It turned onto the gravel road that led to the mill a half-kilometer away. The second truck moved quickly into the vacated space, so smoothly that the great shovel did not have to slow its pace.

"Damn!" cried Herve Santiago as another load of ore poured onto the ground three meters short of the truck bed. He slammed his fist against the control panel in the shovel's cab. "Can't Mboya see what she's doing? That's the fourth load that's missed the truck. How can her aim be this bad? She's supposed to be a professional.'' His finger hovered above the manual override switch; then he pulled his hand back, stuffed it into his pocket, and looked out the side window. ''What's going on over there, Johnston?''

''This 'dozer is just shoving sand back and forth. We haven't touched the rocks Mboya wanted us to move. It's as if the boulders aren't where the operator thinks they are.''

''And the trucks aren't where Mboya thinks they are. The spook is showing her a truck that isn't there.'' Santiago watched the second truck pull away empty. ''And it's telling the drivers that they have full loads when the truck beds are empty. Something is altering the data stream between the vehicles and the spook.''

''But it's not the same problem Elissa had five days ago. She knew that the shovel wasn't obeying her commands. Mboya and her team seem to think that everything is fine,'' said Johnston.

''Only a very sophisticated device could cause this kind of trouble. What if our saboteur believed Chief Durant's announcement that we had corrected the first problem and were ready to start mining? He could have altered the device's programming just enough to let our operators think the equipment is working correctly. If we weren't sitting in these vehicles it might have taken two or three days before someone realized there was a problem.''

''That's right,'' said Johnston. ''The mill is automated; we probably wouldn't have known anything was wrong until we tried to load our first shipment for Nagashimi-BOEM.''

Santiago reached for the communications unit. ''There's no point in continuing the test. I'll call Nevarre. You pull the cartridges from the cameras. Then we'll head back to the base.''

Jeff Grund used the narrow access ladder attached to the side of the engineering building to climb down from the hangar's roof. The brisk spring breeze caught at his open jacket and lifted it away from his back as he descended through the long metal safety cage that surrounded the ladder. The slender rungs were damp and slick and chilled his fingers.

It had taken him an hour to inspect the roof antenna and the heavy coated cable that ran from it to the building's outer wall. He had found no suspicious splits, no breaks, no splices in the visible cable, but he was not discouraged. Ninety percent of the cable's total length was hidden in the walls of the building. The saboteur could have accessed the hangar's wiring schematic and cut into the cable in any inconspicuous spot.

Grund reached the ground and tugged his jacket close about his body. He was rarely cold, but the damp wind on the roof had chilled him. He strode around the corner and into the hangar, grateful for its relative warmth.

The cable entered the building at the corner opposite the mine room. Grund stopped at a workbench and picked up a pair of wrenches and a long, heavy-bladed screwdriver. Then he climbed the stairs to the gallery where offices lined the outer wall. The corner room was the engineers' lounge, furnished with a few comfortable chairs and a beverage dispenser. He moved the chairs away from the wall and applied a wrench to the recessed bolts that held the smooth inner panel in place. In moments he had popped the panel free and exposed the wall's interior structure. He began tracing the cable from the point where it entered the building.

Jan Mboya watched the twin holographic projections with wide eyes and open mouth. On the left was the mine as she had seen it through the spook; on the right, Santiago's view from the mining shovel's cab. Load after load of ore spilled across the soil even as the spook showed ore pouring into the truck beds. "It's impossible!"

"It's a fact," said Griswold, looking around the conference table. "Does anyone here still doubt that we have a saboteur in our midst?" No one answered her.

Alec Harwood reached over and turned off the display. "Just what kind of sabotage are we dealing with?"

"Some sort of device is interrupting the data stream between the mine room's central processor and the mining equipment," said Jeff Grund. His fingers flew over his computer's keypad. "It alters the data stream just enough to make the spook useless. It's impossible for the controllers and the equipment to communicate with each other in any meaningful way."

"Can't we circumvent it?" asked Griswold.

Grund nodded. "I'm trying to do that. I've traced the cable from the antenna halfway through the building and haven't found anything spliced into it yet. I'll get back to the search as soon as this meeting is over."

"The device might not be spliced into the cable," suggested Joli Nevarre. "It could be a receiver and transmitter set up to intercept the radio signals and alter them before retransmitting them. If that's the case, we'd have to find the device and deactivate it, or set up a new communications link. That means laying cable or building microwave towers between the base and the mine."

"That would take days," protested Elissa. She feared Griswold would once again choose the conservative option. "We don't have enough time for that. Our first shipment of ore is due on the twenty-fifth."

"Couldn't we vary the parameters of our communications—change the wavelength at random or something?" asked Harwood.

"Won't work." Grund did not look up from his keypad. "A device this sophisticated would easily track and respond to any changes we make."

Mboya leaned back in her chair and stared at Griswold. "You can't meet your contract if you try to mine that ore with the spook. If your plan is to wait until you get that equipment operational, you might as well cede the mine to Nagashimi-BOEM. My team and I can pack our gear and return to *Nairobi* tonight.''

''Or you can stay and help us.'' Elissa picked up a stylus, began making notes on her electronic memo pad. She had an idea, one that she was certain Griswold would veto if it was not presented properly. ''You've had a lot of experience controlling heavy equipment, Jan. I watched you to handle that shovel during the on-site test. You are just as competent in the cab as you are when you're hooked to a computer link. Are you willing to try mining firsthand?''

Mboya smiled. ''I thought you'd never ask me. I really enjoyed sitting in the cab of that big machine. The spook just isn't the same as the real thing.'' She pointed to Selati. ''Mammo has driven trucks in the field. With some help from your engineering team, I think we might get that first shipment ready in three days.''

''Assuming everything works,'' said Elissa, watching Griswold out of the corner of her eye.

''Just what are you proposing?'' Griswold looked from Mboya to Elissa and back again. ''You can't seriously intend to go out to the mine and run the equipment on-site!''

''Why not?'' Elissa jotted some figures on her pad. ''Shuttling operators back and forth between the base and the mine will be a nuisance, but we can handle it. With Jan and Mammo, Herve and a couple of people from his crew, we can run one full shift a day.''

Griswold shook her head. ''It's too dangerous. I won't subject anyone to the risks involved in operating that equipment on-site.''

''You didn't object to the tests we ran two days ago, or to having Herve and his crew sit in the cabs this morning. That was more dangerous than what Mboya is proposing to do. We know the equipment works under manual control,'' said Elissa, ''and I'll be at the mine, monitoring every movement of the shovel and trucks.''

''It's the only way to fulfill your contract,'' offered Mboya. ''Either we do this, or you pack up and turn the base over to Nagashimi-BOEM.''

Griswold hesitated, took the time to look each member of her staff in the eyes. None of them offered an objection to the plan. ''All right, but this must be a high security operation. I'll announce that we've solved the last of our problems and begun mining. No one but the crew and the occupants of this room is to know that we're not using the spook.'' Griswold began making notes. ''Nevarre, I want you and Grund to set up an alternate communications link so that we can reactivate the spook as soon as possible. Harwood, locate and disable that disruptive device, and get me some proof—fingerprints or something—so that I can issue a warrant for the saboteur's arrest before Secretary Sandsmark gets here tomorrow.

''Nagashimi's *White Crane* will arrive in the morning. Sandsmark and Austin Duerst are scheduled to inspect the mine in the afternoon. I'll see if I can postpone that until the following morning. Let's try to have something other than spilled ore to show them.''

''Alec!'' Elissa ran to catch up with the Security Chief. ''This clears Sinykin, doesn't it?''

Harwood looked around, then pulled Elissa into an empty office. ''What gave you that idea?''

''Someone had to reprogram that device. At first it just interfered with the commands the spook was sending to the shovel. Now it's actually substituting false information in the data stream.''

''That doesn't clear Sinykin,'' said Harwood.

''He's nowhere near the spaceport. He must have reached Port Freewind by now. How could he be the saboteur? He didn't even take a transmitter with him.'' Elissa was dumbfounded. Had Harwood begun to believe Griswold's accusations?

''We have no proof of Sinykin's whereabouts.''

Elissa slammed her palm against the desktop. ''Damn it, Alec! You know Sinykin. How can you believe he would do this?''

''I don't know that he's the saboteur, and I don't know that he's not. We haven't concluded our investigation.''

''Investigation! Your Security team can't even keep the coneys out of my hangar. How are you going to catch a saboteur?'' Anger put a hard edge in Elissa's voice. She turned away from Harwood, took a deep breath. ''I'm going to do some investigating of my own.''

Harwood touched Elissa's arm, then let his hand fall. ''Stay out of it, Elissa. You'll only draw more attention to Sinykin. Let my people do their jobs.''

''I won't stand by while they ruin my husband's reputation and his career.''

''We'll find the guilty party. Trust me, Elissa.''

''Damn you all,'' muttered Elissa as she walked away, ''including you, Sinykin, for making Jaime and me go through this.''

Chapter 21

Port Freewind, Ardel

Ilakri stood on the top of a dune. He looked out across the sand at the ocean. It was filled with more water than he had ever seen, more water than he had ever imagined could exist. It moved, not in one direction like the river, but back and forth, flowing toward him and then away. It made a sound unlike anything he had heard before. He was listening to it when he dropped the relic.

His mind realized that suddenly his left arm was lighter. He looked down, saw that his hand was empty. The ancient twisted red thing lay on the sand at his feet.

He thought about picking it up. He remembered how his body had felt before his mind had separated itself from its physical connections. His head had ached, his limbs had hurt, and fever had made him tremble. His mind had freed itself from that pain. It would have to touch his body again, feel the pain again, if he was to recover the relic. His mind would have to tell his body to bend over, stretch out an arm, reach all the way down to the sand. Then his hand would have to close on the relic, and he would have to straighten up without dropping it again.

It was a complicated process. He did not think he could do it.

Ilakri turned to the bright being who danced beside him on the dune, the being who possessed too many arms and too many legs. He thought to the being, *Can you help me?* The bright being did not answer him.

Ilakri looked down the dune to where the water touched the sand. The five-fingered Master stood there, his back turned to Ilakri. *Can you help me?* Ilakri asked with a thought. The Master vanished. Ilakri was not surprised.

I could leave it here, thought Ilakri, remembering the warm caves of home and his mates' gentle hands. *I can take my body with me and leave the relic behind.*

No! The word was not spoken, but it echoed in his thoughts. Ilakri knew that it came from the bright being who danced beside him, the being who had traveled with him since he had carried the relic out of the ancient ruins. He knew that the being would not allow him to leave the relic behind.

Ilakri looked to the north. He could see the buildings of the fisher port, nestled in the curve where river met ocean. The buildings were unlike the caves of home, unlike the ruins where he had found the relic. He saw people moving among them, adults like himself but with strange blue lines on their faces, and younglings. Many younglings. Some of them even moved on the water, floating in large containers and casting nets over the side in some mysterious rite. Ilakri had come so far to find these fishers. He tried to lift an arm, to wave to them. He did not know if they could see him.

The relic! The words were unspoken but Ilakri heard them in his thoughts. He knew that the bright being would not let him rest until the relic was once again in his hand. Ilakri turned his back on the fishers' city and reluctantly let his mind sink down until it reconnected with his body.

Pain washed through him. Pain from the infection in his torn palm, pain from the salt-rubbed wound on his knee, pain in the back of his head, all but overwhelmed by the fever that made his hands shake, his legs tremble, his breath come in strangled gasps.

The relic still lay at his feet, and all around him bright beings danced, waiting for him to pick it up.

He bent over, reached down, felt the little strength he still had drain from his body. His legs gave way. Ilakri collapsed in a heap on the sand.

The fingers of his left hand closed on the relic before the bright being, and the rest of the world, disappeared.

Chapter 22

Port Freewind, Ardel

"What is all the excitement about?" Sinykin Inda surveyed the narrow, chaos-filled street from the back of his alep. Other spectators watched from doorways and shop windows. A hand of younglings, tentacles and eyestalks waving, scattered before a group of running Masters. Shrill voices shouted words Inda could not understand. "Are they coming to greet us?" The tattooed fishers looked more like they were bent on driving strangers from the town.

Arien jumped from the back of his alep. "They are calling for the Master Healer." He dashed across the road to pound on a yellow door and shout something that Inda could not understand. His abandoned mount brayed and backed away from the noise.

"Damn," said Inda. The fishers were carrying someone whose head lolled to one side as if he were unconscious or dead. Inda tried to dismount so that he could help them with their burden, but his alep dropped its ears and did a six-legged side step, bumping into Arien's animal. Each alep snorted a challenge. "Jeryl!"

"Sit square in your saddle and rein in your mount," advised Jeryl. He leaned down, snatched the dangling rein of Arien's alep. "The animals are sometimes frightened by noise. Do not let your mount raise its center legs; it will try to throw you and run away."

The alep transferred its weight to its powerful rear limbs. Inda felt its center of gravity shift. He leaned forward, tightened his grip on the rein, and grabbed the alep's neck fold with his left hand. "Everything's all right," he whispered in the animal's ear. He tugged at the rein, turned the alep's eyes away from the running crowd. "If you throw me now, there'll be no one to stable you and feed you. If you calm down, I'll find you a nice stall and fresh straw for the night."

Arien's pounding finally caused the yellow door to burst open. A short, stocky Master appeared and shouted more words that Inda could not interpret. The intricate blue tattoos that circled his eyes and snaked down his cheeks seemed to move as he spoke. Arien gestured. The tattooed one looked up the road and saw the fishers' burden. He pushed Arien aside and ran into the street, still yelling.

Inda's alep sidestepped again and brayed. Inda sawed at the rein, tried to bring the animal back under control. He pulled its head to the right, felt the alep's strong muscles bunch beneath the saddle, knew it was getting ready to throw him. He cursed again and tightened his grip on the alep's neck fold. "Jeryl!"

Jeryl spun his own mount away from Arien's quieting alep. He grabbed the bridle of Inda's mount in his right hand, smacked the frightened alep between the eyes with his left. The animal bawled a complaint. Inda felt the tension leave its muscles.

"You can dismount now," said Jeryl. "Give me the rein."

Arien and the cranky tattooed Healer had pushed to the heart of the crowd. Now they emerged, the body of the ill Master supported between them. The fishers regrouped and followed, quieter and almost respectful in the presence of the Healer.

They bore their burden into the building from which the Healer had emerged. Inda grabbed his pack and sprinted after them. The other fishers stopped outside the yellow door. Inda was a physician first, a diplomat second; he followed Arien and the Healer into the building.

Three platforms shared the center of the room. The Healer settled his patient on the first one. A huge skylight flooded the area with sunshine; Inda saw beads of sweat on the patient's face and sand in his dark hair. His face was free of the blue fisher tattoos. His sallow skin had flushed gold around his unseeing black eyes and down his slender neck. He was shaking; not shivering with cold but shaking hard, like a palsy victim. Sometimes he flung his head from side to side and gasped.

The Healer spoke again. Arien answered him in the clan dialect which Inda understood. "He is Sinykin Inda, the Terran Healer. He brings you the plague-stopper." Arien turned to Inda. "This is Master Healer Hanra-bae."

Inda nodded. "May the great sun smile on you today, Master Healer."

Hanra-bae grunted but did not look up. His hands hovered, palms down and fingers spread, a few centimeters above his patient's body. They moved in slow, deliberate circles down the heaving torso, then traced each quivering limb.

"Is it plague?" asked Inda. The Healer's fingers twitched. Inda thought he saw a blue spark jump between fingertip and patient's skin. He blinked twice, afraid he had imagined the flash. Then he saw a second spark, and a third, and he knew that they were real.

"It might be." Hanra-bae still had not touched his patient. He walked to the room's far wall, began gathering bits and morsels from the baskets, jars, and pots that lined its shelves. "Will your plague-stopper help one who is already ill?"

Inda sighed. He wanted this answer to be "yes," and it was not. "The vaccine is a preventive measure. It is given to healthy people to keep them from falling ill. It will do nothing for one who already has contracted the plague." Inda wondered if the blue sparks were a manifestation of the plague or of the Healer's powers. He dropped his pack, took a step forward, bent over the ill Master. He touched the patient's forehead, passed his fingers over the flushed cheeks. No sparks leapt from his fingertips. He pressed a hand to the patient's chest and felt the rapid beating of his heart and the quick, shallow rhythm of his breaths. He observed the dry lips, the swollen tongue, the clenching fingers. "Fever and dehydration. Convulsions soon, if we cannot cool his body."

"Yes." Hanra-bae walked to the hearth, poured his trove of dried botanicals into a bowl, and added steaming liquid from a pot. "This infusion should help."

"We need something that will work quickly. We should immerse him in cold water," suggested Inda. "That will pull heat from his tissues and give us time for your medicine to work."

"Immerse him!" The Master Healer turned on Inda. His facial tattoos almost fluoresced against his pale gold skin. "He is not dead. I will give no living person to the water!"

The angry onslaught made Inda step back. "He is dying. The fever will kill him if we do not bring it down quickly. Cold water might save his life." The Healer's expression did not change. "Immersion has saved others who have had high fevers. The water will draw the heat out of his body. It may prevent the convulsions."

"And it will kill his spirit!" Hanra-bae was adamant. "He will not be put into water."

Inda stared at the Master Healer. He remembered the funeral at Bentwater, the body set adrift in its wicker coffin. This dread of immersion was cultural conditioning; he could not overcome it in time to save this patient. Yet Hanra-bae's potion would not reduce the Master's fever quickly enough to prevent convulsions. He would have to try something else. He turned to the fishers waiting outside the open door.

"Bring me buckets of water, the coldest water you have. And cloths, clean cloths to soak up the water. Quickly!"

They stared at him. No one moved.

"Arien, translate for me." Inda pushed the GuildMaster toward the door. "Make them understand." Then he bent over the patient and began to pull the heavy tunic from his torso.

"Lift his head," said Hanra-bae. "The potion is ready. We must make him drink it."

Together they struggled to pour tiny portions of the vile-smelling brown liquid into their patient's mouth and make him swallow. They had emptied half the bowl before he choked and spewed most of it out again, soaking them both.

"He must drink all of it." Hanra-bae lifted the bowl again, pressed it to their patient's lips. "He is not one of my people. He comes from the Southern Desert, probably to trade with us. The plague must have followed him on his journey north."

Inda tightened his grip on the southerner's shaking shoulders. The heat of the Ardellan's skin burned against Inda's forearms. The southerner's chest heaved and his head jerked back, bruising Inda's shoulder. Hanra-bae's potion spilled across the platform and the bowl clattered to the floor.

"Convulsions," said Inda. "I cannot hold him alone." A cloud obscured the sun, darkening the infirmary. "Where is that water!"

"Here." Arien was at Inda's elbow, a dripping wooden bucket in his hand.

"Strip off his tunic and leggings." Inda looked at Hanra-bae, anticipating an objection. The Healer said nothing; he was struggling to hold their patient's thrashing legs. "Did you get the cloths?"

A youngling ran up, loops of fabric trailing from its tentacles.

"Throw half of them in the water," instructed Inda. "Then get another bucket and more cold water."

"He will not survive," said Hanra-bae. "Once the convulsions begin . . ."

"We can walk away, and he will surely die. Or we can stay and try to reduce his fever."

The southerner's back arched off the platform. He kicked his right leg, caught Hanra-bae under the chin with his bare foot. The Healer grunted, pinned the leg beneath his left arm. "I am willing to try new methods, but I will not allow you to immerse him in water."

"I understand." Inda turned to Arien. "Squeeze the water from the cloths and lay them on his skin. Begin with his shoulders and work your way down to his feet. The cold cloths will draw the heat from his body."

Their patient gasped when the dripping fabric was spread across his chest. He shuddered, arched his back again, and threw his head against Inda's shoulder. Inda winced, gingerly moved his bruised collarbone. The southerner gasped once more, flung out his arms, kicked with both legs. Hanra-bae lost his grip, caught a foot in the abdomen. He doubled over, retching. A youngling ran to help him. The Healer pushed it away.

"See to our patient." Hanra-bae stumbled to a table and straightened up, coughing. He picked up a mug and drank. "Sul, Hep, Min, get in here! Bring straps to tie this southerner's legs."

Inda struggled to keep his grip on their patient's arms and shoulders. Suddenly the southerner sighed and the tension left his muscles. He sprawled across the platform, right leg hanging over the side. Arien moved quickly, lifting the leg and wrapping it in cold, dripping fabric. Then he walked around the platform, began wrapping the other leg.

The younglings arrived, carrying broad strips of pliant leather. Arien held the southerner's feet while Hanra-bae and the younglings bound his ankles together and secured them to the platform. The southerner lay like a peaceful sleeper throughout the procedure. Inda pressed a palm to his chest.

"His heart beats very quickly, and he hardly breathes. Is he close to death?"

Hanra-bae waved everyone away from the platform.

He bent over their patient and again moved his fingers in slow circles above the still body. In the darkened room the Healer's hands seemed to glow with soft blue light. Inda closed his eyes, took three breaths, opened them again. The light was still there. Bits of it broke away and jumped to the southerner's body, like static discharging.

"I know of your healing powers, that you can speed cell growth and regenerate damaged organs. Can you do nothing to reduce his fever?" asked Inda.

The Healer's hands stopped moving. Hanra-bae stared at Inda, his face a mask that revealed nothing. "The kind of healing you speak of increases activity in the patient's body and generates heat. I know of no way to slow a patient's metabolism, to steal heat away from his body, except with snow or the help of a potion. Perhaps we once had the power to do it; many of our healing techniques have been lost."

Inda nodded. "My own people have lost and rediscovered some healing methods many times. I think it is the nature of our profession." The clouds above the skylight parted, permitting the angled beams of late afternoon sunlight to brighten the infirmary. The disconcerting blue glow around Hanra-bae's hands faded. Inda sighed and lifted the cloths from the southerner's chest. They felt warm and clammy, and the southerner's skin was still flushed and hot. Inda dropped the fabric into a fresh bucket of water, let it soak a moment, then wrung it out. He spread the cold, damp cloths on their patient's skin. "His breaths are too slow and shallow. I fear that he will suffer brain damage before we can reduce his fever."

"His death is a certain thing," said Hanra-bae. "Your treatments may delay it, but I do not believe that you can cure him."

"Then perhaps we should seek out the council of Mothers." Jeryl stood in the open doorway, a dripping bucket in each hand. "I am not content to fetch water for a futile cause when there is work to accomplish."

"It is not futile," insisted Inda. He squeezed some water into the southerner's mouth, then wiped his face and neck with a cold cloth.

Their patient's unseeing eyes suddenly closed. They opened again, lively and focused, tracking some movement through the skylight. His fingers clenched, then relaxed, clenched, opened again, clenched and stayed that way. Tendons stood out on his wrists, twined by blood vessels clearly visible beneath his pallid skin. Greenish circles ringed the chitinous ovals at the tips of his fingers.

He gasped, and let the breath out with a shudder. His legs stiffened, began to tremble, strained against the bindings. His arms stretched upward, reaching for something only he could see. His dry lips moved, forming words without sound.

Another gasp, another shudder, and the southerner's back arched off the platform. He lifted his head, flung it back against the wood. It struck with a sickening thud.

"Hold him down," cried Hanra-bae. He ran to the platform, kicked over a bucket as he threw himself on top of their patient. Water puddled on the slate floor, turned the dust on Inda's boots into mud. Hanra-bae forced the southerner's arms down, pressed his back to the platform. "Hold his head!"

Inda slipped a cloth beneath their patient's head. A golden stain slowly spread across it. Inda smelled the heady scent of Ardellan blood. The southerner's eyes stared upward, and his lips continued their silent appeals. Inda laced his fingers together, pressed his palms to their patient's forehead to hold his skull immobile. "He is bleeding. He must have lacerated his scalp."

"Or fractured his skull," suggested Hanra-bae. "He will not live much longer."

The southerner might have heard them. He sighed. His muscles relaxed. He stopped breathing.

"Damn!" Inda released his forehead, tipped his head back to open his airway.

Hanra-bae slid off the platform. His left hand hovered over the southerner's chest. The blue glow was back, and a steady stream of sparks descended from his fingers to the southerner's body. "His spirit will soon leave his body. You will feel his death cry as it moves out toward his home."

"No!" Inda picked up a bucket of water and splashed it across their patient, drenching himself and Hanra-bae. He bent down, grabbed another pail. "Get those straps off his ankles." Arien rushed to help.

Inda poured more water over the southerner's face and chest. Their patient gasped, choked, coughed, and sputtered.

"He's not dead yet!" cried Inda. He reached for a third bucket. "How serious is the wound on his head?"

Hanra-bae looked at Jeryl and shrugged. Then he bent over their patient. "It is just a cut. It has already stopped bleeding. If he survives the night, it will heal."

"He will survive." Inda watched the southerner's chest rise and fall in the slow rhythm of normal breathing. He sounded more confident than he felt. Their patient's fever was subsiding; perhaps Hanra-bae's potion had finally taken effect. The potion or the cold water, or both, had given the southerner a slim chance at life.

"It will be dark soon. Light the wall sconces," said Hanra-bae to the younglings. Then he turned to Inda and his companions. "Let the younglings watch our patient for a while. They can put cold cloths on him and give him water to drink. We must eat and restore our strength so that we can be ready when he needs us again."

Inda shivered. The air temperature was dropping and he was soaked to the skin. Food was less important than dry clothing right now. "Jeryl, do you have my packs?"

"Beside the door, with the rest of our gear."

The crowd of onlookers had dispersed. Inda checked the street, saw a youngling fastening shutters on a building across the way. Another trudged toward the infirmary, a strange object clutched in its tentacles. The youngling stopped outside the door and peered at Inda. Its eyestalks slowly crossed. It said something in the fisher dialect.

Inda shrugged and stepped aside. The youngling sidled past him, one trembling eye trained on Inda while the other was scanning the room. Inda smiled. "I won't bite you."

The startled youngling dropped its parcel.

Hanra-bae shouted something that Inda could not understand. The youngling replied, eyestalks and tentacles waving. Inda bent down, reached for the fallen parcel. Its fabric covering parted at one end, revealing a dark red ceramic surface streaked with dust. Inda's hand closed on the thing.

The wide river flowed slowly over Javelicohmo's many feet. He felt the mud squish through his pedicles. The water was low, at least an arm's length lower than during this season last year. It was saltier, too. His feet could taste the difference. Javelicohmo looked up, smiled at the intricate patterns made by the sun's rays reflecting off the red and yellow and blue buildings of the settlement. He was composing a new dance to celebrate those patterns when someone called his name.

"Healer Inda, are you all right?"

Inda looked up into Arien's face. The GuildMaster was reaching for him. "I'm . . . fine." Inda looked down, slowly shook his head. His right hand hovered just above the youngling's half-open parcel. He could feel the redness of the object it contained, smell its antiquity. He remembered the river and the settlement and the dance, and he knew that those memories were as ancient as this object. They were not his memories, and that frightened him. He drew back his hand.

Arien picked up the parcel, unwrapped it. "The youngling says this was found on the beach along with our patient."

"Yes, that would be correct," said Hanra-bae. He wiped the dust from the object with a damp cloth. "Southerners sometimes bring these sculptures north to trade for goods and dried fish. This one is especially beautiful. I have not seen this shade of red before."

"Beluki," whispered Inda. His hand was shaking. Just six . . . no, seven days ago he and Elissa had talked with Jaime about Beluki artifacts. He had never imagined that there might be Beluki ruins on Ardel. Now he had touched one of the famed artifacts, seen unexpected evidence that the remnants of a Beluki settlement existed somewhere in the immense Southern Desert. He looked at Hanra-bae. "Do you know where the southerners find these things? Does anyone know?"

"Somewhere in the desert." The Healer shrugged. "The sculptures have no real value, other than their beauty."

"They have great value to Terrans. We have found them on many planets, in the ruins of ancient settlements. Some Terrans devote their lives to studying those settlements, trying to learn about the people who built them."

"Ah," said Hanra-bae, "the colorful people with too many arms and too many legs."

Inda was puzzled. "Who do you mean?"

"The people who created these sculptures."

"Are they still alive?"

"No. Many of the southerners have told us of seeing their spirits in the ruins. They say that the colorful people with too many arms and too many legs still walk among the broken houses and tumbled towers. They splash through invisible waters on the salt plain and climb the cliff face to the plateau. They talk to the southerners who visit them and tell them where to find these beautiful things.''

They talk to the southerners, thought Inda. *Some Ardellans communicate with the ghosts of the Beluki!* He took a deep breath, reached out, and pressed his right palm to the smooth surface of the relic. He closed his eyes, tried to see again the broad river and the colorful settlement.

No vision came to him. *Did I imagine the many legs, the feel of mud on strange feet? Was it unreal?* The thought frightened Inda. He pulled his hand back, bent, and reached instead for his pack.

''If the thing belongs to the southerner, should we not leave it with him?'' asked Jeryl. ''He might awaken and ask for it.''

''It will be miraculous if he wakes at all,'' said Hanra-bae. He put the sculpture on the floor beside the platform. ''Follow me. There will be a fire in the kitchen and hot tea and food waiting for us.''

Inda dropped his sodden coveralls in a corner of the guest room. He drained half his mug of tea in a single gulp, then wet one of the rough towels the youngling had left him and scrubbed the trail dust from his body. The clean, dry clothing he put on felt luxurious against his skin. By the time he finished his tea, he was warm and comfortable.

He stepped into the courtyard, looked through the kitchen windows at the bright glow of the fire and the younglings arranging platters of food on the table. His stomach growled. The food smelled delicious and he was hungry, but he turned aside and walked to the infirmary to check on their patient.

The southerner was still in danger, and his survival had suddenly become imperative. Locked in his fever-ridden mind was the location of Ardel's Beluki ruins. Inda stood beside the sickbed, watching Sul and Hep and Min swathe their patient's body in cold, wet cloths. The southerner's heart and lungs were working within reasonable limits, and the convulsions were at least temporarily at bay. He might live through the night.

Inda looked at the twisted artifact that lay beside the platform. How many years, how many centuries, had passed since that red ceramic object was fashioned by Beluki digits? Inda imagined it lying in dusty ruins until this Ardellan found it. Or had it passed from hand to hand among the southerners, a treasured heirloom or a sign of personal wealth?

And the scene he had experienced when he touched it—was that memory or something else? Inda reached down, extended his forefinger to stroke the artifact's shiny surface. *The southerner must live,* he thought. *He must wake and be lucid, must lead me to the Beluki ruins. They will be a treasure far greater than any titanium deposit. Ardel will become important for more than its minerals. The archaeologists will come to work in the ruins side by side with the Ardellans. They will make Ardel a center of Beluki research and study, keep it safe forever from corporations that want to exploit its resources. Sandsmark will surely name me envoy if I can only find those ruins.*

Chapter 23

Elissa walked out of the mine room with a cup of coffee in her hand. She took a sip, discovered that the coffee was as cold and bitter as her mood. She poured it down the recycler and punched for a fresh cup.

A day in the repair-bot's control chair had stiffened her back. She stretched, rotated her shoulders, felt two vertebrae pop. A fleeting pain made her catch her breath. She slowly released the air from her lungs and felt the cramp beneath her right scapula relax. She was hungry and tired, but she still had work to do. She picked up the fresh cup of coffee before going on to her office.

Sinykin's latest letter was still on her desk. She sat and stared at the half-page note, wondering why he had bothered with it. There was no real information in the few lines he had scrawled at Bentwater—just word that he was going on to Port Freewind. No mention of Griswold's recall request, no remorse that he had not been here when Jaime needed him, and no suggestion of when or if he would return to the spaceport. Elissa crumpled the letter and tossed it into the recycling bin.

An Ardellan messenger had brought Sinykin's note to the spaceport that afternoon, and she had sent him away with another letter for Sinykin before she read it. Now she was sorry that she had wasted valuable time composing the letter, warning Sinykin that Griswold was accusing him of sabotage. She had hoped that it would make him come to his senses and return to the spaceport, but his letter had convinced her that he would do as he pleased, without regard for regulations or for her needs or Jaime's. She looked at the holo of Sinykin and Jaime on the corner of her desk and wondered if it was time to replace it with one of Jaime alone.

Elissa had never really understood Sinykin's fascination with the Ardellans. She knew only that contact with them had changed him, had seduced him away from his family and the Terran community. She was losing her partner. She could fight another human for him, but the Ardellans had weapons that she did not understand and could not defend against. Riding after him was not a reasonable solution. She would be compounding their problems by violating more regulations. Her absence would endanger the mining project, making it more likely that the Union would lose the spaceport to Nagashimi-BOEM.

The mine and the ore shipment due in three days were her main concerns now. She turned to her computer, asked for a visual readout on the afternoon's production. It presented her with a graph and a list of figures. Elissa whistled. Jan Mboya and her crew had managed to dig and load two hundred tons of ore before darkness forced them to return to base. She ran some calculations, determined that they should be able to mine at least another fifteen hundred tons in the next three days. That much sand would keep the mill working at half capacity, refining the ore for shipment to Nagashimi-BOEM's reduction facility orbiting Hecate. If Mboya dug the richest sand, they would have just enough high-grade ore to make that first shipment on time.

Those figures were based on twelve-hour workdays at the mine, clear weather, and no breakdowns. Elissa was all too familiar with Murphy's laws. She knew that something would happen to slow down production. The questions were what, and when, and would she be able to correct it.

"Elissa?" Jeff Grund was standing in the doorway.

Durant smiled and pointed to a chair. She checked her chronometer; it was past midnight. "I didn't know you were still here. I thought you'd be home with Marta and Tommy by now. Jaime's staying with you again."

"That's good. He keeps Tommy out of mischief."

"It's kind of you to say that, but I don't believe it. I don't know what I'd do without you and Marta to help me with him right now. Without Sinykin . . ."

"I know. He'll be back soon."

Elissa shook her head. "I don't think he will. He's infatuated with the Ardellans, with some kind of magic he's found out there. He may never come back." She shook her head again, then turned her attention to Grund. "What have you been up to?"

Jeff frowned. "I just finished tracing the cable from the antenna to the spook. I had to tear apart half the offices on this level to do it."

"Did you find anything?" Elissa fervently hoped so; she almost crossed her fingers. It would be so convenient to cut a wire away from the cable and trace it to its source. Surely then they would be able to start mining with the spook, and she would be able to prove Sinykin innocent of sabotage.

"Not a damn thing." He shook his head, then swept the unruly hair from his eyes with his right hand. "The cable is clean. Nothing's been attached to it or cut into it."

Elissa sighed. That was indeed bad news. "Then there must be a transmitter interfering with the radio signals."

"That's right. It has to be capturing and modifying the signal, then retransmitting it. And it could be hidden anywhere on the base, or in the wasteland between here and the mine," said Grund. "It'll certainly be shielded. We'll need sophisticated equipment to locate it." He shook his head again, this time letting his hair fall across his forehead. "Mboya and her team will have to keep working at the site. How much ore did they ship to the mill today?''

A noise in the hall outside the office forestalled Elissa's reply. The building was supposed to be empty at this hour. She gestured for Grund to be silent, then rose from her chair and tiptoed to the door. He followed her.

Coni Mattrisch's head appeared around the door frame, quickly followed by the rest of her body. She grinned. ''Chief Durant! Dr. Grund! You surprised me. I didn't think anyone was in the building. Will you be staying much longer?''

''I'm finished here,'' said Elissa. She did not want to continue this discussion in front of anyone, not even a member of the Security team. She looked at Grund. ''Have you eaten yet, Jeff?''

''No. I'd like a sandwich before I go home.''

Elissa turned to Mattrisch. ''I suppose the commons is closed at this hour?''

The guard shook her head. ''You should be able to get a beer and a sandwich. There's usually someone in the kitchen around the clock.''

Elissa went back to her desk and spoke a command. The computer's display faded. Another command dimmed the room's lights.

''Are you patrolling the hangar tonight?'' asked Grund.

''Harwood has all of us on rotating assignments. We're never sure where we'll be from one hour to the next.'' Mattrisch walked with them down the hall. ''Have you heard anything more from Dr. Inda?'' she asked Durant. ''I hope that his medical mission has been successful.''

Elissa suddenly realized that she had discounted the reason for Sinykin's absence from the spaceport. He was not adventuring with the Ardellans, he was trying to save their lives. She sighed, felt the bitterness leave her heart as the air left her lungs. Sadness and frustration welled up to take its place. She turned and strode down the walkway beside Mattrisch. "Sinykin won't be able to judge his mission's success until midsummer, when the plague is at its height. If his vaccine works, the death rate among the Ardellans will be much lower than it was last year."

"When you write to him, tell him that I bear him no grudge for the way he left the compound." Mattrisch rubbed her shoulder, then shrugged. "I'd have let him ride away without interference, but I had orders to let no one go through the gate."

Elissa nodded. "I'm sure he didn't mean to harm you or to cause you any trouble. He knew the consequences he would face when he rode away from the spaceport, but sometimes he forgets that what he does affects others. When he decides on a course of action, he won't let anyone or anything stand in his way." Sinykin's single-minded idealism had seemed so attractive when they met. He had been the young physician out to save the universe, or at least the part of it that he could reach. Elissa had thought he was noble then. Now she wondered when her mind had transformed that perception of nobility into one of selfishness. Why was she now unwilling to grant him the same freedoms that he had always granted her?

"Sinykin will be glad to know that you aren't angry with him," said Elissa. Her boots clattered on the stairs. Grund was right behind her, the hangar door just ahead.

Grund turned to Mattrisch. "Are you finished here?"

"I still have to check some of the workshops," she replied. "I'll let the two of you out and lock up behind you. We'll be patrolling the hangar all through the night."

Chapter 24

Port Freewind, Ardel

Sinykin Inda pressed the mouth of the injection gun to the fleshy part of Hanra-bae's arm. He pushed the dispensing stud, heard the hiss of compressed air escaping from the cylinder, saw the Healer flinch as the vaccine was propelled through his skin. Inda released the stud and pulled the gun away.

Hanra-bae flexed his arm, examined the small golden bruise. "That is all? An instant's prick, and I am now protected from the plague?"

"It takes a few days for the protection to become effective," said Inda. "Then it will last for the rest of your life."

"Remarkable. If I show no ill effects, tomorrow you can begin vaccinating all who wish it."

Arien offered his arm to Inda. "I would like to be vaccinated today."

"Of course, GuildMaster." Inda wiped Arien's gold-tinged skin with an alcohol swab, then administered the immunization. Arien did not flinch. "We also should vaccinate those who are caring for the southerner. It is just a preventive measure. The plague is usually passed by insects, but we shouldn't take any risks."

"That is sensible." Hanra-bae turned to a youngling waiting beside the door. "Fetch Sul and Hep and Min from the infirmary. Then go to the kitchen and ask the other apprentices to come in."

"It might be best if I train you and your staff to vaccinate your people," said Inda. "The fishers of

Bentwater refused the vaccine, even though Jeryl vouched for me. They might be willing to accept it from a Healer.''

"You are a Healer," said Arien. He stared at Inda, his brow furrowed and his hands raised in a gesture of apology. "If there was any fault in our negotiations with the Mothers of Bentwater, it was mine. I was not an adequate translator.''

"That is not true.'' Jeryl stopped behind his friend and squeezed his shoulder. "The blame lies within the closed minds of the Mothers.''

"No one is to blame.'' Inda offered the vaccination gun to Hanra-bae as the younglings trooped in. He recognized more important concerns than the Mothers of Bentwater; they were in no immediate danger from the plague. The fishers of Port Freewind were at risk. The southerner had carried the plague to them. How many red fliers had fed on his blood, become infected, were now feeding and spreading the disease among the port's fishers?

Hanra-bae took the gun. "Line up," he said to the younglings. "I am going to give you a prick that will help protect you from the plague.''

"Select a fleshy place on the youngling's upper leg.'' Inda pointed to a spot on Sul's body. "Clean the skin, then press the nozzle of the gun against it and push this stud. You'll need to use both hands.''

Sul jumped at the hissing sound, then rubbed its leg when Hanra-bae pulled the gun away. "May I go back to the southerner now?'' it asked the Healer.

"No. Eat, then get some sleep. One of the other younglings will take your place in the infirmary.'' He continued with the vaccinations.

The southerner lay, limp and quiescent, on the platform in the center of the infirmary. His face had lost its golden flush. The shape of his skull was clearly visible beneath the pallid skin that loosely covered his bones and muscles. Dehydration and fever had exhausted his reserves. The delicate tissue around his swollen lips was cracked and peeling. His black eyes stared, unfocused, through dilated pupils.

"Rapid, shallow respiration," said Inda to Hanra-bae. He pressed his hand to the southerner's chest. "His heart is beating quickly. The fever has subsided a bit. I don't think he's in danger of having more convulsions."

"Perhaps not," replied the Healer, his left palm hovering above the patient's forehead. His hand moved slowly, carefully, past the southerner's eyes, nose, mouth, then stopped above his neck. Inda watched, waiting for the blue glow, the bright sparks of healing energy that he had seen the night before. They did not manifest. "He is still very ill," said Hanra-bae. "It is unlikely that he will recover."

The southerner's Beluki artifact lay on the floor at Inda's feet. Inda looked at its red curves, remembered the vision that had come to him the first time he touched it. He could still feel water flowing around his ankles. He bent down and grasped the relic in both hands, half-expecting to be thrust again into that alien world of many-legged beings. Nothing happened. He straightened up, set the relic carefully beside the southerner. Jeryl gave him a strange look. Inda shrugged. "He carried it all the way here. Perhaps he needs to know that it is still with him."

"It certainly did not protect him from the plague," commented Arien.

"But he is aware of its presence." Jeryl pointed to their patient's face. His eyes still stared at something the rest of them could not see, but his hand clutched the twisted ceramic artifact and his lips moved.

Inda bent close, heard soft syllables he could not interpret. He looked at Hanra-bae. "Can you understand him?"

"Only a few of the Mothers can communicate with southerners. Their dialect is very difficult to master."

"It does not matter," said Arien. "He is already drifting into sleep. We will get no information from him now."

He was right. Their patient's eyes slowly closed, and his clutching hand relaxed its grip on the artifact. Inda was acutely aware that the location of Ardel's Beluki ruins might stay forever locked inside the southerner's fevered brain. He might even carry it with him into death.

Hanra-bae turned to the younglings. "Give him water whenever you can, and wrap him in cold cloths if his fever rises again. We have an appointment with the council of Mothers. If you need us, send for us at Cobran's home."

Port Freewind had no town square. Its oldest stone houses were scattered across a low bluff that overlooked the ocean and the estuary of the White River. A wide path traced the bluff's edge, and from it Inda looked down on piers and fishing shanties clustered along the riverbank. Huge nets, some still attached to oddly-shaped floats, hung drying on wooden frameworks; boats, large and small, bobbed and rolled on the choppy water along the shoreline.

Cobran's house perched near the edge of the bluff, its only visible opening facing away from the water and the ocean winds. Like the others Inda could see, the house was round and built of multicolored irregular stones set with mortar. Its roof rose to a center peak. It had no windows or door. Inda followed Hanra-bae and Arien through its single opening and down a dark, narrow passage that followed the curve of the outer wall. The passage suddenly turned and doubled back, then spilled them into the house's single room.

Inda blinked in the soft light of a half-dozen tiny oil lamps. The room smelled of damp earth and roasted tubers and fish. *Fish oil in the lamps?* he wondered. Lush tapestries covered the stone walls, and thick woven rugs were scattered across the floor of cut and dressed stone tiles. Wooden benches, tiny tables, a small loom, and a single chair were the only furniture. Decorative objects filled every available niche—under benches, on a narrow shelf near the top of the wall, on the tables, and beneath them. Inda saw shells as small as the tip of his little finger, others larger than his fist; multihued stones, polished smooth by water; crystals, singular and clustered, transparent and colored, their smooth faces reflecting lamplight. Delicate carvings of fish and animals, painted in realistic colors, covered the top of one table.

The largest object lay on the floor in front of the loom. Its dark blue surface gleamed even in the shadows. Inda stepped to the side, looked at the object from a different angle. It seemed to disappear, leaving an oblong hole in reality. He blinked and again could see its undulating surface, the two knobs at its end protruding like truncated antennae. The disappearance was a trick of the shadows.

"Are you interested in the relics of the southerners?"

Inda looked up. A Mother stood beside the loom. She had not been there a moment before; he was certain she had not been in the room. "I did not see you, Mother. Pardon my rudeness."

Arien stepped forward, said something in the fisher dialect. The Mother lifted her hands and shrugged.

"We will use clan-speech so that the others can converse with us," she admonished Arien. "It would be impolite to exclude them from our discussion."

"As you wish, Mother Cobran. These two are Jeryl, Mentor of Clan Alu, and Sinykin Inda, Healer to the Terrans. We have come to talk with you about the Terran's plague-stopper and about this season's caravan schedule."

"And about the relics of the southerners," added Inda. He wanted to touch the blue artifact. Would it allow him to access more of the Beluki memories? He wiggled his toes inside his boots, remembered mud oozing between alien pedicles. The feeling was as vivid as the touch of his sock against his foot.

Cobran settled her slender body into the chair and pointed to the benches with a tentacle. "Sit. We will share refreshments." She leaned back, watching them with lively gray eyes, one hand toying with the neat plaits in her pale hair. Her short yellow robe fell in soft folds above matching leggings and boots. "Tell me about this plague-stopper."

"It is called a vaccine, Mother. The Terran has brought devices that force the vaccine through the skin and into the body." Hanra-bae rolled up his sleeve and showed her his upper arm. "It makes a quick sting, like the bite of an angry insect, and leaves a small bruise. Within a few days it makes the recipient immune to the plague."

"Excellent. Is it safe?"

"It is," said Inda. "The injection cannot make someone ill with the plague. Sometimes a patient will have a reaction—will feel ill and have a fever for a day. That is very rare."

"And what is your opinion of this vaccine, Master Healer?" asked Cobran.

"My staff and I received injections this morning. If we experience no problems, I think it will be safe to immunize the rest of our people tomorrow."

"Then I leave the arrangements in your capable hands." She turned to Arien. "It is good to see you again, GuildMaster. We look forward to your annual visit and the caravans of merchants that follow it."

Hanra-bae rose. "Mother, I apologize for interrupting you. There is one other matter that I must mention before I return to the infirmary. A southerner was brought in yesterday. He had collapsed from fever and dehydration—plague, we think. He carried a relic with him. He survived the night, but he may not live much longer. This morning he spoke in words that none of us could understand."

"I see." A youngling appeared, carrying a tray of steaming mugs and small plates piled with appetizing tidbits. Cobran gestured for the youngling to serve her guests. "When we have disposed of our business here, I will come to the infirmary."

"Thank you, Mother." Hanra-bae turned and disappeared down the dark passageway.

Inda accepted a mug and plate from the youngling. He had expected tea but instead found that the mug contained a rich vegetable broth. Its spicy tang reminded him of Jeff Grund's hot and sour soup, and the many dinners he and Elissa had shared with Jeff and Marta. It seemed so long ago, a different world or a different lifetime. What was Elissa doing right now, while he sipped his broth and nibbled fish dumplings?

"I wonder, Mother Cobran, if your people might have trade goods that would please the Terrans?" Jeryl leaned forward, resting his arms on his thighs. "All trade with the Terrans is conducted through Clan Alu, and we are open to increasing that trade base. The Terrans offer iron and copper in exchange for those things which they value."

"And what goods of Ardel have they found to be of value?" asked Cobran.

"Sand that we will mine from Alu's lands," said Inda, "and handcrafted goods—embroidered tapestries, beautiful leathers, woven rugs. And artifacts, like the piece the southerner brought with him and the one you have there." He pointed to the blue Beluki artifact. "We have found relics like that in many places, yet they are among the rarest and most valued of our possessions."

"More valuable than the strange metal you take from the sand?" asked an unfamiliar voice. Inda turned, looked over his shoulder. Two Ardellans, one of them dressed in Metalsmiths' red, were standing at the mouth of the passageway. The smith spoke. "Would you give us iron in exchange for some of those relics?''

Cobran rose, extended her hands to the newcomers. ''Reass, Mikal, welcome to Port Freewind! It has been too many seasons since we last saw you. Please join us. Do you know my other guests?''

Jeryl turned his palms toward the newcomers in a warding gesture. A red tinge stained his aura, and his words were sharp with anger. ''These two are no strangers to us. What brings you to Port Freewind, GuildMasters? Do you track us for a purpose, or just for sport?''

''Jeryl!'' Arien stood, stepped between his friend and the newcomers. His voice was stern. ''I had not expected to see you here, Reass. Have your palms healed well?''

Inda heard the warning in the words, remembered the last meeting he had witnessed between Reass and Arien and the fireball that had burned Reass' hands. He shuddered and moved out of the line of fire.

Reass ignored the question and raised his hands to Cobran in greeting. ''Mother, we thank you for welcoming us into your home. Mikal and I offer our apologies for not sending word that we were coming. We have been pursuing your other guests for several days, with good reason.'' He turned to Inda. ''Healer, we ask you to bring your plague-stopper to Berrut. Our guild members need to be vaccinated. In exchange, you may choose whatever goods you wish from our trade stock, or we can pay you in iron.''

''I require no payment for the vaccine.'' Inda rose. He was familiar with Reass' easy acceptance of things Terran, and he was skeptical about the smith's motives. ''We discussed this when I vaccinated you at Alu Keep. I told you then that I was committed to coming to Port Freewind.''

''You did, and I have no wish to interfere with your work here. When I returned to Berrut, I spoke with the other GuildMasters about your plague-stopper. They were adamant that I follow you and offer you whatever you ask, if you will protect our guild members from that deadly illness.''

Inda nodded. ''It will cost you nothing to have your people immunized. However, I must vaccinate the fishers first. The plague has already struck here.''

''Will you come to Berrut when you are finished in Port Freewind?'' asked Mikal.

''Perhaps,'' said Inda. Mikal was taller and thinner than stocky Reass, and soft-spoken where Reass was aggressive, but Inda trusted him no more than he trusted the smith. ''How many people live in Berrut?''

Mikal offered a figure that made no sense to Inda.

''About eight thousand in your counting system,'' said Jeryl.

Too many, thought Inda. He would have little vaccine left after he finished with the fishers. Neither Reass nor Mikal had threatened him, yet he felt uneasy about denying their request. They must have come to Port Freewind for more than the vaccine; they could have gone to the spaceport for that. He was glad of Jeryl's solid and supportive presence at his right hand, and of Arien's at his left. They could protect him better than any Terran weapons. Sinykin nodded to each of them before turning back to Reass and Mikal.

''I do not have enough vaccine with me to immunize all of your people. There is more vaccine at the Terran compound. As I told you at Alu Keep, you can send your Healers to me at the compound. I will give them the vaccine and the equipment they will need to administer it.'' *If Griswold will let them into the compound,* he thought, *and if she doesn't have me locked up by then.* ''It will take only a moment to teach them how to use the equipment. Is that acceptable?''

Mikal deferred to Reass, who shrugged. ''We will do what we must to protect our guild members.''

''Then sit, all of you,'' said Cobran. She turned to

the youngling. "Mas, bring more refreshments for my guests.

"We were discussing the season's caravan schedule and the trade goods sought by the Terrans. We fishers can offer colorful shells of all shapes and sizes, ink from the belly of the black wriggler, cutting tools made from the yellowfin's giant scales, and more than a few of the southerners' relics. We always need iron, but we seldom use copper. Would you give us iron for any of these things?" she asked Inda.

"Indeed we might, Mother. We are certainly interested in the relics and their source." Inda looked to Jeryl for approval. Clan Alu held an exclusive trade contract with the Union; Inda could not make any promises until he confirmed the arrangements with Jeryl. He expected that Alu would allow the Terrans to trade iron for Beluki artifacts. Whether Alu agreed or not, the presence of Beluki ruins on Ardel would change the planet's status from mining colony to major archaeological site.

Cobran acknowledged Inda with a wave of her hand. "And what of you, Reass? What have you to offer the Terrans?"

"We have all the riches of Berrut. Sturdy works of iron and copper; delicate gold and silver decorations; beautiful tapestries and woven rugs; fine leather harnesses and saddles. I fear that the Terran representative has never seen examples of our goods. Alu shows only those which *it* wants to trade.

"Our merchants have brought caravans to Port Freewind for many generations, always under the guidance of the FreeMasters Guild," continued Reass. "We hired the guild to provide us with guides and translators. Now the FreeMasters are the allies of Clan Alu, and they control our trade with you fishers and with the Terrans. We have become too dependent on the arrangements they make for us. It is time we dismiss the FreeMasters. We must negotiate our own schedules and make our own agreements."

A ruby haze of anger spread through Arien's aura. "This is just a ploy to make your own trade arrangements with the Terrans. I thought that our last encounter had convinced you not to meddle in Alu's business, Reass. The Assembly ruled long ago that Alu has exclusive rights to trade with the Terrans. If you try once more to interfere with that contract, I will see you punished. As for your trade with the fishers, that has always been your own business. I would have stopped in Berrut as usual and informed you of the caravan schedule before I returned to my guildhall."

"We have the right to offer our goods to the Terrans!" cried Mikal.

Inda rose and spread his hands, palms upward in a gesture of apology, before Cobran. "I am sorry to be the cause of this controversy, Mother. Thank you for welcoming me into your home. I must leave now."

"Will you not discuss trade with us, Terran? You could dismiss these two," suggested Reass, pointing to Jeryl and Arien. "Then they could not interfere in our talks."

"I cannot make trade arrangements with anyone but a representative of Clan Alu. The Terran Union has a contract with Alu, and I am bound to honor it." *Until Sandsmark appoints me envoy*, thought Inda, *if that day ever comes. Then I will have some latitude to negotiate a new treaty.* "It is best that I leave now. Mother Cobran, thank you again for your hospitality." He turned and entered the narrow passage that led outside.

Jeryl moved to follow him. "I will go also. Thank you, Mother. Perhaps we will talk again later."

"Cobran was angry," said Jeryl as he and Inda stepped from Cobran's house into the bright morning sunlight. "We offended her other guests."

"I think they offended us first." Inda trod the path along the bluff's edge and gazed down on a pair of younglings mending nets. Others were cleaning fish and hanging the gutted bodies on wooden racks. Inda's thoughts were not on the fishers but on the great Southern Desert in which precious Beluki artifacts were hidden. If the southerner survived, he might be able to draw a map of the route to the ruins. With that and an artifact in hand, Inda could return triumphantly to the spaceport, his appointment as envoy assured. Griswold's threats to have him recalled would dissolve. He would have power and support, and would at last be able to accomplish things for the Ardellans. "We ought to make some compromise with the guilds, Jeryl. There must be a way to satisfy them without sacrificing Alu's interests."

"Let me know when you think of one," said Jeryl. "I will present it to the council." He pointed up the trail. A youngling was running toward them and shouting; several others milled about in its wake.

Inda moved aside to give the youngling a clear path. It ran toward the edge of the bluff, stubby legs pumping and tentacles flailing. Then it saw Jeryl and tried to slow its pace. It stepped on a rock, tripped and fell, bounced up and ran headlong into Jeryl. The two of them tottered near the sheer drop to the riverfront. The youngling squealed and twined its tentacles about Jeryl's waist. Inda grabbed the Mentor's arm, pulled him onto safer ground. The youngling followed. It never stopped chattering.

Only two words of its garbled speech made sense to Inda: "Hanra-bae" and "Arien." Jeryl listened for a moment, then pointed back the way they had come. "Cobran," was all he said to the youngling, who released him and ran toward the Mother's house.

"There is trouble at the infirmary," said Jeryl. "I think Hanra-bae sent the youngling to fetch Arien."

"The southerner!" Inda's bright vision of Terran archaeologists at work in the Beluki ruins faded. It was replaced by an image of the southerner dying or already dead, his knowledge of the ruins' location going with him into the afterworld. Inda shook his head. He would do everything he could to keep the southerner alive. ''There may still be something we can do for him. Come!'' He ran toward the infirmary.

Chapter 25

Terran Spaceport, Ardel

Howard Sandsmark twitched a muscle in his hip, directing his hover cart down *White Crane*'s passenger ramp and onto the glassy heat-sealed tarmac of the landing field. The installation before him looked like a hundred others spread among the settled worlds. The gray maintenance hangar, its huge door rolled back to reveal its cavernous interior, dwarfed the spaceport's other buildings. Windmills and paved roads, fences and gardens and chicken runs had left a Terran imprint on the barren landscape of Ardel's wasteland. The golden sun hovered, impotent, above distant snow-covered mountains. A chill wind blew from the heights across the landing field, making Sandsmark shiver. He turned up the collar of his jacket.

The Ardellan air was thinner than Terran standard, the gravity only slightly greater than that on *White Crane*. Sandsmark flexed his muscular arms in appreciation. He would be able to pull himself in and out of his cart without help, something he could no longer do in high-gravity environments.

Two figures waited for him at the edge of the field. One was a stranger; the other he immediately knew was Anna. The wind fluttered the hem of her long blue coat, just as it had so many years ago on another landing field. She had always been the one who waited, greeting him with laughing eyes when he returned from adventures. His memory gave her smooth skin and a bright smile. It was only when she walked out to meet him that he saw the wrinkles around her eyes and mouth, the steel-gray hair streaked with white. Ardel had aged her. No, twenty years of life had aged her. He was sure he looked no better.

"Hello, Howard," she said. Her words had hard edges.

"Hello, Anna." He wanted to say more, knew there was nothing more to say. The past was written. Neither of them could go back to change it.

Her office was cold and impersonal, except for the holos and photographs on the walls. They were better than the ones Sandsmark remembered, clearer and cleaner with sharply delineated lines. No living things appeared in them.

Anna had become cold and impersonal, too. She stood at the window in her blue dress tunic and looked out at the spaceport instead of at Sandsmark. The silver Administrator's insignia at her breast glittered in the sunlight.

"I'm afraid we're going to lose this one, Howard," she said.

Sandsmark longed to hear passion and anger in her voice, heard only resignation. Had time changed her that much? He did not want to believe it. "We'll only lose if we give up and let Nagashimi-BOEM take the mine away from us. I'm not ready to do that."

"What are you ready to do?"

Her bitterness stung him. He refused to be baited into an argument, changed the subject instead. "Has Inda returned to the spaceport?"

"Not yet. We'll lock him up as soon as he comes in."

"On what charges?"

"Defying orders, leaving the compound without permission, suspicion of sabotage. . . ."

Sandsmark kept his voice dispassionate. "This isn't a military organization; you can't lock him up for crossing you. What evidence links him to the sabotage?"

''It's just circumstantial right now, but we'll have proof once Security finds the retransmission unit. That's how the spook has been sabotaged. The unit captures radio signals from the equipment at the mine site, alters them, and transmits them to our receivers on the base.''

''Then it's an inside job.''

''Damn right.'' Griswold turned away from the window and glared at Sandsmark. ''Dr. Inda had access to technical information through Chief Durant. He left the compound just before the problems at the mine became apparent. That's enough evidence to justify requesting his recall and initiating a full investigation into his activities.''

''It won't stand up before a review board, Anna. You need more than your suspicions and a few coincidences to justify recalling Inda.'' Sandsmark saw her eyes darken, knew that he had put her on the defensive. ''We have to investigate this, but we shouldn't concentrate on Inda to the point of ignoring other suspects. A half-dozen people assigned to this base have some connection to Nagashimi-BOEM. Did you know that Jer Robinson went to school with Austin Duerst's brother? Or that Joli Nevarre worked for Braddock-Owen Extraterrestrial Mining before it merged with Nagashimi Interstellar Drives? Even your Security Chief once interviewed at Nagashimi.''

''Then we'll investigate them all,'' said Griswold. ''I still want Inda recalled. You may be willing to tolerate his insubordination, but I'm not. His unauthorized contact with the Ardellans has put this entire installation at risk.''

''We'll discuss it after the Nagashimi-BOEM situation is resolved. If we lose this base to the corporation, Inda's status won't matter. You'll all be recalled and reassigned. Nagashimi-BOEM has plans to mine iron in the mountains and turn this plain into a vast manufacturing center. Duerst even mentioned building ships on Hecate. You should be worrying about that, not about a personality conflict with Sinykin Inda.'' A shock of white hair fell across Sandsmark's forehead. He brushed it back with his right hand. His fingers trailed across the bald spot that felt unfamiliar even after ten years of thinning hair. He was a legless old bureaucrat who had stretched his political neck a little too far with the Ardellan project. If the project collapsed, the Union would have to scramble to save face. His superiors would surely demand his resignation.

Griswold stared at Sandsmark for a long moment. Then she pursed her lips and leaned forward as she unleashed the anger he had known was locked within her. He should not have been surprised that she turned it against him instead of Inda or Nagashimi-BOEM.

''You've undercut too many of the decisions I've made here. You question my judgment and overturn my rulings. I can't be an effective Administrator when you second-guess me.''

''You won't be effective until you learn to trust the people who work for you. That means all of them, even Sinykin Inda. You've made decisions that hobbled him and left him no choice but to defy you.'' Sandsmark looked away. He and Anna had shared too much history to be really objective with one another. He had chosen to gamble on keeping her in his department despite that. Perhaps it had been a mistake. She might have been better off making a career elsewhere, away from his influence. He turned back, locked his eyes on hers. ''You're a good Administrator. Don't become obsessed with the actions of one subordinate. Let it rest for now. Inda's transgressions mean nothing compared with the possibility of losing this installation. You should concentrate on saving the base and the mine.

''What are you doing to fulfill Nagashimi-BOEM's contract? Is the spook operational now? Have you been able to mine any titanium at all?''

Griswold sighed. She stepped away from the window, sat down in the chair behind her desk. "We're mining on-site. Mboya and her team are out there now, operating the shovel and the big trucks. They can only work during daylight hours, but Durant thinks we can push just enough ore through the mill to make our first shipment on time."

"Duerst wants to tour the mine room this afternoon and the mill tomorrow. He is planning to follow the first ore hopper up to the reduction facility on the twenty-fifth," said Sandsmark. Duerst would brook no delays. The man was as punctilious as he was obnoxious. "How many people know that you're mining on-site instead of using the spook?"

"The mining team, some of Durant's engineers, and a few people from Security. Joli Nevarre and Jeff Grund. That's all. We've told everyone else that the problems have been corrected. They all think the spook is operational."

"We need to make Duerst believe that, too." Sandsmark nodded, tapped his fingers on the arm of his cart. He had wanted to wipe the self-satisfied smirk off of Duerst's face ever since he'd boarded *White Crane*. This might just be the way to do it. "Is the second shift of miners out at the site?"

"No. Mboya took only her best people."

"Then let's call the second shift in and set them up in the mine room. If we do it right, Duerst won't know that they aren't really controlling the equipment."

Griswold tipped her head to the side and frowned. "Just what are you planning?"

"A bluff, Anna. Didn't you ever learn to play poker?"

Chapter 26

Port Freewind, Ardel

The smell of decay pulled Inda up short at the infirmary door. Someone had died, but not within the past few hours. A day ago, perhaps two. And the odor was not coming from the infirmary. Inda looked in, saw the southerner still sprawled on the platform, a pair of younglings attending him. His condition seemed unchanged.

"Out here," said Jeryl. He pointed up the street. Inda turned, saw Viela and another Healer standing in the road. A weary alep rested between them, head down and ears drooping. The alep carried a blanket-wrapped bundle across its back. Fishers and younglings had come out of their shops to gape at the strange trio. They pointed and muttered and moved well upwind of the alep.

Jeryl approached Viela. "The smell of your alep's burden tells me that you should have had a funeral ceremony performed yesterday. I would be glad to remedy the problem and remove the source of these fishers' distress."

"Not you," spat Viela. His rose-tinged aura flushed ruby red. "We have sent for Arien and a funeral urn. We do not desire your help."

"And you, Bantu?" asked Jeryl of the second Healer. "Do you defer to the wishes of Viela?"

Bantu shrugged. "He is my GuildMaster, at least until the Healers can meet and select another."

Inda saw the sudden tightening around Jeryl's mouth, then the smoothing of his facial features, the relaxation of his expression. The Mentor's aura momentarily clouded, then cleared to its usual soft white glow. "My respects, GuildMaster," he said to Viela, "and may I know what became of your predecessor?"

Viela laid a hand on the blanket-wrapped bundle. "He died on the trail."

Jeryl lifted his hands in a gesture of respect. "My condolences to you and your guild. It is difficult to lose a leader, more difficult when it is unnecessary. Someone of his great age should not have been traveling."

"So I told him," said Bantu. "I could have handled the situation on my own."

Viela snorted. "You cannot keep even the guildhall in order!"

Bantu's reply was cut off by Hanra-bae, who appeared in the infirmary's doorway. "Arguing among yourselves will not solve our present problem. Your dead GuildMaster is polluting Port Freewind's air and creating a health hazard. If you will not allow us to give him to the water, you must cremate him immediately." He offered a beautiful covered basket to Viela. "Will this meet your needs?"

"Do not be foolish. Kelta's ashes will escape through the weave." Viela turned his face to the sun. "These fishers cannot even supply us with a suitable urn."

"You may have my teapot," said Hanra-bae.

"You insult your guild and your GuildMaster. A cooking utensil is not an appropriate funeral urn. Have you no unused herb pots?"

Hanra-bae shrugged. "I have no clay pots, since I store my herbs in baskets. There may be something else in the infirmary that would honor Kelta." He turned, went back inside, returned a moment later bearing Inda's aluminum equipment box. The lid was open, and Inda could see that the vials of vaccine and the packing material had been removed. "This will certainly not burn."

"That is a Terran thing!" Viela was outraged; the ruby glow in his aura darkened and spread.

"The box will not burn, and it will protect Kelta's ashes until you can get them home to his urn." Hanra-bae reached under his tunic, brought out the previously-offered teapot. "You have three choices. You may use the Terran's box, or my teapot, or we will set your GuildMaster adrift on the river. Which do you choose?"

Viela glowered. Bantu stepped forward and took the ocher-colored teapot from Hanra-bae.

"A wise choice," said the fisher. "Now where is the FreeMaster?"

"Here!" Cobran strode up with Arien at her side. "Let us quickly dispose of this dead person. The odor of decay befouls my streets."

"Clear the center of the road," said Arien. He stood before the burdened alep and turned in a circle, motioning the onlookers back with his hands. His FreeMaster's cloak shone like silver in the sunlight. "The cremation will take only a few moments. Then you can go about your business."

Inda stepped back, found that he was standing between Jeryl and Cobran. He saw Reass and Mikal across the road, watching from the shadows between two buildings. They were leaning close to one another, as if sharing a whispered conversation.

Arien bent low, pressed his right palm against the roadway. His lips moved in an inaudible incantation. Then he straightened, raised both hands, traced arcane signs in the air. He spread his arms wide. "Viela and Bantu, lay your GuildMaster on the stones at my feet. You need not remove his blanket."

The two Healers struggled with the bindings that fastened Kelta's body to the alep's saddle. Bantu gave up, pulled out a dagger, and cut the ropes. "Wasteful," muttered Viela. The body slipped down into his arms, and he carried it as easily as he would a bundle of dry twigs. He knelt in the street before Arien and gently lowered Kelta's body to the ground. The dead GuildMaster made only a small hump in the blanket.

"Step back," warned Arien. He repeated his caution for the audience. "Everyone stay at the edges of the street." Then he took the teapot from Bantu and set it at Kelta's feet. "Do not be frightened of the flames. The fire of transformation will not harm you or your property."

Arien removed his sheathed dagger and tossed it to Jeryl. Then he raised his arms again and held them wide apart, his hands level with the top of his head. His fingers were spread and his palms were turned slightly inward.

A priest blessing the multitude, thought Inda, *or preparing to accept and focus the energy of a god.* Inda slitted his eyes, concentrated on Arien's aura. It shone with brilliant white light, like a form-hugging cloud of shimmering energy. The light was brighter at Arien's feet. The brightness moved upward along his body and down his arms to his hands. Inda watched the movement, saw the energy being drawn up until Arien's palms glowed with power.

Hands held high, Arien strode three times around the body. He stopped at each of its corners—left foot and right, right shoulder and left—then faced toward the blanket's center. The last circuit brought him back to the teapot. He bent down, lifted off the lid and set it to one side. Then he walked to Kelta's head.

The crowd was silent as Arien raised his palms and turned them once again toward Kelta's body. He pointed his fingers at the center of the blanket. The energy that had gathered at Arien's palms discharged along his fingers, then shot outward in a bright stream to strike the blanket on Kelta's chest. Light flared. Inda closed his eyes against the sudden brightness. He could not shut out the flames. Their images danced on the inside of his eyelids, and their heat warmed his cheeks.

The fire died as quickly as it had been born, leaving

only the teapot and Arien in the road. Arien lowered his arms, walked over to the teapot, bent down and settled its lid in place. "Done," he said as he handed the pot to Bantu.

"The Healers Guild thanks you," said Viela.

"As do the fishers." Cobran offered her hands to Viela, who touched her palms with his own. "We share your grief at the death of one who was so important to your guild. The wheel of life turns, bringing a time of regeneration and rebirth to the Healers. Use this opportunity wisely, GuildMaster."

Cobran turned and knelt near the spot where Kelta's body had lain. She leaned over, touched the stones as if afraid they would burn her hands. "No heat," she said. "They were not even warm. And I see no ashes. What have you done with the body?"

Arien pointed to the teapot. Its ocher glaze was suffused with soft amber highlights. "Kelta's ashes and the little that was left of his spirit are in the pot. Touch it, and you will feel the warmth of life."

Cobran repeated his words for the fishers. They crowded around Bantu, their outstretched fingers reaching to test Arien's statement. Inda knew that it was true, for he remembered the warmth of Sarah Anders' urn beneath his hands and his awareness of her presence when he stood at the mourning wall. Her body had been cremated by Arien and Jeryl in this same mystical manner. Part of her spirit remained in that urn in Alu Keep.

Across the road in the shadows, Reass and Mikal still whispered together. Mikal waved his arms as if protesting something Reass had said, then turned away and walked into the street.

"Mikal!" called Viela. He strode toward the merchant, pushing fishers out of his path. The ruby flush had returned to his aura. "Where is my sibling Reass!"

"Here, Viela." Reass stepped into the sunlight.

Mikal moved away from him, as if he feared to be in the Metalsmith's presence.

"You are more foolish than I had believed, sibling. You should have run back to the protection of your guildhall. Here even Mikal will not stand with you." Though Viela spoke in the clan-speech that most fishers could not understand, his anger was evident in his tone and his aura. The fishers left the road, seeking refuge in the workshops on either side. Viela took up a stance of power—feet spread and hands raised—and fear quickened Inda's breath. Arien had faced Reass just this way when Reass had challenged him. Inda would never forget the bright discharge of energy, the burnt flesh of Reass' palms. He moved closer to Jeryl.

"Reass, I accuse you of causing the death of Kelta by deliberate action," intoned Viela. He turned his palms toward Reass. Sparks erupted from his fingertips. "You are not a FreeMaster, yet you have shown me that you possess power. I have power of my own. I challenge you, Reass. Enter the circle of dispute with me. Only one of us will emerge alive!"

Chapter 27

Port Freewind, Ardel

"No!" cried Cobran. "We do not settle our disagreements by killing one another!" She pushed her way past the watching fishers and confronted Viela. Her voice was quiet and firm, and her sparkling aura showed no trace of the angry flush that colored Viela's. Cobran was accustomed to being obeyed. "You and your clan ways try my patience, Healer. Turn aside your palms. I will not countenance your threats in my city."

Inda took an involuntary step backward as the ruby cloud of Viela's aura billowed toward Cobran. The Healer's rage was tangible even five meters away. Inda shuddered at its power.

"You shelter a killer within your city," Viela asserted. "Reass owes me a life-debt. Will you continue to protect him, or will you walk away and let me do what I must?"

Neither Cobran's will nor her slender body swayed before Viela's anger. Her arms remained at her sides and her tentacles lay quiescent against her chest. "Your accusation is not proof that Reass killed your GuildMaster. Is there someone who will support your charge?"

"Bantu!" cried Viela. He turned, searched the crowd for his companion, found him still holding the teapot. "Tell her, Bantu. You saw Reass kill Kelta. Tell her!"

Reass stared at Bantu over Viela's shoulder, as if forbidding him to confirm Viela's words. Bantu's hands were shaking. He spared the smith a single glance before he addressed Cobran.

"Reass and Viela fought," said Bantu. "Kelta stepped between them. I do not know which of them killed him."

"Mikal will testify for me," called Reass. Inda wondered if the green-tinged haze in his aura meant that he was concealing something. "Mikal was with me. He knows I meant no harm to the GuildMaster. My argument was with Viela."

Viela ignored Reass. He dropped his hands and advanced on Bantu. Dark patches flowed in his aura like thunderclouds. Bantu stepped back, clutching the teapot to his chest. Was he trying to protect it, or did he hope it would protect him? His fear was evident, even to Inda.

"One funeral is enough today. Remember your oath, Healer." Arien took Viela's arm, pulled him up short. "This kind of revenge will compromise you. There are other ways to reveal the truth and exact justice." He pressed a palm to the center of Viela's chest. The Healer's expression relaxed, and the murky clouds cleared from his aura. His anger was still evident, but now it was controlled.

"It is true, Viela," said Cobran. "Go and rest. Master Healer Hanra-bae has a room for you and another for Bantu. Tomorrow I will hear testimony from each of you, and from Reass and Mikal. I will decide the truth of this matter and hand down judgment according to our customs. Until then do not look for Reass. He has our protection."

"I will honor your request, Mother, and await your judgment because I have great respect for you and your fishers. I will listen to your decision, but it will not bind me. Reass must answer to the Healers Guild!" Viela pushed Arien away, glared at Reass, then took the teapot from Bantu and followed Hanra-bae out of the street.

* * *

"Do you think he is right?" asked Inda.

Jeryl squinted at him. "Who?"

"Viela." Inda and Jeryl stood outside the infirmary, watching the crowd disperse. Reass turned and strode after Cobran, his red cloak billowing in the ocean breeze. The ends of the long thong that bound his hair danced against his back. His walk was sure, bolstered by confidence or bravado; Inda could not guess which. Mikal followed more slowly, his hands pinning his cloak against his body as if he were hiding something. "Did Reass kill Kelta?"

"Viela seems to believe so."

"And what do you believe?" Inda watched Jeryl out of the corner of his eye. He was learning to perceive Ardellan auras most clearly with his peripheral vision. It was like having a new sense, one whose input he could not yet fully interpret. "Is one of them lying?"

"Deception is beyond Viela. It is a Terran custom that he despises," said Jeryl.

Inda's back stiffened and he felt a sudden tightness in the muscles around his mouth. *Did Jeryl mean to offend me?* he wondered. *Can he read my reaction in my aura?* "What do you mean? Ardellans lie."

"Of course we do. We do not expect our lies to be believed. They are only a way of avoiding the truth."

"That makes them virtuous?"

"We do not attempt to deceive." Jeryl's aura was so white that it seemed to sparkle. "We had no word for deception until Terrans came to Ardel. The concept was impossible for us to imagine. Only the head-blind can fool one another with lies."

"Although some Ardellans are masters of trickery and misdirection," said Arien as he joined them. "Do not be taken in by Jeryl's righteousness. We can be tricksters and thieves and even killers. We only go about it in a different way."

"Enough!" said Jeryl. His aura had flushed the faintest pink. "Shall we check on your patient?"

They turned and went into the infirmary. Two younglings were caring for the southerner. Inda surveyed their bodies, saw that each one bore the tiny golden bruise of a vaccination. The younglings differed from one another in shape and size and manner, yet he could not identify them. They could be any two of the younglings who had passed before him that morning.

"Hep, how fares your patient?" asked Arien.

"He has had no more convulsions," said the first youngling. "He sleeps, but he is still restless and feverish."

The second youngling turned its eyestalks toward Inda. "We change his wrappings often and wet them with water from the coldest well, Terran Healer. We do this just as you showed us."

"How is it that you know clan-speech?" asked Inda. He touched the southerner's forehead, then opened his eyes and peered into them.

"All apprentices who wish to become Healers must learn the speech of the clans before they can take instruction at the guildhall in Berrut," said Hep.

Inda nodded. "You will both make good Healers. Has the southerner spoken to you?"

"A little." Hep's eyestalks crossed. "Always in words we cannot understand. His eyes never open. I do not think he knows where he is."

"He is still very ill." Inda pressed his palm to the southerner's chest, counted his pulse—slower than it had been yesterday—and his respiration—deeper. Were Ardellans subject to pneumonia? He considered fetching the diagnostic equipment from his pack, realized it would be futile. He had no Ardellan norms with which to compare this patient's condition. It was one thing to clean and dress a wound, or temper a fever by cooling a patient's body, another to understand the workings of alien organs and biochemistry. He would have to leave that to Hanra-bae. "Have you been forcing liquid into him?"

"The Master Healer brewed a decoction this morning." The youngling pointed to a bowl on the hearth.

Inda lifted the plate that covered it, sniffed the murky greenish-brown liquid. It smelled of the same herbs that the southerner had spewed all over him yesterday.

"How often?" asked Inda.

"Whenever we change his wrappings. We give him as much as he will swallow."

"Good." Inda went back to the platform, looked at the Beluki artifact that lay beside the patient. He stroked its smooth ceramic surface with a fingertip. Would the southerner ever regain his senses enough to tell Inda where he had found it? "Do you think that he knows this is here?"

The southerner muttered something incomprehensible.

"He knows," said Arien.

Inda looked up. "When I touched it yesterday, I saw strange things—people and places like none I have ever known."

Arien exchanged a glance with Jeryl. "From holding it?"

"Yes. Come here, touch it yourself. Tell me what you see." Inda stepped aside to make room for the others. "Take it with both hands." He watched Arien pick up the artifact, hold it, study it. There was no change in Arien's expression or his aura. Inda was disappointed. "You see nothing unusual?"

"Nothing," said Arien. He offered the relic to Jeryl.

Jeryl took it with both hands. He held it much the way Inda had, palms pressed to the shiny hard surface, fingers wrapped around its spiral curves. He looked at it for a long time before glancing at Inda. "I see nothing. That does not mean there is nothing here to see. Some people are gifted in one way, others in another. Perhaps your gift is one that Arien and I do not share." He thrust the artifact at Inda.

Inda shrugged and stepped back. He dared not touch the thing now. What if the vision had only been his imagination running wild? The boundaries between fantasy and reality were blurring more each day. Had

Kelta's cremation been real? Was the shimmer-light that sometimes danced in his palm imaginary? He pointed to the platform, watched Jeryl set the artifact beside the patient. It was a real thing, and it was magical, and for now it belonged with the southerner.

Chapter 28

Port Freewind, Ardel

He goes away, said the soundless voice inside Ilakri's head. *The five-fingered Master leaves!*

Ilakri struggled to wake, to cry out and stop the strange Master. The bright beings danced around Ilakri, urging him to act. Why did they not help him? They could touch the Master, speak to the Master, yet they did nothing.

Call to him now, said the voice. *Stop him, make him return. He must take the relic!*

Words formed on Ilakri's lips. "Come back, strange Master," he said, and heard the words as if someone else had mumbled them. He turned his head, tried to open his eyes. Someone touched him, pressed something cold and wet to his face. He shuddered.

You have failed, said the voice inside Ilakri's head. *The five-fingered Master is gone. You must prepare yourself for his return. You must make him understand you. You must tell him that the relic is his.*

You must tell him of the things we show you. . . .

The heat in Ilakri's body, the cold dampness of the cloths against his skin, the pain in his head and his chest receded from his awareness. He had no thoughts of his own. His attention was focused on the bright beings and the soundless voice. The beings still danced, graceful movements of too many arms and too many legs, colorful clothing floating about unseen torsos. They made pictures in Ilakri's mind, visions of things beyond his comprehension. Huge metal boxes that flew through the air, carrying more of the bright beings inside them. Towers of metal stretching to the sky. Buildings like herders' huts but much larger, made with walls of thick flowing stuff that hardened and turned shiny in the bright sun.

A village at the base of a cliff, peopled by bright beings who came and went from the cliff-top in the flying boxes. Mysterious implements scattered along the banks of a wide river. Bright beings wading, water swirling about their legs. Dancers moving wild and free around a huge fire that gave light but no heat.

And the other beings they brought to the village—aleps and wool-deer, huge silver tols and tiny blue lizards, plump and tentacled climbers with stubby legs and eyes on stalks.

Younglings, thought Ilakri, *those are younglings!* But the visions swept on before he could pose a question.

More comings and goings, larger metal boxes, more people. Sun chasing moons chasing sun across the sky. River narrowing, widening, narrowing again. *Seasons*, thought Ilakri, *seasons passing. A long time*.

The unexpected flash was bright, so bright that Ilakri shut his eyes against the metal image. When the brightness faded, the village was changed. The great towers no longer touched the sky. They lay bent and scattered on the earth beside the river. Some of the buildings had broken open like cracked eggs, spilling their contents across the soil. Bright beings still danced, but there were fewer of them. The metal boxes no longer came and went from the cliff-top.

The river dwindled and the number of bright beings dwindled over many seasons. The buildings were never repaired. Some of them housed a small herd of wool-deer, a flock of fowl, lizards in rough cages. The people brought wood from the cliff-top and burned it for light and heat, and they seldom danced. Sometimes they burned their dead.

The bright beings lived in the ruined village for a long time before the last one died.

Chapter 29

Elissa Durant watched the scene in the wasteland unfold on the mine room's monitor. The huge mining shovel scooped a dipper full of titanium-rich ore from the mine, then turned and poured it into a truck's long bed. The full truck pulled away, bound for the mill, and an empty one took its place. The action looked as if it were occurring in realtime, as if the virtual reality equipment were functioning normally, but Elissa knew that this was not so. The holo-images were being produced by a tape of yesterday's abortive test of the spook. At Sandsmark's order she was watching the same tableaux that Mboya and her team had seen through the mine room's equipment, a set of false images produced by the saboteur's retransmission unit.

Sandsmark hoped those fictitious images would convince Austin Duerst that the spook was operational. He was gambling with the future of Ardel's inhabitants, both native and Terran. It was a greater gamble than Elissa wanted to take, another demonstration of the artifice of bureaucrats and politicians. At times like this she was glad to be an engineer, responsible only for executing decisions made by her superiors. "How much time can you give me?" she asked Grund.

He glanced up from the micro-board he was prepping and frowned. The shape of his eyes was distorted by the magnifying lenses of his goggles. "The uninterrupted portion of the tape is less than an hour long. We can't edit it—Duerst would notice any jumps in the action. He'd know that he wasn't watching a realtime view.''

''Then we'll have to limit his inspection to less than an hour. Forty minutes from the time he enters the room until he leaves—that gives us sufficient margin for error. Do you think this tape has any chance of fooling him?'' Sandsmark's scheme was making Elissa feel itchy all over.

''I'm less worried about the tape than I am about the miners. They'll have to synchronize their actions to the movements of the equipment as they see them through the spook.'' Grund made one more adjustment to the micro-board with a needlelike tool, then slid the board into place in the tiny processor box beside the monitor. ''I've provided each of the control chairs with separate but synchronized access to the tape. Each operator will see the same scene, but from the point of view of the equipment he or she is controlling.''

Elissa nodded. ''You shut down the transmitters, didn't you? I don't want the actions of the miners in this room interfering with the work that is going on down at the mine.''

''All the equipment at the mine site is on manual control. Even if we did transmit, the machines would ignore the orders.''

''Then you can call the miners in here and have them practice matching their moves to the images on the tape. I don't know how much experience Duerst has had with this type of equipment. We'd better be prepared to look good.''

''I think we should put someone in each of the control chairs,'' said Grund. ''If we leave one empty, Duerst might sit down and try to control a piece of equipment himself.''

Elissa shuddered. ''That would certainly give us away. Tell the miners not to respond if he asks one of them to move.''

Grund nodded. He finished putting away his tools,

then reset the monitor to the beginning of the tape. The shovel scooped up another load of sand, turned on its base to center its dipper over the truck's box. "There's one good thing abut this bluff, Elissa. If it works, if we can convince Duerst that the spook is functional, it might make the saboteur careless. He could tip his hand by trying to get to his equipment to find out what's gone wrong."

"We can hope so," said Elissa.

The intercom in Elissa's office chirped. Elissa pressed her hands together, felt them slip as her sweaty palms met. She took a deep breath, said, "Clear," and nodded when the computer display before her vanished. "Open intercom," she commanded. There was a second chirp.

An image of Jer Robinson's face appeared before her. His hair and the top of his forehead was cut off as always because of his height. Elissa usually ignored the distortion, but now she coughed to suppress a nervous giggle. She made a note to have someone adjust Robinson's imager. "Yes, Jer?"

"They're on their way up, Chief," he said.

"I'll be right out." Robinson's face followed his hairline into oblivion. Elissa pushed her chair away from the desk, hesitated before standing. She hated inspections, not because she feared that her department would be found less than competent but because she disliked bureaucrats and executives. In the past they had poked their noses into things they did not understand, had asked stupid questions, and then refused to listen to the answers. Elissa believed that they were only attempting to demonstrate their perceived power over her and her people, and that irritated her.

Today's visit was more than an inspection. It had taken on some aspects of a sideshow and others of espionage. Elissa intended to hustle Duerst through the department before he noticed anything amiss. She looked down at her coveralls (her newest pair), brushed some lint from the sleeve, and tugged at the waist before giving up in disgust. The damn things never would fit properly. She ran her fingers through her curls as she walked out to join Robinson beside his desk.

Anna Griswold was the first to come through the door. She nodded to Durant and Robinson, stepped aside to make room for a tall, dark-haired man dressed in a black business tunic and trousers. The man's hazel eyes swept the room with a cold, appraising glance that belied his friendly smile. His gaze paused on Robinson's face for a moment, then moved on to Elissa's.

"Mr. Duerst," said Griswold, "this is Chief Durant and her clerk, Mr. Robinson. Chief, this is Mr. Austin Duerst, Vice President of Nagashimi-BOEM. Secretary Sandsmark has gone ahead to the mine room. Are you prepared to give us a full demonstration of the mining equipment this afternoon?"

"I am," said Elissa, her eyes locked on Duerst's. She sensed that he was wary and perceptive, and would not be an easy man to fool. "Good afternoon, Mr. Duerst. Welcome to Engineering and Maintenance. If you'll follow me, I'll take you directly to the mine room." She shifted her gaze, strode past him into the hallway.

Sandsmark was waiting in the glass-walled observation cubicle outside the virtual reality room. Mboya's second shift of miners occupied the room's control chairs. They were "riding the spook," eyes hidden behind opaque goggles, hands encased in black mesh gloves or gripping wire-draped joysticks. The miners moved with silent grace, heads turning so that their eyes could track objects unseen by Elissa and the other observers, hands moving on controls of which only they were aware.

The monitor screen before Sandsmark showed the scene at the mine—a scene identical to the one Elissa had watched a dozen times since mid-morning. It was three minutes into the tape, three minutes cut from Elissa's margin for error. She looked at the chronometer above the monitor, marked off forty minutes in her mind. By then Duerst would have to be on his way out the door.

"Duerst!" called Sandsmark. He turned his hover cart to face the newcomers. "Come and look at this monitor they've set up for us. We can see everything that's going on down at the mine."

"The monitor is part of our standard equipment, sir. Our technicians use it to verify sensor calibration," said Elissa. She knew that Sandsmark was aware of that—he seemed to be playing the fool for Duerst's benefit.

Duerst walked over, drew a finger through the dust on top of the monitor. His easy smile faded, was replaced by a frown. Concern furrowed his brow. "This monitor is an older model. I was told this installation was equipped with the latest technology."

"It is." Griswold pointed to the circle of contour chairs in the adjoining room. "The virtual reality gear that the miners are using has all the new modifications. Some of the supporting equipment is a generation older. It's all in good condition and doesn't degrade the functioning of the spook."

Duerst was unimpressed. His gaze took in the entire room, one cubic meter at a time, as if he was appraising the value of its contents for auction. "What about the actual mining machinery?"

"The shovel, which you see here," said Elissa, pointing to its image on the monitor, "was designed for the Ardellan mines and assembled on-site. It's capable of moving twenty tons of sand with each lift of its dipper. We currently have two trucks and a 'dozer in operation, with more trucks scheduled to go on line next month, once the mill doubles its handling volume to full capacity."

"And the ore? Is the quality as high as was originally reported?" asked Duerst.

Sandsmark grunted. "You've seen the same assays that I have. The spot evaluations are high, and we expect the early yields to exceed our previous predictions.''

"The black sand that is found in some areas of the desert is rich in titanium ores—mostly titanium dioxide,'' said Elissa. She eyed the chronometer, counted fifteen minutes of the allotted forty gone. "We selected our initial mining location based on the original mineral survey and a more recent color-density analysis of the soil. Current assays are showing exceptionally high yields.''

"Yes,'' added Griswold, "and we're investigating the feasibility of mining another titanium ore that is scattered throughout the wasteland. You might know of it—the semiprecious stone sphene. The indigenous people cut and polish it to make beautiful but fragile gems.''

Duerst did not comment. He was watching the miners, his fingers drumming quietly against the desktop. "You've employed a Kenyan mining team.'' It sounded as if he disapproved.

"They came highly recommended,'' said Griswold. Her white-knuckled fingers caught and twisted a loose thread at the hem of her tunic. "I'm satisfied with their work thus far.''

"But their transport ship is still in orbit around Ardel. Why?'' asked Duerst.

"You'd have to ask that question of their leader. She's not working on this shift. I can leave a message for her to contact you this evening if you like.'' Griswold pulled out her electronic notepad, made a verbal notation in a low voice.

"It's not necessary,'' said Duerst after she had finished. "I was just curious.'' His eyes tracked the movements of the miners' hands, traced the slender, bright-colored wires that linked goggles and gloves and joysticks and footpads to the central processor. "I'd like to try one of the control chairs now. I've been checked out on this sort of equipment at some of

Nagashimi-BOEM's mining stations. I'm sure I can handle what you have here.''

Elissa's chest tightened. She looked at Sandsmark, wondered if he realized in what an impossible position Duerst's request put them. ''All the stations are in use right now. I'd rather not interrupt the miners' work.''

''Nonsense!'' The drumming stopped. Duerst faced Elissa, his startling eyes pinning hers with a glare. ''I just told you I'm capable of handling this equipment. Give me one of the trucks. You won't notice any change in the routine. You can watch me on your monitor.''

''Really, Mr. Duerst,'' said Griswold, shouldering Elissa aside and commanding the tall man's stare, ''you can't expect us to pull an experienced operator off the job so that you can play with the equipment.''

''That's exactly what I expect you to do.'' The fingers of Duerst's right hand twitched against his thigh.

Sandsmark leaned forward and nosed his cart closer to the glass wall, forcing Duerst and Griswold to step away from one another. He peered into the mine room, his balding head moving from side to side as he watched the miners. ''The contract does allow Nagashimi-BOEM to inspect every aspect of the mining operation. Mr. Duerst has a right to ask for a personal demonstration of the spook. In fact, I'd like one myself. This equipment has always fascinated me.''

''It'll have to wait until tomorrow,'' said Elissa in the firmest voice she could manage. ''You can 'ride the spook' during the morning shift change. I won't have you delaying production right now. We have a deadline to meet, you know.'' A deadline that they might not meet, even with Jan Mboya's miners working full-time at the site. If Duerst agreed to wait until morning, she could drag the bluff out for a few more hours. Perhaps it would be enough time to catch the saboteur.

''I think that's a reasonable compromise. Don't you, Duerst?'' asked Sandsmark. He turned his cart and began moving toward the door. "I think we've completed the rest of this inspection. Captain Suwa is expecting us to join her for dinner aboard *White Crane*."

Duerst hesitated, looked back over his shoulder at the miners. Elissa checked the chronometer again—only five minutes left of the forty. She turned, caught the reflection of Duerst's face in the glass wall. His frown had deepened and an angry light glinted in his eyes. She held her breath. He knew what was at stake here.

"You have too great an interest in food, old man." Duerst blinked. His meaningless smile returned, but the look in his eyes did not change. He turned away from the miners, nodded to Griswold and Elissa, then followed Sandsmark to the door. "All right, we'll 'ride the spook' in the morning."

Elissa sighed. Once Duerst hooked into the spook he would know about their ruse. She could drag out Sandsmark's bluff for only a few more hours. Perhaps it would be enough time to catch the saboteur and clear Sinykin's name.

Chapter 30

Port Freewind, Ardel

Inda wandered into the elongated courtyard between the compound's kitchen and the private rooms. The stone walls sheltered him from the chill spring breeze, and the afternoon sun warmed his face and arms. He bent to look at the raised garden bed, saw tiny red leaves forcing their way up through the loose soil. Some of the leaves were long and narrow, others round, still others curled in miniature rolls or spirals on fragile stems.

The cycle of death and rebirth was evident wherever he turned on this planet. Kelta's ashes rested in a tea-pot, but they might as easily fertilize these infant herbs. The plants in turn would mature and increase Hanra-bae's pharmacopoeia. The complex chemicals manufactured in their leaves and stems and roots would help to heal and sustain the fishers in future years, until they, too, died and were set adrift to nourish the life in the sea. Sea fed land, and land fed sea; out of every death came life.

Inda sighed. Terrans had long tried to transcend that natural cycle. Yet there was a kind of peace in accepting it, in understanding his own place on the wheel of birth and death. He thought again of his dream, of his dead daughter Miranda running into the sea with the shade of Sarah Anders. What gift had they offered him wrapped in a cloak of darkness? He remembered reaching for it, watching it vanish just as his hand touched it. His mind suddenly transformed the image into another vision, a memory: a youngling offering him a parcel wrapped in a dusty cloak. The cloth parting, revealing the dirty red Beluki artifact.

A premonition? A message from Miranda and Sarah Anders? The skin on Inda's arms prickled. He straightened, turned away from the garden. There were many mysteries on Ardel.

Inda walked into the kitchen, poured himself a mug of tea from the inevitable pot on the hearth. This pot was chipped and battered, a castoff pressed into service when its newer cousin became Kelta's urn. It still brewed excellent tea.

A plate of bite-sized breads was on the table. Inda popped a morsel into his mouth, was surprised at the burst of sweetness when he bit into it. Its center was chewy and tasted of nuts. He ate two more with his tea, then left the empty mug on the table and walked back to the infirmary.

Hanra-bae was vaccinating younglings. He looked up when Inda entered. "Have Arien and Jeryl left?"

"Yes," said Inda. He grabbed a vaccination gun, took the next youngling in line. "Cobran sent a youngling to fetch them. They were going to have a private trade discussion."

"Things have gotten much more complicated since Reass and Mikal arrived."

Inda nodded, then wondered what that gesture meant to a fisher. "They certainly have. And I don't have authority to negotiate with Reass and Mikal." It galled him to admit that. Would he ever become envoy?

"Trade does not concern Healers." Hanra-bae pulled the empty vial of vaccine from his gun, inserted a fresh one. He turned to the next youngling. "Come here, little one. An instant's sting could save you from deformity and death. This," he waved the gun, "is nothing to fear."

The youngling approached, its eyestalks jutting in opposite directions and its tentacles hanging limp. It seemed ready to flee.

"Master Healer?" queried someone from the doorway.

"Yes?" Hanra-bae finished the immunization before he looked up. The youngling limped away, stroking its leg with a tentacle.

"Master Healer," said a young fisher waiting just outside the infirmary, "my neighbor Belra is ill. Will you come and see him?"

"Of course." Hanra-bae put down his equipment, shooed the younglings over to Inda. He spoke to the fisher. "What is your name, and what troubles your neighbor?"

"I am Mosra. Belra has a fever. Two of his younglings are also ill." The fisher paused, looked across the room at the southerner. "The younglings found the southern visitor on the beach yesterday. They helped to carry him to the infirmary."

"So," said Hanra-bae. "Did they see red fliers about?"

"They did not say."

The Healer rose. "Sul, bring my pouch!" he called.

The youngling appeared with a black leather sack. The sack had a long strap and many pockets that closed with bone buttons and tiny leather loops. Hanra-bae opened several of the pockets and checked their contents, then added items from the many baskets that filled the room's shelves. "Are you finished there?" he asked Inda. "You can accompany me if you wish."

Inda swiftly immunized the last youngling and set aside his vaccination gun. "I'll get my pack and meet you in the street."

"I once worked on a fishing boat," said Hanra-bae as they followed Mosra along the bluff's edge that overlooked the piers. "Most of our younglings do. My name was Han then. We earn the honorific 'ra' when we become Masters.

"We took the boat out one day and the weather turned rough. The wind swept me overboard. My

Master swung the boat about and tried to reach me, but a creature of the deep had caught my leg. It was dragging me through the water toward its cavernous mouth when one of my siblings speared its eye. It screamed and released me, and the others pulled me to safety. I have not been on a boat or in the water since that day.''

Inda shuddered. Water and death again, intimately connected for all the fishers. ''It is fortunate for your people that you were spared.''

''It is more fortunate for me,'' said Hanra-bae. ''All of my siblings died on the boats.''

Mosra turned away from the bluff and led them to a small house not far from Cobran's home. Its gray stone facade wrapped up and over two weathered red boulders that crouched like sentinels on either side of the entranceway. Several fishers and a hand of younglings had gathered outside the house. They whispered among themselves and pointed at Inda as he followed Mosra and Hanra-bae inside.

The single room was as cluttered as Cobran's home. Inda scarcely noticed; his attention was immediately drawn to the fisher and younglings resting on pallets on the floor. A Mother sat beside the hearth, her hands clasped in her lap and her tentacles dancing among the folds of her clothing. Hanra-bae had already dropped his pouch and knelt beside her mate. He ran his palms over the fisher's aura, examining him as he had the southerner. Blue sparks flashed from his fingertips to the fisher's chest and forehead. The Mother conversed with Hanra-bae in the fisher dialect.

''This is Mother Katran,'' said Hanra-bae. ''Belra is her mate. She is very worried about him. She said that he and the younglings were feverish when they returned from fishing today.''

''How serious is their illness?'' asked Inda, remembering the southerner's seizures.

''It might be the early stages of plague, or just a minor upset and fever. It really makes no difference.

Red fliers have been seen along the beaches. When they appear, the plague quickly follows. I wish I had a way to kill them.'' Hanra-bae grabbed his pouch, opened a half-dozen of its pockets, and dropped bits of their contents into a bowl on the hearth. He poured in steaming water, releasing the heady and comforting scent of his botanicals. ''Belra and the younglings are not yet in danger of having convulsions. This potion should ease their fevers and allow them to rest through the night. We can do no more for them.'' He spoke more of the unintelligible syllables to Katran, and she replied in kind.

A youngling's eyes peered around the edge of a partition at the back of the room. They fastened their gaze on Inda. He stared back at them, wondering at the weird image of eyeballs seeming to float in midair. The eyes quivered on the ends of their stalks, then withdrew. ''Are there any herbs that will keep the red fliers at bay? I can vaccinate Katran and her other younglings,'' suggested Inda. ''If you are facing an outbreak of plague, we should immunize everyone now.''

Hanra-bae agreed. ''You may begin with those fishers waiting outside. They are probably Belra's friends. If this is plague, they will be the next to fall ill.''

''All right, but send the other younglings out to me, and make certain you immunize Katran. She is in great danger.'' Inda reached into his bag, pulled out the gun and a fresh vial of vaccine. Katran looked at it, said something incomprehensible.

''She wants to know if that is a weapon,'' said Hanra-bae. ''She asks if you would kill her now, and save her the pain of the water.''

Inda stared at him. ''What do you mean?''

''If Belra dies, she will have to follow him into the water.''

''You can't mean that!'' Inda saw Katran start and instantly regretted the force of his exclamation. This

Mother feared for her life. He returned the gun to his
pack, offered up open palms in apology.

"I do mean it," said Hanra-bae. "This is the custom of my people."

"That's barbaric. Why would she kill herself?"
asked Inda even as he thought, *Like the wife-burnings
in old India. Widows threw themselves on their hus-
bands' funeral pyres, and no one tried to stop them.
They had become unwanted burdens to their families.*

Hanra-bae patted Katran's hands and whispered
something to her. "Belra would do the same if Katran
died before her time. Their family would be irrepara-
bly broken. There would be no reason to continue,
nothing to live for. We do not become FreeMasters as
Jeryl and Arien did when their mates died."

"Then we must keep Belra and the rest of the fishers
alive," said Inda. He could not accept the idea of Katran's suicide. It was enough that the sick died of
plague; how could he stand by and watch it kill healthy
people? He turned to the entranceway, looked back
over his shoulder at Hanra-bae. Did he see approval
in the Healer's eyes? "Send the younglings out to me."

"I will."

Some of the younglings waiting outside had already
been vaccinated. They pointed to Inda's gun and the
bruises on their thighs, chattered an explanation for
the others. The Masters stood back, watched Inda immunize the other younglings before they offered him
their bare arms. Katran's healthy younglings appeared;
Inda vaccinated them and sent them back in to help
Katran. Hanra-bae came out at last, as Inda was packing away his equipment.

"How are they?" asked Inda.

"We can do no more for them tonight. They have
all taken their first dose of the potion. Katran will give
them more through the night, and will send for me if
their condition worsens." Hanra-bae looked at the
low-hanging sun. "I think we must vaccinate as many
people as we can tonight. If the day is warm tomor-

row, more red fliers will hatch and the plague will spread with them.''

''You are right.'' Inda shouldered his pack. ''Where shall we start?''

By the time Inda crawled into the furs, he was certain that he had vaccinated every fisher in Port Freewind. There were more people in the city than he had expected, and his supply of vaccine was depleted. Three vials nestled in their foam wrappings at the bottom of his pack. They would immunize three hundred more Ardellans. Then he would have to return to the spaceport for more vaccine.

That was a chilling thought. Inda longed to see Elissa and Jaime, but he had no wish to face Griswold. He checked the date on the glowing dial of his chronometer. Sandsmark should have arrived at the spaceport by now. Perhaps he would smooth things over with Griswold and they would finally resolve the issue of Inda's appointment as envoy. He had to be realistic, though. Jeff Grund was now Assistant Administrator, and Elissa had hinted at other problems—with the mine, and with their relationship. Griswold was ready to ship him off the planet. His immediate prospects at the spaceport were not pleasant. It would be so easy to stay outside, to cross over and live as an Ardellan. Would anyone come looking for him?

Inda held out his hand in the darkness, conjured a tiny flame of shimmer-light to dance in his palm. This ability was part of him now, and whatever happened he would let no one, not even Elissa and Jaime, take it from him. He watched the flame for a moment, then let it die before he slipped his arm back under the furs. He yawned. It was time to sleep.

The shouting woke him just after midnight. He picked out two voices but could not identify either one. The owners might have been standing outside his window or at the far end of the courtyard. Their words were incomprehensible, but the noise carried well in

the still night air. Inda buried his head in the furs, to
no avail. The fight and the noise level continued to
escalate. Finally Inda rose and went to the window.

Moonlight illuminated part of the courtyard. The
adversaries stood beside the kitchen door, their faces
in shadow. They waved their hands and pointed at each
other to punctuate their enraged exclamations. Their
deep red auras formed incandescent halos about their
bodies.

Suddenly another figure appeared, stalking across
the courtyard from one of the sleeping rooms. "Reass!
Bantu!" said the newcomer. His voice was low and
forceful. "Take your argument elsewhere. You know
better than to fight in my compound. My patients need
rest and quiet!"

The shouting and wild gestures ceased. The two
turned toward the intruder, their faces becoming visible in the moonlight. Inda saw pale skin, shadowed
eyes, mouths twisted by emotions he could not identify. One of them spoke to Hanra-bae, more words that
Inda could not discern. Then they both went into the
kitchen and closed the door. Hanra-bae crossed the
courtyard again, probably returning to his bed. Inda
sighed. His feet were cold, and the warm furs beckoned.

Cobran and Hanra-bae were taking morning tea
when Inda wandered into the kitchen. A tray of sweet
breads sat on the table, and a pot of boiled grain was
warming on the hearth. Cobran was eating grain. Inda
settled for tea and bread.

"I visited the southerner this morning and listened
to his ravings," said Cobran. "I think his name is
Ilakri, and he recently emerged from the coccoon. He
spoke of bright beings with many arms and legs, and
of following a five-fingered Master. Also something
about a box that flies like a bird. He said other things
that I did not understand, but he did not answer my
questions. I do not think that he heard my words."

Inda sipped tea and considered the "box that flies." Was it some kind of southerner magic, or might it be a spacecraft or shuttle? Where would Ilakri have seen such a thing? A five-fingered Master—that would be a deformed Ardellan, or perhaps a Terran. Jeryl or Arien might know of a deformed Master. He would ask them. And the bright beings with many arms and legs—who were they? Were they connected to the "box that flies"? Did they have something to do with the Beluki artifact? "Did he speak of the relic?" Inda asked Cobran.

"Not in any way that I understood. Much of what he said was nonsense."

"Fever will sometimes cause people to see and hear things that are not there," added Hanra-bae.

"Hallucinations." Inda used the Terran word. "Precipitated by chemical changes in the brain." High fevers sometimes caused brain damage in humans; the same thing might happen to Ardellans. Perhaps Ilakri would never fully recover from this illness, would never be able to explain where he had found the relic. The Beluki ruins might remain hidden in the Southern Desert. Inda could not contemplate that thought without a thrill of foreboding. The fall and disappearance of Beluki civilization was a mystery that had fascinated Terrans for almost a century. The ruins on Ardel might hold the key to understanding who the Beluki were and why they had suddenly vanished from the settled worlds. Perhaps on Ardel they would learn that something more remained of Beluki civilization than broken buildings, ruined ships, and those strange ceramic artifacts.

Cobran swallowed the last of her tea and set her mug aside. "Have you seen Viela this morning? The council is waiting. We are ready to hear his testimony about Kelta's death."

"He was meditating in the back garden," offered Hanra-bae. "You will probably find him there."

Bantu walked in from the infirmary. "Viela has

completed his meditation and is waiting for you in the courtyard, Mother.''

"Then I will take my leave. Thank you for the tea, Hanra-bae. You kitchen is excellent, as always." Cobran exited through the door by which Inda had entered.

"Have you finished vaccinating all of the fishers?" asked Bantu.

Hanra-bae snapped his fingers and a youngling came to clear the table. Inda grabbed one more sweet bread before the youngling took the tray. He bit into the bread, let Hanra-bae answer Bantu's question.

"Not all of them. We should finish this morning, after we check on the southerner and on Belra and his younglings. I hope that the vaccine will put an end to this outbreak of the plague."

Bantu swiped a bread from the tray as the youngling passed him. "I have not been vaccinated. Viela would not approve, but I would like to try the vaccine. I know that Reass has been vaccinated, and he and Mikal would like you to come to Berrut, Healer Inda."

"My vaccine is almost gone," said Inda. "I must return to the spaceport to get more. If you would bring some of your Healers to the spaceport, I could give you the vaccine and teach you how to administer it. Hanra-bae has already mastered the technique. It is not hard to learn."

"Viela would never permit it. He would like to end all contact between your people and mine."

"I know." Inda finished his tea. "Viela has reason to distrust us."

"Come to the infirmary with us," said Hanra-bae to Bantu. "I will vaccinate you."

Bantu followed them. He looked away as Hanra-bae loaded the injection gun. A faint golden flush colored his face. "Please do not tell Viela."

"We will not."

Bantu winced at the hiss of compressed air from the gun. Across the room the southerner muttered something incomprehensible. Inda bent over him, listened to the alien syllables, and wondered what they meant. He touched the patient's brow, noted the rhythmic rise and fall of his chest, listened to the beat of his heart. "His fever has broken," Inda called as Hanra-bae put away the injection equipment. Bantu rubbed his arm, looked down at the tiny bruise left by the vaccination.

Hanra-bae joined Inda at the southerner's bedside. "His fever was down when I checked on him after midnight. There is a good chance he will recover from this plague."

"I hope that your other patients are as fortunate," said Inda. "Has there been any word about Belra?"

"Two more younglings are ill. Only Katran has been spared."

Spared, thought Inda, *to drown herself at her mate's funeral?* He bit back a sharp comment. He did not want to anger Hanra-bae. "Were you planning to visit Katran's house this morning?"

"Yes." Hanra-bae checked the supplies in the pockets of his leather pouch, replenished some with leaves and bark from his pharmacopoeia. "I hope you will accompany me."

"May I come also?" asked Bantu. He was standing near the southerner's relic, tracing its red curves and curls with his fingers.

"Of course you may. I welcome the help of all Healers."

There were busy younglings and Masters in the street, more of them than Inda had seen on other days. He followed Hanra-bae to the bluff. From there, he looked down on the fishing boats tied to the piers. Some fishers stood at wooden racks mending nets, others worked on the boats. Younglings swabbed decks and swept piers, checked rigging and greased pulleys. Not a single sail was unfurled. Inda saw no one at play, heard no joyful shouts.

"They will not take the boats out today," said Hanra-bae. He stood beside Inda, his shoulder brushing the Terran's. "They are afraid of the plague, afraid of what they will find when they return from the sea. So many died last year. We have just begun to replace the lost families."

How many died needlessly, following their mates into the sea? wondered Inda. He kept imagining Katran's delicate face disappearing beneath the waves. The vision chilled him. "We should check on Belra."

Hanra-bae turned away from the estuary and led Inda and Bantu inland to Katran's house. Someone had fastened a strip of red fabric near the entranceway. The wind ruffled it, reminding Inda of the fluttering red wings of the insects that carried the plague. Today there was no gathering of fishers outside Katran's home. Hanra-bae walked in without knocking.

Katran was still sitting beside the hearth. Belra and four younglings lay on pallets on the floor. Hanra-bae knelt beside Belra; Bantu bent to check one of the younglings.

"It is plague," said Hanra-bae, his hands slowly sweeping a few centimeters above Belra's body. Again the blue sparks leapt from his fingers to his patient's chest. "His fever is very high. Convulsions will begin soon."

Inda bent down, touched Belra's forehead. His skin was hot and dry, his pupils dilated and staring at something beyond Inda's field of vision. "He's burning up. We have to cool his body. He should be immersed in water right now."

"Katran will not permit it," said Hanra-bae.

"Ask her. It may be the only thing that will save him." Inda saw a pitcher of water on the table. He carried it to Belra's side, pulled a cloth from his pack and dipped it in the water, used the cloth to wipe Belra's face.

Katran murmured something. Hanra-bae answered her.

"She thinks that the water will make him worse. I have told her that you are a good Healer, that you

helped to save the southerner with your wet cloths."
Hanra-bae pulled aside the furs that covered Belra,
then began to loosen his clothing.

"What about the younglings?" asked Bantu.

"Get some cloths and soak them in cool water,"
said Inda. "Put them directly on the younglings' skin.
We must change the cloths as they get warm. The idea
is to draw some of the heat from their bodies. Perhaps
we can keep them from having convulsions.

"We should take Belra down to the waterfront and
immerse him in the water," suggested Inda. "That
would be the fastest way to bring down his body temperature."

Hanra-bae looked at Katran. "She will not understand. She will think he is dead or dying, and she will
try to drown herself. Belra is not as sick as the southerner was. I think the wet cloths will save him."

Inda picked up the pitcher, poured water over Belra's body. Katran shrieked and jumped up from her
chair. She stumbled around a youngling, tried to pull
the pitcher away from Inda. Hanra-bae grabbed her
hands. He pushed her back toward the hearth, speaking softly to her in the fisher dialect. She was trembling.

"Find more cloths," said Inda to Bantu. "See if
you can find a healthy youngling to fetch water." Bantu
grabbed the empty pitcher, then disappeared around a
partition at the back of the room.

"Master Healer!" The shout came from outside the
entrance. There was more, a phrase that Inda could
not understand.

Hanra-bae grimaced at Inda, shouted something to
the intruder. "The youngling says I am needed now.
I told it that I am treating patients. It must wait until
I come out."

The youngling shouted again. The words were unintelligible, but the tone was urgent. Inda saw Hanra-
bae's expression darken.

Bantu returned with the dripping pitcher in one hand

and a bundle of rags in the other. He tripped on the edge of Belra's pallet, splashed water on two of the younglings. Katran squealed. Hanra-bae murmured something to her and pushed her into a chair. Then he turned to Bantu.

"One of the fishers has collapsed on the pier. The youngling fears he is dying. I must go to him. Will you stay and care for Belra and the younglings?"

"Of course," replied Bantu. "Go!"

Hanra-bae grabbed his pouch, pointed to Inda's pack. "Bring your things and come with me. We must hurry."

Inda snagged his pack and followed Hanra-bae from the house. The waiting youngling ran to the bluff, disappeared over its edge. Hanra-bae followed. Inda stopped at the edge of the bluff, gazing down at the narrow steps cut into its face. The youngling was nearly at the bottom; Hanra-bae was halfway down. Inda hesitated. Hanra-bae looked up at him.

"It is safe. Come down. We must hurry. Plora is ill."

"Plora?" Inda put his left foot on the first step, then his right on the second. He pressed his right side against the stone bluff as he descended. "Who is Plora?"

"Cobran's mate! If he dies, she will follow him into the water!"

Chapter 31

Terran Spaceport, Ardel

"Jaime! Breakfast is ready!" Elissa pulled the steaming cakes from the heater, set them in the center of the table. She had made enough for both of them, even though her stomach was too full of butterflies to have room for food. In less than an hour she would watch Sandsmark and Duerst "ride the spook." Sandsmark's ruse would be revealed (although he was sure to blame it on someone else—probably her) and Duerst would demand an explanation. There was nothing she could say to him that would excuse the lies.

Jaime bounded into the room, his bright eyes and happy smile denying that Elissa had awakened him at the Grund's home after midnight and brought him back to sleep in his own bed. He climbed into the chair that Inda usually occupied, scooped up two cakes with his fingers and dropped them on a plate. His fingertips immediately went into his mouth. "Hot," he mumbled around them.

"Then use a fork, and let the cakes cool before you try to eat them," said Elissa. She poured coffee for herself, soymilk for Jaime. "Put your fingers on the cold glass. They'll feel better."

"Dad's coming home tomorrow!"

"What?"

Jaime gulped down half the milk, then obliterated a white mustache with his fist. "Tomorrow will be ten days since he left. He said he'd be back in ten days."

"I don't think so, honey." Elissa's first sip of cof-

fee had killed the butterflies but soured her stomach.
Now she felt a twinge of impending heartburn, an
inflammatory reminder of the deceptions—hers and
Sandsmark's and Sinykin's—that had overshadowed
truth in her life and Jaime's. "Your father said he'd
be gone at least ten days. That means it could be
longer. He promised to write and tell us when he'll
be back."

"He said he'd be back in ten days," repeated Jaime.
His smile was gone, replaced by tight lips and a set
jaw. He spoke with the naive certainty only children
and innocents possess.

Elissa bit her lower lip, told herself the tears welling
in her eyes were the result of the pain. She wanted to
spare her son this disillusionment. "Dad's last letter
said he was on his way to Port Freewind. I'm sure he's
still there. He would have written to us if he was coming home."

"No! You're wrong!" Jaime pounded the table with
his fist. His plate jumped and clattered. Milk splashed
in his cup. "You're lying to me. You sent him away
and you don't want him to come back!"

"Jaime!" His intense attack shocked Elissa. Anger
flushed the poignant tears from her eyes. Her right
hand came up, its palm reaching for Jaime's face. He
flinched but never stopped staring at her. She pulled
her hand back without slapping him, pressed her palm
to her chest. The thumping of her heart startled her.
"That's a horrible thing to say. I miss your father as
much as you do."

"You don't. You're glad that he's gone. You'd be
happy if he never came back to me!"

"That's not true." Elissa had never before heard
Jaime use such an insolent tone. She managed to keep
her voice calm, despite an unreasoning rage that urged
her to grab Jaime and shake him. She gripped the table's edge with white-knuckled fingers.

"I don't believe you. I hate you. I don't want to live
with you anymore." Jaime was on his feet, his break-

fast and burned fingers forgotten. "I'm going to talk to the guards at the gate. I'll bet you haven't told me about all of Dad's messages." He stormed out of the kitchen.

Elissa rose and followed him to the door. She leaned against the wall, watched as Jaime pulled his jacket from its peg and scooped up a handful of textbook disks. He was nine years old, suddenly behaving like a teenager. She wasn't prepared to handle a rebellious child alone. "Where are you going?"

"I'm going to ask Tommy to go to the gate with me before school. And I'm not coming home until Dad gets here."

"All right. You talk to the guards. You can ask them to have a FreeMaster take a message to your father." Elissa stifled an urge to brush the soft brown curls from her son's forehead. She made fists of her hands and tucked them between the small of her back and the wall. Jaime looked so much like Sinykin that it brought an ache to the center of her chest. "You can stay at Tommy's tonight. I'll drop off your clothes on my way to work." Perhaps a letter from Sinykin would arrive today. She was as anxious as Jaime to know if he was all right, and when he would be returning home.

Elissa found Jeff Grund staring at the monitor outside the mine room. The screen showed the huge shovel dumping a load of sand into one of the trucks. The flow of sand slowed to a trickle, the bottom of the dipper closed, and the shovel backed away from the truck. Elissa looked through the observation wall, saw Jan Mboya sitting in one of the chairs, her eyes hidden behind goggles and her hands moving on controls.

"It looked good from here," said Grund. "How did it look to you?"

"Fine," said Elissa. "When did you get it working?"

Grund jerked, turned to look at her. He smiled, showing perfect white teeth. "Good morning."

"It didn't look so good out here." Herve Santiago's voice came from the com-unit. "She dumped the load three meters shy of the truck bed again."

"Damn!" Mboya released the controls, stripped off the goggles and glove. "Everything seemed perfect. I don't understand how that retransmission unit can project such a convincing false image." She walked out to join them beside the monitor.

"It's got to be pretty sophisticated," said Grund. "Right now that's to our advantage. We can put Duerst in a chair and let him play with one of the trucks. If you can't tell that you're not seeing what's actually happening at the site, he certainly won't be able to tell. He doesn't have your training or your years of experience. We should be able to convince him that the spook is working."

"Are you out of your mind?" asked Elissa. "If anything goes wrong, he'll just cry 'fraud' and the court will award the mine and the base to Nagashimi-BOEM. We've already pushed this bluff too far. I think we should stop now."

Grund shook his head. A strand of black hair fell forward and dangled before his right eye. He brushed it away. "We can't stop now. We still don't have any proof of sabotage. We have to keep bluffing him until we find something we can use against Nagashimi-BOEM."

"It's only two more days," added Mboya. "Our production was very good yesterday. Once Duerst and Sandsmark leave the mine room, we'll switch the equipment back to manual control and start mining again. We should have enough ore at the mill by late afternoon to make that first shipment tomorrow. Then Duerst will be gone and we'll have some time to resolve this problem."

Elissa shrugged. She knew they were right, but she

had a bad feeling about the scheme. Something was going to go wrong.

Howard Sandsmark steered his hover cart into the mine room with a twitch of his hip. Austin Duerst was already there, standing at one of the chairs between Anna and the miner Mboya. Once again Sandsmark envied Duerst. His long, lean body was not youthful, but it was whole and healthy.

One of the reclining chairs had been moved out of the circle. Chief Durant was waiting beside the spot where it had been, a glove and a pair of goggles in her right hand.

"We thought it would be easier if you stay in your cart, Secretary," she said. "This station controls the repair robot. You can run it without the use of foot controls."

"Thank you." He maneuvered his cart into the vacant space. That placed him across the circle from Duerst. "Which piece of equipment will Mr. Duerst be controlling?"

"One of the trucks," said Mboya. "I'll be riding the shovel from the chair on your right."

Griswold nodded. "Mboya will be watching out for you. Make sure you carefully follow her instructions. We can allow you only ten minutes on the equipment before we must bring in the next mining team and get back to work. We're pushing a deadline, you know. Our first shipment is due tomorrow."

"I wanted to try out the shovel," said Duerst. He ignored Mboya's glare, took the glove she offered him and smoothed it over his left hand. The slender cable hung from it like a party streamer. He settled into the waiting chair. "You're wasting time, Sandsmark. I was hoping to see you climb into one of these chairs."

On the day you die . . . thought Sandsmark. "That would take even more time. Let's just get on the system and see what we can do." He took the glove

from Durant's hand, pulled it onto his own. Its soft
mesh fabric formed to his hand like a second skin.
It felt light and natural, stretching with him as he
flexed his fingers and made a fist. The connectors
lay like threads along the backs of his fingers and
hand, then converged into the ribbon cable. He
touched it.

"The designers tried using micro-cables," said
Durant, "but operators would forget that they were
there and tear them out when they moved too far
from the equipment. The rainbow cables are heavy
enough to feel and colorful enough to notice. That
means we have fewer repairs." She handed him the
ear jack.

"Sensible," said Sandsmark. Across the room
Mboya gave Duerst a pair of goggles. Sandsmark
reached over, took his pair from Durant. A tiny mi-
crophone was suspended from the left side on a slender wire armature. He tapped it, heard the sound
through the jack. When he looked up, he found Duerst
staring at him. Sandsmark felt as if they were oppos-
ing knights being armored for battle. "I'll meet you
out there," he said. Duerst nodded. They each donned
their goggles.

The world was transformed. Sandsmark looked out
on a broad wasteland, on clear blue-green sky and the
huge orange ball of the rising sun. He turned his head,
and his view panned along the horizon until the mine
came into sight.

"Put your right hand on the joystick," said Mboya
through the ear jack. "Your fingers should nestle into
the indentations. The stick controls your vehicle's
speed; the studs at the finger positions bring up an
array of graphics programs. You steer with your left
hand."

Sandsmark pressed the stick forward, heard the buzz
of an engine powering up. His view advanced as the
repair-bot moved toward the mine. He saw one of the
trucks begin to move in the distance.

"What will the graphics tell me?" asked Duerst.

"That varies depending on the equipment," said Mboya. "Your truck has load level and capacity graphics to tell you how much sand you're carrying, and a program that shows you where the truck's center of gravity is located. The sensor graphics fill in the ground-level view to help you identify and avoid road hazards.

"The repair-bot has many specialized graphics programs that are used in maintaining the other equipment. And we all have access to the basic mining graphics. If you press the second stud beneath your index finger, you'll bring up the graphics for titanium concentration."

Sandsmark fingered the tiny button. His view of the mine suddenly was overlayed by a swirling rainbow of transparent reds, violets, and blues. Mboya's huge shovel ground forward on its treads, stopping near the largest red patch. Then the heavy articulated arm extended over the sand. The dipper dropped down and cut into the rich, red ore.

"Back your truck over here, Mr. Duerst," ordered Mboya. "Keep it on the firm ground. I'll drop this load of sand into the box."

The dipper lifted away from the ground, sand trickling out between its tines. Duerst's truck backed into view, stopped five meters away from the shovel. Sandsmark watched the ease with which Mboya backed the shovel away from the mine, then turned its bulky body and centered its bucket over the truck's bed. If this wasn't real, it was the best simulation he had ever seen. Sandsmark maneuvered the repair-bot in for a closer look as the dipper's bottom fell open and sand poured into the truck.

"Excellent," said Mboya. "You positioned the truck very well, Mr. Duerst. I think that's enough of a demonstration. My miners are anxious to get to work."

"Not yet," said Duerst. His truck was moving

again. It pulled away from the mine, sped toward Sandsmark's repair-bot. Sandsmark pushed forward on his joystick, moved his left arm to turn the repair-bot out of Duerst's path. Duerst pursued him. They began to circle the mine, moving faster than Sandsmark thought was safe.

"Once around the pit, Sandsmark," called Duerst. "Is that robot easy to handle?"

The image before Sandsmark's eyes jumped, then settled again. Something had changed, but he did not know what it was. "Enough!" he said, and turned the repair-bot out of Duerst's path. "Shut us down, Chief Durant. We're finished here." The image of the mine jumped again, then vanished, leaving his eyes staring into darkness. He released the joystick and peeled the glove from his left hand before he removed the goggles.

Duerst was already climbing out of his chair. He shot Sandsmark a dark glance, then turned his charming smile on Mboya. "Thank you for the demonstration. I hope we haven't delayed you too long."

Mboya did not reply.

"Gentlemen." The sharp edge was back in Griswold's voice. "We have a transport waiting to take you to the mill. Shall we go?"

"I heard that you're running a demonstration in here," said Coni Mattrisch from the doorway.

Elissa pointed to the scene on the monitor. "We've just finished. One of the operators got a little wild with his truck."

Mattrisch walked in, glanced through the observation window, then looked over Elissa's shoulder at the monitor. "Does that really show you what's going on out at the mine?"

"Yes, it does." Elissa turned, looked at the mine room. Duerst was already out of his chair and following Griswold to the door; Sandsmark was maneuvering his hover cart out of its slot in the circle. They would all be out of the mine room in a moment. Mboya was busy replacing gloves and goggles on their storage pegs. She looked worried. "Have you met our guests?" Elissa asked Mattrisch.

"No." Mattrisch's fingers toyed with the loose end of her belt, slipping it in and out of its loop. "I shouldn't stay. I have to get back on my rounds. I was just curious about the test." She turned and left the room just as Griswold and Duerst entered through the other door.

"Your transport is waiting in the hangar," said Elissa to Griswold. "The mining team is on the way up. I'd like to stay and help them get started."

"That's fine," replied Griswold. "Please follow me, gentlemen," she said to Duerst and Sandsmark, leading them into the corridor.

Elissa waited until she heard the lift doors close behind them. Then she opened the direct channel to the mine. "Herve, how do things look out there? Is the equipment all right?"

"Chief, this is Genesee. Herve is injured. We need help out here."

The butterflies were back in Elissa's stomach. "Do you need an emergency transport?"

"No. Li is already bringing Herve in. Call the hospital and tell them to expect a head injury. You could send out a tow truck and a repair crew, though."

"What happened?" Elissa felt a hand on her shoulder, turned to see Mboya standing beside her. "Call Robinson," she whispered. "Tell him to get Jeff Grund over here right away."

Genesee's voice was shaky. "Herve was riding in Duerst's truck. Duerst had it traveling pretty fast when he sideswiped the 'dozer. Herve was thrown around the cab. He's unconscious and bleeding."

"And the truck?" asked Mboya.

"We'll have to tow it in for repairs. It's not usable right now."

Mboya shook her head. "Then we're finished. With

only one truck, we can't transport enough sand to the mill to meet that contract deadline.''

"Damn," said Elissa. The contract was the least of her worries now. Her best maintenance engineer was seriously injured, possibly dying. Sandsmark's deception had exacted much too high a price.

Chapter 32

Inda scrambled down the narrow steps toward the waterfront. His left foot slipped on a pebble, slid perilously close to the edge of the stairs and the sheer drop to the shore. He leaned his right shoulder into the stone wall of the bluff, kept himself from tumbling down the last half-dozen steps.

A chattering crowd had gathered around the prone figure on the pier. Inda looked over, picked out Arien and Jeryl standing among the fishers. Hanra-bae was already on the sand, running. Inda jumped over the last two steps, hit the sand hard. He ran after Hanra-bae.

The Master Healer hesitated at the broad steps to the pier. Inda could see him staring at the water, could see that the sight of it made him cringe. Then Hanra-bae shuddered and turned his eyes toward his patient. He placed first one foot and then the other on the steps, his soft boots making no sound on the weathered wood. In a moment he was on the pier. He shouted something, began shoving his way through the pack of fishers. They moved aside, clearing a path to the fallen Master. Hanra-bae dropped to his knees beside Plora, his hands extended to read the fisher's aura.

Inda took the steps two at a time, watching Plora. From five meters away he could see the trembling that presaged convulsions. He ran. The pier's planking reverberated under the hard soles of his boots. He stopped abruptly, dropped his pack at Hanra-bae's side. One of the fishers was speaking, more words and phrases that Inda could not understand. Frustration welled in the Terran physician, forced him to act. He bent down, pressed his palm to Plora's face. The fisher's skin was hot and dry. Tremors twitched the muscles of his cheek, misshaped his mouth. His respiration was irregular—fast and shallow, then absent as a spasm shook his neck and shoulders, then a sigh followed by more shallow breaths.

"Plague," said Inda to Hanra-bae. Worse than Belra's case, worse even than the southerner's. Plora was dying.

"Yes," said Hanra-bae, his hands still tracing his patient's aura. "He was mending nets. He told his friend that he did not feel well. He walked out on the pier to check on his boat, to see whether the younglings were properly greasing the pulleys. He started to tremble, and then he collapsed."

"How long can he survive if we don't stop the convulsions?" asked Inda.

Hanra-bae glanced at Inda through clouded eyes. His face had aged years in the past few moments—the lines on his forehead had deepened and a network of tiny wrinkles surrounded his eyes. He hesitated, then shrugged. "Plora will be dead before nightfall."

And Cobran with him, thought Inda. He jumped at the touch of a hand on his shoulder, turned, and found Jeryl and Arien standing behind him. Beyond them was Port Freewind's natural harbor, the estuary of the White River. Water lapped at the pilings of a nearby pier, dampening the wood a half-meter below the high tide mark. "How deep is the water here?"

Arien looked over the side. "Deeper than a youngling is tall."

"Too deep." Small boats crowded the shoreline; larger ones were docked along the piers. There was no place to wade into the water. Inda looked seaward, thinking of broad beaches and tidal pools. The trembling had spread to Plora's arms and legs; convulsions would begin soon. "We must get him into the water," he said to Hanra-bae.

Cobran appeared on the pier. She knelt beside Plora, gathered him into her arms. A damp red stain marred the front of her golden tunic. Its odor of tea and spices complemented the fresh smell of the sea breeze.

"Master Healer." Inda squeezed Hanra-bae's shoulder. "Our only chance is to immerse him in cold water. Is there a shallow pool along the shoreline? One where the water would come no higher than your waist?"

Now Hanra-bae was trembling. He stared at Inda, his mouth working but producing no sound.

"You need not enter the water," said Inda. "I will take him into the pool. Just show me where. It is his only chance."

Cobran looked at Inda with wide eyes. "Plora is not yet dead. You must not take him into the water before his time."

Inda reached for Cobran but did not touch her. "The cold of the water might stop the convulsions. It could save his life."

She looked at Hanra-bae. "Is this true?"

"Cold water helped the southerner," said the Healer. "I can do nothing else for Plora. He is too ill for potions, too near death for my skills. The Terran's way is his only chance."

Cobran turned back to Inda, stared at him as if trying to read his alien soul. "It is not only Plora's life which concerns us here. It is my life and the life of our house. If one dies, all die."

"I know." Inda knelt, slipped his arms under Plora. The muscles of Plora's back quivered. The fisher's body was light, his limbs limp. Inda easily lifted Plora, then lurched to his feet. "I need a shallow pool of cool water."

"There is a shallow place away from the harbor." Cobran pointed toward the sea. "The younglings go there to find shells and smooth stones. The water is very cold this early in the season."

"That is what we need, Mother." Inda followed

Cobran along the waterfront. Hanra-bae walked at his side, pouch in hand. Jeryl and Arien followed with Inda's pack. Most of the fishers trailed after them. "Will they understand what I am doing?" asked Inda.

Hanra-bae waved his hand. "I do not believe so. I can try to send them away."

"Please." Inda did not relish a hostile audience. The tremors in Plora's limbs were becoming more intense. Plora's left arm was trapped and twitching against Inda's body, but his right was free. A spasm jerked the right hand up and away from Plora's torso, then dropped the arm to swing awkwardly at his side. Inda stumbled as Plora's center of gravity shifted. Hanra-bae caught Inda's shoulder, kept him from falling. Plora's body seemed heavier with each step Inda took.

Hanra-bae dropped back and spoke to the fishers. One of them replied; Hanra-bae spoke again. Several fishers shouted objections to his comments. Hanra-bae shouted back. Inda kept walking. He could see Cobran's shallow place—not a tidal pool, but a sheltered spot behind a rocky breakwater just beyond the river's mouth. Cobran was running toward it, as if her actions would speed Plora to the life-giving water.

Jeryl walked at Inda's side. "Arien is helping Hanra-bae with the fishers. They think you are going to harm Plora," he said. "I can help you carry him. You must be getting tired."

"No," Inda lied. Momentum propelled him. Only thirty meters more to the water. Cobran was already there. Her feet had left a trail in the damp sand. Inda followed the prints; it was easier to watch the ground than to look ahead. His arms ached, and a cramp tore at the right side of his neck. He needed things to help Plora in the water. Jeryl could get them. "Bring me some floats, the ones they use on the fishing nets. And a short rope, a supple one."

The fishers still argued with Hanra-bae and Arien. Their shouts followed Inda to the water's edge. Cobran had stopped there, her feet sinking into the sand. Water lapped at her boots, staining the leather. Inda did not pause to speak to her. He carried Plora into the water. Behind him people argued, shouted, ran. Inda shivered and kept walking. He gasped when the cold water reached his crotch. Plora twitched in his arms.

The fisher's body shook with hard spasms. Inda felt the convulsion start, knew he could not hold Plora alone. "Arien! Jeryl!" he called, certain that Hanrabae's fear of the sea would keep him on the shore. "Help me!" Inda let Plora's legs fall into the water. He moved his left arm up, wrapped it around Plora's chest beneath his arms and held on tight. Plora's breaths were fast and hot against Inda's neck. His body stiffened, his feet bruising Inda's shins in the water. Plora flung his head back. His mouth opened, and a sigh rattled through it. His chest deflated as if all the air had left it.

"Damn!" Inda heard splashing and shouts behind him. He struggled to turn around with Plora in his arms. "Breathe, damn you!" he exhorted the fisher, though he knew Plora could not hear him.

"Let me help."

Inda looked into Arien's face, saw the same assurance he had seen there one strange and desperate night in the Iron Keep. Sarah Anders had described Arien as "angry and distrustful" in her journal. That description no longer fit him. Perhaps it never had. "Take Plora's sash," said Inda to Arien. "Tie it securely around his waist. Make it loose enough so that you can slip your hands through it."

Plora gasped at Arien's touch, began to shake in earnest. Inda clamped his arms around Plora's chest, bent forward to lay more of the fisher's body in the water. His own clothing was soaked, and the crisp sea breeze increased his shivering. The cold water would slowly reduce Plora's body temperature, counteracting the heat-generating effects of his illness. It would also reduce the body temperature of Inda and anyone who waded in to help him, putting them in danger from hypothermia. Immersion in water less than ten degrees above freezing could cause loss of consciousness in half an hour, death in another hour. Inda wondered how soon his mental processes would be impaired by the chilling of his body. Could he stabilize Plora before he had to leave the water and warm up?

Jeryl splashed through the surf towing a string of bright-colored floats. A half-dozen fishers broke away from the crowd and tried to follow him. Hanra-bae and Cobran, wildly gesticulating, turned them back at the shore.

"Get a tight grip on Plora's sash," said Inda to Arien. "Do not let him sink more than a hand's breadth beneath the surface." Inda inched his way along Plora's torso toward his head, holding the fisher's shoulders above water. Plora gasped and stiffened again. His arms shot out, one hand striking Inda's shoulder and the other hitting Arien in the face. Arien yelped and jumped back. His left hand lost its grip on the wet sash.

Plora's soaked clothing dragged his body deeper into the water. He kicked and twisted, tossed his head back. Water splashed his face. His eyes opened but did not focus, and his breath came in ragged gasps.

Jeryl was at Plora's shoulder. "Let me help," he said. The string of floats bobbed on the water behind him like gaudy party balloons.

"Fasten a float on either side of his neck," said Inda. He struggled to keep Plora's head above water while Jeryl tied the floats to the shoulders of the fisher's tunic. The cold water had already chilled Inda to the bone. His teeth chattered, and his feet were numb in their sodden boots.

"The floats will keep his head above water?" asked Arien.

"They will help. One of us must still hold his head, but we will no longer have to support his shoulders."

"And how long must he stay in the water?"

Inda looked down at Plora's blank eyes, his flushed skin, the twitching muscle in his cheek. Tremors still shook his limbs. "Until the convulsions have stopped. His skin is already cold. We must bring down his internal temperature."

"The water is so cold," said Jeryl. His fingers were fumbling with a knot. They tugged and twisted the wet rope, could not seem to adjust it to his satisfaction. "I cannot make my fingers work properly."

"Try to fasten some floats to Plora's sash. Then go back to shore and warm up." Inda's legs were shaking from the cold. He pressed his knees together and tried to wiggle his toes. He could not feel them.

"I think you must go first, Healer," said Arien. "You are shaking, and you look unwell."

Hanra-bae and Cobran were still arguing with a crowd of fishers on shore. Inda watched the altercation and wondered how long they could keep the fishers from stalking into the water to rescue Plora. "I can't leave my patient. One of you should go."

Jeryl finished with the floats. Plora hung suspended beneath them in the water, his head supported by Inda while Arien kept his body from drifting. The trembling in his limbs was easing. His respiration was more regular, though still shallow. Inda slipped a hand inside Plora's tunic and pressed it to his chest, trying to feel the beat of his heart. His fingers were too numb to sense anything.

"Inda! Healer!"

Inda looked toward shore, saw Hanra-bae waving a flask in the air. He spoke to Jeryl. "Get the potion from Hanra-bae, and ask him to send for furs and blankets and a litter for Plora. We must strip off his wet clothing and wrap him in furs after we take him from the water."

"You should go, Healer." Arien touched Inda's face with a fingertip. "Your lips are turning blue."

"I'm just a little cold. I'll be all right," said Inda. Jeryl pulled up his sodden tunic and began to wade toward shore. Plora's body turned in the gentle current. Inda shifted positions, trying to keep Plora's face dry. He was tired. The strain of holding Plora's head above water cramped his neck and sent needles of pain shooting across his shoulders and down his arms. His muscles were numb with cold and exhaustion. He could not keep his arms from shaking.

Inda watched the figures on the beach. Beyond Hanra-bae and Cobran, beyond the crowd of fishers, beyond even the cluster of frightened younglings, two people stood together on a dune. One was tall and slender and long-haired, the other small like a child. They were too far away for Inda to make out their features, but he knew them. He had seen them in his dreams. His daughter Miranda and Sarah Anders held hands and waved to him, beckoning him to join them on the warm sand.

Inda took a step forward, could not feel his numb foot touch bottom. He balanced on his other foot, let the current sway him. He watched Miranda and Sarah turn away, begin walking down the back of the dune. Their legs disappeared first. Then Miranda's body and head vanished behind the sand. All he could see of her was her hand clutching Sarah's. Then that, too, was gone, and Sarah followed it into oblivion.

Inda's knees collapsed, and he sank into the water with a surprised yelp and a splash. Cold enveloped his chest and arms. He gasped, tasted salty water, coughed. The water covered his nose, his eyes, his forehead. He wanted to float in it with Plora, to rest and sleep.

Chapter 33

Terran Spaceport, Ardel

Anna Griswold paced back and forth across the waiting room, her small, boot-shod feet making a surprising amount of noise against the tile floor. Elissa glared at Griswold for a moment. She was suddenly conscious that her own left hand was tugging and twisting a single curl of her hair over and over again. She looked over at Engineer Li, saw that she was leaning back on the couch with her eyes closed and her Oriental features composed. Elissa sighed, released the curl, and clasped her hands in her lap.

"Pacing won't make the microsurgery go any faster," she said to Griswold. She had little patience left for the clap-clap of Griswold's steps. "Why don't you go back to your office and get some work done. I'll call you as soon as Herve comes out of surgery."

"No." Griswold was adamant. "I let Sandsmark talk me into that stupid stunt, and that's what got Santiago hurt. I'm responsible. I'll stay here until I know that Santiago's all right."

Elissa shrugged and went back to twisting her hair. She would have contested Griswold's claim of responsibility, but doing so was pointless. Instead she sipped cold coffee, grimaced as it hit bottom and lit a flare of heartburn. She drank it anyway. The pain was not enough punishment for what she had let Sandsmark and Duerst do to Herve.

Griswold was at the far side of the room when the door to the surgical suite opened. She stayed there, frozen by fear or something else Elissa could not name.

Li opened her eyes and rose in a single graceful movement. Elissa scrambled to her feet. She and Li met Jamal Addami just inside the door.

"How is he?" asked Li.

"He's still unconscious. We've removed the blood clot from beneath the skull fracture and stopped the bleeding. We won't know anything more until he wakes up," said Addami.

"Which will be . . ." Elissa realized she had been holding her breath. Her hands were shaking.

"Tonight, or perhaps tomorrow morning. It's hard to tell with brain injuries. His scans show the potential for return to normal function, but sometimes things don't go the way we expect them to. I can't make any promises right now. He's lucky to be alive."

"I know," said Li. "May I see him?"

Addami shook his head. "Not until tomorrow. Then for only a few minutes at a time."

Li nodded. "Thank you. I'll be back in the morning." She reached for her parka.

Elissa offered her hand to Addami. The physician grasped it, held it longer than politeness dictated. His gaze sought and captured Elissa's.

"The accident wasn't your fault," he said in the same quiet, matter-of-fact tone that Sinykin used when he was comforting the friends and relatives of his patients.

Elissa shook her head, then shrugged. "I didn't cause Herve's injuries, but I could have prevented them." She glanced at Griswold, could not read her expression. Elissa turned back to Addami and rewarded him with a small smile. "Thank you for everything, Jamal. I'll call in the morning to check on Herve."

"Go home and rest. You've been working too hard," said Addami. He squeezed her hand, then released it. "Will Sinykin be returning to the base soon?"

"I don't know." Only a few hours ago Jaime had accused her of keeping him from his father. She wished now that it was true, that she could call Sinykin back with a wave of her hand or a simple message. Instead she and Jaime were alone. She would have to face Jaime before nightfall and deal with his anger and the fear that was at its heart. Intuition warned her that it would not be a pleasant encounter. "Please have someone contact me if there's any change in Herve's condition. Thank you again, Jamal."

Li was waiting beside the couch, Elissa's coat in her left hand. Griswold had already fled the waiting room. Elissa saw the back of her head through the plexiglass pane of the exit door.

The infirmary doors faced east, toward the landing field. Elissa followed Li through them and found the afternoon unexpectedly balmy for early spring. The sun warmed their backs as they walked together toward the hangar. The fresh breeze ruffled Elissa's curls and flushed the disinfectant smell of the infirmary from her nostrils.

White Crane still squatted on the landing field, her ramp drawn up and her well-kept hull gleaming in the sunlight. Li's transport was parked a dozen meters from the ship. They stopped at the cab. Elissa looked through the window, saw Herve's blood on the seat.

"Is *White Crane* still scheduled to depart in the morning?" asked Li.

Elissa nodded. "She's supposed to follow the first ore hopper up to Nagashimi-BOEM's reduction facility." She stuffed her hands in her pockets to keep from pulling open the door and touching the blood. "We may not have enough ore ready to make that shipment tomorrow. I wish she'd leave now and take her passengers with her."

"So do I." Li's face was still an impassive mask, but her words were angry. "May I pick up Duerst and Sandsmark at the mill? I'd like to chase them both around the wasteland with the transport for an hour. I wonder how fast Duerst can run?"

"They deserve worse treatment than that," said Elissa. "Harwood and a security team went with them to the mill. He wouldn't let you have them. Why don't you go back out to the site and see how the miners are doing?"

"Okay, Chief." Li opened the door and climbed into the cab. She seemed to take no notice of the blood. "We'll all be going home if we miss that shipment in the morning, won't we?"

"I'm afraid so." Elissa closed the door, then stood back while Li pulled the truck onto the road that led to the mine. Then she turned and followed the pedestrian path toward the hangar's side door. It took her past the residential units. Marta Grund's front door was open. Elissa looked at it for a long moment, wishing that she had time for the hot coffee and companionship she always found in Marta's kitchen. She reluctantly walked on to the hangar.

The mine room was empty. Elissa sat at the console and asked for the latest production figures. They appeared on the screen, neat bars of red and violet telling her how much sand had been shipped to the mill and how much ore was ready for the hopper. It looked good, only about two hundred tons short of a full load. Mboya must have been wrong when she said they could not transport enough sand to fill the shipment. She and her crew easily could dig and ship two hundred tons before sundown, even with only one working truck.

"Don't believe it."

Elissa looked over her shoulder, saw Jer Robinson standing in the doorway. He offered her a notepad. She took it, looked at the figures scrawled across its screen. "Are these correct?" She could not keep the disappointment out of her voice.

"Mammo Selati has been reporting the manual readings from the mine site," said Robinson. "They don't match the computer's figures."

"I can see that." Elissa cleared the console, then climbed off the stool. She suddenly felt tired. "We're short a thousand tons of sand. There's no way we can have enough ore prepared for shipment tomorrow.'' Sandsmark had gambled and lost. But unless word of Herve's accident had reached them, he and Austin Duerst did not yet know that.

Chapter 34

Port Freewind, Ardel

The sounds of shouting and splashing disturbed Sinykin Inda's rest. The noise seemed to come to his ears from a great distance. It moved toward him, growing louder. He willed it away. Then he felt hands on his shoulders, other hands under his arms. The hands pulled at him, tugging him from the womb where he floated, lifting him from its safe caress. They drew him into the cold, harsh air. He choked, spat a mouthful of salty water. Someone pressed his chest, forced out another gush, and another. He gasped.

The next thing he became aware of was the hard, lumpy ground beneath his back. Alien fingers tugged at the fasteners on his clothing, gave up and slit the weave with a blade. They peeled the damp fabric away from his clammy skin. He felt another rush of cold air, tried to shiver, and found that he was already shivering. Dry, rough cloth rubbed his skin, warming it.

Inda opened his eyes to clear sky and bright sunshine. He heard the mutters of fishers on one side, the soft lap of waves on the other. Ocean smells filled his nostrils. He could still taste the salty water. His chilled synapses slowly summed the data from his senses, fired recent memories to find the one that fit. "Plora!" he cried, pushing away helping hands as he struggled to sit.

Arien turned Inda toward the water but would not let him rise. "Cobran and Hanra-bae are with Plora. His convulsions have stopped. They soon will remove him from the water.'' He wrapped a fur around Inda's shoulders. ''You saved his life.''

''And who saved mine?'' asked Inda.

Arien settled another fur over Inda's bare knees. ''Does it matter? You are alive, and so is Plora.''

Inda just sat and stared at Hanra-bae. The Master Healer moved through the waist-deep water as if he had never feared it.

The infirmary's kitchen was warm and dry. Inda sat near the fire, soft furs wrapped around his naked body and a mug of steaming tea clutched in his fingers. It had taken him nearly an hour to stop shivering. He felt as if he could sleep for days. The soft murmur of voices in the infirmary and an occasional youngling trudging through to get a bucket of cool water from the well assured him that Plora was still alive and receiving the ministrations of Hanra-bae and Cobran. Inda intended to offer them his help once his hands stopped shaking and he poured another mug of tea into his stomach.

Viela stalked into the kitchen while Arien was brewing a second pot of tea and Jeryl was peeling fruit at the table. The Healer glared first at Jeryl, then at Inda and Arien warming themselves beside the hearth. He passed through the room without a word and stepped into the courtyard. Inda heard him muttering outside an open window, but could not make out his words.

''Viela was to present his case against Reass this morning,'' said Inda in a hushed tone. ''Did Cobran make a judgment?''

''She announced her decision just before she was called to Plora's side,'' said Jeryl. He did not moderate his voice. Viela's mutterings outside the window ceased. ''Viela could not prove that Reass killed Kelta, and Bantu did not come to testify for him. Reass and Mikal both claimed that Kelta's death was due to exhaustion and old age, that witnessing the argument between Reass and Viela was too much for the ancient Healer. He became excited and collapsed.''

Inda shook his head. "Yesterday Bantu said that either Reass or Viela killed Kelta during a fight."

"But Bantu withdrew his testimony, and Reass now says that he and Viela did not raise their hands against one another. He claims that he does not have the power to kill," said Arien as he refilled Inda's mug with fresh tea.

"Reass was lying," said Jeryl. "I think Cobran knew that, but Viela presented no evidence to refute Reass' statements. Cobran could do nothing but dismiss Viela's accusations."

Inda shook his head. "There is something more going on here. I heard Reass and Bantu arguing in the courtyard last night. They woke me, and they woke Hanra-bae."

Arien shrugged. "It proves nothing. Cobran considers the matter of Kelta's death resolved. She has decided to open trade talks with Reass and Mikal."

Jeryl cocked his head and looked at Arien. "Where does that leave the FreeMasters?"

"Unemployed, for now. The Berrut guilds will organize their own caravans this year."

"They are fools." Jeryl offered his tray of fruit to Inda and Arien. Inda took a ground-plum. "There is more to guiding a caravan than loading goods into a cart and driving it down a road."

"You and I know that," said Arien. He scooped up a handful of scarletberries, popped several into his mouth. They left red stains on his fingertips. "The merchants will learn. They will find dealing with recalcitrant borras and broken cart wheels a challenge."

Inda laughed. "I would like to watch Reass argue with a borra. I don't think he and the merchants are really interested in running their own caravans. They want to trade for Terran metals and to have access to Terran vaccines and technology. They don't like buying only what Clan Alu will sell them, so they try to punish Alu by depriving her allies of their livelihood. It is a tactic born of desperation."

"I know that the guilds want free trade for Terran goods," said Jeryl, "but the trade rights belong to Clan Alu. The ores that you Terrans take from Ardel come from Alu land."

"The ores do. There are other things that could be traded, things that Terrans value. The guilds could barter leathers and weavings and gemstones for Terran iron and copper. Could we not find a way for them to trade with the Terrans and still safeguard Alu's rights?" asked Inda. Sarah Anders had died trying to end an Ardellan dispute over trade rights. It was time to resolve this argument once and for all, to forge an accord that would benefit the clans, the guilds, the fishers, and the FreeMasters. As envoy, Inda would have had authority to negotiate a new pact. Instead he was a self-exiled physician following his conscience and hoping that Terran leaders would accept a new trade pact when he presented it to them. "We could meet with Reass and Mikal this afternoon to discuss changing the trade agreement."

Jeryl and Arien exchanged glances, a silent communication that Inda could not interpret. Then Jeryl spoke.

"I do not lead Clan Alu; I only guide Alu's council. Any change in the trade agreement would have to be approved by the elders."

"It is the same with me," said Inda. "Any changes in the pact would have to be acceptable to my superiors." In his mind's eye he saw Griswold frowning in disapproval while Sandsmark gave a shrug of resignation. This move on Inda's part would force the Secretary to take action, to either appoint Inda to the post of envoy or recall him from Ardel in disgrace. His long wait would be over, and his dream, or his worst fear, would be realized.

Inda offered his right hand, palm upward, to Jeryl. His fingers had stopped shaking. He closed his eyes and reached inward for the soul-fire that had almost been extinguished by the sea's cold waters. It flamed merrily in the center of his chest, and with concentration he coaxed a bit of it into his palm. He opened his eyes when he felt the shimmer-light's warmth against his skin. "You taught Sarah Anders to make shimmer-light because of your friendship with her. Your apprentice taught me because he was grateful for my vaccine. If we, who do not share even the same number of fingers, can aid one another and call each other 'friend,' you and Reass can surely find common ground."

"Perhaps," Jeryl said softly.

Inda let the shimmer-light disperse. He still felt tired, and now he was ravenous. He devoured the ground-plum, then left the hearth and scooped up three bite-sized breads from the tray on the table. He washed them down with more tea.

"You should sleep," suggested Arien.

"I want to see Plora first. Then I can nap." The thought of lying down among warm furs was comforting. He would rest for an hour, then arrange to meet with Reass and Mikal. He set down his mug, ran his hand over the coveralls hanging beside the fireplace. They were still too wet to wear. He pulled the fur close against his bare skin and walked into the infirmary.

Ilakri was sitting up, spooning aromatic soup into his mouth from a large bowl. His gaze followed Inda across the room, focused not on the Terran's face but on his hands. It made Inda so uncomfortable that he hid his hands beneath the fur. The twisted red Beluki relic lay at Ilakri's feet, gleaming in a sunbeam. Someone had cleaned the dust and salt from its ancient surface. Inda longed to touch it, but he was not ready to approach Ilakri.

Plora lay on the far platform, swathed in wet cloths. Cobran and Hanra-bae and a pair of younglings tended him, changing the cloths for fresh, cool ones and feeding him sips of one of Hanra-bae's potions. Cobran wore a borrowed robe tied at the waist with a length of rope. Her feet were bare. Hanra-bae had stripped to his damp leggings; a rough towel wrapped his shoulders and swung down behind him like a short cape.

Inda walked to Plora's side, laid his palm on the patient's forehead. He could feel Ilakri's eyes on him. "How is he?" he asked, meaning Plora.

"Alive," said Hanra-bae. "His fever is under control, and we have stopped his convulsions. He may yet survive the plague. He would have died if you had not carried him into the water."

"And I would have died if you had not lifted me out of it." Inda understood the great fear that had kept Hanra-bae away from the water for most of his life. Hanra-bae had managed to overcome that fear, if only for a few moments. "You kept me from drowning. Thank you."

"You deserve our thanks," said Cobran. "Your vaccine will save many of my people, and your actions today have postponed and perhaps prevented the death of my line. What can I do to repay you?"

You could promise me that your people will no longer follow their prematurely-dead mates into the water, thought Inda. *You could promise me that you will support life over death, that you will find a place in your community for those who no longer have mates.* It was a request he dared not make. He would not impose his values on a culture he neither lived in nor understood. He had another proposal that might benefit the fishers and all Ardellans. "I would like to meet with Reass and Mikal, to suggest to them and to Jeryl some changes in the trade agreement that may make it more acceptable to the guilds without denying the rights of Clan Alu. I would be pleased if the fishers would join in these talks."

Cobran lifted dripping cloths from a bucket and wrung the water from them. "Your meeting has my blessing. I would like to attend, but I must stay with Plora. I will not leave here until he is out of danger."

"You could hold your meeting here, in the courtyard," suggested Hanra-bae. "Then Cobran could take part in the discussion." He patted the Mother's hand. "I would call you if Plora's condition changed. I will stay with him."

"All right. Send younglings to fetch Reass and Mikal," said Cobran. "When shall we begin?"

Inda looked at the bright street outside the infirmary's door. It was mostly deserted. He saw a few Masters in the shops across the way and a hand of younglings digging in a garden. Viela was the only person in the street, striding toward the outskirts of town with his dusty traveling cloak thrown open and a worn pack slung over his shoulder. Port Freewind's spirit had been subdued by the arrival of the plague. "Mid-afternoon," he said, "in Hanra-bae's courtyard." Their proximity to the infirmary would remind all the participants that there were more important things in life than trade agreements.

Hanra-bae's assistants had dragged a table and some benches from the kitchen into the courtyard. The table nearly filled the paved space down its center, so that Inda was forced to walk along the rock wall that edged the garden and risk crushing the Healer's herbs. The sun, tracing its afternoon path through the western sky, had already covered half the table with shadow. Cobran had claimed a seat in the remaining sunshine. She still wore the borrowed robe, but now her feet were covered by a pair of soft boots. Her limp hair framed her face in pale strings. Inda was pleased that she had come despite her obvious exhaustion. Her presence meant that Plora still lived.

Bantu wandered in from the kitchen, a mug of tea and a well-laden plate held close to his chest. "Do you know where Viela is?" he asked no one in particular.

"I saw him on the street at midday, walking out of the city," said Inda. "I have not seen him since."

Cobran shrugged. "I do not think he has returned

to the infirmary.'' She looked at Bantu's water-stained tunic and torn leggings. ''You seem to have had an adventure in Belra's household today. How do he and his younglings fare?''

Bantu's face twisted in the odd grimace that Inda had begun to think of as a smile. ''They are out of danger. Every piece of cloth in Katran's house is wet. We managed to keep all our patients cool to prevent convulsions. One of the younglings may lose an eye, but they will all survive. Katran will nurse them now that their fevers are under control.'' He sighed. ''I have not practiced so much healing in many seasons. That is the unfortunate fate of a teacher and administrator.''

''Then perhaps you should return to healing and let those who cannot heal administer your guild,'' suggested Arien.

''An admirable idea, especially if Viela remains GuildMaster,'' said Bantu. ''For now, I think I will eat and sleep. This day has been exhausting.'' He carefully skirted the table and wandered down the courtyard to his room.

''His disposition seems much improved. I wish that all of us could reap such benefits from the plague,'' commented Jeryl as he paced up and down the narrow path to the kitchen. ''What is keeping Reass and Mikal?''

''Nothing!'' Reass spoke from the gate at the end of the court. ''We have come to hear you out, Sinykin Inda. What kind of trade agreement do you offer us?''

Inda was on his feet, offering his palms in a welcoming gesture. ''Come and sit with us, Guild-Masters.'' He ushered Reass and Mikal to the table and seated them beside Cobran. Arien and Jeryl took the opposite bench. Inda joined them, but sat apart. ''We would first hear your complaints, GuildMasters. What is it that troubles you about the present trade pact?''

Reass and Mikal exchanged looks that in Terrans

Inda would have called skeptical. He could not label the Ardellan expression. Mikal withdrew his hands from the tabletop, but Reass left his visible, fingers intertwined.

"The issue is Clan Alu's monopoly of Terran metals," said Reass. "Part of the Iron Keep was destroyed this past winter. The miners lost their leaders and many of their workers. They have stopped shipping iron and copper to the Metalsmiths Guild. Without metal we cannot work. We have no livelihood."

Inda gazed at his hands while Reass spoke of the Iron Keep. His own part in the disaster was still too fresh a memory for him to be objective. He knew that the miners who sought to work the weather had brought about their own destruction and the demolition of their keep's great tower, but he still felt that he might somehow have prevented it. The miners had objected to Alu's trade in Terran iron and copper because it destroyed their ancient monopoly. Instead of creating a free market, it seemed that the Terrans had caused Ardel to trade one monopoly for another.

"All of the guilds depend on the smiths for their tools, for metal parts, for iron blades and copper implements," Reass continued. "All trade is based on iron—we even measure value by the knife-weight, the amount needed to forge a good blade. We can barter without iron, but the leatherworkers cannot make new harnesses, the weavers cannot repair their looms, the dyers cannot replace their boiling pots until the smiths have iron. Even the Healers come to us for copper wire and copper disks for their rites.

"Clan Alu trades with the Terrans for metals, yet little of that iron and copper reaches my workers. We Metalsmiths must be able to trade directly with the Terrans. Only then can we be certain of our supply."

Inda could feel the heat of Jeryl's ire, could see the blush spreading through the Mentor's aura. In a moment this meeting would degenerate into angry shouting. He took a deep breath and spoke before Jeryl could.

"These are legitimate concerns, GuildMaster. It was never our intention to transfer the metals monopoly from the Iron Keep to Clan Alu. We had hoped only to increase your supply of iron and copper.

"You must not blame Alu for the shortages this past season. Severe storms kept some of our ships from landing. We did not receive all of the metal we had expected."

Reass shrugged. "Since the weather-workers of the Iron Keep destroyed themselves, you should no longer have problems with storms. We know that the weather-workers tried to demolish your ships and your spaceport so that you could no longer bring metals to Ardel. They were jealous because we preferred the quality of Terran metals to those the Iron Keep produces.

"Although the storms are over, we still do not receive the metals we have requested from Clan Alu."

Jeryl's aura blushed ruby red. "You have never 'requested' anything. You demand what you feel is your due, regardless of the needs of other guilds and clans."

"Alu has a legitimate claim to the trade rights," said Inda. "The ores we Terrans dig come from Alu lands. We must compensate Clan Alu for the special minerals we take from those ores, and for the land on which our mill and our spaceport are built. That does not keep us from hearing the concerns of the guilds and the other clans. Still, our first obligation is to Alu. Jeryl, what does your clan require to protect its rights?"

"We require payment in iron and copper for our minerals and our land. We also reserve the right to decide what Terran goods may be traded and with whom."

Arien spoke for the first time. "Tell them the reason for your last condition."

"Some Terrans once brought weapons to Ardel, powered weapons that killed at a distance. Ardellans died. My mate was among them," said Jeryl. "The Terrans also brought shuttles, flying metal boxes that carried people from place to place. Terrans could come and go like the wind, and no Ardellan could stop them." He turned to Inda. "Weapons you may have, within your compound. Shuttles you may have, only for traveling back and forth to your great ships in the sky. No weapons, no shuttles may leave the Terran compound."

"It is a fair agreement," said Inda. "The Terrans will continue to abide by it. But we can trade with the Metalsmiths and the merchants and the fishers without violating that agreement. I offer a proposal that could satisfy all of you and put an end to this dispute."

Reass shifted in his seat as if preparing to bolt and run. Jeryl's aura darkened. Cobran lifted her hands from the table, laid one on Reass' arm and the other on Jeryl's. "I would hear the Terran's proposal."

"My thanks, Mother." Inda rose and walked to the end of the table so that he sat with neither Jeryl nor Reass. "The Terrans have much to offer to all Ardellans, and you have much to offer Terrans. I agree that the restriction on weapons and shuttles is a good one.

"However, it may not be good that all trade passes through the hands of Clan Alu. Alu could set a fair price for its land and its minerals. The Terrans will bring that much iron and copper to Ardel. Any clan or guild could trade with the Terrans for iron and copper, paying a fair value in trade goods. The payment would go directly to Clan Alu, as part of its reimbursement for the land and resources it has given to the Terrans. Alu would also receive a reasonable portion of the Terran metals—one-twelfth, perhaps.

"Some things that the Terrans have will not be sold. Vaccines and medical information will be given freely to any Healer who requests them. Other technological information will only be disseminated with the permission of Alu's council."

"This seems to me a reasonable compromise," said

Cobran. "Each party benefits. The Terrans continue to dig the sands that they value, Clan Alu receives metals and trade goods in payment from the Terrans, and the other clans and guilds and we fishers can trade with the Terrans for the metals we need. When the miners of the Iron Keep are once again ready to offer metals for trade, we will have two sources of iron instead of one."

"No!"

The exclamation came from the far end of the courtyard. Inda turned, saw Viela standing in the gateway, his back to the street and his hands making a warding gesture toward the table. Viela reached back, pulled a sheaf of vegetation from his pack, and lifted it above his head.

"You negotiate with a murderer," cried Viela. "I have come to prove that Reass killed Kelta. Come out and face me, Reass, or turn your back and run from me and show that you are both a killer and a coward! The rest of you, come out and witness the fall of mighty Reass, GuildMaster of the Metalsmiths." Viela backed away from the gate into the street, still waving the gray-green sheaf of grasses above his head.

Chapter 35

Port Freewind, Ardel

"Come, Reass! Will you face me or will you run in fear?" cried Viela as he backed from the courtyard into the street. The sheaf of immature grain that he held above his head shook in the rising wind. Dark clouds obscured the late afternoon sun, deepening the shadows and blurring their edges.

Bantu's face appeared at a window. "Who makes all this noise?" he asked, rubbing a hand over his eyes.

"Your GuildMaster does," said Jeryl. He rose from the table and followed Viela into the road. "Your GuildMaster is not satisfied with Cobran's judgment. He wishes to try Reass again. Take your case to the Assembly in Berrut, Viela! Let them decide Reass' guilt or innocence."

"No! Today I will prove that Reass is a killer." Viela drew a dagger, held it before him with its point turned toward the smith's chest. "Come, Reass. If you are innocent, you have nothing to fear."

Cobran was on her feet, moving with Arien into the street. Mikal hung back, his hand on Reass' arm, and he whispered in the smith's ear. In that moment Inda heard only the rush of the wind in the trees and the pounding of his heart. Its beat was so loud that he thought the others must hear it, too.

"You behave like a fool, Viela," called Hanra-bae from the infirmary door. "Lay down your weapon and act like a Healer."

Reass pushed aside Mikal's restraining hand and

strode into the street. He faced Viela, offering his empty palms to the Healer. "What is it you want from me, sibling? We have already argued this before Cobran. I killed no one. Kelta died because he was too old and too feeble to travel. The excitement of our quarrel caused him to collapse."

"He was burned, Reass! Burned by the power you had intended for me!" Viela advanced on the smith, still pointing the dagger toward Reass' chest. Viela's aura was a seething ruby cloud, Reass' a sickly green-tinged haze. "How did you come by that power, Reass? Mikal has no such power. Cobran has no such power. Only those who have outlived their mates possess powers such as yours. You are neither FreeMaster nor Healer, yet you can channel energy and make it into a weapon. How many mates have you outlived, Reass?"

"The mating practices of my guild are not your concern." Reass stood his ground, legs spread and palms still offered in supplication. "Put up your dagger, Viela, or I shall be forced to take it away from you."

The threat made Inda shudder. He had once seen Ardellans attack one another, had heard the crackle of energy discharging from their fingertips, had smelled the acrid odor of burnt flesh. Sarah Anders had died when she tried to stop one of those fights. Inda was not so brave nor so foolhardy. He stayed with Mikal at the courtyard gate, peering out from behind a sheltering stone wall.

Viela's cloak sleeves had fallen back. The delicate blue lines of his tattoos glowed and writhed against the pale skin of his arms. He turned the tip of his dagger up and took another step toward Reass. "I am leader of the Healers. If you expect us to aid your guild, you will answer me. How many mates have died in your arms?"

"Viela!" Jeryl approached the Healer, one hand

held out as if to take the dagger. "Remember your Healer's oath. Give me your weapon!"

Viela ignored him. "I will have your answer, Reass. How many times have you mated? How did you gain the power that killed Kelta?" He stepped closer to Reass and brandished the sheaf of gray-green grasses in the smith's face. "Take the seeds, sibling. Chew them. You have nothing to fear. They will only help you tell the truth." Viela flicked his dagger and sliced through the stalks, letting the seed heads tumble into Reass' hands. Then he pressed the tip of the dagger to Reass' chest. "Chew them!"

"I will not!" Reass swept the dagger aside with one hand, sending it and grass seeds and stalks flying. He brought the other hand up, palm facing Viela and fingers cupped. Sparks flashed at his fingertips.

"No!" Cobran tried to move toward the Healer, but Jeryl restrained her.

Viela stepped back, his hands beginning a warding gesture that would never be completed.

Sparks leapt from Reass' fingers, joined to form a bright stream of energy. The power shot away from his palm. It struck Viela's hand and then his chest.

Viela screamed. He stumbled backward, his cloak flaming as he fell.

"Reeeeaasss!" Arien turned on the smith, his own hands raised to attack. Power flashed a second time. Reass had no time to ward, no time to turn the attack away. His scream was cut off as the energy discharged in his face.

The stench of burning flesh filled the air. Inda stumbled into the street, choking back bile, driven by a need to stop this carnage. Hanra-bae was already kneeling at Viela's chest. Bantu was stripping away Viela's cloak. Inda passed them, dropped to the ground beside Reass.

The smith's eyes were gone. His face was a scorched and peeling ruin. Breath rattled through his open

mouth, past exposed bone and cartilage. He was alive.
Inda had no idea how to help him.

A mournful wail sent prickling shivers up Inda's
spine. He turned, saw Cobran standing with arms
spread wide and head thrown back, keening. Other
voices joined hers as fishers came out of the workshops and homes. Their lamentations echoed up and
down the street.

"Viela is dead," said Hanra-bae. "He was killed
by Reass. We witnessed it."

"Viela provoked Reass! He attacked Reass with a
dagger," protested Mikal.

Jeryl shrugged. "Reass easily disarmed Viela. There
was no need for him to kill the Healer. He could have
turned his back and walked away."

"Stop arguing!" cried Inda. "I need help here.
Reass is still alive." Inda could not predict how long
the smith would survive. His wounds were terrible.
Shock might kill him in an hour, or he could succumb
to infection in a week. Inda needed plas-skin, a sterile
field, antibiotics that would kill Ardellan bacteria
without harming the patient. He had none of these.
Reass moaned, turned his wrecked face from side to
side. He reached one hand toward his ruined cheek.
Inda grabbed the smith's wrist, pulled his hand aside.
"Lie still." He tried to reassure Reass. "The Healer
is coming."

Instead Arien knelt beside Inda. "I intended that
he live. I only burned away his ability to focus
energy. He will never again raise power to attack
anyone."

"Nor will he see again," Inda said softly.

Bantu pressed his hand to Arien's shoulder. "Leave
us. I will help the Terran care for Reass. He would not
want you near him."

"Just make certain he survives," said Arien as he
walked away.

The sky had grown darker. Thunder rolled in the
distance, interrupting the fishers' keening. A sudden

flash of lightning followed by more thunder sent them scurrying back to their workshops and boats. Inda looked skyward, was rewarded with a splattering of raindrops on his face. He bent over Reass to keep the rain out of his wounds.

Chapter 36

Terran Spaceport, Ardel

Elissa Durant turned away from her computer's display. Staring at the numbers would not change them. "Clear," she said to the empty room, and the display disappeared. It did not matter; she knew the figures by rote. The mining team had dug enough sand to fill Nagashimi-BOEM's ore hopper to three-quarters capacity with high-grade titanium ore. It was not enough to meet the terms of the Union's contract with Nagashimi-BOEM.

In a way she was relieved that the struggle for Ardel was over. Now she and Sinykin and Jaime could get on with their lives on some other planet. They could leave behind Griswold's animosity and Sinykin's fascination with the natives. In a few weeks all the Union personnel would be withdrawn from Ardel, and this spaceport and the mine would belong to Nagashimi-BOEM.

"Shut down," she said, and the computer's indicator light dimmed to standby. She was tempted to dump the machine's memory. Best to leave as little information as possible for the new owners, but that could wait until tomorrow. She pushed her chair away from the desk, checked her chronometer, rose, and stretched. It was nearly Jaime's bedtime. She would have to go straight to the Grunds' if she wanted to see him tonight. She grabbed her jacket and left the office.

The hangar was dark and silent. Her staff had gone home to dinner hours ago, unaware that their days on Ardel were numbered. Only she and Jer Robinson and the miners knew that they would fail to make the required first shipment of ore. Even Sandsmark and Duerst had not yet been notified.

The safety lamps along the balcony shed enough illumination to light Elissa's way. She strolled to the stairs, leaned against the rail, and surveyed the hulking, shadowed shapes of the equipment on the floor below. Tomorrow she should send out a vehicle to tow Herve's damaged truck into the shop. Or perhaps she would leave the truck at the mine for Duerst's people to deal with. Elissa liked that idea. After all, Duerst had caused the damage. He did not even know that he had almost killed Herve.

The hangar was as familiar to Elissa as her own bedroom. She had helped to construct the building, had designed the repair bays and had ordered the tools, expecting that she would be the base's Chief Maintenance Engineer for many years to come. She would be sorry to walk away from everything she had built on Ardel.

She was halfway down the stairs when she saw light where none should be. A thin line of brightness was spilling out from beneath a closed door at the back of the hangar. All the rooms in the building were equipped with automatic lighting to conserve power. The computer should have turned off the lights when it no longer sensed motion in the room.

Elissa slowly crept down the stairs, trying to keep her boots from clattering on the metal treads. She counted doors from the outer wall; the light was coming from workshop number four, where the spare electronic gear was stored. Her feet touched the hangar's plasticrete floor. She ducked into the shadowed alcove beneath the staircase, where the tool caddy was kept. Her fingers traced the outlines of a half-dozen tools before she found the big wrench that she wanted. She hefted it, decided that it would make a good weapon.

Something rattled behind the lighted door. Elissa kept to the shadows, slinking along with her back against the hangar's wall, the wrench ready in her right hand. She passed the first three workshops, stopped beside the door to number four. Someone was moving in the room. She heard footsteps and the scraping sound of equipment being shifted on one of the benches. Feeling like a protagonist in one of her vintage mystery novels, Elissa unlatched the door with her free hand and pushed it open.

The person standing at the far bench spun around to face the door. Her Security badge flashed in the light.

"Oh, Coni, it's just you!" cried Elissa, feeling relieved and silly at the same time. She walked into the room, dropped the heavy wrench to her side. "I didn't know you were still trapping coneys in here." She peered around Mattrisch at the equipment on the bench. It was not like any live trap she had ever seen. It looked like a circuitboard of a transmitter, but not one that Elissa had requisitioned. She stepped closer to the bench. "What is that you're working with?"

"Just some surveillance equipment," said Mattrisch. She moved in front of it to keep it from Elissa's sight. "You shouldn't be in here. Chief Harwood said no one was to know about this."

"He did?" Alec had not mentioned any secret project at the last staff meeting. He always kept the other chiefs informed about his department's actions. Elissa took another step forward and leaned around Mattrisch. The circuitboard, with its streets of wire winding through a miniature city of shielding boxes and walls, was indeed a transmitter. Elissa traced the telltale antenna lead to the wall and up. It joined a wire that stretched around the room, tucked in a joint of the wall's pegboard. She looked back at the open box, searched out the ground wire. "That's a transmitter, Coni. It's probably the one that we've been looking for. What did Chief Harwood tell you to do with it?" She did not want to believe that Alec Harwood was a saboteur, but the evidence was right here, before her eyes.

Mattrisch pushed aside some tools, grabbed the transmitter box and settled it over the circuitboard. "He just told me to check on it," she said. Her voice was huskier than usual.

"You don't know anything about electronics," said Elissa. Then she noticed the miniature tools and the tiny solder gun scattered across the bench. She stepped back. "Do you, Coni? Know anything about electronics, I mean?"

"I know enough," said Mattrisch. She advanced on Elissa. "You shouldn't have come in here. Now I can't let you leave."

Elissa backed toward the door. The wrench was still in her hand. She lifted it above her head and shook it. "Keep away from me!" She could not believe how incredibly stupid she had been, giving Mattrisch the run of the hangar and the mine room. She should have guessed that there was more to Coni's questions than a Security officer's curiosity. "Don't try anything. I can crack open your skull with this wrench." She was angry enough to do it.

Mattrisch circled to the left, her hands up and her eyes on Elissa. She bounced on her toes. Her right leg shot out, the foot connecting squarely with Elissa's forearm. The wrench flew across the room, clattered against a bench.

Elissa doubled over, clutching her arm and moaning.

The next kick struck the back of Elissa's head.

Chapter 37

Port Freewind, Ardel

Bantu and Mikal carried Reass through the downpour to the infirmary, where they laid him on one of the bare stone platforms. Mikal conjured a ball of shimmer-light. The younglings lit the wall scones. Lightning flashed above the city, sending unanticipated bursts of illumination through the windows.

Inda and Bantu and Hanra-bae bent over Reass, clearing the dead tissue from his burns. They worked without speaking, moving as would a well-trained team. By full dark the wounds were clean. Hanra-bae brought a pot from his pharmacopoeia and spread its golden salve on the open, weeping tissues.

"This will help to keep his body's moisture from leaking away," said the Master Healer. "It also contains herbs that will prevent infection."

Inda stared at the ruined face and shook his head. A Terran this badly burned might survive if he was treated in a well-equiped facility. He would have to undergo reconstructive surgery, nerve regeneration, and skin grafts, not once but a dozen or more times. Even then his rebuilt face would not work quite like the original had. Reass had only Hanra-bae's salves and potions, herbs and decoctions to heal him. He would be horribly scarred, if he survived at all.

"There must be something more we can do for him," said Inda, thinking of sterile fields and intravenous fluids.

"There is." Hanra-bae wiped his hands on a damp

towel before accepting a mug of tea from a youngling. "Tonight Bantu and I will enter a healing trance. We will help Reass begin the long process of healing his wounds from the inside out.

"Come sit with us in the kitchen while we prepare."

Rain still beat against the kitchen window. Inda watched the water splash against the pane and slide down in sheets. An occasional lightning bolt lit the sky, flashing over the harbor. Wind whistled through the courtyard, and distant thunder rattled the shutters. It appeared that the storm would last all night.

Arien and Jeryl were at the table, wolfing down cold roast fowl and slabs of bread. Inda's metal equipment box lay between their plates, with Viela's badge of office resting on its lid.

"It is done, then?" asked Hanra-bae.

"Viela has been cremated." Jeryl touched the box. "I know he is not pleased with this funeral urn," he said to Bantu. "The one he had chosen is probably among his belongings at your guildhall. You may have any FreeMaster transfer his remains from this box to the urn." He pushed the box across to Bantu. Viela's medallion slid off the top and clanged as it struck the table.

Arien picked up the medallion and offered it to Hanra-bae. "Master Healer, we join you in mourning for Kelta and Viela. Your guild is once again without a leader. Viela had no chance to name a successor. Will you come to Berrut and take his place as GuildMaster?"

Hanra-bae took the badge of office with two fingers and held it away from his body. He looked at it with the wary stare of a hiker skirting a poisonous snake's lair. "I am no GuildMaster. I have no desire to leave Port Freewind. The fishers need my healing skills. And I hate the winters in Berrut!" He turned the medallion over, examined the other side. "Bantu worked

with Kelta for many seasons. He knows what a
GuildMaster must do. This badge of office belongs to
him.''

"I was to be Kelta's successor," said Bantu. "He
turned instead to Viela because he believed that I had
betrayed the guild. He was wrong. I only did what I
thought was necessary to insure the welfare of the
Healers. The world is changing, and we must change
with it or die. Kelta and Viela refused to accept
that.''

"Then the medallion and the office are yours."
Hanra-bae handed the badge to Bantu. "Your appointment must be confirmed by the other Healers.''

"I understand." Bantu slipped the medallion's thong
over his head. The copper disk slid down to the center
of his chest and nestled in a fold of his blue Healer's
tunic. "I will notify all of the guildmembers once I
return to Berrut. For now, let us get on with our work.
We must begin Reass' healing tonight.''

"The smith's sight is gone forever, but the flesh
of his face can be rebuilt and the nerves and skin
that were burned away can be regenerated," said
Hanra-bae. "It will take many days for the new tissue to grow. He must spend much time in trance,
guiding and directing the cells of his body. Tonight,
while the wounds are fresh, we will prepare the way
for him.''

Arien waved a hand in negation. "He is unconscious and in shock. You cannot join with his mind
under such conditions. You could be drawn down with
him, could lose your way back to your own body. It is
too great a risk.''

"Healing is always a risk," said Bantu. "I will aid
Hanra-bae. I can be his anchor to the outside world
while he enters Reass' mind and body.''

"No." The blue tattoos on Hanra-bae's face came
alive in the flickering light. "I need you with me.
Reass will need both your strength and mine to begin
this healing. We must enter the trance together.''

"Then who will be our anchors?" Bantu clutched his new GuildMaster's medallion with trembling fingers. "Who will monitor us and guide us back to our bodies?"

Hanra-bae shrugged. "You can choose either Jeryl or Arien as your monitor. They are both capable of doing what is necessary." He laid his hands, palms upward, before Inda. "I ask that the Terran be my anchor."

"What?" Inda shook his head. He did not understand what the fisher was asking of him. Lightning flashed outside the window, momentarily brightening the kitchen. Inda shut his eyes against the impossible sight of Hanra-bae's writhing tattoos. He pressed his hands to the table to keep them from shaking. "What do you want of me?"

"I want you to lay your palms in mine," said Hanra-bae.

Inda did as Hanra-bae bade him without opening his eyes. He felt an electric tingle in his right hand as his skin touched the fisher's. Power danced up his arm and across his chest, then flowed to his center where his soul-fire burned. The flame flared high, sent rivulets of answering power down Inda's left arm to his palm. He gasped.

"Look at our hands." Hanra-bae twined his fingers with Inda's. "Open your eyes and look at the light."

Their hands were engulfed in blue flames that did not burn. Inda forgot the storm, forgot the fisher's tattoos, forgot everything but the power that coursed through his body and Hanra-bae's. "What must I do?"

"You will stay with me while my mind travels into Reass' body. You must make certain that I breathe, that my heart continues to beat, that my body is kept warm while I am away from it. You must be prepared to call me back if my body begins to fail. Will you do it?"

Inda looked into Hanra-bae's eyes. They stared back at him, a golden light shining in their depths. The blue lines that circled them had stopped writhing. The fisher's tattoos flowed across his cheeks and around his mouth, then down his neck to disappear beneath his tunic. They glowed with the same light that surrounded his hands and Inda's. Inda's heart beat faster; he heard the rush of blood in his ears. The connection he forged with Hanra-bae in that moment was so intense that it felt almost sexual, yet it had nothing to do with hormones and body parts. It was mind-centered. Inda bared his psyche to the fisher's gaze as he answered him. "I will monitor your body and be your anchor."

Reass had been moved from the infirmary to a sleeping platform in a smaller room. He was still unconscious, his face swathed in bandages, the rest of his naked body wrapped in soft furs. Four wooden chairs, their seats and backs cushioned by thick tapestries, had been arranged in an arc beside his platform. A heavy curtain covered the single window and another muffled the alcove that led to the door. The rest of the room was empty. Neither light nor sound entered it from outside.

Bantu and Hanra-bae settled into the central chairs. They sat close together, their bodies touching at shoulder and hip and knee. Jeryl took the chair beside Bantu and turned it slightly toward the fisher before he sat. Inda mirrored Jeryl's actions on the opposite end of the arc.

Jeryl blinked, and the fire in the wall sconce flickered and died.

The room was dark and still, except for the sounds of breathing—the rhythmic inhalations and exhalations of the Healers and their monitors, and Reass' ragged wheezing. Inda let the darkness and the silence envelop him. He no longer held Hanra-bae's hands. His right palm rested on the fisher's forearm. He felt the slow, steady beating of Hanra-bae's heart, the gentle expansion and contraction of the Healer's chest as he breathed. Inda sensed the life energy flowing through both their bodies. They were connected to each other in a way that he did not understand but he could not deny.

A shining blue aura surrounded Hanra-bae. Inda felt it more than saw it. It tickled his palm, intersecting with his own less-visible aura where his skin touched Hanra-bae's. The aura ebbed and flowed about the Healer's body in a complex dance to the rhythms of his blood and breath.

Inda narrowed the focus of his senses, turned all of his attention on Hanra-bae. He counted the Healer's pulse and respiration, waiting for the drop that Hanra-bae had told him would come with trance. The sudden change surprised Inda despite the Healer's warning. Hanra-bae's muscles relaxed and his head lolled forward. Inda leaned against him to keep him upright in his chair.

The Healer's aura changed with the relaxation of his body. It expanded, extending outward in a fuzzy oval that engulfed Bantu and Inda and Reass. A feeling of well-being settled over Inda, the second state of the trance as Hanra-bae had described it. He breathed with the slow rhythms of Hanra-bae's pulse, let his awareness of his own body recede as his senses monitored the workings of the Healer's body.

For a long time nothing changed. Then Reass made a low, choking sound. His breath rattled in his throat and he struggled against the furs that wrapped his body. Hanra-bae's aura glowed brighter and his pulse quickened, then slowed again. A thrill of fear ran up Inda's spine.

Reass moaned. The sound broke Inda's concentration, changed the focus of his attention from the Healer to the patient. He heard the swish of furs sliding to the floor, the scrabbling of fingers tearing at bandages, more moans. He squeezed Hanra-bae's forearm with his right hand, reached with his left to pull the smith's hands away from his face. He was gripping one of

Reass's wrists when he realized something was wrong. The blue aura that encircled him and Reass and Hanra-bae was becoming more diffuse.

His fingertips searched out the Healer's pulse, found it beating a slow, fluttery tattoo. Inda released Reass, pressed his left hand to Hanra-bae's chest, felt only shallow, irregular inhalations. Reass continued to moan and thrash. Inda feared that Hanra-bae was caught in his patient's panic, trapped deep in Reass' body and mind. The Healer was no longer able to break away from the trance on his own. He needed Inda to call him back.

Inda settled into his chair and took both of Hanra-bae's hands in his own. He closed his eyes against the disquieting sight of the Healer's disbanding aura, closed his ears against their patient's moans. Instead he thought of the golden light in Hanra-bae's eyes and the power that had flowed through both their centers. That power could bring Hanra-bae back to his body.

Inda looked deep into his center, just as he had when he made shimmer-light. He found the soul-fire that burned in his chest and tried to make it flow down his arm, but the flame would not be coaxed from its safe nest. Inda touched his own doubts and knew that he was afraid.

Hanra-bae's hands were cold. His feeble pulse was barely perceptible. His body was dying.

Inda took a deep breath and turned his attention inward once more. He and Hanra-bae had shared the power before; there was nothing to fear in doing it again. He pressed his palms tight against the Healer's. Inda's soul-fire flared. Blue light flowed upward and across his chest, down his arm to his palm. He felt the tingle as it passed into Hanra-bae's body. He fed more energy into the Healer, waiting expectantly for the answering surge of power at his other hand.

It did not come.

Inda's soul-fire danced and flickered and grew

smaller as its power flowed into the Healer's body. For the first time Inda understood the nature of the fear that had made him hesitate. He felt his own reserves of energy dropping and knew that he would soon be forced to withdraw. In a desperate rush he pushed more power down his arm and through his palm.

And felt an answering tingle in his other hand.

Energy surged into him, completing the circuit. His soul-fire flared again. He felt Hanra-bae's palms twitch. Then the Healer's fingers reached up to twine with Inda's. They were warm.

Mikal was waiting outside Reass' room when the Healers emerged. His eyes asked questions that he seemed afraid to voice. Hanra-bae ignored him, but Bantu stayed and took him in to see Reass. The others walked to the kitchen for hot tea brewed with Hanra-bae's restorative herbs.

They had just poured from the second pot when a youngling answered a knock on the kitchen door and found a bedraggled figure standing on the stoop. Water dripped from the visitor's sodden cloak to puddle at his feet. He raised one arm, swept back his hood, and peered into the kitchen.

"Septi!" cried Jeryl. "Come in! Strip off that cloak and warm yourself by the fire." He sent a youngling scurrying for towels and another for a dry tunic and boots. "It is a horrible night to be out. Did you find the stable for your mount?"

"I did," said Septi. He let Arien pull the cloak from his shoulders. A leather pouch tumbled out of it and slipped to the floor. Septi stooped and snatched it up. "I bring messages for you and for Healer Inda." His fingers argued with the latch and won. He pulled out a blue envelope and handed it to Inda.

"And where is my message?" asked Jeryl.

"Yours did not require runes." Septi brushed limp wet hair away from his face, then pulled off his damp tunic. "Ertis sends word that he is ready to mate. Mieck will emerge from his cocoon tomorrow."

Jeryl slapped his palms against the table, then rose and began pacing before the hearth. "I must leave for Alu in the morning. Mieck has no mate. He will need my guidance to reclaim House Ratrou and found the new line."

"If he emerges from the cocoon whole and healthy," said Hanra-bae.

Jeryl touched the medallion on his chest. "Mieck is the first youngling Alu has cocooned without a mate. If he is whole and healthy, I will keep my pledge to honor the old ways. I will make a sacrifice in the mountains at midsummer."

"And I will join you there," promised Hanra-bae. He picked a ground-plum from the tray and popped it into his mouth. The tea had improved his color, and his hands no longer trembled.

Inda tore open the blue envelope and pulled out a single sheet of paper. He read it quickly, then read it once more before crumpling it and tossing it into the fire. The excitement of the day had driven thoughts of Griswold and the spaceport from his mind. Elissa's words brought them careening back. Griswold was accusing him of sabotage! He looked at Hanra-bae, regret tightening his chest. Much as he wanted to remain in Port Freewind, he would have to leave. "May I travel with you tomorrow, Jeryl? I must return to the spaceport as quickly as possible."

"Of course," replied Jeryl. "We will leave at dawn."

"As will I," said Mikal from the doorway. "Bantu tells me that Reass will not be fit to travel for many days. I must return to Berrut now." He turned to Inda. "I would like to take your offer of a new trade agreement back to the guilds."

Inda looked at Jeryl and Arien. Neither voiced an objection. "I think we should all take the proposed agreement back to our people and see if they will accept it."

"Good. I will send word of the guilds' opinions to Alu," said Mikal. "It is late. I will take my leave now. Thank you for everything you have done for Reass." He slipped out to the courtyard.

Inda swallowed a last tidbit of sweet bread. "I must speak with Ilakri before we leave," he said. "I hope he will tell me where he found that artifact. What room is he sleeping in?"

Hanra-bae shrugged. "Ilakri left this afternoon. He took his cloak and his boots and that relic and he walked out of the infirmary. I have no idea where he went."

Inda muttered an oath under his breath. His hope of returning to the spaceport in triumph had walked out with Ilakri. Without a map or an artifact he could not prove that the Beluki had ever been on Ardel. If he mentioned them at all, Griswold might assume that he was lying. She had already decided that he was a spy and a saboteur. Bringing that artifact to the spaceport might have given him a chance to remain on Ardel and be appointed envoy, but the artifact was gone, spirited away before he even had an opportunity to barter for it with the southerner. There was no time to chase after Ilakri now. Inda drained his mug and rose. "I must get some sleep if we are to ride at dawn. Good night." He followed Mikal into the courtyard.

The rain had finally stopped, and the wind had swept away the clouds. The night air was damp and cold. Moonlight brightened the courtyard, making the droplets on the leaves glisten and the surface of the puddles shine. Inda crossed to his room. Light shone through the shuttered window; a youngling must have lit the sconce for him. He pulled open the door and gasped.

Ilakri's red relic was on the table.

Beside it lay Inda's pouch, its flap open and most of

its contents spread around the room. It took Inda ten minutes to gather and inventory everything. The only things missing were his iron bars and Sarah Anders' stainless steel flatware.

Chapter 38

Terran Spaceport, Ardel

Elissa's head hurt. The pain encased her skull as a giant thumbscrew would. Then it cascaded down her neck and across her shoulders, bounced along her lower vertebrae, and wrapped around her chest to clutch at her right arm. The rest of her body might as well have disappeared for all that she was aware of it. The pain occupied all of her attention.

She was certain that she had two eyes. She could feel them throbbing to a strident rhythm, pain swelling first through the left and then through the right. It was a small pain compared to the blinding agony that spread around the back of her skull. She moved her head a fraction of an inch, felt the gorge rise in her throat. The floor shifted under what was left of her body. She clung to it, hoping that the earthquake would take her to oblivion.

The nausea convinced her that there was no earthquake.

Eventually she opened her eyes, but she could see no better than when they were closed. The room was pitch black. Perhaps that was good. She was afraid that light would have made the pain in her head worse.

The second time Elissa woke the pain was no better, but at least it did not surprise her. She lay still for a long time, taking inventory of her body. The parts that did not hurt instead prickled or were numb from lack of blood and pressure on nerves. The plasticrete floor was hard and cold beneath her, and pressed relentlessly against her elbows and knees. She considered moving, decided that it might be a bad idea.

She wondered how long she had been unconscious.

Then she remembered how she got that way.

And changed her mind about moving.

She began with a finger, then let the idea of motion spread through her hand and wrist to her forearm (the one that was numb, not the one that ached). She gasped as she freed her arm from beneath her body. Blood surged down Elissa's arm, sending prickles of new life through her hand, but she took no notice. The computer had detected the movement and turned on the lights.

Even without moving her head she could see that the workshop was a shambles. Someone had pulled tools and coils of wire from the walls and strewn them across the benches and floor. Tiny components had been pulled from their boxes and scattered about the room.

She correctly guessed that the transmitter was gone.

The third time Elissa woke she heard noises in the hangar. In spite of the pain and nausea (or perhaps because of it) she crawled to the workshop's door. The handle and latch were impossibly out of reach. She propped her shoulders against the wall and, biting her lower lip, inched her way up to a sitting position. She tasted blood before she was finished.

She grabbed the latch with her good hand, released the catch and tugged at the door. It swung inward. She propped it open with her foot, sat across the doorway with her back to the wall and her leg extended, tears of pain streaming down her face. The world tilted around her. She closed her eyes and tried to catch her breath. It did not occur to her to yell for help.

She had no idea how long it took her engineers to find her.

Howard Sandsmark guided his hover cart into the infirmary room with a twitch of a muscle. Anna Griswold was already there, sitting in a chair beside Durant's bed. Sandsmark tried not to stare at Durant. Her pallor surprised him, as did the bruise that covered her right arm from elbow to wrist.

"You put up a good fight," he said, smiling. "How do you feel?"

"Exhausted. Sore." Durant shrugged, then winced. "The medication they gave me didn't do much to stop my headache."

"You have a concussion," said Griswold.

Durant glared at her. "So would you if you'd been kicked in the head."

Sandsmark ignored the sarcastic edge in Durant's voice. He laughed. "I'm glad to see that your assailant didn't rob you of your sense of humor."

"My assailant," said Durant, "was one of our Security guards. Her name is Coni Mattrisch. I caught her fiddling with an unauthorized transmitter in that workshop."

Griswold rose and walked to the window. "Chief Harwood is searching the base for Mattrisch right now."

"She cleaned out the workshop after she assaulted you," said Sandsmark. "Her fingerprints are all over the tools and benches, but there's no sign of a transmitter or an antenna. She must have taken them with her."

Durant nodded, then winced. She gingerly laid her head back against the pillow. "Have they finished loading the ore hopper yet?"

"Duerst rejected the shipment because it didn't meet contract specs," said Griswold. "The hopper has already returned to Nagashimi-BOEM's facility."

"With Mattrisch and the transmitter aboard," suggested Durant. "How can we prove that our equipment was sabotaged?"

Sandsmark shook his head. "We can't. The evidence is missing, and so is Mattrisch. We would have to link the transmitter to Nagashimi-BOEM, and right now we can't even prove that it existed. Your testimony will help, but we have no physical evidence to support it.''

Griswold walked back to the bed and laid a hand on Durant's shoulder. ''You did a good job. I'm just sorry that it won't keep us from losing this base.''

''Don't think about that right now,'' said Sandsmark. ''There's someone waiting to see you.'' He motioned for Griswold to follow him to the door.

Jaime Inda burst into the room. ''Mom,'' he cried, ''are you all right?''

Chapter 39

Approaching the Terran Spaceport, Ardel

Sinykin Inda's body was sore and tired. Inda shifted position in his saddle and stretched first one leg and then the other, trying to ease the aching muscles in his calves and thighs. Then he arched his back and rolled his shoulders to relax the knots in his neck. He had ridden fast and hard all day and all night, and his body was not accustomed to that kind of exercise. It was developing pains and blisters in unexpected places.

He and Septi and Jeryl had said farewell to Hanra-bae and Cobran at Port Freewind's stable the previous dawn. Inda had given Hanra-bae the last of the vaccine and a promise to send more; Cobran had given Inda a cloth-wrapped bundle and her thanks. The bundle contained a surprising gift—the dark blue Beluki artifact that Inda had admired in Cobran's home. After his experience with the southerner's relic he had been almost afraid to touch the shiny blue surface of Cobran's gift. Now the two artifacts rode together on the back of his saddle, wrapped in soft cloth and tied with strips of leather and nylon rope.

Inda and the two Ardellans had traveled all day, changed mounts that evening at Bentwater, then had ridden the forest trails by moonlight. This new morning found them still a half-day's ride from the spaceport. Inda was exhausted and hurting and wanted to rest, but the thought of Griswold's accusations kept him in the saddle. He needed to refute her claims and clear his name, and he could only do that at the spaceport. He leaned back, felt the firm pressure of the bundled artifacts against his buttocks and lower back. They would forever change the way Terrans viewed Ardel. That made the hard ride worthwhile.

Neither Jeryl nor Septi had spoken in a long time. Their aleps trudged along the trail, moving more slowly as the morning progressed. Septi's eyes were closed. Jeryl was watching the scenery.

Inda yawned. His head dipped toward his chest. An instant later he straightened up with a start, eyes wide open and heart pounding. He looked all around, saw nothing out of the ordinary.

Soon he yawned again. The rocking motion of his alep's six-legged gait was relaxing. Inda drowsed, his eyes closed. His head fell forward again, and he slept.

Bright and laughing people with many arms and many legs were all around Inda. He counted their arms, and the number kept changing. He tried to count their feet, but their feet moved too quickly through the dust and he could not see them all. The people swayed and danced beside the trail, traveling with him.

Eventually one of their number approached him. Inda knew this one. The name was bright in his memory. Javelicohmo. Javelicohmo, who had once stood in the wide river, feeling the mud squish through his pedicles. Javelicohmo, whose feet had tasted the salty water. Javelicohmo, who had celebrated the glorious patterns of the sun's reflected rays with a dance.

Javelicohmo spoke, and Inda listened. The words came from inside Inda's head, not outside it. He heard them with his mind instead of his ears. They tripped through his brain on light little feet, dancing as the bright laughing people danced.

"Keep the long dark twisted thing, the one that is the color of scarletberries," were Javelicohmo's words. "Keep it, for it is my soul and my memory and my life. Keep it, and it will teach you great secrets."

Then Javelicohmo disappeared among the other dancers.

* * *

Inda woke to the sound of an alep snorting. He started in the saddle, looked around, was surprised to see the spacesport sprawling before him. Guards waited at the newly reinforced gate, and he could tell that they were armed. He wondered if they were planning to imprison him.

Then he remembered the dream.

And Javelicohmo's instruction.

He pulled his mount up short. "Jeryl, Septi," he said, "I must speak with you before we approach the gate." He untied the bundle from the back of his saddle and held it in his lap.

"Things have changed at the spaceport," said Jeryl. He was eyeing the guards.

Septi agreed. "There is too much hostility here. I would rather not go closer."

"Good." Inda unwrapped the bundle. He looked at the southerner's artifact and at the long blue relic that Cobran had given him. His fingers trailed along their smooth ceramic surfaces. He did not want to give up either one. "My people will not allow me to keep these. They will send them to another place, where there are many scholars. The scholars will study them to learn more about the people who made them.

"I had a dream, and the dream told me that the red one should not be taken from Ardel. The southerner left it with me and took my iron bars, but he also took something of Septi's." Inda looked into Septi's eyes. "You loaned me Sarah Anders' flatware. I promised to return it to you. I cannot do that because the southerner took it as part of his payment for this relic. Therefore the relic also belongs to you."

"It is not mine," protested Septi.

"But it must be yours," said Inda, offering it to Septi, "for if it is only mine, it will be sent away from Ardel. You can keep it safe within Alu's walls. I beg you to do this for me. I will come for it when I can."

Septi leaned forward and touched the artifact. Its

dark red surface shimmered in the sunlight. He cradled its wide middle in one hand and wrapped the fingers of the other around its narrow end. "I will keep it just until you come for it."

"Which must be soon," said Jeryl. He made a warding gesture in the direction of the Terran compound. "I think you must leave the spaceport. Come to live with us in Alu Keep."

Inda stared at him.

"Bring your mate and your youngling—your child. We will give you a house and everything you need," Jeryl assured him.

Inda made a conscious effort to close his slack-jawed mouth. He had hoped for this invitation ever since his first reading of Sarah Anders' journal. To live among the Ardellans as she had, to experience daily the magic that they took for granted, was his greatest dream. Now that it was being offered to him, he seemed to have lost the power of speech.

"Come to Alu as soon as you can," urged Jeryl.

Inda swallowed. "I will," he said, although he wanted to say much more. The words would not come. He sat on his alep and watched Jeryl and Septi ride back down the trail toward Alu Keep. When they passed out of sight around a bend, he turned his mount and rode toward the spaceport. Cobran's Beluki artifact was still in his lap. He wondered if it would be enough to buy his freedom.

Anna Griswold paced back and forth before the windows in her office. Howard Sandsmark watched her and wondered how long she would be able to hold her temper. It was always difficult to lose a post. He had done it a half-dozen times in his career; this would be Anna's first. She was fighting Duerst and Nagashimi-BOEM with every resource at her disposal.

"Coni Mattrisch is being charged with the attempted murder of Elissa Durant," said Griswold to Duerst. "We've searched the entire base and we haven't apprehended Mattrisch. My Security Chief is going to search *White Crane*, and if she's not on board he'll be sending a shuttle up to your reduction facility. Mattrisch might have stowed away on that ore hopper that went up yesterday."

"I can't give you permission to board *White Crane*," said Duerst. He lounged in a chair, one long leg draped over the arm, foot swinging. His fingers drummed a gentle tattoo on his thigh. "She's not my ship. You'll have to talk with Captain Suwa. I'm sure she'd prefer to conduct her own search."

"Chief Harwood is with Captain Suwa right now," said Griwsold. "She has already agreed to help with the search. We should have their report within the hour. *White Crane* is, after all, a small ship."

Duerst shrugged. "You'll need a warrant to search the reduction facility. That's Nagashimi-BOEM's corporate policy."

Sandsmark put on his best bureaucrat's insincere smile. He was going to enjoy poking holes in Duerst's defenses. "Administrator Griswold is empowered by the judiciary to issue warrants when there is no judge within twelve hours one-way communication range. Ardel is an outpost world. I've certified that the nearest court is fifteen hours away. Your warrant's being generated right now."

"This Mattrisch has probably gone native," said Duerst. "You may never locate her if she jumped the fence to the Ardellan side."

"We'll keep looking until we find her." Griswold stopped at her desk and picked up a printout. "We now have enough titanium ore to fill the order for your first shipment. The hopper can pick it up at the mill any time."

"No." Duerst shook his head. "The Union has defaulted on the contract. Our legal department is filing a motion to have the mine and the spaceport ceded to Nagashimi-BOEM. The courts usually allow the dispossessed party six weeks to clear out of a facility.

You might as well pack your things and arrange transportation off Ardel.''

Griswold turned on Duerst, her eyes flashing. "I have no intention of abandoning this base to Nagashimi-BOEM until the courts tell me that I must. File your motion to take over the mine. We have enough evidence of sabotage to warrant a full judicial investigation. I can tie up this dispute in the courts for at least a year. You won't be able to touch the mine during that time, and if you accept a shipment of ore from us you'll be validating the contract and that will put an end to your motion.''

She had played the bluff well. Sandsmark followed her lead. "How much will it cost to maintain your reduction facility while it sits idle for a year? Your stockholders won't be pleased to learn that the return on their investment has been indefinitely delayed.''

Their threats did not alter Duerst's demeanor. His fingers drummed to the same slow rhythm. "You have no physical evidence of sabotage, just a lot of suspicions and the word of one concussed engineer. That won't be enough to delay the court's decision. This base will be Nagashimi-BOEM's within a week.''

Bluff called. Sandsmark feared he had no choice but to fold. Perhaps he should have gutted Duerst at dinner that night aboard *White Crane*. It would have proved to be only a temporary solution because Nagashimi-BOEM had a dozen young executives ready to vie for his place and power, but it would have been so satisfying. Sandsmark maneuvered his hover cart closer to the desk and picked up the sheaf of legal documents Duerst had brought with him. "I'll need some time to review these.''

Duerst shook his head. "You've had all the time I intend to grant you. Read them now. I want them signed before I leave for Hecate Station.''

Inda was nearly at the gate before he recognized either of the guards. He had become so accustomed to

Ardellan features that the Terran faces appeared almost alien. After days spent in compact Ardellan structures, the buildings behind the guards seemed huge and unfamiliar. Then Inda's perception shifted. He remembered the guards' names, remembered walking among the buildings with Jaime and Elissa. The spaceport was home, and for the first time he was glad to be returning there.

"Heditsian," he called. "Rashad. It's good to see you."

The guards came out to meet him at the gate, their weapons drawn. They were not belligerent, but neither of them smiled. One of them drew his weapon.

"Dismount," ordered Heditsian. "Keep your hands where I can see them."

Inda peeled his stiff legs away from his saddle and slid from his alep's back. He hit the ground with a knee-jarring thud, his right hand still clutching Cobran's gift. His entire body ached. He leaned against the weary alep and patted its nose. "Fresh grain and a warm stall for you, and no more work today," he whispered.

Rashad motioned with the muzzle of his weapon for Inda to step away from the animal. "Someone will come from the stable to take care of your mount."

Inda straightened up. "What about my gear?"

"Leave it. Chief Harwood will want to inspect it. He'll return anything that's not needed as evidence."

"Evidence?" Inda chuckled, thinking of the filthy coveralls that were stuffed into his packs. Harwood would hate picking through his dirty socks and underclothes. "Am I still suspected of being a saboteur?"

Heditsian shook his head. "Mattrisch is the saboteur. We'll soon have her in custody." He opened the gate and escorted Inda into the compound. "Griswold has a different complaint against you. She's charged you with insubordination."

"It's not the first time," muttered Inda.

"What are you carrying?" Rashad pointed to the wrapped Beluki artifact. "Is it a weapon?"

"No. It's a gift for Griswold from the leader of the fishers. I'd like to take it to her right after I see my family."

"I'm sorry, Dr. Inda," said Heditsian. "We have orders to lock you up until Harwood and Griswold are able to question you. I'm placing you under arrest." He turned to Rashad. "Call another Security team to the gate. We'll escort Dr. Inda to the administration building as soon as they relieve us."

Rashad walked back to the guard shack. Inda watched Heditsian close the gate. He considered trying to overpower him, knew he had nowhere to run. There were too many things he needed to do at the spaceport—see Elissa and Jaime, give the artifact to Griswold, speak with Sandsmark. He would do those things sooner in custody than as a fugitive. After all, he had the trump card in his right hand. If it could not set him free, nothing would.

He offered his bundle to Heditsian. "Have you ever touched a Beluki artifact?" he asked.

The intercom in Griswold's office beeped. Griswold stalked to the desk to respond. "I told you not to interrupt us, Lindy."

"I'm sorry, Ms. Griswold. Security just brought in Sinykin Inda. They say he must see you immediately."

"I'll speak with him later." She jabbed at a stud on the control plate with her forefinger. The office door opened before she completed the motion.

Inda strode in, leaving his escort at the door. He smelled of sweat and dust and alien animals. Sandsmark found his enigmatic smile intriguing.

"I'm sorry to disrupt your meeting, Anna," Inda apologized. He nodded to Sandsmark and Duerst. "Please forgive me, gentlemen. This is a matter of the utmost importance." He set a dirty cloth bundle on Griswold's desk.

"Dr. Inda, this is quite inappropriate," began Griswold.

Inda did not let her finish. "Please unwrap the bundle, Anna. It is a gift for you and for all of us, from Cobran of the fishers. Her mate was dying of plague and I helped save his life. She was grateful."

Griswold opened her mouth to rebuke him, closed it again as he shoved the bundle closer to her. She shot Sandsmark an angry glance. He only shrugged and said, "Open it." Her fingers tugged at the cloth. It fell away, baring the gleaming blue Beluki artifact. Griswold gasped.

So did Sandsmark.

Duerst's fingers stopped drumming.

Inda did not seem to notice. "The fishers have more artifacts," he said. "They find them somewhere in the Southern Desert. Septi of Alu Keep was given a red one."

Duerst was already on his feet, leaning over the desk. He poked at the artifact with a stiff finger. "This will have to be authenticated." The angry set of his mouth and the blackness of his eyes attested to his fear that it was genuine.

"It's real," said Griswold. She stroked its gentle curves. "In case you have any doubts about that I'll dispatch an analysis and holograms to the Beluki Institute on Titan tomorrow. It'll be several weeks before we receive their response, but no court will rule on the fate of Ardel without it." She was smiling.

Sandsmark had forgotten how much a smile softened Anna's features. It pleased him almost as much as did the scowl on Duerst's face. He clapped Inda on the back. "Congratulations. We'll talk more about this later, and about your appointment as envoy. Right now I think you should go home. Your family has been waiting for you. And we," he smiled at Duerst as he dropped Nagashimi-BOEM's documents into the recycler, "have some business to discuss."

* * *

Inda strode across the compound toward home, dodging a pair of laughing children who were jumping rope on the paved walk. Spring had come to the spaceport while he was away. The last of the winter's snow had melted, leaving behind boggy soil and the emerging scarlet blades of the native grasses. A light breeze carried the earthy scent of the chicken coop across the compound. In the distance the windmills turned, creaking.

The house seemed no different. Inda stopped before the closed door, suddenly afraid of the changes he might find within. He peered through the window, smiled when he saw Jaime watching a holofilm on the entertainment unit. His right hand worked the latch and pushed the door open. He stepped inside, his senses quickly cataloging the familiar sounds and smells, and reached for his son. "Jaime!"

"Huh?" Jaime dragged his gaze away from the holofilm. "Dad!" He jumped up and threw his arms about Inda's waist, then leaned back and glared at his father. "You're late! You promised you'd be home yesterday."

"I'm sorry." Inda hugged him. "There were lots of sick fishers at Port Freewind. I had to make sure they would get well. I came home as soon as I could."

Jaime squirmed free of Inda's grasp. "People here needed a doctor, too." He held up his hand, showing off the fine red line of a healing cut on one finger. "I hurt myself, and I had to bandage it all by myself. Dr. Addami had to take care of Mom. You should have been here."

"Elissa!" called Inda, his heart thudding against his ribs as he remembered her last accident. She had escaped from her crushed vehicle with only bruises and a broken wrist. Had something worse happened to her this time?"

"Sshh! She's sleeping," said Jaime. "Dr. Addami said she has to rest. She has a con . . . a con . . ."

"A concussion." Elissa stepped from the hallway.

Inda gasped. Contusions had swollen Elissa's right cheek. A purple bruise spread from the corner of her mouth up to her right eye, and she carried her right arm bent and pressed against her abdomen, as if the arm hurt her. "Lissie!" He rushed to her side and gingerly slipped an arm around her. "You shouldn't be on your feet." He guided her to the couch and helped her sit. Then he began a gentle examination of her injuries. His fingers touched a large, firm bump on the back of her head, and she winced. "What happened?"

Elissa's words came slowly. It seemed to take a great effort for her to talk at all. "Coni Mattrisch beat me."

"What?"

"I was working late. Trying to find a way to make the shipment on time." Tears welled in her eyes. Jaime had settled on the floor at their feet; she stroked his hair with her good arm. "We lost the base."

"No. Everything's all right," said Inda. "Why did Mattrisch do this to you?"

"I saw a light in a workshop. She was in there. With a transmitter. She was the saboteur."

"And she fought with you?"

Elissa nodded, then closed her eyes and shuddered. "She knew I would turn her in. She knocked me out."

Inda was no longer sorry he had kicked Mattrisch when he left the compound. He should have kicked harder. A broken shoulder would have kept her from harming Elissa. "I'm sorry, Lissie. I should have been here."

"You couldn't have done anything to stop it."

Her easy acceptance made him feel more guilty about being away. He had read the anger in her letters; she seemed to have passed beyond that to indifference. That made him afraid. Had he sacrificed his family for Ardellan magic?

Elissa stared out the window. The holofilm played on, its sound track muted. "When did you get back?"

"Just now—an hour ago. Security took me to see

Sandsmark and Griswold right away. Austin Duerst was with them. He wasn't happy to see me.''

"Why not?'' She turned to look at him. Her eyes no longer had the sparkle he remembered.

"Nagashimi-BOEM won't be taking this base away from us.''

Jaime jumped to his feet. "You mean we're not going back to Terra?''

"No, Jaime. I don't think we are,'' said Inda.

"I have to go tell Tommy!''

"Later,'' said Elissa. "Let's wait for the official announcement.''

Inda flinched. She did not believe him. "I found a Beluki artifact at Port Freewind,'' he said, watching her eyes. She stared back at him, unsmiling. "Two of them, actually. Septi took one of them to Alu Keep. It's as much his as mine. I gave the other to Griswold. She says it's authentic.''

"A real artifact? Can I see it?'' Jaime climbed up beside his mother and bounced on the couch. The gel inside it gurgled.

"Please don't do that, Jaime,'' said Elissa. "I'm sure if it's really a Beluki artifact Ms. Griswold will let everyone view it before she sends it to Titan.''

"It is real.'' *More real than you can imagine,* thought Inda, remembering the vision of the many-legged beings that had come to him when he first touched the red one. "The fishers have seen many more artifacts. They come from the south, beyond the great desert. There must be a Beluki ruin down there. And that means Ardel will be protected from further development while we search for the ruin. Nagashimi-BOEM can't take the mine away from us now.''

Elissa sighed. "I hope that's true. After Duerst wrecked one of our trucks and Herve got hurt I thought we'd lost the base for good.''

"Herve Santiago?'' asked Inda.

"Yes.'' Elissa's voice broke. She looked away and cleared her throat before continuing. "He was in the cab of a truck that crashed. He has a skull fracture, but he's recovering. Jamal says he'll be all right.''

Inda shuddered. He leaned toward Elissa, wrapped one arm around her and the other around Jaime. This mine had cost them all too much. He wanted to take his family away from the spaceport, to share with them a simpler life among the Ardellans; but he feared Jaime and Elissa would see only the things they would be giving up, not the riches they would gain. He stared at the portrait cube on the table, the last family hologram taken before Miranda's death. His daughter smiled at him, just as she had in his dreams. He released Elissa and Jaime and sat back.

''I want to show you something.'' Inda lifted his right hand and closed his eyes. He concentrated, searching for the flame that burned in the center of his chest. It was difficult to coax it out into his palm; the flame hid as if it feared Terran skepticism. Inda heard Elissa gasp at the same moment he felt the warmth of shimmer-light against his skin. He opened his eyes.

Jaime and Elissa were staring, openmouthed, at the flame in his hand. ''Jeryl's apprentice taught me to do this. I can teach you. It's a simple thing, something the Ardellans do with hardly a thought. They make this kind of magic every day.

''They've invited us to live among them—all three of us. Jeryl would like us to come to Alu Keep. He has promised us a house and anything else we need. I know it means giving up our jobs here, being away from our friends, having a different kind of life. But it would also be a great opportunity. Sandsmark is going to make me envoy. Jaime will keep up his education by computer link—Jeryl said we could bring personal computers with us. And, Elissa, there is so much you could learn about the Ardellans' engineering skills—some of their homes look as if they're carved from a single piece of stone—and so much you could teach them.

''Will you come to Alu with me?''

''Yes!'' cried Jaime, his fingers reaching toward the shimmer-light.

Elissa said nothing.

Inda let the shimmer-light die. ''Jaime, why don't you go and visit Tommy for a while?''

''Okay.'' He gave Inda a swift hug and was out the door a moment later.

Inda reached over and picked up the holo-cube. He held it so that Elissa could see Miranda's smiling face. ''I learned about other kinds of magic from the Ardellans, Elissa. I learned that the spirits of those who die on Ardel are not lost to us. Sarah Anders came to me in my dreams, and she did not come alone. Miranda was with her.''

Elissa just stared at him.

''She is a happy little girl, Elissa. Sarah watches over her, and together they watched over me. They helped to save my life in Port Freewind. I know they'll come to me again, but not here at the spaceport. We have to leave the Terran settlement in order to see them.''

A single tear rolled down Elissa's left cheek. Inda leaned forward and kissed it.

''Will you come with me to Alu Keep?'' he asked again.

Elissa closed her eyes. ''I'll think about it,'' was all she said.

Chapter 40

2262:9/30, Terran Calendar

Jessica Caves, High Southern Dessert, Ardel

Ilakri stood for a long time at the mouth of the narrow arroyo, staring at the random scatter of rocks and boulders on its floor. The path to his home cave was unchanged, yet everything about his life would be different once he walked that path. He turned away, looked down the wide salt plain toward the sea. He was tempted to retrace his journey, to again seek out the five-fingered Master. His right hand slipped into the pocket of his torn cloak and toyed with the iron bars and the strange metal tools that he carried there.

Jaella had warned him to return to the cave before their younglings were born. Ilakri felt an obligation to her and to Yaro for transforming him from youngling to Master. Duty outweighed desire; he turned back to the arroyo and picked his way toward the cave.

Pebbles still covered the narrow steps to the cave's entrance. Ilakri brushed them aside as he climbed.

The odor of smoke and frying bread and the sounds of younglings at play welcomed him at the cavern's mouth. He poured the last of his water into the storage barrel, tossed the empty skin onto the pile of those waiting to be refilled. Then he conjured a ball of shimmer-light and strode into the cave's dim heart.

Jaella was waiting for him in the chamber that was the home of their trine. Her body was round with the younglings that were growing inside it, yet her face was thin and wan and her aura had almost disappeared. She rose when Ilakri entered and offered him tea and sweet cakes.

Yaro had not yet left the cocoon, though he had begun to move inside it. Jaella's time was near. Soon the younglings would burst from her body. Ilakri made her lie down, arranged the furs to keep her warm. Then he knelt beside her. He brought the iron bars from his pocket and showed them to her. She seemed pleased, but she did not speak. He did not show her the strange tools; those he wanted to keep secret, along with his memories of the five-fingered Master.

Ilakri knelt there for a long time, waiting for the cycle of death and rebirth to play itself out.